Reaper's Claim

Simone Elise

Inkitt

This book is published by **Inkitt** – Join now to read and discover free upcoming bestsellers!

Prologue

It was a love so strong that it was undying, impossible to destroy. It was the type of love that filled novel pages and romance movies aimed to feature. Every bone in my body ached with warning; every muscle stiffened with fear at the thought of him, but the stubborn person I was didn't listen to my own body's warning.

He was a flame able to burn through me. He was the flame, and I was the moth, unknowing of the harm this man could cause or the power that he would one day hold over me.

If I knew then what I know now, would I still let myself be drawn to him? I often asked myself this question.

As I stared into his misty gray-black eyes, I had my answer; I would do everything the same because I loved him, and this love was worth everything I faced for being with him—every torment, every second glance, every argument I was sure to have with my father. It was all worth it.

Chapter 1

Abby

Everyone gets an upbringing. Everyone is taught the essentials of life by their parents, and sometimes the parents' essentials of life aren't always the best. I learned to roll a cigarette before I was taught to tie my shoelaces. I suppose in most families this is considered odd, but in ours, it was normal.

My father, Jed Harrison, was President of Satan's Sons Mother Charter. He was a hard, rough man who was absent for most of my childhood. My sister, Kim Harrison, was tall and blonde, and eyes were naturally drawn to her. She had the ability to draw the attention of any man and didn't have to do much to hold it. She was also my twin.

We shared similar features—both tall, slim, and blonde, but if you looked closely enough, we had noticeable differences. To most people, the differences were too small. It didn't help either that we lived with only males.

The MC was positioned in the bushland on ten acres at the top of a large hill. The main house, garage, and pub were fenced off with barbed wire, which sent the clear message—fuck off.

The clubhouse wasn't a traditional one. It was a large four-story brick house. Dad had renovated it to fit the needs of the club. This meant extra bedrooms, a boardroom, and an open living space.

When we had larger functions, the larger bar was opened. It was complete with pool tables, TVs on every wall, and rooms down the hall for when couples could not make it back to the main house.

Kim and I were brought up on the brother's code and understood the world that to most was a mystery. We knew the differences between club women and "old ladies." Dad always said, a brother's old lady only knows what he tells her, and we are never to interfere. So we kept our mouths shut.

Dad often made us tag along on club runs, the non-dangerous ones. He took our safety seriously and didn't trust anyone with it.

Mom left us, but she didn't do it by choice. Breast cancer took her from us. Kim and I were only young, barely ten. It didn't just hurt losing her; it tore us apart. Kim and I once got on. After Mom's death, we couldn't be in the same room without wanting to kill each other.

Dad did his best, but he wasn't born to be a parent and hell, he never wanted to be a dad. He was meant to be the distant dad that showed up every once in a while, told us he loved us, then rode off again, but he had to take us on full time, and that really threw a firecracker in his idea of parenting.

So we grew up in the clubhouse; not the best of places to raise two growing girls, but the boys took us under their wings, too, and not once did they hurt us.

My best memories are ones around bikers—tattooed, criminal bikers.

Kim threw herself into shopping, flirting, and makeup. I threw myself into art, study, and removed myself as far away from people as possible. Kim loved high school; I hated it.

Dad, or Roach as he was known around the club, didn't care what we did as long as we were happy, and I guess in our twisted way, we were.

Kim was happy stealing smokes from biker's jackets and sneaking off with boys. I was happy in my room drawing in my notepad. The years slowly moved on, and before long, I was sixteen; or should I say, we turned sixteen.

My interests stayed the same: I drew, went to school, and I guess, all in all—minus swearing and the occasional punch-up— I was a model student and the daughter that didn't cause Dad's

3

head to explode every five minutes, unlike my sister.

Kim's interests in boys had disappeared, and while I strongly believe it was because she screwed her way through them all already, she would say it was because she grew up. The real reason was that she had the hots for Dad's Vice President, Trigger.

My dad was blind to Kim's open attraction for Trigger, but the rest of the world wasn't; at least, I wasn't. Every time I looked up, it seemed one of the two was giving the other suggestive looks.

What Kim saw in him I didn't know and why she would want to go there—where oh so many other women had been before—was beyond me. He was a man, she was barely a girl, and yet those factors didn't seem to stop either of them.

Trigger was the stereotypical biker. When he wasn't checking out my sister, he was either bashing someone's brains in or working on his Harley. He had the height that shadowed everyone, muscles that bulged, and he wore a pissed-off look really well.

Dad had told me Trigger was the best Vice President he could have asked for. He was one that didn't mind to "get his hands dirty." Personally, he creeped me the fuck out and if I could avoid him, I would at all costs.

Being brought up in a clubhouse meant two things—I knew what sex was before any other kid my age, and I was bartending as soon as I could hold a glass and pour a steady drink, which pretty much led me to this point of my life—me serving drunken, swearing bikers from behind a bar and Kim over in the corner giving Trigger "fuck me" eyes.

***

I poured Gitz—his real name Brad—another stiff shot. He, unlike everyone else, wasn't into the roaring party that Dad held for a visiting charter gang. He hadn't left the bar, and he hadn't stopped pushing his empty glass back to me, either.

Gitz was in his early twenties; he swore a lot and slept with a lot of the club women, but one called Lilly always had his attention. She had left the previous week, and even though Gitz had voted against it, Dad let her leave the club after seven years of service.

Club women are owned by the club and, like the bikers, they are sworn in. Unlike the bikers, though, they aren't given respect and are usually referred to as club pussy.

I guessed that was why Gitz drank so heavily and ignored the party around him. He wouldn't admit it out loud, but he liked Lilly, and it was his stupid pride that stopped him from claiming her as his old lady. From what Lilly told me, that was part of the reason she left.

"Abby, sweetheart!" Dad slammed his beer down on the counter, his face red and flushed with excitement. "Ya need a break, darling?"

Bartending was not where I saw my life heading, but I didn't fight it. "No, Dad, I'm fine." I flashed him a smile, refilled Gitz's drink, and then pulled a few beers out of the fridge.

"Have a break, sweetheart; you've been filling Gitz's drink all day now." Dad waved his drunken hand for me to leave and not wanting to get into an argument, I stepped out of the way and let another guy, Tom, take over.

"I might get some fresh air then." I patted Dad on the shoulder and walked past him. When Dad drank, his hard exterior slowly softened. It was one of the rare moments when I was reminded of my childhood father. Not the 'Roach' that everyone knew my father as.

I weaved my way through the crowds until my hand landed on the back door and I stepped outside into the fresh air.

The dimly-lit alleyway was centered between the pub and the house. It was where we kept the rubbish bins, and it wasn't the door we mainly used, but it was my quick getaway. I headed up the alley when I heard the back door open behind me.

I turned around, interested. No one else used that door, and I froze when my eyes landed on his drunken ones. My blood ran cold, and I knew instantly I was fucked.

Reaper

A drunken man has a happy soul—my dad brought me up believing that, and there I was, twenty years old, staggering out of the back door of the clubhouse. *The Mother Charter knows how to throw a welcome party.*

I leaned against a rubbish bin, trying very hard to keep the booze down, when I heard a scream. Glancing around the darkened backyard, I couldn't see anything out of place. Then I heard the scream again followed by a hushed conversation. The thumping music from the clubhouse and loud roar of drunken men muffled the sounds, and I couldn't be sure if it was my drunken mind playing tricks on me.

Placing one hand on the wall, I followed it around until I reached the end of the pub. She screamed and slammed her tiny fists on the man's shoulder. I blinked away the drunken blur that was creeping across my vision, fighting not to pass out.

"I'm not Kim!" she yelled, frantic, and continued to hit him.

The more she moved, the more she was trapped. He had her pinned against the wall, rubbing himself against her. He wasn't interested in what she was saying, and I knew there was only one thing going through his mind.

I took a step back and thought to back away completely—it wasn't my place to get in the way—but found myself moving towards them.

"Get off, Trigger!" she yelled. The terror and panic in her voice coated each word.

"Oi!" I screamed down the alley, and I knew he would have heard me, but being the drunken prick he was, he ignored me.

6

"You heard her. Get off her!"

Trigger got his name because he was always the first to pull the bloody thing. He was a full-on dick, and we had been in numerous punch-ups.

"Fuck off, Reaper. This is between me and my girlfriend." Rage spread across Trigger's face as he spat the words at me.

Although the Brother's Code was to never get in the way of another brother's dick, I took one step closer to him, giving him plenty of warning. "She's not into it. Now back the fuck off."

Temper control wasn't my strong point, and the alcohol fueled my rage. I glanced at the girl; she was terrified, tears pouring down her cheeks.

"I'm not fucking Kim," she yelled in his face and pushed him again with all her strength, but it didn't even move him.

She was weak, small, and after taking a second glance, it was apparent that she was young, too.

I warned him; he didn't listen. I let my temper get the best of me, moved forward, and grabbed him by the back of the neck. "Did ya not fucking hear me? I said get the fuck off her!" Grabbing his collar, I threw him backward, ripping his flirty hands off her.

He fumed. I could nearly see the steam coming out of his ears. I baited him with my eyes, wanting him to charge at me—nothing like a fight over a woman—though, in this case, it might be a girl.

"Whatever." He glanced at her, his eyes scorching. "I'll fuck you later, Kim."

I watched him stagger off, bastard of a VP he was. Prez actually had respect for that little shit.

I turned back to look at her. Her breathing was heavy as she leaned against the wall. Her eyes met mine, and that was it; she went into meltdown. Her tears flowed faster, and they weren't stopping. I hated crying women more than I hated the fucking law, but I didn't leave her.

"Come on, darling, calm down. He's gone now." I placed my

hand on her shoulder, dropping my head so I could look into her blurry eyes.

I didn't know what the fuck I was doing. I stood there, looking more like a noob with every second that passed.

Her sobs soon turned into hysterics, causing her breathing to sharpen.

Fuck. What the hell do I do? I wished I had paid more attention to fucking Dr. Phil, or some other shitty daytime TV program.

I brushed the blonde hair from her face, which stuck to her pearly white skin. I had never seen anyone cry as much as her.

"Come on, darling, calm down." I rubbed her shoulder, standing in front of her awkwardly. I was so far out of my fucking depth; I should have just stayed at the fucking rubbish bin.

She dropped her head onto my chest and I wrapped my arms around her, and she continued to weep, soon soaking my tee shirt with tears.

My heartbeat drummed faster. This young girl trusted me enough to let me touch her. She didn't even know me, but she clung to me for dear life. Her small frame curved into my chest perfectly. I kept my arms wrapped around her, feeling like I was protecting her from the whole darn world.

"I... he..." she stuttered into my chest. "If you hadn't come..." She pulled her head away from my chest and looked up at me. "Thank you."

I stared down into her crystal blue eyes, which were framed by red puffy circles.

"Thank you, Kade." Fat tears slid down her cheeks, but she kept her eyes locked on mine.

"You know me?" I would remember meeting her because she didn't have a face or a body any man would ever forget.

"You're Satan's Sons Western Charter's VP." She swallowed sharply. "Everyone knows you."

"Not everyone, sweetheart." My lips twitched into a smirk, and I couldn't stop myself from wiping underneath her eyes with the back of my sleeve. "You ok now?"

She nodded her head. "I think so." Her long eyelashes blinked up at me. "Thanks, Kade. I owe you one."

I could count on one hand how many people called me Kade: my mother, father, my brother, my Prez when he was pissed off, and this sweet girl.

I was called 'Reaper' before stepping into the VP position I was in charge of, ridding the world of dead weight.

"Do you want me to take you home?" I asked the girl, watching as she continued to wipe away angry tears. Though when I thought about it, I was far from a fit state to be in control of any motor vehicle.

How a sweet little thing ended up here, I didn't know, but hopefully, this would teach her to stay the hell away from places like this and the people that dwelled in them.

"No." She shook her head. "I live here."

At the Satan's Sons clubhouse? I looked her up and down again. She looked too young to be a club whore or as some refer to them, club property. She didn't look like one either. She didn't look like the type of girl that should be hanging around a clubhouse filled with dirty bikers. She looked like the type of girl a guy like me would never have a chance with.

"How old are you?" I asked her. I felt my curiosity build each time I stared down into those crystal blue eyes.

"Sixteen." Her eyes locked with mine. "Why?"

If you were legal, baby girl... damn the gods for creating such temptation.

"Bit young to be hanging around here, aren't you?" I placed my arm on the wall, keeping her there. Her eyes did not drop from mine once.

Darn, girl, you don't even know how powerful those blue opals of yours are yet.

"Like I said, I live here." She closed her eyes briefly and then looked down at the ground. "Can I ask something of you?"

9

She could ask me anything, and I would answer. Her beauty was worth going to war for. I could only imagine what she looked like in the sunlight. I was sure these dark shadows and the night sky were hiding most of her beauty from me.

"Sure, sweetheart, ask away."

"Don't tell my father." She placed her hand on my chest. "He loves Trigger. Kim is just a fucking idiot."

Who the fuck is Kim? More important, who the fuck was her father?

I was about to ask her both questions but stopped when someone called my name.

"REAPER!" Banger roared. His drunken arse walked around the corner.

I hurried to block her from Banger's view. "What?" I roared up the alley at him.

"Prez wants ya." He took a long drink of his beer and then tossed the bottle to the side.

I glanced back at the girl, but she wasn't looking at me; she stared down at the ground. The black Metallica t-shirt gripping her body had worked its way up, exposing the soft skin of her midriff.

"Are you alright by yourself?" I asked. I really didn't want to leave her, and that bothered me. Why the hell did I care if this girl was alright or not? I had done the gentleman thing—my duty to her was over, but still I didn't move.

"Yep." Her blonde hair fell to the side as she glanced up at me. "I'll be fine."

I didn't believe her, but Banger snapped at me to hurry up. I nodded my head regretfully, taking three steps before pausing and looking back at her. "Pity you aren't fucking legal."

"The forbidden is always more desirable." The corner of her lips twitched upward, and for the first time, I saw her smile. I knew right then it wasn't something I would ever forget, and I wanted to punch myself for admitting that.

10

I nodded my head, shooting her a grin before walking up the alley to Banger, who was ranting about me taking my sweet time. I didn't look back at her, but I fucking wanted to.

***

Roach was a hard, cold, mean bastard of a man. If you didn't know him, you wouldn't give him a second look for fear he might rip your throat out. He was the Satan's Sons MC President. His VP, Trigger, was sitting next to him, and both of them were sitting directly across from me and my Prez, Dane. A few other people occupied the table, too: Banger and Bleach on our side, and Gitz and Cameron on theirs.

I lit a cigarette and glared at Trigger.

"We agreed to help shift ya guns, brother, but we didn't agree to inherit your war with the Soldiers." Roach took a long drag on his cigarette.

"The Soldiers aren't worth our bullets," Banger barked. "We're dealing with it; got nothing to do with you."

"They shot up my garage, brother. That makes us a part of it," Roach barked back.

It appeared that the meeting was not going to solve anything. Everyone was hungover and nerves were raw. Before the boys could open their mouths and begin a pointless argument, a blood-curdling scream roared throughout the room. Everyone jumped.

"Oh fuck me; shit just got real." Gitz shook his head, and within a minute the double doors behind them blew open and in walked a very angry redhead.

"Dad!"

Roach spun around in his chair. "What the fuck have you done to your head?!" he roared, getting to his feet.

Dad? *Roach has a daughter*. I glanced at Dane, but he didn't seem shocked by it.

"I didn't fucking do it! I fucking woke up with it!" she screamed at him. "It was fucking Abby!"

She was swearing like a man and screaming like a maniac. I guess the apple didn't fall too far from the tree with these two. I wondered how long it would be until she too was shooting people and blackmailing cops.

"Abby!" Roach screamed.

"We came for a fucking meeting, not family drama," I hissed in Prez's ear. They were wasting time. I was all for spending time with brothers and shit, but I was hungover and the last thing I needed to witness or hear was a whiny, spoiled brat complaining to her old man. This is why you shield up before entering any woman.

"Brother, you'll be thanking him in a minute." He grinned with a knowing look in his eyes.

I glanced back up and then there she was, wearing the same tee shirt from the night before, only now with a pair of shorts that were extremely short.

She crossed her arms and glared at the redhead. I looked between the two and ran my eyes over the features of the redhead. They were fucking twins—identical twins—and the only difference was the red hair.

"What did you do, Abby?" Roach fumed. "Why did you dye ya sister's hair?"

"Because it was either dye mine, dye hers, or cut all her hair off." Abby shrugged her shoulders but kept her face deadly calm. It was the kind of calm you would expect to see before a storm.

"Red, Dad, *fucking red*!" The evil twin stomped her foot, threatening to cry.

"Abby, ya better start fucking explaining yourself!" Roach roared at her, and I couldn't stop the glare that I shot his way.

Roach was the size of two normal-sized men. He was big, intimidating, and I really didn't like him speaking to her like that. I didn't know why it bothered me. I lit a cigarette and couldn't look away even if I wanted to.

"I felt like it," she hissed at him with fire in her eyes.

"We are about to get a show," Bleach sneered.

"I sometimes feel like fucking throwing you two out on the streets. *Doesn't mean I'd fucking do it!*" he roared.

"It's red, Dad," the redhead sobbed.

"Now look what you've done, Abby," Roach patted the redhead on the back.

"Oh god forbid, Kimberly cries," she spat, glaring at her sister.

"ENOUGH!" Roach pointed a finger at her. "Fucking explain ya-self, Abby, before ya end up living on the fucking streets."

"Oh come on, Dad. I've done her a favor. Now she can re-fuck her way through every guy in town as the red harlot."

"DAD!" Kim roared and reared back her fist to hit her sister. Roach stepped in between them, keeping them separated.

"Every fucking day I wish... I wish I had fucking boys!" he roared.

Abby continued to glare at her sister, and I had a strong feeling I knew why she had decided to attack her sister's hair.

Trigger leaned back in his chair, grinning. "You know, Kim. I like it. Makes you look older," he spoke up, running his eyes over Kim.

Kim blushed bright red.

Would Roach be okay with his VP fucking his underage daughter? The look of rage on Roach's face gave me my answer.

"She's still fucking sixteen," Roach roared down at his VP. "And you better stop fucking looking at her like that before I rip ya cock off."

I guess he didn't know about what his VP got up to with his daughter after all. I glanced back at Abby, only to have her eyes lock with mine.

I had gone unnoticed until now. She gulped, and then her eyes snapped to the ground.

13

My seat creaked as I sat up straight. I wanted her to look back at me. *Why the fuck won't she look at me?*

"Boys. All I wanted was fucking boys," Roach muttered under his breath, glancing between his two girls. "Well then, how are we going to settle this?"

"I want to kill her," Kimberly snarled.

"With what, Kim? A pair of your high heels?" Abby scoffed.

"You think you're so bloody clever, bookworm." Kim spat, glaring fiercely at Abby. "Why don't you do the world a fucking favor and go back to your fucking bedroom and stay there?"

"Do you even know how to spell the word 'favor?'" she threw back, taunting her sister.

I liked her. I fucking liked that fire in her eyes.

"Enough!" Roach roared over their ranting. "I'm in a fucking meeting." He waved his arm around the room. "This is *my* fucking CLUBHOUSE." The veins in his neck bulged.

"Calm down, Dad." Abby's eyes softened, and she patted her old man's arm. "You'll give yourself a heart attack."

"Yeah, Dad, chill, would you." Kim patted his other arm.

"I need a break," he snarled, "from your bullshit and your bullshit." He looked between the two. "Always fucking fighting, always fucking ranting. ALWAYS FUCKING BRINGING ME INTO IT!"

His roaring was enough to make the windows shake, and every man in this room flinched, but Abby and Kim didn't seem the least bit fussed by it.

"Look what you've done," Abby snapped at her sister.

"What *I've* done?" Kim glared back, taking the bait. "You dyed my hair, bitch!"

"Yeah, and we both know why," she snapped back. "And if you don't settle down your fucking rant attack, I'm going to tell Dad."

Roach stood solidly between them while they threatened each other, acting like he wasn't even there.

"Tell me what?" he piped up.

"Do you want to kill him?" Kim's voice had an edge to it.

It was as if I was watching a fucking movie, though Abby was hotter than any actress. *Down, Kade. Underage, remember?* Abby was an underage pussy that I had no right to be thinking about.

"I would love to." Abby crossed her arms. "You know I have nothing to lose."

"You want me dead, Abby?" Roach roared into the conversation.

"Shut up, Dad; we aren't talking about you." Kim raised a hand in her father's face.

Trigger looked a hell of a lot more nervous now. He knew what he had been doing the night before.

One glance at the twins and I could tell them apart now, and it wasn't just the red hair.

Abby had softness in her eyes. She was slightly taller; her breasts appeared to be made for my hands, and she had an ass all men would watch when she walked away. Kim's breasts were smaller, and she had a flat ass. Not to mention, she looked and dressed like a club whore. One glance and you would know who was who.

"Fine. I'll back down." Kim crossed her arms.

"You don't have to. Really, I would love to tell Dad what you told me last night." Abby applied a bit more pressure to the situation until her sister spun around, her long red hair flicking around her face.

"Sorry for bothering you, Dad. We have this all sorted." Kim shot her dad a big grin and then put her hand out. "I need money."

"For what?" Roach sounded a bit more relaxed.

"For a new wardrobe. I have red hair now."

"I didn't know whore came in any other color," Abby spoke up.

"Says the ugly twin." Kim rolled her eyes.

Roach slapped a big wad of cash in Kim's hand. "Get out. Fuck off, the two of you."

Kim planted a kiss on her dad's cheek. "See ya tonight, Dad." She shot a glare in Abby's direction and a lustful wink at Trigger, and then walked out.

Abby started to follow her, but Roach wrapped his hand around her upper arm, stopping her. "Abby."

"Yes, Dad?" She turned around and looked up at him with no expression.

"You gonna tell me what really happened?"

"No."

"Did someone hurt you?"

"No."

"Are you lying?"

"No."

He shook his head, his face softening. "You're lying, little one."

I had seen Roach kill a man in cold blood. I had seen many sides to this man, but I had never seen the soft, gentle one. I looked at Dane, and he grinned back at me. *I guess being a father does weird things to a grown man.*

"I'm fine, Dad. Sorry for interrupting your meeting." A weak smile traced her lips.

He pulled her into a hug, ripping her up from the ground. Then finally, she looked me in the eye while hugging her old man, looking over his shoulder at me. Her feet dangled in the air as Roach hugged her.

Darn, she was beautiful.

"Do you want to stay for the meeting, little one?" He put her down, rubbing the top of her head. "We're talking about the Soldiers."

This was club business. Skirts did not belong in the middle of club business.

"I think the room is a bit full. I'll see you tonight." She was

16

blocked from my view, but I could still hear her voice.

"Righteo, little one. Off ya go then."

Abby closed the two large wooden doors behind her. Roach slumped back in his chair and reached for his bottle of beer.

"Don't have fucking girls. Let that be a lesson to you young blokes," he grunted.

Dane grumbled a deep laugh as both of them shared some fatherly joke together.

The meeting continued, but I wouldn't lie and say my mind wasn't on a sixteen-year old's blue opal eyes and killer body.

Abby

Embarrassment was something I was used to. Growing up around so many men and being as clumsy as I am, it just came with the territory. But this morning, I got a huge dose—close to an overdose—when I was not only ranted at by Kim but also had told off my dad, all in front of the man I hadn't been able to stop thinking about all night.

Kade Wilson; also known as Reaper.

No woman could lie and say they didn't find him attractive. He had a bad-boy appeal, and even a saint would fall for his looks— those deep dark eyes, that sexy smile, and that body. I knew it wasn't just my hormones lusting after him because any female with a pair of eyes would be doing the same.

I was singing off-tune, loudly, to a Metallica track when my dad broke into my bedroom.

"Dad, ever heard of knocking?" I snapped before bending down and swooping up my paintbrush. *Great, another stain on my carpet.*

"Better start explaining why the hell I just got a letter from the school, Abby." He waved a piece of paper in my face.

I snapped it from his grasp and read over the finely written letter, which detailed a suspension—my suspension.

"I didn't do anything." I was gobsmacked. The letter stated I was being suspended for abusing a teacher. Sure, I might be a bit of a spitfire at times, but I couldn't remember one occasion where I had abused a teacher.

"The letter is telling me otherwise," Dad grunted, not buying my denial.

"I didn't do this." I gave him back the piece of paper. "They must have gotten Kim and me mixed up because I don't even have Mrs. Matthews as a teacher!"

I watched as Dad thought it over. Finally, he blew out a deep breath and turned around sharply. "KIMBERLY!" He closed my door on the way out and roared down the hall.

Kim was suspended, again. What a surprise.

I looked back at my painting. There was something off and I couldn't decide what it was, but something was missing from the abstract piece of art. Maybe I just needed a break from it.

I was cleaning the paintbrush in my bathroom sink when I heard Dad's big boots storm back into my room.

"Abby, I can't find Kim."

I looked up at my mirror and saw my dad's reflection staring behind me.

"Well, I wouldn't have a clue where she is." I could guess, though; it was the same place Trigger was. I did like my sister—just a little bit—and I knew that telling Dad that Kim was sleeping with Trigger would bring a whole lot of hell down on her.

"You cut yourself?" Dad stepped closer, looking into the sink filled with red.

"No, just paint." I showed him the clean brushes. "I'm not that stupid, Dad."

"Good. Don't want you doing any of that cutting with razors shit. Too pretty for scars, baby girl." He ruffled my hair. "I'm heading out for a while. I'll be back before the party tonight."

"Um, Dad," I spun around. "Is the Western Charter still staying?"

"They haven't ridden out; I expect them to in the next few days though." He narrowed his eyes, looking down at me with suspicion. "Why?"

"Just wondering how many I will be bartending for." I hid my real reason behind a smile.

Kade was still here. He hadn't left, which meant maybe I could redeem myself. I didn't want him to look at me like I was a little girl.

***

The booming laughter came from the lounge in the clubhouse, which could be heard from my room two floors up.

I closed my bedroom door and walked up the hallway. Kim popped her head out of her room.

Red hair… I couldn't help the evil grin. Serves her right for not controlling her boyfriend and letting him loose; Trigger knew it wasn't Kim the night before.

But Kim, in her rage, wouldn't hear of it. Instead, she ranted about how he would have done me a favor finally popping my cherry. She was disgusting at times, but I knew she said it out of rage: she didn't mean it.

She was more hurt that Trigger couldn't tell us apart when we were complete opposites. He could darn well tell us apart now; I made sure of that.

"Are you going out tonight?" Kim asked, walking next to me.

"Yep." This always happened. We would have a major fight, and then hours later we would pretend it didn't happen. It was easier than saying sorry.

"Trigger is meant to be breaking away from Dad later. I was hoping you could stay home and make sure we weren't missed."

She had the guts to ask for a favor. God, she knew how to outdo herself.

"Just give Dad a few beers. He will soon forget about where his gay VP is. He was looking for you this morning."

We took the stairs two at a time.

"Yeah well, he found me. Stupid school. Honestly, they have it out for me. Please, Abby." She grabbed my arm, stopping me. "Please do this for me. Come on, my hair is fucking red for god's sake!"

After a few seconds of tossing the idea around, I sighed. "Fine, but you better warn that boyfriend of yours. If he comes near me again, I'm telling Dad."

"Yeah, yeah." She waved her hand, making light of it.

"Not yeah, yeah, Kim. I mean it."

We walked up the hallway and into the bar. The lounge and bar were an open space; it was huge and completely filled with bikers.

The girls weren't wearing much, and the blokes weren't hiding their lust. Many of them had hands up the shirts of the whores and had them pinned against walls, against the bar, on the couch, on the pool table. It was funny how I was so used to it that I didn't even look twice.

"I'll see you later," Kim whispered in my ear before stalking off, making fuck me eyes at Trigger.

God, those two make me sick.

Within five minutes, I watched Trigger disappear out the club door following Kim's footsteps.

I swiped a beer from the counter and made my way over to the pool table. Gitz and Cameron were attempting to play, though I was sure it was harder to play having a woman wrapped under your arm.

"Are you heading out, Abby?" Gitz asked me, holding a pool stick and sitting at the table, some woman's hands all over him. He seemed a lot better since last night. He was either putting on a brave face or he really was over it.

"It's your turn, Gitz," Cameron shouted before driving his lips onto a brunette's.

I sighed and slumped into the couch. The music was pounding and so was the laughter; everyone seemed to be having a great night. Then there was me, sitting here, bored shitless.

I scanned the crowd and spotted Dad leaning against the bar, laughing and talking to the Satan's Sons Western Charter's President, Dane.

If he was still here, I wondered if that meant Reaper was, too.

I walked across the room, and then when Dad was within arm's reach, I swooped in under his arm.

He kissed the top of my head and wrapped his arm around me, all the while keeping up with the conversation.

I could hear his heart beating through his leather cut, and I loved it. It reminded me of my childhood, all the times I fell asleep by his side after having a nightmare.

"Are you alright, darling?" Dad looked down at me.

I nodded my head and just held on to him a bit tighter.

Most guys in the room had a whore clinging to them, not their daughter, but I knew Dad didn't mind. He never minded.

Dane and Dad kept talking, laughing, and joking. The hours slowly ticked by.

I let go of Dad and yawned. "I'm going to get a drink."

He nodded his head and let me go.

I leaned across the bar and poured myself a drink. The bartender was busy up at the top end filling order after order.

"Should you be drinking that, sweetheart?" Reaper's voice whisked across my ear, and I could feel him standing behind me. His chest pressed against my back, and he reached around me and wrapped his hand around the glass in my hand. "Or should I be taking that off ya?"

My eyes were glued to his hand. It engulfed mine, and the metal of the reaper ring he wore pressed into my skin.

"I'm allowed to drink." My heart was pounding faster than a heart attack, and I was sure my voice wavered with nervousness.

His laughter was deep and thick and it rumbled through his body, sending chills through mine.

"I've been waiting for ya to leave ya Dad's side."

I slowly turned around and looked up into his deep dark eyes. He kept his arm behind me, pinning me between him and the bar. Not a bad place to be pinned, I thought.

"Why would that be, Kade?"

"Wanted to see if you were alright after last night. Did you tell anyone about what happened?"

"I told Kim."

"Bet she didn't believe ya. Nice work on the hair, by the way."

A smile twitched on my lips. "Thanks."

"Seems those two aren't anywhere to be found."

"Hence why I am trying to make sure that Dad doesn't pick up on that." I sipped from the plastic cup—Dad made sure the bar only stocked plastic cups after so many incidents with glasses.

"You're covering for her even when she is a complete bitch?" He frowned. "You are twisted, woman."

Woman.

"I'm sure she will do the same for me when I need her to." I swallowed the whiskey quickly. It burned my throat on the way down.

Kade's eyes went darker for a moment before he pulled away and scanned the crowd. "Ya old man looks busy. Can we split for a bit?"

Did Kade want to go somewhere with me? He wanted to talk to me, alone. For an instant, I thought I knew how a heart attack must feel like. Swallowing sharply, I ordered myself to keep my shit together.

"Ok." I glanced at Dad, who was still busy chatting with Dane. He didn't seem to notice that I wasn't around. "Where do you want to go?"

A dangerous smile spread across his face, one that would be sure to scare a smart woman away. "Only one place a biker wants a girl."

"In his bed?" I raised an eyebrow, teasing him. Why I felt relaxed around him, able to flirt with him, I didn't know. Being around him brought out a confidence I didn't usually have around men, but at the same time, he had the ability to make my confidence crumble. *What do you call that?*

"Nah, babe." He leaned closer, dipping his head to the side, his eyes not leaving mine. "On the back of his bike."

He pulled his keys from his pocket and shot me a wink. Then it happened. It wasn't Kim following the biker out; it was me.

How many times had I promised myself I wouldn't be that girl? I wouldn't be like her, but there I was, following Kade aka 'Reaper' out into the club's car park.

I'm supposed to be the smart one.

Chapter 2

Reaper

The road was dead, the night sky as black as the sea, the air whipping through me. Her thin arms were wrapped around me, clinging to my back, holding on tightly.

I had an angel on the back of my bike. Sure, she was young, and there was no fucking way anything was going to happen, but still she was on my bike, clinging to me.

I had gotten her out of the club party, stealing all her attention.

The bike glued to the road as we climbed the hill, turning into the corners. The park was dimly lit, but the view was as good as I had remembered.

I pulled the bike to the curb and cut the engine.

"The view is amazing," Abby gushed. She was quick to get off my bike to admire it. "I haven't been up here in years."

I didn't like the fact she wasn't clinging to me anymore, but I would deal with it. I *had* to deal with it. She unclipped my helmet and handed it back to me.

"How did you know about the Black Hill Lookout?" she asked, walking off into the park.

The city lights were below us, and I was quick to put the kickstand out and lean the bike down to follow her.

"Not my first time in town, baby." I pulled a cigarette from my leather vest and lit it, not taking my eyes off her back.

Damn that frame, so bloody perfect.

She whipped around, her blonde hair swiping across her face. "How come you haven't been to the club before if you've been in town?"

"The clubs weren't always brothers." I smirked at her innocence. She had too good of a soul for the likes of me.

Her mouth formed an "O" in understanding and then slowly, a smile spread across her lips.

"So you were the enemy once."

"I suppose, darlin'. What are ya getting at?"

Before the charter was patched over to Satan's Sons, our club was known as Widowers. Now I rode for a club name that I once shot up; it was just the way the brotherhood worked, I guess.

"I really know how to pick them," she muttered to herself, shaking her head before turning back around and looking at the city lights. "How long are you in town for?"

"Ride out tomorrow."

"So tonight's your last night in town?"

"What are ya getting at, babe?" I moved to stand behind her, placing my hand on her small hip. She froze at my touch, and my heart rate quickened. Fuck. I shouldn't have touched her. Then she relaxed, slowly turning around.

"Nothing." Those opal blue eyes stared up at me. She let out a long sigh. "Why did you bring me here,?"

"You were bored; I could see it in ya eyes. Thought ya might like to get away."

I played it smart. I wanted to steal all her attention, and then she might not think I was a complete stalking prick.

"Thanks." She smiled. "So, Kade..." she slowly bit that juicy bottom lip of hers, amusement flashing across her face. "You going to kiss me already or are you going to just keep staring at me?"

I took a sharp breath. "What the fuck did you just say?"

I didn't need her to repeat it. It burned into my ears, but still I didn't believe it. She looked smart, but right now she wasn't acting it. I was too old, too dangerous for this angel.

"I said," she took a step closer to me, placing her hand on my chest, "are you going to kiss me?"

I ran the back of my knuckles down the side of her face. Her

25

skin was just as soft as I had imagined it to be. I wanted to kiss her. I wanted to do a whole lot more to her, but I was too old for her, and she was way too young for me.

"No, sweetheart, I'm not gonna kiss you." As much as I wanted to, I couldn't fucking do it. She was underage. She was the forbidden fruit.

While I was having a mental breakdown, I didn't notice her rise to her toes before she planted a soft kiss on my lips.

She barely grazed it, but it was enough. It was enough to get a taste.

"What the hell was that?" I hissed. She had just hooked me on a drug I couldn't get a real fix of, not for two fucking long years.

She pulled her head back, staring into my eyes. "I never said I wasn't going to kiss you."

"I'm too old for the likes of you, Abby." Too old, too dangerous, and too fucking scarred for her.

"But yet I still want to kiss you again." Abby smiled, a real full-blown smile. "You know, Kade, you really need to loosen up."

"Ya flirting with fire, Abby," I grunted as I walked past her, intending to sit on top of a picnic bench.

Stupid teenagers. They didn't know what was good for them. Abby didn't realize what she was doing.

"Kim can't tease me anymore." She followed me, grinning like a bloody teenager.

She is a teenager.

I was used to women—cold, loose, and used. Not this bubbly, happy, grinning shit. It reminded me again just how far she was out of my reach.

"What ya talking about, darling?" I searched my cut for my pack of cigarettes, but at the rate I was going, I was going to smoke the whole pack before I got her back to the clubhouse.

"Well, it's not like I've lost my virginity or anything, but still, the first kiss is something." She shrugged her shoulders and pulled herself up on the picnic bench next to me.

"That was your first kiss?" I couldn't believe that bullshit.

"Yep." She stole a cigarette from my pack before I even had a chance to get one out.

"That wasn't a fucking kiss," I growled. A primal instinct flooded my body; I couldn't fight it if I wanted to.

Her eyes went wide with fright. "I'm sorry... I didn't... I'm sorry," she stuttered.

"Stop." I put my hand under her chin. I flicked the unlit cigarette from my hand and twisted around, placing my other hand on the side, framing her perfect face with my hands.

If my place in hell wasn't already reserved, it sure as hell would be now.

I dipped my head, so she knew. She knew what was about to happen and she didn't pull away; she didn't run off screaming. She took a shaky breath before I claimed those perfect lips. I couldn't be gentle; it wasn't me. I kissed her hard, and rough, and the small moan that came from her lips told me she liked it.

Her hands wrapped around my neck, and she kept a tight grip on me. I placed my hand on her hip and moved my other hand to grip the back of her head.

She kissed me back hard.

My hand was itching to reach up under her tee shirt and feel those hard perky breasts of hers, but I didn't. I kept my hand glued to her hip.

She broke the kiss, taking gulps of air.

"You ok, babe?" I brushed the wild hair from her face.

"Don't stop." She drove up, pressing her lips hard against mine.

Her small, warm hand touched mine, and she tried to guide it up her shirt. I froze.

"I can't, babe." I pulled away, planting kisses down her neck.

She begged me to touch her. "Please, Kade, please."

"I can't, darling." I just couldn't do it.

She grabbed my hands and instead of moving it up, she moved it down, causing my eyes to double in size and my heart to nearly explode from shock.

She pulled herself up on me. "Come on, Kade. Please."

I shook my head and kissed up her neck.

"Kade, please," she begged in my ear as she pressed her body into me.

Growling, I pushed her back down onto the table and went to unbutton her jeans. I would regret this later, I knew it. But I was only human.

I slipped a finger into her, and immediately her eyes closed, and she moaned.

"So darn tight, baby," I grunted, squeezing a finger inside her.

Sweet sixteen.

I started to pump my finger, and she was rocking against it. I couldn't fit two fingers in her; she was too darn tight, I knew it would hurt her.

"Babe, look at me." I gripped her head. I could feel her tighten and clench around my finger. She was gonna burst, and I wanted to see it on her face when she did.

Her eyes fluttered open, and those big eyes were painted with lust and desire. Her pussy clenched itself around my finger, and her body started to rock, her back arching.

"Don't fight it, darling." I kissed down her neck.

Her arms shook around me, and she put a death grip on my finger. *So darn tight.*

She moaned loudly, and my name escaped her lips in the last breath. I wasn't just hard anymore; I was dead stiff hearing her moan my name as she came for the very first time.

Her forehead was sweaty, and she pressed it against mine. "Thank you." Her sweet words washed over my face.

"Don't have to thank me, baby." I kissed her softly. "It was my pleasure."

I knew I was never going to forget that look on her face and in her eyes when she came.

I had taken her first kiss. This little sweet sixteen-year-old girl just gave me something that I would never forget.

Looking into her flushed face, those eyes, I felt my heart squeeze. I felt something I hadn't ever felt before.

***

I braced the bike as she eased herself off. The club car park was dead quiet; there were a few passed out bodies lying around.

She shivered in the night air, and I kicked the stand out, getting off my bike.

She wouldn't look me in the eye. Instead, her eyes were locked on my bike. I didn't know what to expect. I had never deflowered a girl with my finger before.

"Why is that bit blank?" She placed her hand on the engine of the bike, where there was a bare spot in the paintwork.

"I've been looking for a picture of a reaper." I scratched the back of my neck. "The guy that did the rest of the work didn't have one I liked."

She nodded her head. "It would look sweet." She looked up, meeting my eyes for the first time since what happened at the park. "Would suit you."

"Yeah." I grinned.

"Well, I better go to… um… bed." She took a step back, her eyes still on mine.

"Night, Abby."

"Night, Kade." She smiled, turning her back and walking towards the clubhouse.

I couldn't stop looking at her, watching her body sway with each step she took away from me.

She was way too beautiful for me. Still, I couldn't stop reliving what just happened. Never would forget it. I knew that when she walked away.

Abby

I woke up to the sound of roaring engines. For a moment, it didn't startle me. I lived at the clubhouse; hearing the roar of engines wasn't out of the norm, but today was different.

I flung the blankets back, staggering out of bed. I ripped the drawing from my sketchbook and scooted out into the hallway. I tripped over my feet and accidently fell down a few steps as I hurried.

I couldn't let him leave without saying good-bye.

I broke open the clubhouse door and scanned the crowd. Dad was talking to Dane, saying his farewells. Kim was awake and still wearing what I last saw her in the night before. Then I spotted Kade on his bike, looking down at his phone.

Smiling, I hurried around a few bodies.

The concrete was cold under my feet, and I really wished I had fallen asleep in my warm PJs instead of shorts and a tight pink tank top.

"Kade." I stood awkwardly next to his bike.

His head darted to me, his eyes shocked for a moment. "You're here."

"I kind of live here." I couldn't stop myself from smiling when I watched his grin bloom.

"You just woke up, didn't ya?"

My cheeks went red as his eyes scanned up and down my body.

"Yeah well." I chewed my bottom lip and then flung my hand out. "I wanted to give you this before you left."

He took the folded piece of paper from me.

"It's just a rough sketch. You don't have to use it, but yeah. Well, I… um, couldn't sleep after you and then, um… well, I started to…" I glared down at my feet. Why couldn't I form words?

He opened the piece of paper. "You drew this?"

"Just a rough sketch. You said you couldn't find one you liked, so I drew that up."

He smiled gently at me. "Thanks, Abby."

My name rolled off his lips. Oh damn, he had me. "No worries." I rocked on my heels and still seemed unable to stop smirking. Darn, was I out of my head? Smart Abby wouldn't do this. Smart Abby would be regretting last night. Not standing next to the man that could be my own form of poison. After how my body was reacting, I was positive I was in over my head.

"Let's head home, boys!" Dane roared and mounted his bike.

"You won't be coming back for a while, will you?" I asked Kade, taking a step closer to him so he could hear me. Why did that get under my skin? Why did I care so much, knowing I won't be seeing him again for maybe years?

The roaring of more engines coming to life filled the car park.

"Yeah, babe. Might be a few years." He looked to be in thought for a moment before he kicked his bike to life, confirming what I was thinking.

"I guess I'll see you then." I wondered if I would ever see him again. Bikers came and went. His commitment to the club might change over the course of a few years. Hell, it wasn't uncommon for a member to jump ship.

"You might be legal by the time I get back here." He ran his tongue across his bottom lip. "Then we can finish what we started."

I blushed. "Well, I guess that means you have to come back then." I chewed my bottom lip, looking at him with lustful eyes.

"You can count on it, babe."

Dane took off, and Kade shot me a wink before taking off after

31

him.

I watched as he tore out of the club's driveway following his president. Count on me to fall for the biker more dangerous and toxic than my father. How the hell was I meant to try and be with a boy now after being touched by a man?

"What did ya give Reaper?" Dad was at my side, and I had been too busy lusting over Kade to realize he had walked across the car park to me.

"A sketch." I crossed my arms, the cold morning air washing across my body.

"Why ya do that?" Dad pressed me for more answers.

"I liked him." I shrugged my shoulders and played down the attraction I had towards a man a hell of a lot older than me. "He reminded me of you." I looked up at my father and kept lying. "A bit of a lost soul."

Dad grunted and then dropped his big hand on my head, ruffling my hair. "All bikers are lost souls, honey. That's why we are all so fucked up."

I shot him up a grin when really my mind was on Kade. Would he ever come back? Two years was a long time, and if I knew one thing for sure, things could change quickly.

Chapter 3

Abby

The years slowly ticked by and to be fair to myself, I couldn't lie and say they were eventful. It seemed every day I was that bit weirder and a bit more left out at school. Finally, it reached the point that I was invisible, unlike my twin, Kim.

She was anything but invisible—captain of the cheer squad, currently dating one of the most popular guys at school. Mind you, she was still slutting it up with Trigger. Trigger, for some strange and most likely perverted reason, liked it.

I withdrew from society, the biker's society, and normal society, and as Kim regularly told me, 'I was a hermit with a pen.'

Drawing was all I had, and to say I spent most of my life doing it was an understatement.

Our eighteenth birthday was fast approaching, which pretty much summed up the reason why I was sitting in Dad's office next to Kim.

"Dad, you promised." Kim huffed and crossed her arms. "You can't go back on a promise."

Dad never went back on a promise. It was his promise to Mom that he wouldn't be hard on us and actually let us date. Kim had a current boyfriend who was still breathing.

"Can't have all those underage girls here, Kim; it would bring trouble I don't want around my club." Dad rubbed his temples, looking like a giant behind his desk.

He had shaved his head a year earlier as a dare, and he liked it. He had been shaving it ever since. Personally, I thought it made him look younger, but Kim said he was doing it because of Leah, his current bed buddy, liked it.

"Dad, most of my friends are over eighteen already and if they want to mess with a biker, so be it." Kim shrugged her shoulders.

"What do you want, Abby?" Dad looked across at me. For the first time this evening, my opinion was actually called upon.

What did I think about having an overly expensive and massive eighteenth birthday party?

"I hate the idea."

"Of course you hate the idea." Kim rolled her eyes and glared at me. "You have no friends."

"Please. You're inviting the whole darn school, Kim, as if they are all your friends."

"Well, not one of them is yours, that's for sure."

She was mostly right.

"Girls," Dad growled with a warning.

"I have friends."

"Yes, two." Kim sneered. "If you classify that black-headed emo freak and her brother as friends."

I got along really well with Kayla Knight, my only friend, and her brother Jace. I considered him a friend, too. Even though he was a year and a half older than us and in college.

"Why are we even calling it a joint fucking party then?" I snapped. Once again, Kim lit a rage within me. "It is your party, not mine. I just want to chill in my room and do nothing. But no. You have to have this big bloody event!"

"GIRLS!" Dad roared, sending us into silence.

Kim glared at me, and I glared right back. We might be turning eighteen, but that didn't mean we had grown up when it came to fighting.

"Fine, Kim, you can have the party, but everyone that enters this clubhouse is to know the rules. The party is to be in the pub only. No one is to enter the clubhouse or the garage. Abby," Dad's eyes shot to me, and for a split second, I saw the pity in them. "You don't have to attend if you don't want to. I know this isn't your type of scene."

"Please, Dad, she doesn't have a scene," Kim piped in.

All through fucking high school, I had to deal with this. When Kim wasn't bullying me, everyone was ignoring me, and right now, I had had it.

"I hate you, Kim," I hissed in her face, "and next time you get bitch-slapped, don't expect me to jump in and have your back."

I pushed the chair back and got up. Why did I always take the bloody high ground? When Kim was being cornered by Megan the day before at school, I didn't even think twice about jumping in to get her off my sister.

Kim couldn't hold her own in a fight if she had to. Though she should learn, because I couldn't count how many times I've had to step in.

"Where are you going?" Dad asked as I opened the door, ready to storm the hell away from both of them.

"Out, and no, I don't know when I'll be home, and no, I'm not telling you where I am going, and yes, I'm going to be drunk when I decide to return to this hellhole I am cursed to call home," I sneered before slamming his door.

I hated Kim, and I hated Dad for never standing up for me.

Reaper

I put my feet up on the desk, reading the newspaper. Once again, Satan's Sons were on its front cover.

"Yo, Prez." Liam knocked on my door before walking in.

I hadn't gotten used to being called Prez, but after Dane was shot down on the streets six months earlier, I had to step up.

"What's up, Liam?" I put the paper down.

"The guys and I have a request." His lips curved in a way that told me it had something to do with women and booze.

"What would that be?"

"You know MC?"

Stupid question, did I know the bloody MC? I wanted to scoff but didn't. I kept my face normal, even though a picture of Abby flashed across my mind. "What about them?"

"Roach's daughters have got their eighteenth birthday party this weekend. Everyone is talking about it. Thought we could be good brothers and offer our help, ya know, and celebrate the girls coming of age."

More like he and the rest of them wanted to fuck some barely legal pussy. "Is that so?"

Abby was turning eighteen. My mind drifted back to that early Sunday morning. That smile on her face. I wondered if she even remembered it.

"So what ya say, Boss?" he asked.

I had been waiting for an excuse to take the seven-hour ride back to her. She probably didn't even remember me. She most likely thought of me as that old guy who took advantage of her in that park.

"Tell the boys we leave in a few hours," I answered him.

Abby might not remember me, but I sure as hell remembered her, and I wanted to see what she grew up like. I wanted to know if she remembered me.

Roach

By Friday morning, I was already dreading the weekend. Kim painted her fingernails at the end of the table, barely wearing fucking clothes, and the men had noticed.

How many times had I told her to cover up?

The Western Charter had rolled in late the night before. It was good to have the brothers back, though I knew the thought of young women had caused the visit.

Still, they were here and once the weekend finished—and we got through this bloody party—we might be able to have a real club party, one that didn't have fucking pink balloons all over my pub.

"Morning, Brother." Reaper walked in, looking like he had a sleepless night.

The dining table was covered with food; the club women had gone to extra lengths with the visit of another charter.

"Ya look like shit, Reaper." I put my paper down, looking over the man who was now President of our Western Charter.

"Morning, Reaper." Kim looked up from her fingernails, flashing that smile I didn't like her giving to anyone.

"Kim, right?" Reaper barely glanced at her and reached for the freshly cooked bacon.

Kim looked disappointed for a split second, seeing he hadn't paid as much attention to her as she had expected. Well there you go, a man not hunting down my daughter. Reaper could stay around as far as I was concerned.

"Yep." She smiled that smile again and blew on her nails. "So, you sleep well?"

"Kim, don't you have shit to do?" I barked.

I won't have her chatting up a bloody man older than her. I might have promised her mother to let them have a semi-normal dating life, but this was beyond that promise.

"Nope." She looked back at me, that taunting grin in place.

"Where's ya sister? Why don't you go and find her, see if she is right for this weekend?"

Abby had been keeping low since she stormed out the other night. It wasn't like Abby to make a scene, but I knew Kim was pushing her.

"I haven't seen her since she left."

"Left?" I got up from my seat. "LEFT WHEN?"

Kim looked at me with a pointless expression. If she weren't my daughter, I would backhand her right now.

"Since she left the other night. You were there, Dad."

"You're telling me Abby hasn't been home for two fucking days?"

"I can't believe you didn't know that." Kim dropped her head to the side, frowning. "Well, looks like she is invisible to you, too."

I already had my phone out, dialing her number, and when she didn't pick up on the third ring, I got concerned.

"Why the hell didn't you tell me she hadn't come home?"

Images of her being raped and left for dead in a ditch somewhere flashed through my mind. Rage boiled within me and spilled out across my face. Why the hell hadn't I checked on her earlier?

Two whole bloody nights she hadn't been here.

It wasn't like my Abby to disappear.

"Dad, you really need to calm down. She will be at Kayla's. Look, I'll call Kayla." Kim dialed a number on her phone, finally acting like a caring bloody sister.

"Hi Kayla, it's Kim. No, I'm not drunk dialing. Look, bitch, drop the attitude. I just want to know if you've seen Abby?" Kim went silent, listening for a moment, and then swiftly hung up.

"Well?" I demanded.

Kim chewed her lip and got up with caution. "Um well, Kayla said she hasn't seen or heard from her since Monday."

"TRIGGER!" I roared. "Keys. I needed fucking keys."

"What's up, Prez?" Trigger held a cue stick, a club whore under his arm.

"Abby is missing."

"I'll get the boys." Instantly, Trigger snapped into the mode I needed him in.

"Has she got any other friends she would stay with?" Reaper questioned Kim.

"No," Kim answered as she pulled on a jacket. "I'm coming, Dad."

"What the fuck for? It's no secret ya hate her, Kim. Stay here."

"I'll get my guys up, Roach. The more eyes out looking for her, the easier it will be." Reaper had his phone, and I nodded my head in thanks.

I prayed to whoever the fuck was in the sky to let my little girl be ok. Trigger barked out orders to the brothers as I straddled my bike.

Where the hell would Abby go, if she didn't want to be found?

Chapter 4

Abby

I got out of my car, and I noticed my dad looking furious—more so than normal—mounting his motorbike.

I feel sorry for the poor bastard that pissed him off.

I was striding to the clubhouse when Kim yelled across the lot, pointing at me. "SHE'S THERE!"

Fuck, Kim, you are getting more brain dead by the day.

Dad's head whipped in my direction, along with every other bikers'. Suddenly, I felt like *I* was the poor bastard.

"Where the fuck have you been?" Dad roared at me, throwing his bike down on the stand and storming across the car park to me.

I felt like a trapped deer; I couldn't move.

"I've been at my art show." I blinked, looking up at him. "Why are you so mad?"

"Mad? Why am I mad?" he spat down at me. "You haven't been home for two days!"

"I was home this morning!" I looked up at him, confused. Then I looked around the car park. Some bikers were looking at me with pity, others with annoyance because I was sure my dad had roared their heads off all because of me.

Suddenly it hit me. *Dad thought I hadn't been home for two days?* He thought I hadn't been home since I stormed out of his office two days ago? It was official; I was invisible not just to everyone at school, but my own dad, too.

"I came home last night!" My fists clenched at my sides. "Who do you think took the cigarette out from your hand and put the bucket next to the couch for you?" At that moment, I hated him. I hated her. I hated school. I hated everything and everyone. I pushed him hard in the chest and stormed past him. "Great parenting, Dad."

Dad hadn't really said anything else; he just let me storm off. After a few hours, I wasn't angry with him anymore. I was angry with myself for making such a scene.

I knew Reaper had witnessed the whole event. I knew that because I caught his blank stare as I stormed across the lot.

Kim had followed me, muttering some empty apology. At the time, I wasn't interested, but now as I thought about it, I wondered why she had bothered.

I was lying on my bed, staring at the ceiling, when there was a knock on my door.

"Come in." I sighed and pulled myself up, throwing my legs over the edge of the bed. I wasn't even half surprised when I saw Dad closing my bedroom door behind him.

Dad looked exhausted. His eyes were locked on my carpet, his hands stuffed in his jeans pocket. It was the first time I could honestly say that Dad looked his age.

"Need to talk to ya." His lips formed a firm line after he spoke, then slowly he looked up.

Just like that, my mind went blank. My stomach fell and my world seemed to freeze. Something was seriously wrong; one look and I could see it.

"Not going to lie to you, Abby. Shit isn't looking too good for me at the moment." His grim words seemed to form ice as he spoke. "I have a bunch of loose ends, and 'til they are all dealt with, I can't have you and Kim around me."

"This morning you were yelling at me for not being home, and now you're telling me you want me to leave?"

"Not leave." Dad moved across the room, then sat down beside me. "I need you to make a break away from this type of life."

"Type of life," I repeated his words.

"I can't have you and Kim paying for my mistakes. Your mom would kill me."

"Dad." I dropped my hand on his knee, looking up into those big green eyes. "What makes you think that we don't want this type of life? It's all we know. Don't push us away. Look, we have dealt with threats before, and each time Kim and I have come through untouched. If you want us on house arrest for a while, we can do that."

Dad seemed torn, and it showed so clear across his face. "What did I do to get two great daughters?" His face softened, and he threw an arm around my shoulder, pulling me to his side.

"So you spoke to Kim?" I asked.

"Yep."

"What did she say?"

"The same thing you said."

Sometimes, on very rare occasions, Kim and I thought alike; this was one of those times.

"You know, Dad," a grin slowly spread across my lips, "you can't cancel our party that easy."

A deep laughter rumbled from his chest. "I guess you're right, kiddo." He gave me a wink before getting up.

Dad said something about a late tea and heading out for a while before he left me alone once again in my room.

I was too young and perhaps too stupid, or maybe I was just so sure that nothing could or ever would really tear our family apart, so I didn't take Dad's 'loose ends' seriously.

It would take something huge to tear the Harrison family apart, and that something huge was coming. It was a hurricane of broken glass, and it would shatter and slice our lives into pieces beyond repair.

But I didn't know that then.

Chapter 5

Abby

Pink and more pink. I had never seen so much pink in my life. I was sure Barbie had come around and spewed up all over the joint. So when Kim asked for my opinion, I couldn't help but voice my honest reaction. "I hate it."

Kim pursed her lips and took a deep breath. "You hate everything. Do you have any idea how much time we have put into this?" She waved her hand around the pub, and her minions that were slumped on bar stools looked more like overworked slaves.

I screwed my nose up when I noticed the pink cups as well. "Well, I never asked you to turn Dad's pub into Barbie's paradise."

"There isn't *that* much pink!" She stomped her foot and as if on cue, Dad walked up behind her.

"Fucking hell," he hissed, looking around his once-manly pub. "This... this... this is rubbish." He pointed around at the pink balloons. "Better be gone by tomorrow morning."

Kim muttered something under her breath but didn't argue. It was the night of the big party, and by the moody expression on each of our faces, it was easy to see we were all just flipping jumping for joy for Kim's pink party.

"I'm not lifting a finger. I had no hand in turning this into...." I looked around the joint and then shrugged my shoulders. "I don't think there is a name for this much pink."

Dad grunted in agreement, and Kim just shot me her classic 'fuck you' glare. She really is just smothering me with sisterly love.

Reaper

She hadn't shown her face once. I took another gulp of my beer and looked over the crowd. How can she not show her face at her own goddamn party? It was after midnight, and the party was in full swing. Lots of teens drinking and lots of grinding, but still there was no Abby.

Kim danced on the top of the bar with another blonde, and Trigger didn't even try to hide the fact he was watching her every move.

Roach, from what I had heard, passed out sometime earlier in the afternoon. I don't blame him; Kim's whiny voice would drive any man to the bottle.

"I'm going to get some air," I yelled in Liam's ear, who was more interested in flirting with the young chick on his arm than listening to what I had to say.

I needed some fresh air, a smoke, and a break from the noise. At first, I hadn't planned on walking over to the clubhouse.

It was stone quiet when I entered the club pub.

If she wasn't at the party, she would have to be here. I took the stairs quickly, and I had already knocked on her door before it hit me: what the fuck was I going to say to her?

Her door flung open and there she was, my own personal minx. Her hair was pulled up into a high ponytail, her cheeks flushed, and those shorts she was wearing would cause a priest to fall down to his knees in front of her.

"Reaper." Her eyes widened slightly as she stood in the doorway with a shocked look on her face.

"Did I piss you off or something?" I leaned against the doorframe, feeling a lot more comfortable seeing how nervous she was. "Not like you to call me by my biker name."

"I..." Her lips pursed and her long lashes fluttered. Slowly, she crossed her arms. "Why are you here?"

"Came to wish you a happy birthday."

"Liar."

"I don't lie, babe."

"Please, that is all your kind does."

"My kind?" I scoffed at that. "We're cut from the same patch."

"Why are you here, Kade? Instead of over there?" She nodded her head in the direction of the party.

"The question is why are you not over there. It's your party, remember?"

Her face slowly fell to the ground, and she stared down at her feet. Guilt crept through my stomach. *Shit, did I say something wrong?*

"I don't have any friends over there. The two friends I do have wouldn't come because, well..." She looked up. "Kim's a bitch."

"So you're hiding out in there then?" I dipped my head at her bedroom.

"Not much else to do."

"Fuck that; get dressed."

Once again those opal blue eyes of hers widened. "What? Why?"

Those scared kitten eyes did something for me. I don't know if it was healthy or right, but fuck it felt good, and I didn't want to stop looking into them.

"I'm taking you out, sweetheart." I leaned forward. Towering over her, I dipped my head to her ear. "You're legal now, remember? Go get dressed."

I heard her gulp, and she didn't pull away from me. Instead, she turned her head and her dangerous eyes locked with mine.

"Give me ten minutes." She put a hand on my chest and pushed me out the door, shutting it in my face hard. It didn't even anger me a bit cause I knew she was getting ready to leave with me.

<u>**Have you ever wondered how Kade, became "The Reaper"?**</u>

 to get a free story from Simone Elise to find out!

Chapter 6

Reaper

*It had seemed like a good idea at the time
but by the look on her face, I doubted
myself. We were at a party, and she wasn't
into it at all, so taking her to a pub or a
club had been scratched out. This seemed
like the right idea.*

"Seriously?" Abby's crystal eyes looked up at me, her perfect red lips curved into a smile. "You're actually going to come in here with me?

"What, babe, don't want me to?" I faked confidence and pretended that her baby doll face wasn't causing my stomach to flip around like a bloody teenager who was seeing a girl for the first time.

She chewed that juicy bottom lip before looking up at me again. "I just didn't think you were the late night shopping kind of guy."

"I haven't gotten you a birthday present; seems only right to get you one now."

I needed her to stop looking at me like that. I needed her to stop batting those long lashes. *Come on, baby girl; you're killing me.*

She ran her dainty fingers through her long blonde hair and looked across at the shopping mall. "I've never been shopping with a guy before."

I liked that. Why the fuck did I like that? It was as if a part of me liked being her one and only even if it was just the first guy to take her shopping.

"Well, babe, it's going to be an experience." I winked at her and reached out for her hand. Was she going to take it or not? Why

47

the fuck did I reach out for her hand in the first place? All the questions melted away when she did take it. Darn, her hand was cold.

We left the bike in the car park and walked towards the huge shopping mall, which before now, I had no intention of ever entering.

The things you do for a woman.

***

I had never seen so much junk and clothes in my life, and we had only been in two stores. I couldn't understand; it was after one o'clock in the morning, and there were still crowds of shoppers around. I guess that is December for you.

I leaned against the shop counter, and the retail assistant was chatting with me, a conversation which I wasn't into. My attention was on Abby as she scanned a rack of clothes.

She frowned at a blue dress. She was stunning, and I wondered if she knew how beautiful she was. *Only eighteen and so flawless.*

A bunch of loud boys entered the shop. It took them a full two minutes before their eyes landed on Abby.

We were in some punk, young-clothes shop. Fuck if I knew the name of it; all I knew was there was a hell of a lot of clothes and Abby seemed to like it.

A tall boy with a cocky grin slowly made his way over to her. My eyes narrowed as I watched like a predator.

"Harrison." The boy stood right in front of her. "Why aren't you at your party?"

"Noel." Abby crossed her arms, and I watched as she took a noticeable step away from him. Her interest in the dress was gone. "Why are you speaking to me?"

"You mean why haven't I pushed you over or backed you into a corner by now?"

48

One more word, cunt, and I'll be giving you a facial. I stepped away from the counter. I didn't want to charge over there in case the prick was Abby's friend. I wouldn't embarrass her.

The kid was young, looked like the type of bloke most girls would go for in high school. Maybe she had a crush on him. That made my stomach burn with disgust and anger.

"You know, Noel, I'm surprised you even bothered to waste a few moments of your pathetic life with me. Looks like your friends are waiting for you; best you fuck off now."

While Abby was speaking, another male made his way over to them.

"Surprised to see you out in public, Harrison." The other male sized her up. I knew that look; it was the same look that I had given a hell of a lot of women.

That was all I needed to see. A need to protect her fired through me.

Abby was stiff as a board, and I could almost feel her anxiety as I approached her. Standing behind her, she must have known I was there because she was quick to take an extra step back until she was pressed against my chest.

She was scared of these fuckers, and that sent a jolt of rage through my blood.

I wrapped an arm around her waist, keeping her back pinned against my chest. Her body melted into me.

Couldn't say I didn't like the feeling.

"You're going to want to take a step back." I threatened, keeping my eyes locked on the kids. One punch and he would be on the ground. If he and his mate knew what was good for them, they would back off. I wasn't below hitting a boy. I saw it as teaching a lesson. I'd call it 'don't fuck with a biker's girl.'

Noel raised his hands, taking a step back. "Calm down, brother. Harrison isn't worth fighting over." He grunted, and the guy next to him nodded in agreement.

Just don't kill him. Just don't kill him. I kept repeating it in my head, trying to keep a handle on my temper.

"Start walking." It wasn't a suggestion so much as a warning.

"Catch you at school, Harrison." Noel shot a look at Abby with a threatening tone to his words before the two of them walked off to join their other friends, who were standing around at the entrance of the shop looking like they wanted to leave.

I kept my eyes locked on them until they walked out of the shop. Abby's breathing was rapid and sharp, and I wondered what the fuck those boys had done to her to get her so worked up and have such a fear of them.

I dipped my head down to her shoulder and whispered in her ear. "Are you alright?"

It took a few minutes before she nodded her head. She kept her hand on my arm, which was wrapped around her. "I'm ok." She tilted her head to the side, staring into my eyes. "Thanks for that."

"Didn't do anything, babe." I wished I had done more, but for some reason, I thought that me punching the guys wouldn't have pleased her. Abby was a gentle soul, the complete opposite of me.

"Can we go?" She pulled out from my grasp, spinning on her heels to look up at me. "I just want to get out of here."

"What about the dress?" I nodded my head at the dress she had just spent at least five good minutes looking at before.

"I wouldn't have any place to wear it to." She glanced at it. "I don't usually wear bright colors; that is more Kim's thing."

I grabbed the dress. "You really need to break out of your shell, babe."

"No, Kade, don't. It's expensive."

My eyebrows shot up at that, my smirk twisting at her sweet, caring smile. "Good thing I'm loaded then."

She continued to natter more excuses why I shouldn't buy her the dress as I walked it to the counter; it wasn't until I handed over the cash that she gave up.

"Do you have a dressing room?" I asked the sales assistant who was looking me up and down like a piece of meat.

Women... so easy.

"Just to the right." She pointed a finger, not taking her eyes off me.

I handed the dress to Abby and gestured with my head. "Go put it on then."

"You want me to put this on?"

"I can put it on you if you want." I grinned at her, enjoying the way her eyes slowly widened.

"Nope. I'm more than able." She was quick to walk off in the direction of the changing room. Damn girl was fine, and I couldn't take my eyes off her as she walked away.

***

It was plain, simple, and elegant like her. The blue strapless dress hugged her body perfectly, and it stopped midway up her creamy thighs. She looked stunning even with the big black combat boots she was wearing.

"I look stupid." Abby snapped. "People keep looking at me, too."

We walked down the street, hand in hand. We had left her other clothes in the shop after she decided they weren't worth carrying around. While I thought she looked amazing, she thought she stood out.

"You care too much." I twirled her around to my side, tugging her under my arm. "Anyway, babe, who says they aren't staring at me?" I whispered in her ear.

That sweet angelic face lit up with a smirk. "You know, Kade, I think you're right."

"That doesn't happen often, trust me."

"Kade?"

51

"Abby?"

She stopped and placed a hand on my arm. "You're kind of alright."

That simple compliment coming from her lips caused a feeling to creep through me. I knew right then that I was falling hard for someone I shouldn't.

Chapter 7

Abby

I had spent the last year complaining about how I was invisible. Never did I think that one day I would be glad I was. When Kade and I arrived back at the house, not one single person had even realized I left. Sure, most of the people that should have been worrying were passed out with alcohol poisoning, but still, I couldn't help but let that tiny little smile spread. I was thankful for being invisible that night.

I was also kind of okay with being invisible at school. While Kim gloated in the aftermath of a successful party, I did everything in my power to remain invisible. I was high on the memory of the other night.

The way his touch just lit a fire within me. The way he looked at me, like I was something special.

"Oi! HARRISON!"

Hearing that voice caused me to walk faster, and I was sure I would have gotten away if I hadn't tripped over my own foot and gone flying to the floor.

The snickering and laughing from Noel and his stupid friend was all I needed to hear.

I reached for my books, only to have Noel kick them away.

"What, Noel?" I looked up at him from the ground, and with no class or grace, I got back up to my feet. "Come on then, get on with the insults so you can leave me alone."

Noel's lips twitched into a grin that would scare any sane person away, and it usually appeared before he said something hurtful.

"Your boyfriend isn't here to back you up now." He took a step closer to me. "Can't go whimpering to him."

Kade. Oh god, I wished he was here right now.

"So?" I challenged him and scooped up my books. "What is your point?"

"Getting lippy, aren't we, Harrison?" He cocked his head to the side and took a few more steps towards me until I was backed against the wall.

It was the end of the day, and I had avoided him thus far. The door to my freedom was at the end of the hall, and I couldn't help but let my eyes flicker to it.

"If you have nothing to say, can I just go?" I asked, but it came out more like a plea.

"Sure, Harrison. In fact, go on, go." Noel stepped out of my way and gestured an arm out for me to leave.

I wasn't going to wait for him to change his mind, so I rushed past him and had my hand on the door before his evil voice spoke to me.

"Oh, and I love what you did to your car. Good to see you are embracing who you are."

What had he done? I pushed the door open and bolted down the steps.

Noel was fully evil, and I was sure he was Satan's actual son. He had made it his personal mission to make my life more miserable.

I reached into my handbag and pulled out my keys. My car was everything to me. I had either been fixing the darn thing or nagging the boys to fix it for as long as I could remember, which was when I first got it when I was fifteen.

Dad had finally coughed up and paid for its paint job as my birthday present. It was beautiful and was only finished last week.

That's why Noel threatening my car had my blood running cold. I spotted my purple beast in the car park. It was sparkling in the sun and looked like it had just ridden out of a magazine.

So when I reached the driver's side of the car and saw what had been keyed into it, it was natural for the tears to swell in my eyes.

'Biker's Bitch' had been keyed, badly and roughly, into the side of my car. I pulled the car cover over it after parking it in the back of the garage. I had managed to get it home without one person seeing it.

I was gutted. It felt like someone had keyed the words into my own body. I hated Noel and if I could, I would kill him. I was tempted to tell my dad.

But what would that prove? It would prove them right, that's what.

I flicked the lights off and closed the door. I knew—because the bikes that normally decorated the driveway in front of the clubhouse weren't there—Dad wasn't home. I wasn't sure if Kade was still around. He hadn't mentioned he was leaving when we last spoke on Saturday.

I couldn't be sure. It was Monday, and it would make sense if they had left to head back home.

Suddenly I felt a lot flatter. I closed the clubhouse door behind me.

"Heard what happened to your car."

My head snapped up. Kim was sitting on the couch, TV remote in hand and looking at me. The normal hate in her eyes was not there.

"I didn't hear about it until it had been done so I couldn't do anything." Kim turned to look back at the TV. "You going to tell Dad?"

I was shocked because Kim was speaking to me and more importantly, she was speaking nicely to me. Which only meant one thing.

"What do you want, Kim?" I shoved my hands in my leather jacket.

"Fine." She looked back at me with a bored expression. "I need you to not tell Dad about it."

"I won't have to, the words kind of tell him for me."

"Just don't drive it then."

"Why? Why should I protect Noel? He is a piece of trash, and a punching from Dad wouldn't be a bad thing."

"Dad has enough stress on his plate; do you really want him chasing Noel down? You know he has a temper." Kim got up from the couch, crossing her arms and looking like her normal pissy self. "Come on Abby, think of him for once and not yourself."

I scoffed, shaking my head and leaving the room before I decided to do something I would regret.

***

I listened to music and tried my very best to work my stress out in the gym when Kim showed her ugly head.

"Dinner is ready. Dad's waiting," she yelled over the music and then slammed the door.

I didn't feel like eating. I felt like doing another hour or so on the treadmill, running my anger off. But Kim's snippy way of saying 'Dad's waiting' meant he was expecting me to make an appearance.

I didn't feel like speaking to a single person, and I really didn't feel like sitting at the table watching bikers scarf down their weight in meat. I wasn't dressed for it either, in my sports crop top and shorts.

By the time I dragged my butt down to the dining room, everyone was already eating and laughing. I snuck into the kitchen and dished out a plate of vegetables.

Just make an appearance and leave, and the less food I had on my plate, the sooner I could go.

I had noticed a full table when I ducked into the kitchen but only as I reentered the dining room did I realize that it was the boys from the Western Charter that occupied some of the spaces.

My dad was at the head of the table, and Kade was on his left-hand side. He was still here.

"Oi, Abby, pass the sauce, would ya?" Gitz asked, and I automatically reached for it off the bench and leaned across the table, handing it to him. "Why you still standing? Come on, have a seat." He gestured to the seat next to him, and I walked around the table, taking the offer.

Kade had thrown me. Once I got in my seat next to Gitz and Bleach, I snapped out of it.

"Abby, where you been, sweetheart? I haven't seen you since I got back." Dad struck up a conversation with me.

"Just ... um ... in the gym." I stabbed a piece of carrot.

"I think we can see that, Abby." Gitz winked at me, causing a sly smile to cross my lips.

"How was school?" Dad asked, seeming not ready to let go of having a conversation with me.

Kim had been talking to Trigger at the end of the table, but when she heard Dad ask that question, her head snapped in my direction.

"Fine." I shrugged my shoulders, "How was your ride?"

Normally Dad would just flash me a smile, nod his head, and say the ride was good but this time, this time he looked at me with a "not buying it" face.

"Really? Because your principal called." Dad put down his fork, and when the man stops eating, you know shit is going to get real. So it made sense that the whole table chose this moment to go silent.

"Principal Frigg just likes talking to you." I brushed it off, but I knew there was a point to this rounded conversation.

"Abby, you can either tell me what happened, or I can ask your sister."

57

"Ask Kim then." I ate a mouthful of veggies and just like that, I passed the buck over to her. She wanted me to lie, well, she could lie for me.

"What's the issue, Daddy?" Kim batted her eyelids and took a sip of her drink. "If this is about Abby being unsociable, I'm sorry, but what do you expect?"

God, the quicker I got these veggies in, the better.

"Abby seems to be getting bullied."

I choked on the carrot in my mouth. Gitz came to my rescue by giving me a firm hard pat on the back.

"Here ya go." He handed me his beer, and I was quick to take a gulp of it.

"What? No, she isn't," Kim piped in. Seems like passing the buck to her was the best idea I had. I sucked at lying.

"Maybe you could explain, Kim, what the fuck you are doing. Why this is happening?" Dad's voice got that angry tone to it, and he seemed to be in full parent mode now.

"She isn't being bullied!" Kim explained.

"Yeah, Dad, she's right. I'm not really." I lied, and my face didn't even give me away because it was already flushed by my near choking experience. "Principal Frigg is just making you worried over nothing."

"Don't lie to me." Dad slammed his fist down. "Kimberly, apparently you are the leading lady when it comes to bullying your sister at school!"

Kim looked at me blankly. Dad was past angry and entering a full-on rage. He never really was good at having a conversation without reeling in his temper.

"Abby, you should have told me." Dad's eyes were scorching on mine. "Now start fucking explaining why you have been giving the school a wrong number."

"Because it's not worth disturbing you about it. Seriously, they are blowing it out of proportion." I kept my eyes locked on his. I was dying of embarrassment right then. Kade was sitting there, quietly, staring down at his plate. He hadn't touched his food, and I wondered if he could tell how awkward this was for me right now.

"You and your sister always come first," Dad spoke with such firmness.

"Oh please, Dad, really? You are going to spin that one?" Kim got guts from somewhere and actually rose to her feet, pointing a finger at him. "The club comes first, and stop trying to act like it doesn't."

And just like that, shit got messy.

"Better reel in that tone, young lady." Dad rose to his own feet, and it seemed like the Harrison family was going to go for gold.

Looked like the boys were in for dinner *and* a show.

"Dad, Kim, calm the fuck down," I piped up in between their glare off.

"What? Dad wants to sit there and pretend that he cares more about us than this club. Well fuck me, I'm not playing along with that anymore."

"KIM!" I snapped at her. Dad was already angry; you don't go fucking poking a bear.

"So Dad, if we come first, where were you last week? When I had my finals? Where were you when Abby got awarded outstanding for exams last month? Hell, where were YOU when we both got in trouble last month?"

"KIM!" I roared at her this time and rose to my own feet, tipping Gitz's beer over in my rush. "WE both fucking promised not to mention that!"

Just drop us in more shit, why don't you, Kim?

"What?" She snapped at me, her eyes firing with rage. "I'm sick of pretending like Dad gives two shits about us. Sure, you love us, but the club comes first, Dad, and you really need to wake up to that."

If a man could burst from rage, Dad was going to. Even a few of the boys were watching him closely, ready to jump up in case he charged at her.

"Kim, you need to calm down and stop saying shit you don't mean."

"NO! I'm sick of it! I'm sick of this club! I'm sick of living in this fucking messed up lie that Dad gives two shits about what happens to us. Hell, Dad, you might want to think you're not the ride-in-and-out dad, but you are!"

Kim was digging our graves one mouthful at a time.

"Kim, this has nothing to do with Dad's parenting skills." My voice was firm; it even sounded strong. I couldn't believe she was giving him a mouthful after she made me feel bad for even thinking about talking to Dad about what Noel had done.

"You're right, Abby, because he is no fucking parent." Kim threw her fork on the table and glared at him with a look of disgust.

"Ok. Clearly, I have missed something because only a few hours ago you were all concerned about his health and that I wasn't to upset him, and here you are yelling at him!"

I don't know when it happened, but Kim and I were now standing in front of each other.

Dad was still standing at the end of the table, shaking with rage.

"You're right, something did change. I just don't give a fuck if he has a heart attack anymore."

I grabbed Kim's arm as she attempted to storm past me. She was not leaving this mess that easy.

"You better start apologizing, Kim, before I knock your fucking teeth out," I snarled in her face. My own temper was boiling over now.

Kim looked at my hand, then looked back at me. "Why are you even bothering to protect him? Since when did you start caring about him? After all, I don't blame you." She looked at Dad with such bitterness. "Where was he when you were assaulted last month? When you were bleeding out in the hospital, and they couldn't get in contact with anyone? Where was he when his Vice

President tried to rape you? Oh, that's right..." Kim slowly turned her head and glared at Dad. "You were too busy screwing your way through any legs that would open." She ripped her arm free and stormed out, leaving me there, speechless.

I was shell-shocked. Only when the boys began to rise from the table did I snap back into the moment.

Trigger was on his feet, my dad's eyes zoned in on him.

"Is it true?" Dad's words were so deeply quiet, so threatening.

I stepped in, grabbing Trigger's arm. There was only a table keeping the distance between them, and Dad could flip that in barely a second.

"Dad, you need to listen to me. Kim made that..."

"Move, Abby!" Dad roared at me.

I didn't listen. Instead, I pushed myself in front of Trigger. He looked shocked, not sure what he should do.

"DAD!" I yelled when Dad seemed zoned in on Trigger, not looking at me. "Kim made that sound like something it wasn't."

"Abby, I think you need to leave." Trigger had his eyes on Dad's, and he placed a hand on my arm, trying to pull me away from him. "Now."

"Don't tell her what to do," Dad spat. "I trusted you."

"Dad, Trigger didn't do anything to me." I spoke softly, quick and direct. I had to get Dad to see reason before he killed the man.

It wasn't fair that Trigger was going to cop all of Dad's rage.

"Dad, it was years ago, and it wasn't what Kim made it sound like."

"Leave, Abby," Trigger spoke in my ear. "Now."

I knew what I had to do, and I knew what would happen if I did, but I had to get Dad's attention on me, so I did the only thing I knew that would get his full attention.

"Mark Defalcon wanted you to know what it felt like to lose something you loved, and he wanted me to tell you..." my stomach twisted with disgust and shame.

"Abby, when did Mark speak to you?" Dad's voice was softer, and just like I had hoped, he was no longer interested in Trigger. He moved around the table and gently grabbed my hand. "Abby, what did he say?"

Trigger did the smart thing and backed right off, leaving me standing there with Dad.

I never wanted to speak these words, and it felt like I was letting Mark win by doing what he asked. But Dad wasn't going to drop it, and he placed a hand under my chin, tilting my head up.

"Abby, tell me now."

A month earlier, I was heading down to the stationery shop when a car pulled up beside me. One second I was walking, listening to music, and the next I was pulled into a car. Mark Defalcon was my dad's personal enemy. They hated each other. Mark led a rival biker group. They were sworn enemies.

I don't remember too much after the third punch. But I do remember the words he whispered in my ear before leaving me in that alley where he inflicted so much pain on me.

'Tell your father that you tasted as sweet and as innocent as your mother.'

I promised myself I would never tell Dad those words. I was found by a stranger, taken to the hospital, and that's when Kim was called in. She promised she would never speak to Dad about it, and it was at that moment I had my sister back. Pity, though, the next day she was back to normal.

I stayed at Kayla's for a few weeks while the bruising went away, and then from that point I tried hard to suppress every memory of that night.

"He said..." I pulled my head from his touch and took a step back. Tears welled up in my eyes. "He said, 'tell your father that you tasted as sweet and as innocent as your mother.'" I squeezed my eyes tight.

All I heard was Dad's breathing; it was sharp and deep. "Please, Dad, don't do anything stupid." I opened my eyes again, looking up into his furious, narrowed ones. "Please, Dad, don't sink to his level."

"Go find your sister." Dad nodded his head at the door for me to leave. "Go on, now."

"No."

"Abby, I need to speak to the boys. Leave."

"Not till you promise you won't hurt Trigger." I crossed my arms. If I had to relive that awful memory, there had to be a reason for it. "Dad, you told me he's the best VP you can ask for and if you are going to do something stupid, you need him by your side, and I won't leave until you-"

"I'm not going to kill him, Abby. Now go find your sister before she leaves."

"What do you want me to say to her?" If I were Kim, I would have already been gone after giving Dad a spray like that.

"Tell her that she can't run away from this family, pregnant or not."

My mouth dropped open. "She's knocked up?"

"Go."

I knew I had to leave, but I couldn't help but give Trigger a small, sad smile. I might have saved him tonight, but he was a dead man if he was the father.

I grabbed Dad's arm and went to my tippy toes to whisper in his ear. "Kim loves you, Dad; don't think otherwise. And he didn't rape me. Neither of them did."

I walked quickly out of the room. Never in a girl's life does she want to bring up her virginity with her dad, and I had to do just that, as well as let him know my darkest secret.

Tonight was the worst night of my life, and I had Kim to thank for it. That hormonal bitch better still be here because she was going to get a piece of my mind.

***

I woke up to my mattress sinking. Opening my eyes, I was shocked for a moment to see Dad sitting at the end of my bed.

I elbowed Kim in the ribs, waking her up.

"You ok, Dad?" I asked.

It was the dead of the night, but my room still had soft lighting from the outside lights drifting through the curtains.

"I let you girls down." His voice was low.

Kim pulled herself up in bed. I knew she regretted what she said because she spent a solid hour crying about it. She was knocked up, and she was angry at Trigger about it. I told her it still wasn't a reason to get Trigger killed.

It didn't help either that Trigger had told her he wanted nothing to do with it, and Dad had pretty much told her the same thing— it was her problem. Neither of them made a smart move by pissing off a hormonal woman.

It made sense now why she didn't want me to mention my problems to Dad tonight— because she was going to drop her own bomb on him.

"You didn't, Dad. I'm sorry." Kim climbed out of bed and went to sit next to him. "I'm really sorry, Dad."

"I should have let you girls go live with my sister. I shouldn't have kept you both."

"Dad, don't be stupid." I got up and flicked the lights on. The blood on his hands and the stains on his white shirt became visible. "Dad, please tell me Trigger is still alive."

Kim went stiff, and her eyes met mine for a moment. For a split second, I saw her regret.

"Trigger knew he was on borrowed time." Dad looked up at me.

"You promised me you wouldn't kill him!" I felt guilt build up inside me.

"I didn't kill him."

"Then who did?"

I knew he was playing with words, and I didn't like it.

"No one did. He got a few punches, but he's still breathing. The same can't be said for Mark." Dad grunted, getting up, looking his age.

"Kim, you're not having that baby. Tomorrow, you're going to the doctor. As for you, Abby," he looked at me, "tomorrow, you're telling me everything."

We both nodded our heads.

"Then I'm calling your Aunty. Next week, you're both going to live with her."

I gasped, and Kim looked like she wanted to kick herself.

"Dad, you can't send us away, it's our last year! I can't change schools now. If I do, it will affect my university choices!" I was outraged at the suggestion.

"We'll talk about it tomorrow." Dad gave Kim a kiss on her forehead. "What you did tonight, Kim, I can't have you speaking to me like that in front of my brothers, but we will deal with that in the morning."

I was frozen and was still chewing over the idea of having to leave and move to god knows where when Dad kissed my forehead.

"I thought you knew, Abby, you could always come to me if you were in trouble." He shook his head. "We'll talk in the morning."

He left, closing the door behind me, and suddenly my thoughts of killing Kim from earlier this evening seemed like a good idea.

"You really fucked things up for us." I snapped at her. "I hope you're happy."

"Can't you see, Abby?" Tears were falling down her face. "I'm fucking thrilled."

She might be regretting it now, but she would be regretting it more when she woke up tomorrow and reality hit us both.

Dad didn't want us here anymore, and it was all her fault.

Chapter 8

Abby

I wasn't a big believer in second chances or forgetting about the past. I was a firm believer in learning from your mistakes. I don't believe in second chances because if you got one shot, by my books, you got one shot too many.

My dad also shared this opinion, which led me to my new problem.

"Dad?" I knocked on his bedroom door. It was the middle of the afternoon, and I hoped, by now, he might be waking up, but by the lack of a response, I knew he wasn't.

"You ok?"

I spun around, shocked to see Kade. He looked like his normal self: black tee shirt, leather vest over the top. He was the picture of what your parents warned you about.

I walked away from Dad's door and towards Kade. "Yeah, I'm ok, but I don't know about Dad." I glanced back at his closed door. "He doesn't usually sleep this much."

"Might have something to do with the fact he isn't here."

My head snapped back at him. "What?"

"Your dad left early this morning. He wasn't really in the mood to answer questions, so no one really asked him where he was going."

I groaned. I knew where he was going, and I had hoped to see him before he left. "He would have gone to see my Aunty."

"That a bad thing?"

"It *is* because I don't really want to live with her, but thanks to Kim's outburst last night..." I looked down at the ground. "Dad thinks that shipping us off will fix everything."

Kade was quiet. Like real quiet. I looked up, crossed my arms, and raised an eyebrow. "Spill it, Kade, what are you thinking?"

It was the emotions behind his cool expression that had me knowing he had an opinion on this.

"Club isn't a place for girls." He leaned back against the wall.

It was just him and me in the empty hallway. I stood a bit taller in front of him. "Girl? You think I'm a girl?"

"You're eighteen, still in high school. Yeah, I think you're still a girl."

A girl? I wanted to hit him. I wanted to punch that thought from his mind. I was not a little girl. "So that is what you think of me? A girl who can't handle herself?"

"No, you're a girl who has been harassed, nearly raped, and hanging around bad ass men her whole life. Having you and your sister around this club just brings drama. Men are men, and you're baiting yourself in front of men with no morals."

Well there it was; he didn't have an opinion, he had a bloody lecture.

"Well, who knew you had such a strong opinion?" I thought he was different. Why did I think he could see me as somewhat equal?

In Kade's mind—everyone's mind—Kim and I were nothing but a problem. A problem they couldn't even bang.

"Nice to know what you really think." I tried to storm away, you know, act my age. But Kade stopped me, wrapping one of his big powerful hands around my wrist.

"I'm leaving, and you're just going to storm off without even saying goodbye?"

He was leaving. Fine, leave. Go. Leave me with this mess.

It was at that moment I woke up to myself. Kade wasn't my boyfriend; he wasn't even my friend. So why did I think I could lean on him for support? He wasn't even a good guy.

"Bye."

"Bitchy this morning, aren't you?"

"FINE, what do YOU want ME to say?"

"Nothing." He let go of my wrist. "Go on then, fuck off." He nodded his head down the hallway for me to leave.

"You know what your problem is, Reaper? You think I care." I gave him a cold look. "You honestly think that I give a shit if you ride out or not? You're just another biker." My words were cold, my face was stern, and god, I had stepped bitch up to whole new level. "And if you haven't noticed, I'm surrounded by bikers. So you're just another dirty, badly tattooed one that seems to have a habit of riding in and out."

I was angry. No! Furious!

First, his face went tight. His jaw clenched and just when I thought he was about to punch through my coldness with his own harsh words, he leaned in and did something I didn't expect.

We stumbled back until he had me against the wall. His hands gripped the side of my face, and his lips drove down. It wasn't loving, and it wasn't gentle. It was raw and hard, and I loved it.

I didn't push him away, but I didn't wrap my arms around him either.

He pulled away, his eyes zoned in on mine. "If any other biker or fucking man for that case touches you, he's a dead man walking." His voice was like a sexual dose that sent my body alight, but the raw threatening tone behind his words sent a wave of realization over me. "You can storm off now, babe. I think I made my point."

I wished I could have kept up that cold expression from before, but I didn't have a chance. My shock and fear washed over my face. I slowly turned and walked down the hall, stunned. My feet were on automatic while my mind went into overdrive, trying to figure out what the hell he meant.

He had made his point? What the fuck did that mean?

Chapter 9

Abby

"This is bullshit," I roared in Dad's face. My temper was out of control. I couldn't reel it in if I wanted to. "This is going to RUIN my life! Can you think of me for once? Just because she hates it here doesn't mean I fucking do!" I threw an arm in Kim's direction.

Dad's face was tight. He let out a long, deep breath. "I told you, Abby, this is decided. I've already spoken to Mandy. You and Kim are going. End of story."

"I think it will be good," Kim piped up.

"Sorry, but when did we ask for the pregnant cow's opinion?" I glared at her then looked back at Dad. "You are ruining my life. I've put all my effort into this high school, and now you are moving me in my final year! Before exams!"

I was angry that he was ripping me away from the only home I knew, but I was furious that he was putting my future in trouble.

"You can take the exams at your new school." He stood up, towering over me. "I've already enrolled you and Kim. You both start next week."

I was gobsmacked.

Kim's stone-cold eyes locked with mine. "I think this is a good thing."

I snickered a frustrated simper at her. "You thought it was a good idea to fuck a guy with no protection, too."

"ENOUGH!" Dad roared. "It's fucking settled. You might as well start packing!"

He was sending me away from my only friends, from my school, from my teachers. I felt like he was taking a part of my life away. I felt robbed, cheated, and mostly hurt. I had always done the right thing. I studied hard, kept myself out of trouble, and this is how I was rewarded?

Tears welled up in my eyes. "If you make me go, Dad, I promise you, you will ruin our relationship." My blurry eyes locked with his stern ones; there was no emotion in his eyes while mine were full of sorrow.

"Then I guess it is ruined. Pack your shit." He turned around and left the room. When he walked out, he also destroyed any respect I had for him and just like that, I lost my dad.

Mandy, or should I say, Aunty Amanda, was a true-blue slut. I hated her. And no, I didn't just hate her because I was being sent to live with her. I hated her because Mom hated her. Why Mom didn't like her, I don't know, but I think Mom was a good judge of character.

I wasn't calling her a slut to be mean, either; she was a slut or as she says, an expensive escort. No matter what she called it, she still spread her legs to make a living.

I hated Dad at that moment, too, for ruining my life. I hated him for sending me away, and I hated him for not even making the five-hour drive here. He sent us with the Western Charter.

The van Kim and I were in slowed down. The gang of bikes in front of us also slowed. I felt like I had swallowed a whole lot of anger, and it seemed to just be spreading through my body.

Aunty Slut Face was out the front of her small brick house. She was dressed in pink and waving like an overexcited Playboy Bunny. Her hair was even bleached blonde.

Kim was quick to slide the door open and jump out. I, on the other hand, wasn't in a fucking hurry. What had made my mood worse was the fact that Kade hadn't even spoken one word to me.

He also had some tramp on the back of his bike with him. Kade, being the gentleman he is, let her ride on his bike.

Sluts don't have rights on the back of a President's bike, but hell, maybe I was old-fashioned. I slammed the van door behind me.

The prospect that had driven the van gave me a dirty look.

"ABBY!" Aunty Amanda exclaimed and let go of Kim.

Kade was off his bike and had made his way over to the happy pair. I glanced at Aunty Amanda, her arms wide open. "Touch me, and I'll break your arms." I walked past her and headed towards the house. I caught a glance of her stunned expression.

I might have always played nicely with her before, but now I had nothing to lose, and I didn't have a father to be 'disappointed' if I did treat her like the piece of trash she was.

***

As I unpacked one of my boxes, Kade came in carrying the last one. My room was directly across from Kim's new room. Fuck my luck.

"We're heading off now." Kade put the box down near my bed.

The room wasn't that big and was filled with boxes. I didn't look up and just kept pulling random shit out of the box. "Ok. Bye."

I heard the door close, and I looked up. Kade stared at me.

"What's wrong?" His tone was deep, and he looked slightly worried. "It isn't like you to be a mean, cold-hearted bitch."

"If you are referring to my treatment of the blonde pinup bitch, then I hate to break it to you, but yeah, that was all me." My belly was full of fire, and I was spitting it out.

He was across the room in two long strides. "You're pissed off that you didn't get your way. I get it. But that is life, so grow the fuck up, Abby, and act your age."

"Oh right, you mean I should act like a girl because that's what I am, remember? A. Girl."

"You want to be treated like an adult, then here is your perfect opportunity to act like a fucking adult. Your aunty is taking you in. Be fucking grateful."

"You know what, Reaper?" I was on the tip of my toes now, glaring into his face. "Fuck. Off. And take your advice with you."

"You're more trouble than you are worth."

"Well, then you must be over the moon now. Because you won't be seeing me again after this." I couldn't be sure why I felt so angry and hurt by that fact. "When you ride out of here in a few minutes, you won't be coming back. There is no club in fucking Rod Valley. There is no fucking reason for you to be back here."

I watched realization flash across his eyes and for a split moment, I thought I saw pity within those big, gray-black, soul-sucking eyes of his.

"And it is not like you are going to come back here to see me, right?" I crossed my arms, taking a step back away from him.

Then he said what I was hoping he wouldn't. "I guess you're right."

I was more than right; I was bloody sure of it. There would be no more running into him at club parties.

No club, no Reaper. It was that simple.

Dad had taken more away from me than just my friends, home, and school. He took my Reaper as well. Maybe that was why the fury in my stomach couldn't be put out.

Kade took a step forward. Slowly, he ran his knuckles down the side of my face. He looked down at me as if I was something special—his something special.

"You're a good girl, babe. Maybe it's a good thing. You were always too good for me." The corner of his lips twitched into that alluring smile I had dreamed about. "You always deserve better than me. This will just make sure you get something better."

"Yeah, something." I felt bitter and robbed, but mainly just sad. "I kind of really liked you, Reaper." My lips formed a tight smile.

He pulled his hand away and without his touch, I felt hollow.

I thought I had dealt with a few hard things during my life, but watching him turn away and walk to my door just blew my heart apart.

He paused, hand on the door. "If you get in trouble and you need me, call me." He didn't look back and why I might have wished he would, I knew it was better if he didn't. If he did, it might be harder for me to let him leave.

"Ok." As soon as the words left my lips, he opened the door and walked out, closing the door behind him, leaving me empty and surrounded by brown boxes.

Chapter 10

Abby

Perhaps it was the fire within my stomach, or maybe I had finally lost my mind. Either way, it still may or may not have influenced my next move. Opening the door quickly, I caught Kade in the hallway.

"Stay the night."

He stopped.

"It's late, and you have been riding for hours now. I'm sure the boys won't mind the stopover, and I'm sure they can find a bar within this shithole town."

I was beginning to think I was talking to myself until he turned around. That look in his eyes, it was the look that drove me insane.

"And why would I do that?" He titled his head to the side. He wanted me to convince him.

I didn't know what to say. I had acted like a hell of a bitch to him for a few days, and there I was asking him to stay around a bit longer.

"Because you want to." The words tumbled out, and when he didn't deny it straight away, my heart swelled. "So what do you say, Reaper?" I stood in front of him, having closed the gap between us completely. "You up for one night of fun?"

What would we do? Where would we go? I had no idea and no plans but all in all, it didn't matter. I just wanted to be with him, and seeing the debate in his eyes, I knew he wanted to be with me just as much.

"What are you two doing?" Kim's voice floated up the hallway. It was sharp and abrupt, just like her.

I looked around Kade but before I could say anything, he spoke first.

"Your sister and I are heading out for a bit." He turned back around. "Got a problem with it?"

Kim wasn't stupid. She knew when to hold her tongue. Her eyes locked with mine for a moment, and I swear she was trying to tell me not to make the same mistake as her, but with a quick nod of her head, she backed away from the subject. "I get it. Just be back in the morning." She looked Kade up and down once more, then looked back at me. "Don't do anything stupid, Abby."

With those fine words of advice, she disappeared.

"Give me a few minutes to shake the boys. Then come out the front when you're ready to leave." He didn't and wouldn't meet my eye.

I suppose this was the perfect opportunity to get changed and try to look more like a girl than a wasted, bitter rag.

***

I always thought that I would get used to it—the second glances, the dirty, scared, envious looks. I always thought that one day, it wouldn't bother me. Maybe I would no longer notice, but as I stood in line with Kade, I knew that it was never going to happen.

Honestly, how could I expect that? Bikers drew attention, and that was that. Look at the guy; I gawked at him, too. He was six feet tall, dominant, broad shouldered, and had *that* look, which caused women's hearts to race and fed her daydreams. He had the attitude, the look, and of course that haunting tint to his eyes. But it was more than just the way he looked. It was the club leather vest, covered in patches and faded from the road. He was part of something that they didn't understand. Some loathed it; others wanted to be involved in it. He walked around wearing something that said 'fuck your rules' to the world, and they loved it or feared it.

"I hate fucking lines," Kade muttered under his breath. He pushed the sleeves of his black shirt up, displaying his tattooed arms. "You would fucking think they would have more than one person serving."

I shrugged my shoulders and suppressed the smirk.

Finally, and I think just before Kade was going to march through the line and demand a seat, a waiter ushered us to a table.

"They'd better serve normal food." Kade slid into the booth, and I went around the opposite side.

"Don't worry, Kade, I'm sure there is a burger on the menu for you." I giggled and swiped the menu off the table. "Do you need help finding the children's menu?"

He gave me an 'I'm not amused' look before looking back down at his own menu.

Since we left, he had been uptight more than normal. I still couldn't be sure if it was because I had roped him into this or he was worried my dad might find out. Either way, it didn't explain the weird looks he kept shooting me.

"Sooooo…" I put my menu down and brought my elbows on top of the table.

"So?" He didn't look up.

"Do you think they serve alcohol?"

He looked up with a dry expression. "They have fucking cupcakes on the menu, what do you think?"

"Tone down the bitchy, would you? I was just asking."

"I've been telling you that for days," he grunted.

"Don't turn this conversation back to me." I hated eating my own words.

"For a smart girl, you do really stupid stuff." He dropped the menu, meeting my eyes.

"Care to explain, Reaper?" I tapped my finger on the table, and while my better judgment was telling me to leave it alone, I poked his question to see if he would tell me what he was really thinking.

He leaned across the table, those deadly gray eyes burning with emotion and questions. "What the fuck is this?"

"This is a café."

"Don't play mind fucking games with me. You know what I mean. This. What is *this*?" He moved a hand behind me and him. "We have tea and then what? Where exactly do you see this night going, Abby, cause I can fucking tell you right now, this isn't a date."

If I was to decide or label this night as something, I would label it as me clinging to the one chance I have at being with him. Hell, might as well just bring it to him.

I leaned in and made sure to lower my voice. "I see this night ending in a cheap motel somewhere, with you and I finishing what you started all those years ago." I made sure to keep my tone in check, and it didn't waver once. My emotion also stayed out of my eyes.

He blinked, then blinked and looked speechless.

"That sound ok, Reaper?" I raised an eyebrow and sneered at him from across the table.

Finally, that taunting smirk of his graced his lips. "It sounds like we are skipping dessert."

I laughed and shook my head. With flushed cheeks, I looked back down at the menu. My stomach flipped and flopped, but my mind was set on the idea, and I wasn't backing down.

Reaper

I was nervous. Never been this nervous. I always held a gun with a steady hand when I was about to take a man's life and always made decisions with a clear mind. But when it came to Abby, my mind was fucked.

Failing to work.

It hadn't been working since she said the words *'finish what we started.'* You don't say that to a man. Especially not me. I never left things unfinished. Abby was different. I never considered us to have unfinished business.

I just considered myself an idiot for having feelings for a woman completely out of my reach. Hell, this was the first time ever I felt something for someone. Of all people, it just had to be her.

"I need you to piss off." I walked up to the motel reception desk. The old guy behind the counter just looked at me with wide eyes. I guess I was abrupt. Maybe I needed to talk in a way he would understand. "How much will that cost?"

"You want to hire the place for the night?"

"You vacant?"

"Yeah, we are empty. Not our rush period."

I doubted this place ever had a rush period. But it was my only option. The other motel, which was slightly better than this, was occupied by The Club. So I couldn't take Abby back there. And this place didn't even have a hotel, or something flash.

This was it.

She deserved better. Hell, she deserved better than me.

"So you still interested in renting the place? Won't be cheap for every room."

My eyes gazed out the window. She was at the pool, putting in one foot, testing the temperature.

"You got cameras?" I looked back at the old man, who was summing up whether to give me a straight answer or not. I wasn't stupid. I knew when people were about to lie to me.

"Yeah we do."

"Turn them off and you have a deal."

He was debating about it. I could see it in his eyes.

"I'll be back at eight in the morning. If there is any damage, I'll be calling the cops. Hand over the cash and some ID."

That problem was now sorted. I had secured a place to spend the night with her. Now what the hell was I going to do? I couldn't let my guard down. I WOULDN'T let myself feel any more of her. If we did have sex, that is all it would be. Wasn't like I was making a commitment to her.

Then again, I had just put more effort into securing a place for her to make sure she felt safe. Normally I wouldn't even care if the girl felt safe or not. Again, I was lying to myself when I said Abby wasn't different.

Abby

I would be a liar if I said I was fine. I can't believe I was here. Then again, I wasn't being suffocated by nerves. I wasn't overthinking it. I was just going with the flow. But I did know if I wanted this evening to go as planned, I would have to push it.

What was taking him so long? How hard was it to book a room? Wondering where he was, I looked up in time to see Reaper walking towards me and the reception lights flick off. Strange. I thought reception never closed.

Guess this was a small town. Maybe they knew there would be no more business coming their way.

Guess this meant there was no room service. I looked up at the stars. One bonus of a small town was the sky really lit up at night. The moon was huge. I had never seen it this big. But did I ever really take much notice of the moon? Maybe not.

The air was still hot and sticky even though the sun had gone down. You would think it would cool down, but it seemed my new home was in the middle of a mean summer.

I had already slipped my sandals off. Sitting at the edge of the pool, I slowly dipped my feet in. God, that was refreshing.

I reached for my clutch, pulling out my cigarette packet. Empty. Well, that's a fan-fucking-tastic way to start the evening.

"Here."

I turned and looked up just in time to see Kade handing me a lit cigarette. My fingers brushed his as I took it off him.

"Thanks."

So, my confidence from earlier was shaking at the mere touch.

I sucked in the cigarette, needing it more now. Just stay strong, Abby. Just stay strong.

"Hot?"

"Yeah," I tilted my head to look at him. "Aren't you?" I looked at him with his tee shirt, leather vest, and jeans, as well as big steel-toed boots. I was hot and I was in a dress. Suddenly, I felt like a complete fool for even saying it. Clearly he dealt with the heat better than I.

"Nah. It's always hot where I am."

Well, that answered my thoughts. I handed him back the cigarette. "I have a feeling it's going to be like that here too. Much to my disgust."

"What? Do you hate the heat?"

"Yes. Who likes sweating twenty-four seven?" Seriously. I couldn't be the only one to think that. He shrugged his shoulders, clearly not sharing my point of view. "You're strange." I shook my head, my blonde hair whipping around.

So now here I was. Finally reaching a situation Reaper and I had been heading for since he saved me.

Withdrawing my feet from the pool, I got up. My eyes slowly scanned his muscular body till I reached his eyes.

They were set on my face. One move, that was all I had to do to make this happen.

Would he take charge once I took the dive?

Going up on my tippy toes, my lips brushed his and just as I hoped, he took charge. Lifting me off the ground, he wrapped my legs around him and suddenly I wasn't breathing air. No, I was breathing Kade. We traded long, deep kisses as he walked us towards a room.

Was I making a mistake?

Would I regret this?

I don't know. But it felt so darn right. So I didn't fight the need to cling to him tighter, or kiss him firmer.

I just didn't care.

Reaper

I ran my hand up her bare back as she slept. I couldn't stop myself from touching her. I hadn't had enough of her. Couldn't get enough of her, which was why I was awake so early. I listened to her inhale softly and exhaling slowly.

I swear, listening to her breathing was calming me and also stopping me from what I had to do next.

I had gotten a taste of her, and I wanted more.

I wasn't ready to leave her.

I wasn't ready to let her live a life without me in it.

So I was going to do what I always did when something came my way that I wanted. I would take it.

I kissed her bare shoulder and got out of bed. Leaving her right now was one of the hardest things I've done. But I had to do it for my plan to work.

I was going to give up my patch. As soon as my eyes laid on her naked flesh, I realized my patch was the least I would give up to spend time with her. I knew Roach wanted a new VP and I had enough experience to get it. Then once that was settled, I wasn't going to rest till she was back at the club where I could watch her every move and when I wasn't doing that, I'd be sneaking her into my bed.

I scribbled a note for her to stay put till I got back. I took another long look at her before leaving.

God darn she was beautiful and if I had my way, she was going to be all mine.

Chapter 11

Abby

I found out the hard way and maybe that was my fault, or maybe I was just as stupid as my sister. It didn't matter as I stood at the reception desk listening to the man order me a taxi. The details of the night before were blurry at best, but this morning's memories were crystal clear.

The feeling of waking up alone in a motel room, the feeling of my stomach dropping when I reached out to the other side of the bed and found that Reaper wasn't there. He didn't even stay long enough to say good morning. Hell, he didn't even stay around long enough for me to wake up.

As I chewed over this morning's events, I found myself becoming more bitter by the moment.

Why didn't he wait? Why couldn't he just wait until I woke up?

"The taxi will be here in about ten minutes."

My head snapped up to the man behind the counter. I could see the pity in his eyes, and that was only making the disappointment in myself grow.

"Thanks," I muttered, scooping my bag off the counter and heading out. The door chimed as I pulled it open.

The morning's air was bitter cold.

I felt like a cheap hooker waiting for the taxi of shame.

I wanted to hit him. I wanted to yell at him. I wanted to whip all this anger I was feeling for him, at him.

I couldn't be sure what was worse: that I wanted to see him, or that I knew he had gotten what he wanted and left as soon as he could.

I knew he had no intentions of seeing me again. Perhaps that's why my anger was being clouded by this feeling of betrayal and hurt.

I thought he liked *me*. I thought we were *different*. All last night, I had somehow convinced myself that we would turn out different, but this morning, I realized there was no *'we.'* There wasn't even an *us*.

"You look lost, love."

I was pulled from my thoughts, and I looked over my shoulder. I hadn't even noticed him when I went outside.

He was leaning against the wire fence, a cigarette in hand and this devilish charm within his eyes. I could see with one look he was born to be trouble. Tall, chiseled features and eyes that could steal your every thought shone in the sun.

"Not lost, just waiting," I replied and for the second time today, I heard the emptiness in my voice. I might be feeling like a depressed train wreck, but I didn't like hearing that in my voice. Why couldn't I put up a front?

"The name's Drake." He flicked the cigarette butt to the ground, stomping on it.

I was freshly burnt. The last thing I needed was to spark an interest with another flame. I gave him a tight smile and turned my attention back to the road. I wished that the taxi would come faster.

"So not the friendly type then?"

While I may not be interested in letting myself be interested, he wasn't following the same reasoning. I let out a low sigh and dragged my eyes up to look at him.

"I'm just not in the mood."

"I get it, being freshly dumped does that to someone."

My face flashed with shock. Was it that obvious?

"You can wipe that shock off your face, love; I'm not a mind reader." He cocked his head to the side slightly. "Just putting two and two together."

"Two and two?"

"It's either A, you gave it up to a dude and he left before you woke up or B, a hooker. And if that is the case, I'm more than interested in the hourly rate."

"You're a pig!"

He chuckled. "Not the second one then. Pity, I was more than keen." He looked me up and down with his seductive gaze. "Come on, I'll give you a ride. Unless you want to stand here longer looking like last night's shag?"

The sting of my last bad decision was still freshly burning, and yet here I was lining up for a second round. So with crossed arms and a suspicious mind, I followed him to his car.

It was just a ride, right? It wasn't like I was going to end up screwing him in the backseat.

I closed the car door and gave Drake a side-glance. "The name is Abby," I muttered.

The engine roared to life and even though I had told myself it was just a ride, I had seen a glimpse of something within Drake's eyes—that look, that flicker—I knew this wasn't just going to be a five-minute ride.

But I wasn't reaching for the handle. Instead, I leaned my forehead against the cold glass. Life was defined by moments and experiences, right?

I suppose I was a sucker for self-punishment.

Reaper

One Year Later

Her blonde hair was ruffled, her cheeks flushed, and an amused smile played across her lips.

I ran the back of my fingers down her bare arm.

She curved back into me. "You know, Kade, if you keep staring

85

at me like that, I'm going to think you're about to burst out with a proposal or something." She giggled.

I hadn't seen Abby so relaxed. So happy, and it was here in my arms. I was seeing it for the first time. Something bubbled in my bloodstream, pride I think.

"You're beautiful. You know that, right?" I looked into her crystal-blue eyes.

Her cheeks tinted red. "You can stop trying to charm me; you already got me."

I rolled her onto her back, keeping my arm behind her. I could feel her naked body underneath me and in this second, I felt like everything was alright. Fuck, what was this feeling consuming me?

She was a gorgeous rare gem that I felt was going to crumble in front of me.

I slowly lowered my lips to hers and she arched up, meeting my kiss.

She reached up, locking her arms around my neck. I was addicted to her touch, to that smile, to her. And when she pulled away, I cringed.

Just before worry consumed me, I looked into her eyes as amusement sparkled within them. "Kade, you're kind of a great kisser." A soft giggle fell from her lips.

Her face began to blur, then fade, and before I knew it, I was pulled away from her. I woke up alone in an unmade bed. Rubbing my eyes, I pulled myself up. My mouth was dry, and I craved water.

Abby's smile was still playing on my mind. Again, another memory of *that night* had managed to take over my dreams. Why couldn't I just have a dream instead of reliving something from the past?

I reached for the beer can beside my bed, and I felt immediate disappointment when I found it to be empty.

Abby Harrison was still playing on my mind, and it had been

over a year since that night.

My bathroom door swung open, and Lea walked out wearing one of my shirts.

"You alright, Reaper?" She looked me up and down. "You look like hell."

"Thanks," I grumbled and got to my feet. *Darn morning afters.*

"Well, I'm heading out, got shit to do." She was freshly showered. "See you when I see you." She gave me a wave over her shoulder before leaving.

That was Lea for you; she wasn't the clingy type.

My phone had numerous missed calls, and I really couldn't be fucking bothered with returning them. My body ached from the long ride, and my brain throbbed from the lack of water.

I found it utterly frustrating that a mere memory of Abby Harrison could still upset me. She had looked at me like I was something special to her, that I was *something* to her, and then she just shut me the fuck out.

It still bothered me, and it didn't fucking help being back here. Roach rarely mentioned them, but still, I picked up on small things.

If I had known that Abby was going to turn as she did, I wouldn't have given up my President patch to be Roach's VP, but karma had it in for me.

Not only did the bitch lock me out of her life, she wouldn't even let me explain my plan, and now I fucking regret ever coming up with it.

I shouldn't have jumped as I did. I should have waited until the waters had calmed down to see what was going to happen between her and me. Instead, I handed in my patch and moved to be her father's bitch. Now I get to regularly be reminded what I wasn't. I wasn't a President. I wasn't Abby's man. I was washed up, regularly drunk, and doing Roach's dirty work.

I pulled my leather club vest over my bare chest and pulled on a pair of jeans. It was the middle of the afternoon, so the clubhouse would just be waking up.

It had been a big weekend with Roach's birthday, a party that neither of his girls showed up to. Abby and Kim haven't been back here since they left.

From what I picked up, Roach didn't really speak to them that much. Which was a fucking good thing if you asked; it kept Abby the fuck away from me.

I staggered down the stairs and could hear conversation from the club kitchen.

"Well if it isn't the Reaper!" Gitz smirked, raising a freshly opened beer.

"Bit early for that, isn't it?" I reached around him, grabbing a glass and heading towards the tap.

"You won't be saying that when I tell you something." Gitz had that evil grin of his, which told me he was about to tell me something that was likely to piss me off, which as a result would give him some joy.

"What?"

"Roach is heading down to see his girls."

"How the fuck does that have anything to do with me?" I wiped my mouth with the back of my hand.

Gitz's grin got bigger, and his eyes narrowed with amusement. Gitz had slowly over time became my best mate, and when I was drunk, I had told him shit that I really shouldn't have.

Gitz was a good bloke though and never repeated it, but still, seeing that grin right now, I regretted telling him anything.

"And Roach wants his VP to ride down with him. Pack ya bags pumpkin, 'cause you're hitting the road." He slapped me on the back, chuckling.

"You're fucking kidding me!" I yelled at his back, but he just kept laughing.

His laughter answered my own question. Suddenly all the missed calls from Roach made sense.

Chapter 12

Kim

A final presentation and an English final were all my mind could focus on. It seemed like all year I had been working towards this goal and now that it was here, I was stressing out.

"Babe." Trent reached across the table, placing his hand on top of mine. "You really need to stop the pen tapping." Those kissable lips of his twisted into a smile.

"Sorry. I'm just, well..." I looked down at my blank piece of paper. "Unsure what to write."

"Well, good thing you have a full month before it is due." He let go of my hands and stretched his arms.

We had been studying for a solid two hours, and I loved that Trent was willing to give up his Friday night to help me study.

"You're right; we should really just have a break." I closed my textbook. "Seriously, I've knocked that paper out of the way and only have one more to go, so why don't we start our Friday night?"

"You sure?" He gave me a challenging look, as if he knew that I would still be thinking about this paper anyway, so why bother pulling me away from it.

"Yes, I'm sure. I want to spend Friday night with my boyfriend." It was settled; no more studying. "So what do you want to do?"

The front doorbell rang, and I knew that Aunty Amanda was at work and Abby wouldn't come down to answer it.

"Ok, hold that thought. I'll just get the door." I shot him a smile, and he nodded his head.

The one thing I loved about living with Aunty Amanda was there weren't strangers coming and going. I felt lame admitting it, but it made me feel a hell of a lot safer, not to mention I no longer needed that deadbolt lock on my bedroom door.

I opened the front door, and my smile dropped immediately. My good mood went with it as well.

"Kim." Drake smiled at me. "Abby in?"

"You know she is." I crossed my arms. I never tried to hide the fact that I hated him.

Drake was a cancerous worm that had wiggled his way into my sister's life. I didn't jump straight to hating him. It went from liking him, to not trusting him, to not liking him, to hating him. Drake looked at Abby as if she was his property.

"Going to let me in?" He put a foot in the doorway, and I didn't budge.

"No."

"KIM, LET HIM IN!" Abby shouted from the stairs.

Huffing, I stepped out of his way to let him in, and boy did he always manage to make himself at home.

"How are you doing, Trent?" I heard him ask Trent as I followed him into the dining room.

"Good, Drake, yourself?"

"Always good, mate." Drake shot him a wink and pulled out a chair.

I moved across the room quickly and went to sit on Trent's lap. I didn't know how Abby could stand to be around Drake; he gave me the fucking creeps.

"So how has your night been?" Drake started a conversation.

"Please don't ask them; they will bore you to death." Abby walked into the dining room and like always, she was wearing that pissed-off look. "Kim, Four Eyes," she shot at us. "Ready to leave?" She placed a hand on Drake's shoulder, and he got up.

"So you're going out?" I asked Abby.

"No, I'm walking out with a bag to sit on the porch." She rolled her eyes at me and handed Drake her bag. "God, you're dumb."

"Well, have a good night." I smiled faintly at her. I never

thought I would miss my awkward, nerdy sister, but I did.

"I would say the same, but I really don't give a fuck if you have a good one or not." She pulled her leather jacket on.

Abby was thinner, meaner, and had this sharp edge to her. I would love to blame it all on Drake, but he really could not take all the blame. Abby had transformed into this mean bitch all on her own.

Trent's fingers were drawing a small circle on my lower back. I knew he was doing it so I wouldn't get upset.

It wasn't till the front door closed behind them that the tension in the air disappeared.

"Sorry for what she said." I kissed Trent's cheek. I didn't care that he wore glasses, he was a great guy, and the old Abby would have thought so, too.

"Don't worry, babe." He grinned at me, and I really don't know what I had done to deserve him to stand by me. When Abby did make an appearance, she was always saying hurtful things, and it was always about his glasses, which I found kind of cute.

Dipping my head down, I pressed my lips against his. Trent was super sweet, and Abby's mean comments slipped away quickly as my mind focused on more important things.

***

"Babe."

"Babe."

I groaned slowly, being pulled from my dreamy state.

"Babe, there is someone downstairs. Are you expecting anyone?"

I rubbed my eyes and sat up and looked across at Trent. "What do you mean someone is downstairs? Is it Abby?"

"I don't think so; they sounded like men's voices." Trent got up from the bed and flicked the lights on. "Do you want me to go down?"

I was wide awake; nothing like the thought of someone uninvited in your house to snap you from a sleepy state.

"No, I will." I pulled open the bedside drawer and tossed my undies around until my hand landed on the cold metal.

"Babe, really?" Trent shook his head in disbelief, eyeing the gun in my hand.

"Sorry, Trent, but I'm still a biker girl at heart." I opened my bedroom door. Trent followed me, and I was kind of glad he was behind me. Trent had a thin build, and I'm certain he hadn't thrown a punch in his life.

I flipped the hall lights on and listened for the voices. I heard footsteps in the living room and then noticed the light had been turned on.

Raising my gun, I rounded the corner. Dad's eyes snapped to me, wide and shock-filled. A wide smile broke out across my face, and I flicked the safety back on and tossed the gun into the recliner.

I threw myself into the brick wall known as my dad. I wrapped my arms around his neck, and he lifted me off the ground, hugging me back.

"Daddy, oh god, I've missed you." I squeezed him tightly.

It had been exactly 55 weeks since I'd seen him and now that he was here, the feelings hit me hard. I had missed my dad and all his oddness.

Dad and I parted, and I realized Reaper was standing beside him. He was sporting a deep glare that was directed solely at me, and it really threw me.

The last time I remembered seeing him was when he left with my sister.

"And who is this?" Dad was looking over my shoulder at Trent. I spun around on my heel. Trent was standing in the doorway with a blank expression.

He knew about my family, but I think seeing them in the flesh for the first time was a bit shocking. Dad was intimidating.

"Dad, this is Trent, my boyfriend." I put my hand out for Trent to take.

I swear I could hear Trent's thoughts as his eyes locked with my father's. He was freaking out.

"Trent." Dad's eyes narrowed and looked him up and down. "What the fuck do you do?"

"DAD!" I threw a hand into his chest. "Don't speak to him like that."

"I'm studying medicine." Trent's eyes flickered to mine. "That's how I met your daughter at university."

"Dad, be nice," I hissed up at him.

Dad grunted something then looked over at Reaper.

"So why are you two here so late?" I looked at the clock behind them, which had just ticked three in the morning.

"Fucking police pulled us over on the way here. Went over the bikes then took us back for every fucking test known." Dad walked over to the couch and slumped into it. "Getting too old to be on the bike that long."

"Dad, don't be silly. You aren't even that old."

I looked over at Reaper. "So are both of you staying here?"

"If that's alright with you." Reaper's eyes were sharp and deadly. The hate within them really threw me.

"Um, yep, fine with me," I muttered and looked back at Dad. "So Trent and I might just go back to bed then seeing as you two aren't burglars."

"Righteo." Dad nodded his head. "Night, Abby baby; see you in the morning."

My eyebrows shot up immediately. "Abby? Did you just call me Abby?"

I couldn't be sure if I was insulted or just really pissed off that Dad had thought this whole time I was Abby.

93

"What, are you going by your full name now?" Dad challenged me, pulling his boots off.

"No, I'm going by Kim." I placed my hands on my hips. "Because that is my name!"

"Kim?" Dad's eyes shot wide, and he was quick to get up, pushing my blonde bangs from my forehead. He looked into my eyes for a few moments before he grinned. "Darn baby girl, didn't recognize you without the red hair."

"I've spent most of my life blonde, Dad." I rolled my eyes. "Now that this is cleared up, I'm going to bed with my boyfriend."

Dad looked stunned but nodded his head.

I shot a glimpse in Reaper's direction, and that hatred that had been in his eyes moments before was completely gone. Looks like he and Abby had some unfinished business, which really stirred my interest.

"Kim, just one thing."

"Sure, Dad, what?"

"Where is your sister?"

I dwelled on that question for a moment. I knew that wherever she was, she was up to no good and would be on the arm of one Drake Collins.

"You really don't want to know. Night."

I walked away, still holding Trent's hand. I wasn't going to blow the lid on Abby; she could face Dad's outrage all on her own. She would need that attitude when she went up against him.

Chapter 13

Abby

Drake and I were far from Romeo and Juliet. What we had was dark and if anything, downright sinister. I hurled my handbag into the backseat of his car, and he started up the engine.

"You been shopping, babe?" Drake asked.

"No, what makes you ask that?"

"Haven't seen that bag before." He indicated into the street.

"It's old." I glanced across at him. "So where are we going again?"

He shot that trademark grin at me, and I knew instantly I wasn't going to like the answer.

"To the club, babe."

So we have it; I was right.

I stumbled up the front steps of the house of horrors. High heels and alcohol were a bad combination for any female, and I was clumsier than most.

The door opened up after I forced my key in it. I hated this place. I hated my aunt. I hated Kim and well, I just hated everything.

"You're going to wake everyone up." Drake followed me in, closing the door quietly behind him.

"Does it look like I give a shit?" I pulled my heels off and flicked the foyer light on.

"Ok, that's it." Drake grabbed my wrist, causing me to fling back around and once he had me facing him, he backed me up against the wall. "What's up, Abby? You're bitchier than normal."

Had I been? I didn't think I had been. If anyone else were in my shoes, I'm sure they would be struggling to find a reason to be pleasant as well.

"The door is behind you if you want to leave," I snapped in his face.

He arched both his eyebrows as if I was proving his point. "Fine, I'll go."

"Sounds great to me."

"You know what your problem is, Abby? You're selfish."

"You know what my problem is, Drake? YOU!"

"Oh, so it's my fault now, is it?" He shook his head, hand on the front doorknob. "You can't take responsibility for your own shit." He pointed the car keys at me.

For someone who was concerned about waking the household up, he didn't seem to be lowering his voice now.

"Maybe I'm just over this." I gestured between the two of us. "One day you want me, the next you want nothing to do with me, and then fuck, you want me again, but only to help you out."

"I told you I don't like labels."

"I'm not asking for a fucking label; I'm asking for some respect." I crossed my arms, and maybe it was the bitch in me coming out or maybe I was just fed up with men thinking they could treat me like this. I took two long strides towards him. "You think you can keep me in the dark. You think I don't know shit, but you're wrong and tonight, I've had enough."

"You're drunk, Abby, sleep it off."

"Is that your excuse tonight? When you had that stripper whore pinned up against the brick wall in the alley?" I shook my head at him, disgusted. "You honestly think that I don't know what you get up to?"

He looked like he had been caught out, and he had. This was the first time I brought it up with him. I had always looked the other way, but tonight, I'd had enough.

"I never promised to be faithful."

"And I never promised to be a ray of fucking sunshine." I glared back at him. "So get off my case about my attitude."

"Fine, whatever." He raised his hands, surrendering. "Hate everyone then and act like a bitch. I'm done."

"You're done again, are you? Well, fuck me, what a surprise. I catch you cheating, and you're done."

"I'm leaving before you say something you can't fucking take back."

"Like what? That I really hate you?" I screamed at his back. I threw my handbag in his direction, but it hit the door. He closed it just in time with a loud bang.

Drake and I fought. Drake and I fucked. Drake and I made up.

This was us, poisonous and unhealthy. I thought briefly for a moment about just leaving my upturned handbag on the floor, but then the thought of Aunty Escort going through my stuff had me on my knees and retrieving the bag.

Maybe I was getting bitter. Maybe I was more of a bitch. But then again, maybe I was just growing up.

I started stuffing my belongings back into the bag. *Why does this bag have so much shit in it?* Honestly, I had only picked it up out of the back of the closet because it matched my outfit. I didn't sort through it at the time, just stuffed in my purse and phone.

I nearly had everything back inside the coffin bag when I picked up the last thing. It was a crumpled, folded piece of paper.

I opened it up, expecting one of my old drawings.

'Abby, be back soon. Gone to sort some shit, don't leave. Kade.'

I read it. I read it again. Then I read that same sentence for the third time, frowning and confused.

Why did I have a note from Reaper? Why was it in my handbag?

I flipped the bag over, taking a better look at it. I was certain that the last time I used this bag was the same day I met Drake and the morning after Reaper and I... well, yeah.

I scooped my bag up off the floor and rose to my feet, my eyes still locked on the letter. It was like I was expecting it to disappear, or the writing to disappear. How had I not seen this that morning?

Maybe I was making this up. Maybe this wasn't even a letter from Reaper, perhaps it was just my drunken mind playing tricks on me, and in the morning, I would wake up to it actually being a receipt from the supermarket.

I dragged my legs up the stairs and headed to my bedroom.

I was sure to wake up to that letter saying something or being something. I had drunk a lot, and *that* made sense—more sense than it actually being a letter from him.

I flopped onto my bed. Sleep was what I needed.

***

I had showered and washed away the previous night's memories and makeup. Still, the crumpled piece of paper in my hand had Kade's scribbled message.

How had I missed this? Did it really make a difference now? I went over that morning in my mind. I remembered waking up and not seeing him there. I was upset. I got dressed as quickly as I could and swiped the contents from the bedside table into my handbag, which explained why I had a coaster from the motel.

Kade could have left this note on my phone, in my purse; it didn't matter because I hadn't seen it.

It was late in the afternoon. I had slept the morning away and had spent a good hour looking at that stupid piece of paper. Twice I had thought about calling him, and just once I thought of apologizing to him. I cringed, remembering the first time he contacted me after that night.

I got up and placed the note in my bedside drawer. At least I wouldn't have to see him anytime soon, if ever again.

That was the only thing making me feel a bit better about the situation; not having to face him. I closed my bedroom door and walked down the passage. I could hear Kim's sharp laughter and Trent's voice from here and by the time I got to the staircase, it was crystal clear. I didn't like Trent, but as Drake pointed out, I didn't like anyone. After Kim had her abortion, she seemed changed. To be honest, it was like she and I had changed roles. She threw everything she had into her studies and university. I just scraped through, and university really wasn't for me.I walked into the lounge looking down at the ground. I hadn't come down to have a conversation with them. I had come down to get my jumper off the clotheshorse, and then I was planning on heading out and maybe seeking out Drake. But all my thoughts and plans for the day changed instantly when I looked up and my eyes locked with a familiar pair of eyes: my father's. Shit just got complicated.

Chapter 14

Abby

Our story was never a love story. It was more of a cocktail of sorrows mixed with the odd good moment. It was short, it was bitter, and it left a permanent scar on my heart, not to mention a bad aftertaste.

I would never and could never deny it; Reaper changed who I was. As my eyes locked with his, all this time later, the memories flooded back to me, and the feelings that were attached to them floated through me. I was being pulled under quickly and going down deep.

I wondered how someone who had such godly looks could be so evil and cruel of heart.

"Abby."

My name pulled me out from the state I had entered, and I looked back at my father. I couldn't believe he was there—with Reaper.

"Dad." I forced the feelings to stay out of my voice. I wouldn't give Reaper the privilege of hearing anything but coldness in my voice. I would never let him get close again. Sure, I had found a letter, but deep down I felt like it hadn't changed much.

"What are you doing here?" I asked.

The timing couldn't be worse. The night after I found the letter that could have changed everything, and Reaper was standing in Aunty Amanda's living room the next day.

"I thought it was time I caught up with my girls." He seemed to be telling the truth because he was able to keep eye contact with me. "Been missing my girls."

Been missing us, has he? Then why didn't he call? Why hadn't he come sooner? Today's world made it so simple to get in touch with someone if you really wanted to. There was no excuse for his silence.

"Well, that's great." A bitter smile crept across my lips. "I'll leave you and Kim to it. Just let me know when you roll back out of town."

I turned to walk out of the room. It looked like I needed to pack an overnight bag and would be crashing somewhere else for a few nights. Surely he wouldn't be staying longer than that.

"Abby!"

"What, Dad?" I sighed and turned around with a deflated look on my face. I wasn't interested in what he had to say, and I wasn't interested in hanging around to listen to it.

"Come back here."

"I really don't see the point."

"You can't speak to me like that."

"Sorry, Dad. I guess I'm just not used to speaking to you." I crossed my arms and gave him a pointed look. "Last time I checked, your motto for being a dad is when things get hard, ship them off to the whore because *she* will be a great role model."

He rose from the chair with the look of a raging bull. "Reel ya shit in, Abby."

"How about I just ride out instead?"

"Dad, just let her go, will you? She will get your blood pressure up," Kim snapped into our conversation. "Really, Dad, just let her go. She won't back down."

"Yeah, Dad, listen to the model daughter of yours." I couldn't help but roll my eyes. "Kim just has so much good advice these days, especially when it comes to getting pregnant and aborting it." I shot her a smug look. She hated me mentioning her abortion, so I did it frequently.

"Abby, that really isn't nice," Trent spoke up, trying to come to the defense of his halfwit of a girlfriend.

"Trent, your face really isn't nice, but yet I have to deal with it regularly." I shot him a tight smile and a "mind your own fucking business" look.

"ABBY!" Kim got to her feet and for once was actually seen off of Trent's lap. After all, since she started dating the walking pizza, she had decided to become a lap poodle.

"Not my fault he looks like a pizza topping gone wrong." I shrugged my shoulders, pretending to come off innocent. To be fair to Trent, his skin wasn't that bad, but I heard Kim mention once he used to have bad skin, and it is sort of a weakness and a sore spot for him.

So being the bitch I am, I take someone's weakness and punch them in it. "Now if you all don't mind, I have places be, with people I actually give a fuck about. So see ya later, and I hope that later isn't anytime soon."

Sure, I was a bitch. I wasn't denying that or making excuses. Perhaps I had grown up to be Satan's Bitch, as Kim liked to refer to me as.

I left the room in silence. No one said anything to me. Nobody stopped me from leaving, either. A large part of me felt pleased with that because I had what I wanted. I wasn't wanted by them. They wanted me gone, and I wanted to be gone.

Funny how sometimes things worked out.

Chapter 15

Abby

Novels; it was something I had yet to give up. I flicked the page. I wished my life was as thrilling as the ones on the pages.

"We need to talk."

Drake walked into the lounge, scotch glass in hand. I closed the book I was reading and arched an eyebrow after taking in his expression.

"What's wrong, Drake?"

He lowered himself into the armchair across from me. "After last night, I didn't think we would see each other for a while and…" he gestured his glass towards me. "You just turn up like nothing happened."

"What do you want me to say?" I pulled my legs off the chair and twisted to face him full on. "Come on, Drake. I was drunk, you were drunk. Two plus two equals us fighting."

Drake dropped his head to the side, studying me. "How many times do I have to push you away till you see it?"

To see that we were the worst possible match ever? I already knew that. I had already seen that. But here I sat on his couch, reading a romance novel, acting like he hadn't cheated on me the night before.

"My dad and his sidekick rocked up this morning. I had to leave the house, and once they are gone, I will leave. Promise." I snatched the novel up from the couch and got up. "Don't worry, Drake, I haven't forgotten what happened." How could I? Even with a fuzzy memory, I still classed it as a fight we wouldn't be coming back from.

"We're still friends, Abby." He got up, grabbing my wrist just before I was about to walk away. "Nothing can change that, so you're welcome to stay as long as you like."

Friends. We were never friends to begin with.

"Sure." I gave him a tight smile. "I guess the whole boyfriend and girlfriend thing never worked out. Perhaps it had something to do with the fact that we never really became boyfriend and girlfriend." We had skipped every step and went straight to the fighting and the sex. "I'm going to go have a nap; didn't get much sleep last night."

"No, you didn't." He gave me a half smile. "You know, Abby, I think we would work together better as friends. No messy stuff to cause our fights, yeah?"

I thought about it for a moment. "Sure, Drake."

I didn't really feel anything about us openly admitting we weren't going back to that fighting, messed-up couple. A part of me, a large part, just didn't care anymore. I suppose I really didn't care about anything.

"Oh, and Abby?"

"Yep?" I spun on my heel, now at the bottom of the stairs.

"Just so you know. Hard and mean doesn't really suit you."

"You haven't known a different side to me," I pointed out.

"Please. I still remember the girl who wouldn't let me leave the house without eating first."

"Maybe I was just worried you would end up skinny." I shot him a wink and started to walk up the stairs.

Maybe I had gotten hard. Maybe I had lost my 'good' side.

I sighed and closed the door of Drake's guest room behind me. Perhaps I needed to snap my life back into focus, but I just didn't see how I could do that, not when Dad was in town with the bloody Reaper.

I dropped the book on the floor and pushed down my jeans, climbing into bed. Maybe I just needed a good few hours' sleep.

Reaper

"Don't like what I'm hearing, brother." Roach put his glass down on the table, sitting directly across from me. He had his judgment eyes on and a cold expression to match. "You either start explaining or hand the vest over."

He wanted answers? Well, I didn't feel like giving any. I stared down blankly at the can of beer. *All because of fucking Abby Harrison.* If it weren't for her, I wouldn't be answering to him. I should have never given up my President patch.

"Shit had to be sorted. I sorted it." I glanced at him. "Family is family, Roach; can't turn my back on them."

"The club is family."

"The club is the club." I swallowed the rest of my can and crushed it in my hand and tossed it in the side bin. "He's all the family I have, and I'm not turning my back on him."

"I'm not asking you to! I'm just making it clear that you stepped over a line and their shit is their shit, and you got no right getting involved in their shit when you're wearing that vest." He gestured to my club vest. "What you *do* affects the club. What you *believe* affects the club, and getting involved with that brother of yours affects the club."

I didn't have the best temper control, and I felt what little control I had slipping away with every word he said. There is a difference between a club brother and a blood brother. I'd never really seen that until now, but I guess no one ever dared to tell me otherwise.

"Not gonna apologize for what I did, Roach." My eyes were sharp as I looked at him. "I'd do it again; ain't gonna pretend like I wouldn't."

Roach looked at me solemnly for a few moments before getting to his feet. "Is that the only reason you agreed to come here? Because of him?"

"Well, I wouldn't come all this way to watch you have a family reunion, would I?" My tone was dripping in annoyance. "Look, ya wanted the truth, now ya got it. I came here for Drake. Blood is blood, and he called me shortly after you told me I had to come here. So it worked out well."

His top lip curled up. "You better watch ya tone."

"Why?" I rose to my feet, gripping the table. "You and I both know this VP shit ain't working."

"Not letting ya walk away, Reaper."

"Not asking." I shrugged the vest off. "I'll always pick blood over the club."

"You of all people know the club becomes blood."

"Roach. Ya telling me I can't help my brother? I'm telling you that where Drake is involved, the club don't mean shit." I stuffed the leather vest in his chest. "I guess you'll have to find someone else to do your dirty work."

"So that's it, ya walking away from the brotherhood for this!?" he roared, grabbing me by the cuff of my shirt and slamming me back against the kitchen wall. "WHAT AM I GONNA TELL THE BOYS? THAT THE REAPER WALKED?"

Gripping his shoulder, I pushed him backward. He might be strong, but I'm stronger; I guess it had to do with the fact I hadn't let my body go yet. "Tell them whatever ya like. I don't give a fuck."

Was I mistaken for walking away from a brotherhood that had been behind me for years? I wasn't sure, but Drake was the only brother I had. He might screw up regularly, but he was all I had.

Abby wasn't here, and I was thankful as fuck for that. The last thing I needed was seeing her judgmental eyes as she watched me turn my back on my club.

I slammed their front door and strode across the lawn towards my bike. Rage fired through my body at a hundred miles an hour. Kicking the bike to life, I had only one destination in mind— Drake's house.

Looks like I'll be crashing with my little brother for a while.

My blood ran hot from the run in with Roach when I pulled up in front of Drake's house. I wasn't in the best mood, I would admit that, but when I saw the trail of cars, the bikes, and the boozing teens on his front porch, I knew my mood was going to go downhill.

Should I have expected my brother not to be throwing a raging party on a Saturday night?

I stepped over a lightweight who had already passed out on the front lawn and headed for the house. I pushed a couple out of my way; it was their own fault anyway. *Who makes out in a front doorway?*

Drake had money. Family money. The house was big, old. We called it the haunted mansion growing up. He had the place to himself after Nanna passed, but by the look of it, he had made himself at home.

The bass of the music was deep, thick, and thumping. I scanned the lounge looking for Drake, then I spotted him dancing with a blonde.

Drake and his women.

I cut through the crowd and gripped his shoulder. Being my brother, it was in his blood to turn and throw a punch; I expected it and ducked.

"BROTHER!" A grin sparked across his face, and he lunged to hug me. "WHAT THE FUCK YA STILL DOING HERE?" he roared over the music.

"Gonna crash for a bit." I gripped his shoulder and yelled it in his ear.

He frowned and noticed the missing vest. I *always* wore a vest. He nodded his head with understanding. "My house is your house!" he yelled back.

Blood. That was what it came down to. I patted him on the back and he handed me his drink. "Enjoy the party, brother!"

He was speaking to me, but his eyes looked over my shoulder. I turned to see who had stolen his attention. In my head, the music faded, and all I heard was the increase of my own heartbeats.

Abby.

She was on the sunken level of the lounge, which was filled with people dancing, drinking. Abby was by herself, hands in the air, swaying to the beat. She looked to be high on something, but it was a sexy high.

Drake whacked me on the shoulder and mouthed "got to go" before cutting his way through the crowd of people.

When Abby threw her hands around his neck, I took a big gulp of the drink Drake had handed me. Looked like Abby wasn't just a guest but Drake's friend.

I didn't know how that made me feel. Pretty pissed off, I suppose.

She laughed as Drake twirled her around and then tightly wrapped his arms around her, pulling her back into his chest. I knew where this was going, and fuck if I was staying to watch. I wished this night was over already. I picked up my bag from the hallway and headed upstairs. I needed to find a room to drink the night away.

Chapter 16

Reaper

*I had my morning scotch, trying to shake
the pain of a hangover, when Drake
dragged his topless arse into the lounge.*

"Pour me one, will you?" Drake dropped down on the couch. "Good night." He yawned, then took the drink from me. "Nothing like a morning scotch to help a hangover."

"True."

We both raised a glass.

"So you bang that bird last night?" I swallowed the remaining dregs of my glass. I glared down at the carpet, remembering Abby draped all over him.

"Which one?"

"The brunette? You know, skinny, curves?" I looked at him.

"Oh," Drake's lips twitched into a smile. "You mean Abby."

He knew her name, more than he would normally know about a girl. Fuck, did he like her? My luck can't be that bad. The bloody woman was ruining my life.

"DRAKE?"

A voice I knew all too well called out. Looked like all my questions were answered.

Drake and I looked across the room, and there she stood, the devil with all her temptation. She was wearing a man's tee shirt. It wasn't mine though; why the fuck did that bother me?

Her legs looked never-ending, and the way her hair was frizzed, looking all sex-kitten like… damn, the woman was dripping in appeal.

Drake had noticed, and he was licking his bottom lip. "What's up, babe? You're awake early. Didn't see that happening till late afternoon."

I needed something stronger than this. I scoffed to myself, looking down at my glass.

"You... what... what are you doing here?"

My eyes shot up, and I saw Abby staring blankly at me. She was talking to *me*.

She tilted her head to the side. "Did Dad send you here?"

"I'm clearly missing something." Drake piped up, pushing himself back into the couch. "Come on, share."

"Reaper knows my dad."

"Your dad?" Drake frowned and looked at me. "Why the hell are you hanging out with her old man?"

"Her old man is Roach." I scoffed. "She didn't share that part, brother?"

"Never came up." Drake looked annoyed and then looked at Abby. "Why didn't you tell me?"

When she didn't answer, I turned to look at her. She froze, not moving an inch, just blinking. Slowly, she raised a finger and pointed it at me. "What... what... what did you just say?"

"Her old man is Roach?" I repeated for her.

"After that."

"What?" I had no idea what she was trying to get at; it was too early for this shit.

"You called him your brother." Her eyes flicked to Drake, "Is Reaper your brother?"

Drake looked reluctant to answer. He exhaled slowly. Looks like my little brother was scared of her.

"Yeah, it is true." Drake shrugged his shoulders. "Sorry, Abby, never came up."

"*Never. Came. Up?*" She looked like a raging bull and was across the lounge in a flash, and for once, her anger wasn't directed at me. "Really, Drake?! It never came up. We were together for a YEAR!" She shoved his shoulder.

"HEY!" Drake grabbed her hand and stood up. "You never mentioned your old man being fucking Roach."

"Well, it just never came up," she snapped at him, ripping her hand back. "I can't believe you."

"You haven't changed, have ya? Still taking your hormones out on people." I rose up. Her sharp blue eyes locked with mine.

"You can go tell Dad I'm not coming back. So piss off, will you?" she snarled, rage flashing across her eyes.

"Not going anywhere."

"Leave."

"He isn't going anywhere," Drake piped up while also taking the empty glass from my hand. "He is moving in." Drake turned back around, pointing a glass at Abby, "And as you agreed to move in last night, I guess I should really introduce the two of you, seeing as we are all housemates now."

Fuck. Me.

"What did you just say?" We both said it at the same time, causing us to share a glance.

"Oh come on, brother, she's hot and a good cook." He winked at Abby. "And Kade is good to have around, Abby. Everyone thinks twice having the Reaper behind ya."

He could say Abby was made of fucking gold, and my opinion of her wouldn't change.

"I can't live here with him." Abby shook her head. "Sorry, Drake, but I've changed my mind."

"Abby, come on! What's the problem?" Drake pleaded with her.

"The problem is he works for my father." She shot me a hot look over her shoulder. "I don't trust him."

"Well then problem solved!" Drake grinned and then handed me a refilled glass. "Reaper isn't a Satan's Son anymore."

"What?" The edge in her eyes had softened as she turned to look

111

at me. I noticed the way her eyes searched for my missing vest. "What happened?"

I threw the drink back and handed Drake the empty glass. "Nothing to do with you."

I wouldn't tell her shit. She would gloat. She would love to hear how I just gave my whole life up for her.

But at the end, it wasn't her fault I walked, it was me. I chose family over the club.

"I'm going back to bed; wake me when your whore is gone."

I left the room, not giving a fuck about the hurt in Abby's eyes. A taste of hurt would be good for her. She had caused me enough pain, and it was about time she got some.

Chapter 17

Drake

I always had a habit of screwing a good thing up, and Abby was a living example of that. I watched her out of the corner of my eye as she read one of those novels of hers on the old couch in the shed. She was the type of girl that didn't mind hanging around the shed. I learned early that as long as you gave her one of her old books, she is happy to be anywhere.

"Keep staring at me, and I'll start to think you want something." Her eyes fluttered up from the book and looked into mine.

"Don't know what you're talking about." I looked back down at the engine I was working on.

Show Abby a bit of interest, and I won't live it down. It was hard enough trying to be her friend. I was just thankful she was at least giving it a go.

"So," she put her book down and got up. "What is the go with Kade? Why the sudden move in?" She handed me a rag to wipe my hands with.

Going from living by myself to living with my brother and ex-girlfriend is going to be a bit of a shock to the system, but hell, I was going to give it a go. "Kade doesn't have anywhere else to go, and when it comes down to it, the house is half his."

"Was he already staying here when you asked me to move in?"

"Does it matter?"

She shrugged her shoulders, but it was the hidden anger in her eyes that told me she wasn't telling me the full story, or at least leaving something out. "Depends if he is always going to be so snippy."

"Yeah, sorry about the comment earlier, Kade just, well…" I scratched the back of my neck. "Kade doesn't really respect women, so don't take it personally. You all are just property to him, or a means to an end, ya know?"

"Oh, I know." There was bitterness in her tone and frustrated, she ran her fingers through her hair, playing with it. It was a habit of hers when she was frustrated. It took me a solid few months to pick up on that one. "So I guess I'll just have to get used to his rudeness."

"I'm sure you can give it back to him, Abby."

She scoffed. "Doubtful."

I poked her with the spanner I held. "Come on Ab, we both know your inner bitch is itching to give him a service."

"He isn't worth it." She leaned back against the bonnet, crossing her arms. "So are you going to help me move my stuff over later?"

"Have you told your aunt that you're leaving?"

A grin spread across her lips. "Maybe."

"You haven't, have you?"

"Well, I'm sure once I start moving my stuff out, she will get the idea." Abby scooped up her book. "Now get your butt into gear and come help me escape from hell."

"Such a drama queen."

"Says the slut," she teased and poked out her tongue.

I watched her walk away and still couldn't figure out how things were going so well between us after everything.

Still wasn't going to question it. Having her around made my life a happier one.

***

"Come on brother, I need help." I knocked on Kade's door before opening it. I wasn't even half surprised seeing him lying on the bed, smoking something I knew wasn't a cigarette.

"What with?" he blew a mouth full of smoke out.

"Abby's bed."

"Busy."

"No, you're not. Come on, I've got a Ute full of her crap I have to bring in."

"I said I'm busy."

I picked up the first thing my hand landed on, which happened to be some old-fashioned vase thing, and threw it at him. I smirked when it hit his stomach. "Get up, you lazy shit."

"I'm not lifting a fucking finger for that bitch," Kade grumbled, pulling himself up from the bed before throwing the vase back at me, which hit the wall and smashed into pieces.

"Tone down the aggression, will ya?" I closed the door behind me. Abby didn't like Kade as it was and didn't need her hearing more shit coming out from his mouth. "Who peed in your beer, bro? Can't think of another reason for you to be so pissed off."

"Fuck off, Drake."

"Can't... need ya help."

He gritted his teeth and gave me the 'Reaper' look. Which was my brother's 'fuck you' glare.

"Come on, for your brother?" I pleaded and just to piss him off a bit more, I shot him a wink.

He was grumbling about how much he hated it here while pulling on his boots. I couldn't stop myself from rolling my eyes as he walked past, muttering about how Abby was ruining his life.

"You know, you and Abby both have a flair for drama." I chuckled, jogging next to him down the stairs.

"Fuck off; we're nothing alike." He snorted.

The front door was wide open. It was the perfect summer day. Abby leaned against the Ute chatting with the neighbor. She looked great; her hair out all sex kitten like and wearing those shorts. Damn, the girl was fit.

Abby spun around, her smile slowly fading. "Hi, Kade." She

gave him her tight, forced smile, causing me to grin.

"Abby, seeing ya using the only muscle you know how, ya mouth." He pulled down the tray of the Ute. "Get out of the way, would ya." He shoved her and started to untie a rope.

Abby huffed and threw a punch into his arm, "Touch me again, and I'll make you regret it."

"Come on, you two, play nice." I stepped in before things got heated and took the other side of the Ute, catching the rope Kade threw over.

"Really?" Kade scoffed and threw her a disbelieving look. "Don't make threats ya can't keep, Abby."

"How about you just go back inside. I'll help Drake."

"With what, Abby? Ya pin muscles aren't going to carry shit."

"We will manage." She was pushing him out of her way.

These two were going to give me a headache. "Abby, cut it out. I can't carry this monster with you." I took the end of the headboard, and Kade jumped up to ease it down to me.

"Fine, but if you drop it, Kade, I will kill you." She huffed and watched with narrowed eyes as Kade stepped off the Ute.

With every item, Abby made it her mission to follow, threatening him the entire way. When we finally had everything in and done, I needed painkillers and a hard drink. Kade looked like he was boiling with rage. He hadn't snapped at her once, which surprised me.

I placed the glass against my forehead and lay on the couch with my legs hanging over the edge. I thought I was going to get some peace now that those two had separated, but that peace was short-lived.

"KADE, GIVE IT BACK!" Abby roared, and I heard her footsteps running down the stairs. "KADE!"

Don't come in here. Don't come in here. I closed my eyes and gritted my teeth when I heard Kade's big footsteps come in.

"Drake, ya know about this?"

Why the fuck did I open my house to these two again?

"What?" I opened my eyes.

Kade held a silver gun. It wasn't overly big, but it looked well taken care of. "This?"

"Give it *back!*" Abby stormed in and charged at Kade; he fought her off with one arm.

"You're seriously letting her have a gun in this house? She will fucking kill herself!" Kade snapped at me, with a serious, pissed-off look on his face. "I bet she doesn't even know how to turn the safety on!"

"Kade, give it back to her." I pulled myself up and rubbed my temples. "It's hers."

"Yeah, give it back." She jumped for it, trying to get it from him.

"Abby, stop jumping," I asked her and stood up. "Give her the gun back, Kade."

"Fuck off; she isn't allowed one, and she doesn't need one either."

"Yes, I do. How else can I make good on my threat when I say "step into my room, I will shoot you." Abby looked smug. "Give me back, Kade, or I'll take your porn collection."

"You've been in his room?" I arched both eyebrows at her.

"Grow a pair, Drake, she's making shit up!" Kade rolled his eyes and slapped the gun down in her hand. "For the record, I'm not ok with this."

"I'm not ok with you being here, but yet here you are," she shot back at him with a burning look in her eyes.

Kade muttered something I didn't catch and stormed out. Abby looked down at the gun in her hands with a smile.

"You don't need that." I pointed my glass at her and gave her a hard look. "And you know it."

She rolled her eyes, "I know, but Kade didn't want me to have it. Call me childish, but it made me want to have it more."

"That *is* childish."

"Guess I'm a child then." She winked and spun away, her hair whipping around as she walked off happily.

It was only day one, and I was already regretting the decision to let them live here. It had to get better from here, right?

Abby

Aunty Amanda wasn't ok with me moving out. Neither was Kim, and I'm sure Dad would have had an opinion, too, if he was there. As my luck would have it, he had just stepped out when I arrived, and he hadn't come back in time to stop me. I was half expecting him to show up halfway through when we had the Ute loaded, but he didn't.

I pulled out a frame, which had a picture of my mom and I in it, placing it on the bedside table. My room felt like my room now.

It wasn't a guest room anymore. It was silly how a few simple things could make such a difference.

It was after midnight, and Drake was passed out on the couch downstairs. Kade hadn't shown his face since the whole 'you can't have your gun' show. I had the perfect opportunity to do the thing I had been dreading since that morning.

It took me a full five minutes to drum up the courage to walk to his door. Finally, I brought up a closed fist and knocked on his door.

I knew he wouldn't get his arse out of bed to open the door, so I let myself in, clearing my throat when I did.

"Reaper, you here?" I closed the door behind me and when I turned back around, my eyes landed on him.

He was shirtless, lying on the bed, one arm under his head. "Wrong room. Drake's two doors up."

His voice was empty of emotion, just like him.

"Can we talk?"

His chest rumbled with a deep laughter.

The moonlight was firing across his tattoos, defining his scars as well. His appeal was rocketing up, and I fought to keep the old feelings under control.

"Not stopping ya." He blew smoke from his mouth and then snuffed his butt out on the ashtray.

My pulse increased, but I kept a calm face on. "I wanted to say I'm sorry." I chewed on my bottom lip, frowning. Why was I apologizing again? Oh right, taking the right road.

"For what, taking off last year and leaving me hanging for months, dodging my calls? Or for playing house with my little brother?" Hurt crept into his words, and while talking, he pushed himself off the bed.

I opened my mouth, but I was still thinking or more like processing what he said.

Kade was tall, and his height dominated me. It was as if his skin radiated sex appeal, like a drug.

"I… I thought you ditched me..." I closed my eyes, cringing as I shared this with him. "I thought you had just left me there. Then the other day, I found that letter, and I'm sorry, you know, I'm sorry for not letting you explain, and I'm... I'm just sorry," I finished in defeat.

A few seconds passed and I opened my eyes. His face had a mixed reaction. I had just expected to see his normal hard, cold expression, but I didn't.

For a split second, I was reminded of the man that took me to that café.

"You should leave." He pushed the words out and took a step away from me, shaking his head. "No point bringing up shit that doesn't matter anymore."

"Doesn't matter? So I don't matter anymore?"

He hasn't seen you in a year, Abby. Wake up. He had called me selfish and a whore since he arrived.

"You're sleeping with my brother," he hissed through his teeth,

119

"Coming in here, looking like that," he waved his hand at me. "It's asking for fucking trouble, Abby."

"Kade, it isn't like that."

One moment I stared into his eyes, and the next I gasped as he gripped my waist and pushed me back against the door.

"What are you doing?" I stuttered as I felt his hand slip up the back of my top.

He tilted his head to the side, watching the fear grow in my eyes for sure. "Drake likes you." He dipped his head down, his mouth hovering over my ear, "Pity he falls for the whores."

My eyes slammed shut, and I squeezed the unwanted tears back. "Let go of me."

"With pleasure." He pushed himself away from me, his hand gone.

I twisted around quickly so he couldn't see how deep his words cut. "For the record, Reaper," I twisted the knob, opening the door, "Drake and I are only friends, which is more than I can say for you and me." I hissed the words at him.

I left his door open and walked back to my room. I shouldn't have attempted to reason with him. I wiped an angry tear away. What had I ever seen in him?

Chapter 18

Drake

My brother had many good qualities. He didn't blink when staring down the barrel of a gun. He didn't flinch when it came to blood. But when it came to a poker face, he just didn't have one.

I slapped down a full house on the table. "That's what you call a flush, brother, now pay up!" I laughed and raked in the cash from the coffee table.

"Bullshit." He pointed his cigarette at me, his eyes piercing. "You're fucking working the cards."

"More like you suck at poker." I threw the remnants of my whiskey back and poured him and myself another. "Told you I had gotten good."

"Cheating doesn't make you good." He grunted. "Four hands, you're fucking cheating."

I chuckled, enjoying his rage. "What do you say to another then?"

"I'm dealing." He swiped the pack of cards from me.

"Whatever." I raised my hands in defense. It didn't make a difference anyway.

I heard the click, click, click coming down the stairs. Abby was wearing heels. That meant...

"I'm going out," She paused in the large opening of the lounge. One of her perfect manicured eyebrows rose when she saw what we were doing.

"Where?" I asked, while Kade muttered something about not giving a shit; he and his bad attitude hadn't changed when it came to Abby.

"On a date." She spoke just before the doorbell rang.

My head whipped to Kade, and he looked back at me. We rose

to our feet in unison, knocking everything off the table in our hurry to get to the door.

"You get her," Kade grunted, sprinting past me as I wrapped my arms around Abby.

"Let go of me." She hissed and kicked her feet.

Kade opened the door, and I pushed Abby behind us. Time to size this kid up and that was what he was, a kid. *Was this guy even legally allowed to drink?*

I shot a disgusted look back at Abby as she crossed her arms. "Get out of my way."

"What you want?" Kade grunted at the young punk on our doorstep. "Come on, spit it out," Kade pressured when the guy just stared.

"Reaper, Drake, get out of my way!" Abby stomped her feet behind us.

I turned to look back at her. "Is this kid even legally allowed to drive?"

"Are you?" She snapped back at me with a bitchy look. "Oh that's right, you lost your license, and yes he is! Now move!" She attempted to push her way through, but Kade and I were fucking bricks; she had no chance of success.

"I'm just taking... um... Abby out," he stuttered. He actually stuttered!

"MOVE!" Abby yelled.

"Are you her... ummm... her brothers?" He looked dumbstruck at us.

Kade's lips twitched, and I knew he was in for some fun. "Can't have sex with a sister, can you? Unless you're some creepy piece of work. You look like that type of freak."

I pressed my lips firmly together, and Kade's very few words sent Abby into a tantrum.

"MOVE KADE, BEFORE I TAKE THE POKER FROM THE FIRE AND RUN IT THROUGH YOUR BACK!" she roared.

Kade laughed and stepped to the side. "All you had to do was ask."

Abby's face was red and she was breathing fire. Darting between us, she grabbed the poor guy's hand and flung him around.

She was storming down the garden path with him in tow. Leaning against the doorframe, I watched them get into his car. "I don't like him."

"Why, scared he might take ya side, bitch?" Kade rolled his eyes at me.

"Didn't have to embarrass her." I gave him a pointed look.

Kade had spilled all about his and Abby's history; history I had known nothing about.

He shrugged his shoulders. "Doesn't matter, she was going to leave with him no matter what I said."

"I still don't like him."

We both watched the car pull away.

"Gay looking kid if you ask me." Kade's eyes met mine; we both seemed to be thinking the same thing.

"Didn't look trustworthy, did he?"

"Definitely not an upstanding citizen like ourselves." Kade smirked then pushed off the wall. "Get ya shit already, I'm not the best tail driver as is."

Looked like we were on the same page. Hadn't planned on stalking Abby and her date, but hell, it wasn't like we had anything else to do. Plus he really didn't seem like her type—not one tattoo in sight.

Chapter 19

Abby

I swirled the red wine slowly in the glass while looking across at Adam Jenkins. He was explaining the terms of my employment, and while I was acting to hang on to his every word, my real attention was on Kade and Drake, who were occupying the seats two tables across from ours.

Kade was screwing his nose up at the menu while Drake eyed the waitress.

"Abby, do you see any issues with this?" Adam asked, and my mind flicked back to the conversation I should have been listening to.

"No, not at all. The hours are reasonable, and I don't see any problems coming up." I shot him a flawless smile and then swallowed the rest of my drink.

I needed more wine.

Adam cleared his voice, and his eyes dropped down to his plate of food. For the first time this evening, he looked worried. "I, um… didn't want to bring this up, but..."

"You're concerned about what happened earlier?" I knew Drake and Kade's stupid behavior would come back to haunt me. Why did they have to do that? Couldn't they have just kept their noses out of my business? Just for once?

"Yes." His word was sharp. "They seem protective of you, and this role might conflict with that protection."

I couldn't suppress the smile. "Why, do you have a feeling they won't like me being used as bait?"

He raised both eyebrows at me, "You know that we'll pay you well because you are putting yourself in a dangerous situation."

"Like I told you in the car, Adam, they are my housemates,

nothing more. They aren't my brothers, and I'm not in a relationship with either of them. So you can tone down the concern."

"Just making sure. I never hire a woman that has strings, because those strings end up screwing everything up." He shrugged his shoulders "And I'm sick of getting punched in the face by them as well."

I nodded my head with a small grin. "You have nothing to worry about."

"So the fact that they are dining here means nothing?" He looked over at the table and then gave me a challenging look.

"It's their favorite place in town to eat." I lied smoothly. I was sure Kade hated it here. After all, it didn't have his two favorite things on the menu—beer and hamburgers.

"Good to hear then." He leaned across the table, lowering his voice. "Because I have a feeling that you and I are going to work well together."

"I'm sure I will just be one of the many."

Adam Jenkins was a twisted and highly clever individual. Many women would fall for his charm and those brown eyes of his. I, on the other hand, have sworn off men altogether.

"Well then, here is to…" He pulled the wine from the cooler and refilled my glass. "A successful and long-lasting business partnership."

I raised my glass to his. "Cheers."

I was either making a good decision that would pay off, or jumping into a pit of fire with the devil himself. My eyes flickered across to Kade, and I realized that if this didn't work out, at least it wasn't the first sticky situation I would be getting myself out of.

***

I flicked through the numerous gift cards that Adam had left. I had gotten home before the boys because they, unlike me, had to pretend they were there for tea. So they hadn't left when he had.

I didn't trust Adam; maybe that was due to what he was employing me to do. Women that do the work that I am about to enter into are known as bait.

We are given someone who is either in a position of power, owed money to someone, or, well, the possibilities are endless. What we do is flirt, charm, and get them where our client wants them, whether that be in a secluded alleyway or in a compromising position.

"You home, Abby?" Drake yelled up the staircase.

Looked like the stalkers were back. I opened my bedroom door, "Yes, now are you going to tell me why you took it upon yourself to stalk me tonight?" I jogged down the staircase and then once at the bottom gave them a hard look. "Really, Drake? Are you going to be one of *those* exes?"

"Calm down, Abby. Maybe we planned on going there." Kade had a smug look on his face as they walked past me. "Not everything is about you, you know?"

"Please, you two had a whole evening of poker and drinking planned." I crossed my arms. "Don't lie; you followed me."

"Whatever," Kade walked off, and I turned to look back at Drake, who was nowhere near as good at lying as his brother.

"Well?"

Drake groaned, "It wasn't like that, Abby, promise." He decided instead of continuing a conversation, he would walk off and follow in the steps of his brother.

"You aren't getting out of it that easy." I followed him into the lounge. "You nearly ruined everything tonight, and you!" I pointed at Kade, "have no right to speak to me like that in front of people! Seriously, what the fuck was with that comment?"

Kade just shrugged his shoulders and turned his back on me.

I may have been mildly angry a few minutes ago, but his noncaring attitude made my temper rise to boiling in an instant. I grabbed his shoulder and pulled on it, forcing him to look at me.

"You're disgusting, you know that?"

His eyes hardened. "Well, my opinion of you isn't that high, either."

"Would you two cut it the fuck out?" Drake yelled at us "You are both doing my head in!"

"Not my fault she is a fucking walking hormone attack. Just got to look at her and she goes for the kill," Kade scoffed in my face while talking to Drake.

I clenched my fists at my side. "And what, you're better, are you? You and your disgusting comments! Not to mention, you seem to just breathe fire on me when I walk into the room, and I am warning you now," I pointed a finger at his chest while glaring up at him. "If you call me a whore one more time, I won't be responsible for how I act."

"THAT'S IT! I'm going out!" Drake roared and stormed out of the room.

Kade and I were too busy glaring each other off to watch him leave, but we knew he was gone when the door slammed.

"Now look what you've done, you've made my brother leave his own house." Kade's eyes were scorching. "Good one, Abby."

"Oh fuck you, Kade! You are a selfish prick, and I don't know what I saw in you."

His eyes rolled with humor, "Come on, babe, you saw what every teenage girl sees, a man she shouldn't have. You only wanted me to piss your old man off."

My mouth fell open. "Do you really believe that?"

He nodded his head with determination in his eyes. "Come on, Abby, admit it to yourself! No one is here, just me, and fuck, I already know it, so go on and admit it." He was towering over me, those eyes staring into mine.

"No."

"Ashamed?"

"NO!"

"Then what the fuck is stopping you?" he roared down at me. For a split second, I think I saw hurt within his black-gray orbs, but that was until he threw his glass across the room.

I jumped at the sound of it shattering against the wall. His eyes were painted in rage while his face remained unreadable. "You never gave a shit, Abby, you just wanted to fuck me, to fuck off your old man, and ya did."

All this time, this was what he thought? This was all he thought of me?

A lot of women would back down in this type of situation. Hell, the rage in his eyes would have men running, but me, well, I'm stubborn. I grabbed his arm, forcing his tee shirt sleeve up. "Would I have drawn this if you meant nothing to me?" My eyes glanced at the picture I drew him all those years ago. "You want the truth, Kade? You want me to admit it?" If he wanted to hear it, fine. What did I have to lose? I lost my pride a long time ago and my self-respect the morning I woke up alone.

"Ever since I was sixteen, I loved you. I fell for the one thing I knew I should never want. You think I used you?" I tilted my head up at him. My heart was burning just touching him, and yet I couldn't pull my hand away. "I couldn't breathe when you weren't around and when you did show up, everything stopped, and all that mattered was you were there, and for those few days, everything felt right." Hearing myself admit it only dug the hurt deeper. I was so stupid.

"I woke up alone in that motel, and it nearly killed me knowing that the one person I trusted that I loved, left." My body was blanketed by the memory. "You didn't break my heart, Kade." My eyes swelled with tears. "You destroyed it."

The anger I felt for him was nothing compared to the pain I carried because of him. The hours I had lost crying over him.

"Do you know the most depressing thing?" My eyes stared into his. "I would do it all again." And that truly scared me.

He hadn't spoken a word. His face held no expression, and his eyes showed no remorse. I took a step back, letting my arm fall to my side. The tears fell while my lungs struggled for air. "You wanted the truth, and there it is."

He just stood there, and why did that shock me? He is called the Reaper for a reason. My lips formed a tight line, and when I couldn't take the silence anymore, I turned my back and walked away.

Time had passed, but the wounds still hadn't healed. How was that even possible?

Closing my bedroom door, I slid down it, leaning my head against my knees. All this time I had thought I was over him when really I had just been covering the wound up. Now the Band-Aid was off and the tears just wouldn't stop.

Chapter 20

Abby

I didn't think it was possible, but the tears did stop. When they did, my clarity followed soon after. I had cleansed him out of my system, and I would love to say forever, but I knew better than to believe that.

"Abby?" Drake knocked on my door before entering. "We're ordering pizza, are you interested? Oh, wow." His mouth dropped open.

"How do I look?" I turned my back to the mirror to face him. I never really cared for a cocktail dress, but it was black. It was meant to be sexy, so I hoped that the two would help me tonight.

He slowly nodded his head, "Um, yep, wow." He finally brought his eyes to mine, "Where are you heading out in that?"

I could tell him the truth, or I could lie. "Nowhere special." I decided to avoid the question altogether. "I will have to give the pizza a miss tonight."

"Clearly," he muttered.

I picked up my oversized purse from the bed and followed Drake out. "So I guess you guys have the house to yourself."

"Are you coming back tonight?" He still couldn't take his eyes off me, which gave me a confidence boost.

"Not sure. I hope so." I gave him a side smile and took the steps one at a time. These high heels could kill me. I was sure of it.

"Abby is heading out, so it's just us," Drake spoke into the lounge while I made every effort not to look at Kade.

"Night." I waved over my shoulder and headed for the front door. It's not hard to say a word, but it seemed like Kade had just forgotten how to speak altogether. Great that he discovered this after I spilled my every secret to him.

***

He wasn't someone important, and why Adam wanted me to flirt with him, I didn't know. But I did it, and I guess I did a good job because after I was done, I got a message saying, 'great work speak soon, Adam.'

I closed the front door softly and pulled my heels off one at a time.

"Starting to think you weren't coming back."

I froze in the foyer, holding my heels, and slowly turned to look through the opening to the lounge. Of course he wouldn't be in bed like a normal person.

"Well, I am." I gave Kade a dry look "Surprised to see you are still up."

"Really?" He walked towards me, "Because I thought it was obvious that our conversation wasn't over."

"You mean the conversation the other night that ended when I walked out of the room."

I wouldn't let him think he had the upper hand. I hadn't been like a little girl, hanging on his every word, waiting for him to continue.

"You can't just dump that on a man and expect him to have an answer, Abby." The fact he was now standing in front of me made it a lot harder for me to think straight.

"Well, next time I will put it on Post-It notes for you." I looked him sharply in the face. "Now if you don't mind, I want to go to bed."

Want to know what the problem is having an argument with a hotheaded biker? They decide when the conversation ends, so I wasn't even the slightest bit surprised when he gripped my wrist, turning me back to face him.

"Reel in the bitch, would you, Abby?" he fumed down at me.

"How about you just fuck off?" I spat up at him, with so much rage across my face. I expected him to fight back, to say something that would make me hate him that bit more; instead, he laughed.

His stomach shook with laughter, "Now that right there is why I can't get you out of my head." His laughter slowly dried up and he let out a low sigh. "Abby, you want the truth?"

Did I want it? I was still shocked by his laughter, not to mention the words that followed. I slowly nodded.

What was he going to tell me? I braced myself, and his fingers traced the side of my face as he looked at me like I was something special. Don't fall for it, Abby.

"You and I just can't work." His mouth spoke in my ear, "And that is the truth."

Heartbreaking? No. Heart-shattering? Yes.

He went to pull away, and I gripped his neck with force. I pulled his head back at me, staring into his eyes. "Don't lie to me. The truth is you are as hung up on me as I am on you." My eyes flickered to those lips of his. "You can say what you want, but I know the truth."

"You don't know anything."

I smiled, "Maybe you're right." I rose to my toes and whispered in his ear, "Or maybe you just can't get me out of your head."

I don't know what I expected, but I sure as hell didn't expect what happened next.

Chapter 21

Reaper

12 Hours Earlier

Pinning her against the wall, I could nearly feel her panic. My eyes flickered down to her lips, which always seemed to draw my attention.

She wasn't a young girl anymore. She had grown up to a sex-teasing, heel-wearing woman that caused every blood vessel in my body to boil with jealousy.

I moved my lips to her ear; her head tilted just slightly. "You and I just can't work." It was the utter truth, and whether she wanted to hear it or not, I didn't care anymore. "And that is the truth."

She had to see it and then maybe once she did, I could stop being so bloody addicted to her.

I went to pull away, and she gripped my neck, forcing me to stare into her eyes. "Don't lie to me. The truth is you are as hung up on me as I am on you." Her eyes raged with passion. "You can say what you want, but I know the truth."

"You don't know anything," I said.

Her lips twisted into a seductive smirk, "Maybe you're right." She rose to her toes, and whispered in my ear, "Or maybe *you just can't get me out of your head.*"

Then she tipped me over the edge, and shit got heated quickly. It took me a flat two seconds to have her legs wrapped around my waist and carry her back in the direction of my room.

12 Hours Later

My door swung open, and the sound of it rebounding off the wall made me sit up straight.

"Fuck, Drake, heard of knocking?" I snarled while my heart pounded at an incredible rate.

Drake scanned my room "Have you seen Abby?"

It was the mention of the she-devil's name that caused my body to stiffen. "Nope."

"Her car is in the driveway, her bag is downstairs, and her phone is on the couch. So it makes me think she must be in the house, but I can't find her." His words had a judgmental tone to them, but it was his eyes that were really judging me.

"So you kicked my door in just to see if I had her?"

"No, I kicked your door in because she is missing."

"Maybe she's just passed out in the backyard."

"Grow up, Kade." Drake growled, "So you haven't seen her?"

"No, I haven't." I didn't like lying to my brother, but it wasn't like I had a bloody choice. "Now piss off, would ya? I don't like early mornings."

Drake didn't back down easy so he stood there a bit longer, staring me down. Wasn't until he finally decided that I didn't know shit that he walked out, closing the door behind him.

Throwing the blankets back, I scanned the bedroom floor, and when shit didn't make sense, I found myself frowning.

My en-suite door swung open, and Abby's wide eyes locked with mine. I didn't know what she was thinking, but my eyes drifted down to her bare legs, and the sight of her half-naked just didn't help my brain to function.

"Drake's looking for you." I strung a sentence together and ripped my eyes away from her. Just don't look at her, then maybe I wouldn't say something stupid.

I heard her scoff and couldn't help but look back in her direction. She tore my top off and threw it at me. In a flash, before I could see anything, she pulled her dress down over her head.

I didn't know what I wanted her to say and it wasn't until she walked out, quietly closing the door behind her, that I realized I wanted her to say something.

Chapter 22

Reaper

Abby was avoiding me. She couldn't make it more obvious if she tried. When I walked into a room, she would walk out. She blocked every call and made sure that I never had an opportunity to speak to her.

I knew why she was doing it. She didn't want to talk about what *nearly happened.* Maybe she was embarrassed, or maybe she just couldn't face me.

I had taken her up to my room, to do what I had wanted to do ever since I laid eyes on her. If it were up to me, the night would have gone very differently.

Instead, she bailed—literally. She freaked out and ran into my bathroom. I don't know how many hours I wasted speaking to that bloody bathroom door, but she wouldn't come out. Not once.

Not until my brother made an appearance.

Was she ashamed? Did she hate me that much?

"Where are you going?" Drake blocked me at the bottom of the staircase.

"Nowhere."

"Bullshit."

"Move, Drake."

"Should I be concerned?" He gave a pointed look at my gun holster. "Not like you to head out with weapons."

"Not any of your business, little brother." I pushed past him. I needed to throw my energy into something else instead of wasting it on a pathetic little sex tease.

I could feel Drake's eyes on me as I walked out the front door. I wasn't in the mood for conversation. I was in the mood for fucking some shit up, but it seemed like my getaway wasn't going to be as smooth as I'd hoped. I didn't like awkward situations and usually avoided them at all costs. But seeing Abby's car pull up behind my bike, I knew I couldn't avoid this one.

Abby slowly got out of her car. I tried to ignore her and headed for my bike.

"Going out?"

I turned my head to look back at her. "Yep."

Closing her car door, she leaned against it. "Kade, we need to talk."

"Got nothing to say." It was the truth now. I had shit to say to her and had been trying to tell her for the past week. Now she was ready to talk, so we should? Fuck that.

"I'm sorry for freaking out."

She continued the conversation, even though I didn't want any part of it.

"Doesn't matter."

She wanted to twist me around, and I sure as fuck wasn't interested in that anymore. I wanted nothing to do with the shitstorm she was creating.

"Abby, from now on, shit between you and me is simple. Got it?" I straddled my bike.

"I guess you're glad I freaked out then." A hint of disappointment lingered in her voice.

I cocked my head to look at her. She was standing on the footpath beside me now, looking unsure of herself. Her hair blew across her face, and if you didn't know it, you would think she was innocent. "You didn't do something you would regret; you should be happy with that." I kicked the bike to life. "Drake's inside."

"Where are you going?" she yelled over the roar of my engine.

I could tell her, but she didn't really want to know the answer. Hell, she wouldn't like it. "Be best if you don't know."

Her hand covered mine, which was wrapped around the handle.

"So are we just going to pretend that everything I said the other night didn't happen?"

"Thought that was what you wanted?"

"I've had a hard week. I'm sorry that I pushed you away." Honesty coated each of her words. "Look, Kade, if you want to just leave us as friends, I'm ok with that, but I need to know because I can't keep going on like this."

We were never friends to begin with. I just wanted to fuck her, and that was what started the sick, twisted relationship that had trailed over many years. How did I put that into words? But if she meant that little to me, why the fuck was I thinking about her and overthinking things she said?

"I need to go," I grunted.

"Just give me an answer."

"Answer to what, Abby?"

"Are we... are we going to keep this..." She frowned. "Whatever this is, going?"

"No."

Her face became devoid of expression. "But I thought you liked me."

"I do, and that is why I don't want this to keep going. I can't promise ya I won't hurt ya, and so far Abby, that is all I've done." I was no knight or gentleman, and the sooner she moved on from me, the better. "Got to call this for what it is. It's fucked up, and I'm not ok with it."

I didn't just like her, I was obsessed with her. The attraction and feelings I had for her were sure as fuck not healthy.

"Then I guess you're right; you should go."

She took one step away from the bike and once she was out of the way, I revved the engine and rode off. I left her standing on the sidewalk. I knew what I said wasn't what she wanted to hear, but she didn't know that I was far from good for her. She needed closure. She needed to move on. While a small part of me was happy to admit that she and I were over, a larger part was twisting and spewing that I had been the one to end it.

Abby

I had royally screwed up any chance of Kade and me, all because I got a classic case of nerves. Why did I have to pick that moment in my life to go all girly and scared?

Kade didn't want a relationship. To be honest, I wasn't sure if I wanted a relationship. All I knew for sure was I didn't want to be *'that girl.'* The one that hovers around blokes who aren't interested.

Kade had every right to call it. Now I wished I hadn't shared my inner thoughts with him. I think when it comes to Kade, I regret everything.

I slumped down on the lounge, hanging my legs over the end. Maybe I should just try and be Kade's friend. I'd rather be that than nothing at all. Maybe that is all we were meant to be.

"Abby, you home?" Drake called out.

"Yeah, in the lounge."

Drake's footsteps got louder as he approached. "How is your sister?"

A groan escaped my lips as I recalled why I hated this week so much. Kim had broken up with her boyfriend. I didn't really see it as a big deal. However, the same couldn't be said for my sister, who had gone all emo on Aunty Amanda.

For Aunty Amanda to call and say that Kim needed me, I knew things were getting desperate.

"Fine, just getting fatter by the moment. I swear the girl has eaten her own weight in chocolate ice cream." I answered.

"Why did they break up?"

"No idea." I shrugged my shoulders. "Could barely understand one word she said. She wouldn't stop crying, or stuffing chocolate in her mouth."

"Poor girl."

I raised my eyebrows at him, "It's Kim we are talking about."

"Still," Drake shrugged his shoulders. "She seemed really hung up on the kid."

"I'm sure she can do better than Four Eyes."

"Can you really do better than a doctor?"

"He's studying medicine," I corrected him. "He is still a pizza boy at the moment."

Drake shook his head and gave me a dry expression. "Can't give the kid a break, can you?"

"Doesn't matter anymore. He is one of the many now." I didn't know why Drake was suddenly all Team Trent. "Where was Kade off to?" I asked, bringing up a conversation that I really did want to have.

"It's Kade now, is it?" Drake's lips twisted with amusement.

"Fine. Where was Reaper going?" I reworded my question, seeing as Drake was reading too much into it.

He crossed his arms. "Don't know."

"Fine, don't tell me."

"No, I really don't know. He was secretive." Drake's expression hardened. "He's bored, and when bored, he goes looking for trouble."

"Well, I can't blame him. This town is about as thrilling as middle school." I grunted, pulling myself up to sit properly. "Maybe he has finally seen reason and will head back to his biker friends."

"Or go join another."

Disgust rolled across my face. "As if. Reaper might be many things, but a traitor isn't one of them."

"You're very opinionated, aren't you?"

"I might not be part of them anymore, but that doesn't mean I don't believe in what they stand for and when it comes to Satan's

Sons, you either stand with them or against them."

"Thought you had nothing to do with the club."

"Like I said, you either stand with them or against them. Just because I left doesn't mean I stand against them." My heart would always lie within that club. "Just because you leave doesn't mean you stop being a part of the club. To be honest, I'm surprised Reaper hasn't been called back by now."

"He left for good reasons."

I gave him a challenging look. "Reasons that you created."

"Blood is blood. Reaper knows that."

"Yes, but you made him choose between the two. So if anyone is to blame, you are." I stood up. "Drake, admit it, you caused him to leave, and if I were you, I would be feeling really guilty about that."

Drake and I weren't arguing. It was more like a passionate conversation, one that was centered on Reaper. It was odd because I thought I would want to throw darts at a picture of him considering the dish of rejection he gave me earlier.

"Then you must feel real guilty for taking him away from his patch?"

I rose and slowly turned around to face him. "What did you say?"

Drake's face was awash with confidence. "I said you must feel real guilty for making him turn in his President patch."

For once, Drake was actually talking about something that I knew nothing about. "You're fucking with me, aren't you?" No way would Reaper hand that over. I had thought he lost it because of something he had done. Like he had been replaced or something.

"You see Abby, my brother doesn't hold his tongue after he has had too many," Drake explained. "So I may have used this to my advantage to get my answers."

"So you got him drunk."

"Yep."

"And he told you what?"

"All about your little hotel fling, and how he was so hung up on you that he left to sort shit with the clubs. Apparently, from what I could understand, he left you in the motel room while he went to get you breakfast. Came back and you were gone. Didn't think much of it. Handed his patch over a few days later, and then took over as your dad's Vice President. Then shit got real messy between the two of you." He frowned, "I think he said something about you turning into a bitch and locking him out of your life or something."

I knew Drake was giving me very little detail, but the detail I was getting was enough to send a flood of guilt through me. "So it was my fault he ended up leaving the club."

"No, I think that was all me. You just cost him his President patch."

"You don't get it. If Kade was still President, he wouldn't have had to answer to anyone. He wouldn't have had my father making him pick between you and the club." Realization hit me harder by the moment. This was all my fault. No wonder he wanted nothing to do with me.

I was the walking reminder of what happened. And he's forced to live with the person who ruined his life. I felt terrible, and the guilt mixed with anger swirled within my stomach.

"I have to find him." I turned sharply, picking my handbag up on the way.

"Abby, wait!" Drake called out to me, and when I didn't stop to listen, he followed. "Come on, you don't even know where he is."

"I'll call him."

"He won't answer."

"Well, I don't care." I pulled the door open and turned to look at Drake. "It is my fault your brother is all depressed and gloomy, and I'm going to fix it."

"I didn't say he was depressed or gloomy." Drake pointed out.

142

"Come on, he will be home tomorrow, tell him then."

"No, I need to tell him now."

"Tell him what? That you are sorry? What will it matter now? Really, Abby?" Drake was trying to reason with me. "Just talk to him in the morning. I doubt he wants to be tracked down by you tonight. Fuck, he didn't even want me knowing where he was going."

My body slumped and I exhaled slowly. "I just feel real bad about it."

"And you can tell him that," Drake grabbed my hand and pulled me back inside, closing the front door, "tomorrow, when he is back."

"You don't think he is going to do anything stupid, do you?"

To my surprise, a grin spread across his face. "It's Kade; all he does is make one stupid mistake after another."

My expression faltered. "Thanks for reassuring me."

Drake laughed. "Don't know why you care anyway. I thought you hated him."

Little did Drake know. I didn't hate Kade at all. I suppose that was the problem to begin with.

***

He didn't come home that night or the next. In fact, three days had passed and he had still yet to show his face. Drake was acting calm and okay about it, but I had caught him calling Kade a few times, but Kade didn't answer.

I hoped he hadn't gotten himself into trouble. I prayed he was still breathing, but all I wanted to know was that he was ok. I didn't even care if he was having a full-on sex marathon with a group of whores. All I cared about was that he was ok.

Therefore, when I noticed Drake calling him again, I hoped

there would be an answer.

Disappointment flooded through me when I heard Drake leave another voice message.

My eyes shot back to the laptop in front of me when Drake walked into the kitchen. "How is the hunt going?"

I pretended like I hadn't been listening to him for the past ten minutes. "Um yeah, nothing yet."

"I'm sure you will find something." He shot me a reassuring smile.

I started to scroll through the course list again. I tried to find something that I wanted to study. Heading back to university seemed to fit with my new plan of getting myself a life. After all, it wasn't like I could really earn good money without qualifications, and I didn't see my career as 'bait' lasting long.

"I've got a job going at the club if you are interested," Drake asked. "Cash in hand. It's just bar work, nothing flashy."

I suppressed a grin because I knew how much he didn't want me to work in his clubs. The mere mention of me dancing in little clothing always caused an argument.

"I've sort of got something going on the side."

He dragged the chair out next to me. "Really?" He had a disbelieving look on his face. "Since when?"

"It's not anything flashy." I threw his words back at him. "And also it isn't any of your business."

"Ouch." He faked a hurt expression. "You're not spreading your legs for a living, are you?"

I whacked his arm. "Don't be disgusting."

"Just checking."

"You're a jerk."

The sound of the front door opening caused us both to go silent. Was it... could it...

"You home, brother?" Drake yelled out while looking at me.

"Who else would it be?" His gruff, hard voice filled the kitchen as soon as he entered.

I had been living with this stomach full of guilt for days now, so I was quick to get up. "Kade, I need to talk to you."

"Abby, at least let the man get a beer," Drake said, amused.

"No, Kade, I'm serious. I have to..." My words dried up, and my mouth slowly fell open as I looked at him for the first time.

It had been three days. Three days!

Kade's eyes widened. "About?" He prompted me to continue, but I couldn't.

It was not the fact that he had shaved his head and got rid of that six o'clock shadow on his face. No, it wasn't his appearance. It was the colors, or more importantly, the leather club vest he was wearing.

"You joined the Vikings?" Bitterness wrapped across my face. "YOU JOINED THE VIKINGS!?"

"Wow. Abby." Drake got up quick to block me. "Calm down."

"Calm down?" I shouted in Drake's face. "He's a traitor!" I pointed an arm at Reaper. "How could you?"

Reaper didn't even seem fussed by my reaction. He just strode past us, heading for the fridge.

"I thought you had something you needed to tell me?" Reaper grasped a beer.

Right now the last thing I felt was sorry for him. The guilt I had quickly boiled into disgust then exploded into raw anger. "You're scum, you know that?"

A smug smirk spread across his stupid face. "No need to talk dirty to me, babe."

"I hate you."

"Don't really give a fuck." He cracked the can open. "Go on, storm off now, Abby." He gestured for me to piss off.

"I don't think so." I crossed my arms, standing my ground. "I hope they burn your tattoos off" I spat in his direction.

Everyone knew when you joined a new club, you got rid of your old club's tattoos. Normally they are blacked out, but in Reaper's case, I hope they burned them off.

"Didn't have any to be burnt." He seemed smug about that. "Now leave, Abby. I need to talk to my brother."

"His name is Drake!" I spat out, sick of the 'brother' references. "And he doesn't want to talk to you."

I didn't normally speak for Drake, but in this case, he had better keep his mouth shut.

"Fuck off, Abby. Now." Reaper's voice hardened.

How could I have ever loved him? EVER! How did I ever have a single ounce of love towards him?

Drake placed his hand on my shoulder. "Go on, Abby. We'll talk later."

"No." I shook my head. I couldn't rip my glare off Reaper. "You're right I wanted to tell you something. I wanted to tell you I'm sorry. I am so sorry for leaving that hotel and ruining your life. I'm sorry you gave up your patch for me. I'm really sorry that you ended up at my father's club." Small tears of anger and perhaps raw guilt slid down my cheeks. "I'm sorry you had to leave the club that you loved because of my father. But most of all, Reaper, I'm sorry that I ever got mixed up in your life because clearly all I have done is fuck it up."

Never in my life had I had so much to say, but now it seemed like I just couldn't stop. Reaper's face was still calm, blank of expression, not giving anything away.

"So there it is." I wiped the tears away, "I'm sorry." I turned sharply, pushing past Drake and moving as fast as I could. I scooped up my car keys off the counter and handbag off the hook. I had to get out of there. I had to get away from all of this.

***

The attraction I had towards Reaper never made sense. Why had

146

I been pulled to a man that was guaranteed to hurt me or worse, one who could kill me? In a way, Reaper *had* killed me; he had killed my innocence.

"Abby?"

My head snapped up, Kim's voice pulling me back to the present. "Sorry Kim, what were you saying?"

Her expression dried with little amusement. "Again? Seriously, Abby, why did you even bother coming around here if you aren't going to listen?" She huffed at the end, crossing her arms.

I was beginning to ask myself that same question. Why had I come here to talk to Kim? It wasn't like we got on. But then I guess desperate times called for desperate measures.

"So Trent hasn't called then?" I chose to change the subject. "Why don't you just bite the bullet and call him?"

"The dumpee doesn't call the dumper." Kim rolled her eyes, clearly not impressed with my lack of knowledge when it comes to break ups.

"But you miss him."

"Doesn't mean I'm going to crawl back to him and beg him to change his mind." She started pulling the kitchen cupboards open at random, looking for god knows what.

"Why did you break up?" All I knew for sure was he was the one to end it, but that didn't really make sense to me because Trent seemed pretty into her. Hell, they rarely were apart.

"I told you." She swung around with a bottle of vodka; that explained the searching. "He called me trash."

I arched my eyebrows, not believing her. "Don't lie, Kim."

She threw me an annoyed look before popping the cap of the bottle off. "I may have run into someone from the past."

"And?"

"And it didn't end well," she snapped before taking a healthy drink from the bottle.

I put my hand out for the bottle, and she handed it to me when she was finished. "Don't we have cups?"

"It's Aunty Amanda's place, Abby, of course she has cups," she scoffed at me. "But the bottle seems more…" She frowned.

"Normal?" I smirked at her with an understanding of what she meant. "So come on, tell me the real reason Trent called it quits."

She sank down into a chair across from me and leaned her elbows on the table. "Ever wished you could take back something you had done?"

God, did I know that feeling. I nodded my head, "Yep."

"You know how Dad came down and shit went down with Reaper?" She started to open up.

Though I wasn't expecting this conversation to go in the direction of Reaper or Dad, again I nodded my head. "Yep. Reaper threw his patch in or something."

"Yeah, well. When news got out about Dad not having a vice anymore, an unexpected visitor showed up at my front door."

"Who?" A frown appeared on my face as I thought hard of who would appear or have the guts to show up here while Dad was on holiday.

Surely they would wait until he got back to the club before trying to get the vice patch.

"Trigger." Kim's eyes flashed with disgust. "After all these years, he just appeared!"

"On your doorstep," I muttered. I knew that feeling; I had felt that feeling.

"Yeah." Acid lingered in her tone and she reached for the bottle. "No hello. Or how are you doing? Or how's the kid? No, just is your old man here?" She was quick to take a mouthful of vodka. "He didn't even say hi."

I opened my mouth to say something but not knowing what to say, I just closed it again.

"The most twisted part of it was that Dad welcomed him with open arms." Kim shook her head with a hurt expression. "Just like

148

that, everything was forgotten."

"So Dad took him back?" I couldn't believe that Dad would do it, especially considering I thought Trigger had been killed. I thought Dad was sure to have killed him by now.

"Did more than that." With bitterness in her voice, she added, "Even invited him to stay here for the rest of Dad's trip."

"He moved in here?" My mouth hung open. "You're kidding."

She shook her head, "Nope. He stayed in your old room. Dad managed to round up a bed for him."

Suddenly I had one more reason not to want to move back into that room. "How long did he stay here for?"

"A week, but it was long enough to do damage."

My mind started to click over the facts and the more I put together, the more I understood Kim and Trent's break up.

"Please tell me you didn't sleep with him?"

Her lips turned into a sad smile. "I nearly did. I still can't explain why I even thought about it. It was as if he pulled me back, you know? Like everything that had happened, hadn't. I can't explain it." She dropped her head into her hands and sighed. "It's like when I'm around him, I lose all sense of control, all sense of thinking. All this time I thought I had grown up, but just a few hours with that man and I'm back to making the same mistakes."

The similarities between her relationship with Trigger and mine with Reaper's wasn't lost on me. I guess it is true what they say about twins; we are similar. Even when it comes to our men, we both seem to fall for the wrong type of guy.

"So Trent dumped you after you told him the truth?" I asked, and her head snapped up.

"No. Trent dumped me when he caught me kissing the stupid prick." Rage filled her eyes. "It was a split-second mistake, and of course Trent walked in at the right time to witness it."

"Well, that explains the trash comment."

She sighed and nodded her head. "He said a few other good

ones, too."

"So what happened with Trigger?"

"I told him to leave." A mournful tone spread into her words. "So he did. He told me he was sorry for screwing up my fresh chance." Tears began to fill her eyes. "And now look at me. I'm failing university. My friends, who all sided with Trent, won't have anything to do with me, and now I'm crying over a man that couldn't care less about me."

I reached out, placing my hand over hers. "Don't be so hard on yourself. Trigger has always cared about you. He wouldn't have come here if he hadn't." Was I stupid to encourage their relationship? I really didn't know. All I knew was I didn't like seeing the pain of a broken heart in Kim's eyes.

"He hasn't even called me." She wiped her tears away. "Not once."

"I'm sure Dad is keeping him busy."

"I'm sure the club whores are keeping him busy."

I bit my lip, knowing that it could be a possibility. Trigger loved his women, though Kim always seemed like his favorite.

"So what do you want to do?" I gave in. "Do you want to go back home?"

Her face was void of expression, giving me no insight into what she was thinking. Finally, she said, "I just want to get drunk, and then tomorrow I want to start a life without him in it."

All this time she had been living a life without him, but it still felt to her that he was there. I wanted to slap myself for doing the same bloody thing.

I had always thought in the back of my head that Reaper and I would end up together. That I would be able to trust him again, and he would get over his pride and want me as his.

"Sounds like a good idea," I agreed. She had to get over Trigger, and I had to get over Reaper.

I couldn't keep letting myself be dragged back to him. All it took was one look at him, and I was his to do with whatever he wanted.

It was time I stopped being so self-destructive.

Kim reached behind her and picked up another bottle of vodka. Handing it to me, she said, "Well then sis, let's drown our sorrows."

***

"This shouldn't be how it is, ya know!" Kim pointed her empty bottle at me "We are the Harrison sisters. Men should be falling down in front of us."

I laughed at her while shaking my head at her ridiculous claim. The alcohol had loosened my lips, which meant I had spilled everything about Reaper, right down to what happened earlier.

"You know what we should do." Kim jumped off the table, which she had been parading on. "We should get them back."

My laughter dried up immediately. "You're kidding, right? What happened to let's better ourselves and move on from them?"

"Screw that." Kim shook her head, "Trigger is the best lay I've ever had."

"Way too much information." I scrunched my nose up, shaking my head.

"So you don't want Reaper back?" she challenged me.

"He isn't good for me." Even with a blurry mind caused by alcohol, I knew that. "And he doesn't want me. He joined the Vikings, remember?"

"Please, once you have him wrapped around your finger, he'll ditch them."

"I don't think it is as easy as that."

"Well, he left Dad's club, didn't he?"

"Because of me."

"Because of Drake." She was quick to correct me. "I think it is time we started doing what we do best."

"What you do best. I was never into skank."

"But you seem to have been doing it so well." She smirked at me, crossing her arms. "So what do you say? At the very least, we have to show them what they are missing."

"You sure you don't want Trent back?"

She stopped pacing the room and looked to be really thinking on the subject. Trent was good for her; I see that now. "He doesn't get my heart pumping." She finally looked up and met my eyes. "I want a man that challenges me and gets my heart racing with just a touch."

"So no more university?" Here I was thinking I was going to head back.

"Nope," A grin spread across her lips. "I have a much better idea for our future."

"What, flirting our way to the top?" I scoffed.

She shrugged her shoulders. "I was thinking more along the lines of joining the family business."

"You're joking."

"We're good at stealing, lying, and making money. Time to face the facts; we are cut from the same cloth as our dad. So it's about time we stop trying to go straight and start embracing our inner offender."

"I'm not liking where this is going." I really didn't like where this was heading.

"Come on, get up. We've got shit to do."

"It's nearly two in the morning!" I pointed out to her as she pulled me up off my chair. "And where the hell are we going?"

"Getting you out of working with Jenkins." She swiped the car keys from the hook, which I then took off her.

"You aren't driving."

"Such a downer."

"One of us has to have some sense."

"Can't we do this in the morning?"

152

"It is morning."

I groaned, stepping out into the cold night air. "This is one stupid idea."

"Well, you're the one who did the stupid thing and started working for the scum."

"I don't see why this can't wait until I've slept off this…" I lost my words trying to recall what I was thinking. "You know what I mean." I clicked my fingers at her.

She shook her head at me but kept walking, which told me there was no way I was getting out of this.

Chapter 23

Abby

Parts of the night were a blur, but some memories were crystal clear. Kim's plan of getting me out of work with Jenkins involved screaming up and down his street and banging on random doors.

Which led to us being chased by a grumpy old man with a baseball bat, and it ended with Kim and me hiding in a rose bush.

There were a few things that I had never experienced and some I had neither intended nor wanted. Passing out with rose thorns stuck to my legs because my drunk sister thought it was a great idea to hide in a bush of roses was one of them.

I cringed, pulling out the last thorn.

The morning really wasn't getting any better.

"Where am I?" Kim groaned while holding her head.

"My place."

"What, you live here?" She eyed the plain room with disgust. "Gee Abby, talk about keeping it to a minimum."

"It's my room." So what if I didn't feel a need to fill it with junk?

I watched as Kim's eyes widened. "So Drake and Reaper live here too, yeah?"

Why did I suddenly get a bad feeling? "Yes."

Her lips twitched with mischief. "I have an idea."

"An idea I'm sure I am not going to like." I didn't even need to hear it before determining that. By the glint in her eyes, I knew I wasn't going to get out of it.

Kim

I heard them in the kitchen. Glancing up at Abby, I gave her a thumb's up. Her doubtful eyes looked back down at me. She didn't think this was going to work. She really could be negative.

Pulling back my shoulders, I strode into the kitchen with attitude and if there was one thing my twin sister had, a lot of it was the attitude. Reaper leaned against the fridge, beer in hand already. Did it even occur to him to hold out until midday? Drake sat at the table eating breakfast.

"Can you move?" I looked up at Reaper with a challenging look on my face.

He swallowed. "Your hair is different."

"So?"

"So why?" Drake's eyes flashed with interest.

"Blondes have more fun. Don't really see the big deal," I snapped at both of them. "Now move, would you?"

God, they are like Abby's guard dogs. How did she put up with the two of them snapping at her heels all the time?

Reaper sidestepped out of the way, giving me access to the fridge. He was still as ignorant as I remembered. God, Abby and I knew how to pick them.

I popped the lid off the fresh bottle of orange juice. It was time to have some fun. I just needed one of them to bite again. Running my hand through my hair, I flicked it to the side.

"Blonde again? Thought you were trying to harden your image." Reaper picked up the bait, and the emotions flashing across his eyes told me that the blonde hair was really bugging him.

"Can you keep a secret, Viking?"

"That's a new one," Drake muttered.

Reaper and I both ignored him.

"You know I can, otherwise we would both have died young," Reaper hit back.

I took a step closer to him, meeting his harsh eyes. "I have this, um friend, and he, well, he has a thing for blondes."

He swallowed sharply. "Who might that be?"

"Oh fuck me, you two are flirting again," Drake groaned from the table.

Time to kick in the acting skills. I flashed a confused look and turned to look at Drake. "Us flirting? Are you joking? I'm simply telling the Viking that I'm heading home this weekend and meeting up with an old friend."

"You're going home!" Drake rose instantly, outraged. "What the fuck for?"

"Trigger is back."

Out of the corner of my eye, I watched Reaper crumple the can in his hand. "That scumbag is back?"

I nodded my head, turning back to look at him. "Yep. He's Dad's new VP."

"You're fucking with me?" He didn't believe me.

"Nope."

"Thought you hated the scumbag?"

"I do." Or at least I was sure Abby hated him. I only wished I hated him.

"So why go blonde for him?"

"I didn't. I'm going blonde for Brad. You might remember him as Gitz." I flashed a bright fake grin. Now I was sure my sister was going red with rage on that staircase listening to this. "Gitz and I sort of have history, and he just broke up with that chick from the valley. So yeah."

"First time I'm hearing about this history." Reaper glared at me. His eyes were on fire, it could and would scorch the devil.

"Dad's throwing that annual club meet. Heaps of people are heading in." I eyed his patch before looking him in the eye. "Even Vikings have a habit of turning up."

If Reaper cared for Abby—really cared—he would be panicking. If he thought for one second that another biker was going to take what he thought was his, I'm sure he would do anything to stop it from happening.

"Anyway. I've got to head out. Picking Kim up, and we're picking up supplies before we leave tomorrow." I waved over my shoulder, feeling satisfied with the destruction I was leaving.

Abby wanted Reaper, and by his reaction, he wanted her, too. If only I were so confident about what Trigger wanted.

Chapter 24

Kim

Abby sucker-punched my arm. "BRAD! Are you crazy!" Her face was red with rage. "I knew I would regret agreeing to your stupid plan."

"Would you shut up before someone hears you?" I smiled evilly at her. "Reaper has a thing for blondes."

"Pity I've still got black hair," she snapped back, stuffing her clothes into a gym bag. "I never agreed to go back home."

"Oh come on, you and I both know you miss it." I let out a long sigh and lay back on her bed. "You know he is going to turn up, don't you?" I dropped my head to the side to see my angry sister.

She muttered something under her breath. I thought her enraged expression was amusing, but the look of terror that captured her face when someone knocked on the bedroom door was even better.

"Coming." I dragged myself up off the bed.

Abby shook her head and mouthed "no" at me.

"Hide in the wardrobe." I hissed at her.

She gave me a deadpan look. "Don't fucking think so."

"You don't have blonde hair, remember?"

"Well fuck it, we can come clean."

"Abby, open up." Reaper's impatient voice roared on the other side of the door.

I arched an eyebrow at her, "You really want to face that?"

A smirk spread across my face as I watched her close the wardrobe door. She was sure to kill me after this.

"Fine, come in, Reaper." This was sure to be interesting. However, it was obviously not going to be pleasurable because

158

Abby would rather hide in a closet than face him.

Reaper's sharp eyes sliced across the room, focusing on Abby's packed bag for a moment before he looked at me. "So you're really going then?"

"Just for the long weekend."

A tormented expression captured his face. "What the fuck for, Abby?"

"Kim wanted me to." That was the truth. I did want to go home to see Trigger. Convincing Abby to go just made sense. I didn't want to face him alone, plus it would do her some good to get out of this shithole.

"So you're really going?"

"No, Reaper, I'm just saying I'm going." I rolled my eyes. God, he was frustrating; no wonder Abby wanted to hide in the wardrobe. "Why do you care anyway? You and I both know you only joined the Vikings to hurt me."

I could see through all their crap, though I was sure Abby hadn't made the connection between the two yet.

"Fuck, you're self-centered."

"Perhaps." I took a step forward, holding eye contact with him. "So are you coming or not?"

"Why would I go back there?"

He wanted a reason, but I knew he already had one. "Because I'm going." My lips twisted into a smile.

It was easier to be Abby than to be myself. God, their relationship was so simple.

"You're cocky this morning." Reaper tilted his head to the side, his black orbs studying me with intensely. "You're not... your normal self."

"Since when did you know my normal self, Viking?" I snapped. The last thing I needed was him figuring it out and then going all biker scary on my arse. "Look, if you come this weekend, great. If you don't, fine." I huffed, and turned my back and started to zip up Abby's pack.

I froze when his hand fell on my shoulder. Oh god… oh god… He slowly turned me around.

"Do you want me to come?" His voice had no edge to it. The honesty behind his words made me lose my voice.

Did Abby want him to come? Oh fuck, why did I push this matter? "Um … well … I …" Why the fuck did he have to be looking at me like that?

His hand slowly traced down my bare shoulder, stopping just above my wrist. His head dipped lower, those eyes wiping away any common sense. "Abby, do you want me to come?"

This never happened to me. I swallowed sharply. "I wouldn't want… I mean I…" My answer was cut quickly when he spun me around, pinning my arm behind my back. "WHAT THE FUCK, REAPER!"

"Tell Abby when she comes back from wherever the fuck she is, Kim, that I want to speak to her, got it?" he hissed in my ear.

Perhaps he really had a thing for Abby to be able to tell the difference. With my free hand, I punched him in the leg, which caused him to let go of me.

"Tell her yourself, wanker." I stumbled backward, gripping the wardrobe door handle and forcing it open.

Abby was standing in the middle, arms crossed with a fierce glare on her face.

"And the bitch shows her face." Reaper's pissed-off glare flickered off me and onto her. Thank god for that.

"Kim, why don't you take our shit to the car. I'll be down in a minute." Abby didn't even take her eyes off him to look at me.

"And leave you with the crazy fucker?" I scoffed. Was she nuts?

"He won't hurt me." She sounded very confident about that.

"So you're actually fucking off back home then?" Reaper's voice dripped with disgust. "Next you'll be telling me the shit she was spinning about Brad was real."

"It was." Abby's voice didn't even flinch with hesitation. "Though I'm not keen on the idea of you coming."

"Liar," I muttered under my breath, and she whacked me with her right arm.

"Car, Kim. Now." She didn't leave room for argument. I didn't like being told what to do, but the intense eye contact between the two told me they had a heated conversation to share.

"Fine." I scooped up her bag and gave her a pointed look. "Make it quick, will ya? It's a long drive." I closed the door, and the pair didn't even wait until I reached the staircase before they started arguing.

I actually felt sorry for Reaper because he didn't have a hope in hell of winning against Abby, and he and I both knew that. The man was doomed from the beginning because well... he loved her.

Chapter 25

Abby

"So what did you and Reaper talk about?" Kim flashed me a small smile, sitting in the passenger seat. "Or should I say, what did you and Reaper yell about?"

"He just wasn't impressed with us lying to him." I kept the details to the minimum. He didn't believe I would leave; he didn't believe that I would head home.

To be fair to him, I didn't think I would go through with it either, but I was.

"Uh uh." She wasn't buying it, but she didn't press the conversation further. "So is he coming or not?"

I doubted he would. "He didn't say."

"I reckon he will show up." Kim had more faith in him than I. "No way he is going to let you spend a whole weekend with horny bikers."

"KIM!"

"What? It's true!"

"It doesn't matter anyway. This weekend is all about Trigger and you, remember?" It's time we got back to the real reason we were heading home.

I glanced at Kim, and that smirk on her face dropped. "Wonder if he'll even care."

"He'll care." If there was one thing I knew for sure, it was that he would definitely care that she showed up.

"Glad you seem to think so." She grumbled and turned her head to look out the side window. "You look better with blonde hair, too."

My eyes flashed up to the rearview mirror, glancing at my blonde hair. "It feels strange."

"You'll get used to it."

"Glad you seem to think so." I smiled, repeating her words back at her.

She shook her head. "Childish."

"Says the girl munching on tiny teddies."

I glanced up at the rearview mirror again, but this time my eyes froze for a minute. "Oh my god." My mouth dropped open.

"What?" Kim's interest spiked, and she turned in her seat to look around.

My eyes snapped back to the road. "It's him, isn't it?"

Kim turned back around with a mocking expression on her face. "I told you he would come."

"He's actually coming," I muttered aloud.

Reaper was behind us on his motorbike, riding alone. He was coming back. He was coming back wearing the enemy's colors. This weekend, though, it wouldn't matter so much.

"Told you. I told you." Kim gloated. "Looks like your weekend just got a hell of a lot more interesting."

"And here I was thinking I would be solely focused on paying you back for the stunt back home." I looked back at Reaper again. How long had he been following us?

"Oh look, a gas station." Kim pointed. "I need to use the toilet."

I looked at her, not impressed. "No, you don't. You just want me to pull over."

Her lips curled evilly. "Pull in, Abby."

"Not going to happen."

"Fine. I'll pee in your car."

I was outraged at the thought. "Like fuck you will." I switched the indicator on. Nerves flooded my body when I saw Reaper also turn off the highway, following us.

Kim clapped with enjoyment when she turned to see if he had. "Great. Now you two get to talk, or yell again." She smiled smugly.

"I knew you didn't need to go to the toilet."

"But I do need tiny teddies." She held up the empty packet.

I pulled the car to a stop at a service station. It was probably a good idea to top up while we were here. It would save us from stopping again.

"I'll take my time," she said over her shoulder before getting out, her eyes alive with amusement at my soon-to-be extremely awkward conversation.

Reaper pulled his bike to a stop behind me and when his engine cut out, I knew I couldn't prolong getting out of the car any longer.

I closed the car door and nodded my head at him. "Hey." I kept my sunglasses down, pretending to be cool, calm, and collected when really I was freaking the fuck out.

He climbed off the bike, pulling his helmet off, placing it on the handlebar. "Thought you left hours ago." He pushed his sunglasses up. "Or are you just a real slow driver?"

I unscrewed the gas cap. "Had to make a stop earlier." Had he not noticed the blonde hair?

He stood in front of me. His hand grasped mine, taking the pump off me. "Explains the hair."

"Thought it was time to go back to my roots." I took a step back while he filled the car for me.

Why did that simple act of kindness make my stomach flutter?

"So you're… um… coming then?" I scratched my arm, trying to make conversation with him.

He turned to look at me. "Yep."

Talk about him giving me nothing to build a conversation on. "Didn't think you would leave, you know, seeing how good you have it with the Vikings." God, it felt like acid to speak those words. "Good thing this is like a rainbow weekend, you shouldn't get a bullet in the head for being a traitor."

"Tell me what you really think, Abby." He grunted, his eyes

mocking me. "Don't hold back."

I crossed my arms. "What, come on, it's not like you aren't going to catch heat. You do realize they are going to give you shit." I felt like I had to remind him of the obvious.

Maybe I was trying to talk him out of it.

"For someone who doesn't miss shit, you sure as fuck are missing the obvious."

The gas pump perked back, and he pulled it out, hanging it back up. What the hell was he getting at?

"Hi, Reaper." Kim appeared beside the car, Tiny Teddies in hand of course. "Where's ya cut?"

I looked back at Reaper, my mouth falling open. Where the hell was his Vikings leather vest? "Have you like left them?" My words rushed out, barely making sense.

"You aren't the only one going back to their roots, Abby." He hung the pump up. "See ya back at home."

Home. He was going home. My eyes widened in size, grabbing his arm in a rushed decision. "You're joining them again, aren't you?"

His cold eyes glanced between my hand and back at me. "Called ya old man, we talked it through."

"But that means, after this weekend, you won't be coming back."

"Yeah, as of Monday, it will just be Drake and you."

That didn't sound pleasing. "Kind of gotten used to you being around."

The corner of his lip twitched, "Better get back on the road, Abby; it will be dark before we get there."

I wished he was in the car with me. God, I hated admitting that. Why did I have such a never-dying attraction towards him?

"Right," I nodded my head. I opened my door, ready to climb in. "Um, feel free to pass me. I can be a slow driver."

He straddled his bike. "Defeats the purpose of making sure you

165

get there safely, doesn't it?" He gave me a half smile.

Tilting my head to the side, "Thought you didn't expect me to be on the road?"

He gave me a wink and before I could question him further, Kim was yelling for me to hurry up. I gave him a wave and got in.

"So lover boy has been stalking us," Kim smirked across at me. "Told you he has a thing for you."

"Yeah, yeah." I turned the engine on. "Oh fuck!"

"What?"

I laughed at my own stupidity. "Nearly forgot to pay." I clicked the car off and searched for my wallet. Only Reaper could make me forget to pay for gas. That man really fucked my head up and admittedly, I loved it.

Chapter 26

Abby

Life is only as simple as you make it. I really had no one else to blame but myself for having such a screwed-up, complicated love life. I took comfort in knowing that I wasn't the only one. Kim had gone a nice shade of white as soon as we parked within the compound.

"You ready?" I asked her, placing a hand on the door.

She slowly nodded her head. "Sure. Let's get this over with."

She may fear seeing Trigger, but her fear was nothing compared to that which I currently had of seeing Dad. My mind wandered to our last conversation and just how rude I had been to him. I suppose the good thing about turning up now was that there were people everywhere. We rather blended into the background.

"Where's Reaper?" Kim walked around the car door to face me. "Thought he was meant to be keeping an eye on us."

"Don't know."

"Did he follow us in?"

I walked around a couple. "He overtook us before we got off the highway. Guess he got sick of my slow driving."

Kim's lips twitched into a smirk. "So you admit you are a slow driver."

I rolled my eyes. What was it with people picking on my driving skills? "Just because I like doing the speed limit, doesn't make me a bad driver."

"No, it just makes you a slow one." She laughed.

Reaper

"I heard you were coming back," Trigger handed me a cold beer. "I thought Roach was talking shit about it, though."

I unscrewed the top, "Thought it was time to come home."

"Rumor on the street said you joined another crew." Gitz shot me a look from behind the barbecue grill. "Heard you were in deep shit with your brother, too."

"Heard your missus married another man." My temper crept up. "Guess shit happens, right?" If they wanted to bring up the past, I could give them back just as much shit.

"Point taken, brother." He gave me a tight smile.

"You coming back to this charter or heading back east?" Trigger wiped his mouth with the back of his hand. "We could use another man at the table."

My head snapped in the direction of loud laughter. Immediately, my stomach swirled with jealousy mixed with pure rage.

Abby and Kim looked like every biker's wet dream. They could barely be told apart now, especially since Abby was not top heavy anymore. It didn't help that they both were wearing the same tight pair of black shorts. It seemed the two of them had decided it was a fantastic idea to wear the same thing; they were both wearing a tight Satan's Sons white tank top as well.

"Is that Abby and Kim?" Gitz stepped away from the barbecue. "Fucking oath it is." With a large grin, he made his way over to them.

"The meat's going to fucking burn!" Trigger roared after him.

I couldn't see Abby's eyes through her large, black-framed sunglasses, but I could tell she was looking my way. The fact that her eyes were hidden did make it harder to tell the difference between her and Kim, but the metal cross around her neck confirmed it was Abby I was staring at.

I dropped the empty bottle into the trash can and watched Gitz engulf Abby in a hug, pulling her off the ground.

"Why are they here?" Trigger's voice hardened. "Roach didn't mention it."

Trigger still had a hard-on for Kim, even after all this time. "Maybe that's the point."

"Surprise visit for the old man?" Trigger cocked me a look. "Like fuck."

Gitz was still busy flirting his arse off with them. "What other reason do they have for showing up?" I pulled a cigarette out. "Something playing on your mind, brother?"

"Nothing worth speaking of." He grumbled, not taking his eyes off them for a moment.

Nerves flooded my body as I watched Abby and Kim walk towards me with Gitz.

Abby scrunched her nose up, "Um, your sausages are on fire." She pointed behind us.

Fuck.

I took a step back while Gitz threw water on it. A strong stench soon filled the air.

"There goes lunch." Trigger glared at Gitz. "Told ya it would burn."

"No harm was done." Kim spoke up. "Kim likes black sausages."

Why was she talking about herself? Abby's arms were tightly crossed across her chest. Her head snapped in Kim's direction.

No. I was positive that… that was Abby. I had watched that arse walk away too many times to not know it was her.

"Is that right, Abby?" Abby spoke to her sister.

Kim pushed her sunglasses up. "Yep."

They were swapping again. Nothing pissed me off more than watching the two of them fuck with everyone's heads. Especially mine.

Abby pulled her sunglasses off and held them up. Her eyes locked with mine, and I was right; it was definitely Abby. "You boys been busy?" She looked between Trigger and me. "Or are you just hitting the bottle?"

"Just rode in." I kept my voice neutral. "You both here for the full weekend?"

Abby's eyes drifted across to Trigger's. "Depends on a few things."

I didn't like the way Trigger looked back at her, and I *really* didn't like the way his fists were clenched.

"Your old man know you two are back yet?" Trigger didn't harness his anger. "Or just planning on showing up, screwing the men, pissing off your old man, and leaving again?"

Kim laughed, "Oh calm down, Trigger. We only came to have some fun." Seemed as if she liked being her sister more than being herself.

"Let's go get a drink, Kim." Kim grabbed Abby's arm. "We're standing out… not having one."

I reached out and grabbed Abby's other arm. "I need a word first." My eyes flickered to Kim. "This will only take a minute."

"Seeing as you asked so nicely." Abby snaked her arm out of my grip. "I'll meet you at the bar."

Trigger glared holes in the back of our heads as I walked Abby across the lot. Once we were out of earshot and we turned the corner of the house, I was quick to get to the point.

"What the fuck was that?"

Her velvet eyes of seduction stared back at me, "Kim didn't want to speak to him."

"So all weekend you two are going to be playing fucking games?"

"No."

"Don't lie to me."

"I came here for her. Shit is complicated, but what I really don't get is why you care so much." Abby placed a hand on my chest.

Somehow, we had managed to get close. I hadn't even realized it.

"You're trying to get in with my dad again, so I'm guessing you are going to want to put as much distance between us as possible." She pushed me backward slightly. "Two days and that is it; then I'll be out of your way."

I didn't want her out of my way. She just didn't get it. It didn't matter where she was or how close she was; she would always be in my way.

"Trigger's got a temper. What if he snaps when you're pretending to be your fucking sister? You could get hurt, Abby, and I am not going to let that happen."

"I don't need a bodyguard, Reaper," she mocked, rolling her eyes. "You worry too much."

My eyes narrowed, "Clearly you don't worry enough."

"If I didn't know any better," her eyes flickered across my face, "I would think you were jealous."

My jaw tightened. "You're clearly just as stupid as you were when you were sixteen."

"Oh," she laughed bitterly, "you mean when I fell head over fucking heels for a no-good biker?"

"Head over heels?"

She shoved my shoulder. "Don't fucking pretend that you didn't know."

"Are we going to do this again?" Didn't we fight about this enough? I broke her heart. I know. The guilt I felt never went away, but it was nothing compared to the regret.

She shook her head. "No, we aren't because you see, Reaper, this weekend isn't about us. There is no us. I'll try my hardest to stay out of your way, and you stay the fuck out of mine, ok?"

Abby usually had a soft edge to her. But right then, the fire-filled woman standing in front of me had no soft edge. Abby's eyes were harsh, hard, and determined, and it turned me the fuck on. God, this was wrong.

"Fine. I'll stay out of your way." I side-stepped, freeing her path. "Fuck off, then."

Her lips formed a tight line. Her expression told me she had more to yell at me about. She loved fighting with me; she just didn't know it.

Finally, she let out a groan and pushed herself off the wall, shouldering me aside as she walked past. This weekend was meant to be about me regaining my brother's trust, but somehow I knew it was going to be all about her. Everything always turned out to be about her.

I turned, catching a glimpse of her blonde hair before she turned the corner.

The only way I was going to get out of this circle was by distracting myself. That meant I needed to get my hands dirty. I needed to get in deep with the club. It was the only way I wouldn't have a moment to think about the blonde ruining my life.

Chapter 27

Abby

I couldn't understand love. To be honest, it completely threw me. I guess that was fair considering my upbringing. The only version of love I had ever seen was Dad keeping the same club whore in his bed longer than a week.

I wished I could remember Mom and Dad together. Maybe then I could understand love better or at the very least know what it looks like.

My stomach clenched as I continued to watch Reaper and the female. Kim had offered twice to shoulder the bitch, but I told her I was taking the higher ground. I wasn't going to let Reaper and his brunette get the better of me. Even if he had his arm wrapped around her and kept giving her that smile that once used to knock the air from my lungs.

"Why a brunette?" I yelled in Kim's ear over the music.

Kim's eyes traveled back to the pair. "You really want to know?" she yelled back in my ear.

I nodded my head. If she had any insight, I wanted it.

"To piss you off." She smiled broadly. "Clearly."

Well, if his mission was to piss me off, he was definitely doing a good job of it. My stomach was so twisted up it wouldn't even hold my liquor.

"Have you seen Dad yet?"

Kim shook her head, "Nope. I still can't believe he isn't around. Is Dad bailing on his own charter party? Typical." Her eyes wandered around the party while she took a long sip of her beer.

"I'm going to take a walk." I sighed. My eyes drifted over to Reaper again. I really needed to put some distance between us.

"I'll join you."

"Nah, don't be silly. Stay, keep an eye on your man." I wasn't stupid. I saw the way she kept looking in Trigger's direction.

"Righteo then, don't be too long."

I gave her a quick nod and began to weave through the crowd. Being back here was harder than I expected. Not because of Reaper, but because it felt like I was home. As wrong as it sounded, I hated admitting that this place *still* felt like home.

The noise of the party softened as I stepped into the clubhouse, the door spinning shut behind me.

"You lost, sweetheart?"

I spun on my heels, trying to see through the darkness. I made out a bulky shadow at the bar.

"Drinking with the lights off? That isn't normal, you know," I spoke while moving closer towards him.

He grunted out a bark of laughter. "Keeps the drunks away."

"The sign on the door saying 'Do Not Enter' doesn't do that for you?"

"Most bikers can't read."

"Most bikers aren't moths, either." I pulled out a stool and sat down in front of him. "Who are you?" I dropped my head to the side and studying his barely visible features. "I don't remember you."

"When a girl doesn't remember her own father, you know the relationship isn't a good one." Dad placed his glass down. "Didn't expect to see you here, Abby."

My mouth dropped open, "Dad?"

"Don't be too surprised, darling; you are in my bar."

I inched closer, narrowing my eyes to get a better look at him. "I didn't recognize you."

"Blame it on the lack of lights."

Guilt flooded through me. "Yeah, I suppose I could blame it on that." It was easier to blame it on the light than the real reason. "Sorry about... well, you know... last time." I chewed on my lip.

"How I acted wasn't acceptable."

"Nothing you girls ever did was acceptable. Thanks for the apology, sweetheart."

"Why are you hiding in here?" When there was a party in full swing outside, the version of my dad that I knew wouldn't be hiding in a dark bar.

His eyes dropped to the shot glass in front of him. "Doesn't matter. Why are you here, sweetheart?" He threw back his shot and then poured another. "Kim here too?"

"Yeah, she is."

"Why?"

Well, Dad, you see, Kim has a hard crush on Trigger, and she convinced me to drag her down here. "No real reason. Just wanted to come home."

The corner of his lips twitched. "Never were a good liar, Abby."

He had a point. "Whatever you say, Dad."

"Get sick of the party, darlin'?" His face soured from the bit of the shot he just swallowed. "Or are you looking for someone?"

"I just needed to get some fresh air."

"From inside?"

I wasn't enjoying the way he made all my actions sound stupid. "I guess." I rolled my eyes. "Why are you hiding in here, Dad?"

His face hardened. "Trying to come to grips with some shit."

I reached for the vodka bottle. "Like taking Reaper back? Or," I leaned over, scooping up a glass, "having Trigger back?"

Dad's eyes froze on mine for a moment. "You knew about Trigger?"

Shrugging my shoulders, "Found out when I got here."

"Heard you were sharing a house with Reaper and his brother."

I left the vodka lid off after pouring myself a shot. I had a feeling I was going to be in need of a refill. "Yeah, I had been. Drake and I are good mates. Didn't know about Reaper being his brother, though."

Dad's chest rumbled from a bitter laugh. "You always had a habit of missing the obvious."

"Don't see how Reaper and Drake being brothers was obvious."

"Not that." Dad shook his head, "Reaper moving in; you didn't put two and two together."

I frowned, "What are you implying?"

"Reaper and I had a fight; it was about Drake. Reaper did something behind the club's back to save his brother's arse. Always is cleaning up after him." Dad rolled the glass around with his fingers. "Reaper took his cut off but soon realized it was a mistake. But by then, he had reached out to Drake, and I heard about you moving in with him so..."

"So you got Reaper to move in with us?" His motives snapped into place. "To what, keep an eye on me?"

"You were off the rails, Abby. You needed someone to watch your back."

"Why are you telling me this now?"

Dad's lips twitched into a smile. "Making sure you got a clear picture and didn't come back here because you were following someone."

God, he jumped to conclusions. "I thought Reaper was in deep with the Vikings. Had no idea he was heading back here." To be honest, if anyone was following someone, it was Reaper following me.

"Then," He placed his glass down and walked around the bar. He opened his arms. "It's good to have you back, darling. Welcome home."

And what a welcome it was.

Chapter 28

Abby

When you grow up with a father called Roach, I guess it was obvious that you don't really get that much love. I suppose it was only natural that as women, Kim and I chased affection. I also guess it was no surprise that this wasn't the first time I was putting Dad to bed.

"Come on, Dad, nearly there." I groaned, buckling under his weight. I pushed open Dad's door, and the old familiar smell engulfed me.

"God, Dad, clean much?" I grumbled and let go of his weight; he collapsed half on half off the bed.

"You were always the good one," he slurred, trying to pat me on the back but instead patted the bedpost. "Never getting in trouble. Always smiling."

Was it terrible of me to be smiling right now? "Yes, Dad. Just sleep it off, okay?"

"Don't go." His large tattooed hand reached out for me. "You can't leave yet."

"I'm not leaving yet. I'll be here when you wake up."

"Promise?"

"Promise." With caution, I made my way back out. This room was disgusting. "You know, Dad, you really need to get someone to clean this."

I closed the door and sighed. Since Dad told me about Reaper, I couldn't get it out of my head. The more I thought about it, the more I wanted to know why and how he managed to lie to me so well.

While the party might be dying down, my night was definitely not over.

Abby had disappeared for the rest of the night. I didn't have the guts to ask anyone where she was. And once the clock ticked two and I still hadn't seen her, I was sure she had left.

That was, until right then as I watched her randomly turn drunk men over in the bar.

"What are you doing?"

She spun around, shocked. "I... um." She straightened up, wearing a startled expression. "I was looking for you."

"In a pile of drunk bikers?" I crossed my arms. "Do I look like the type to pass out?"

"Don't..." She pointed a finger at me and tiptoed over a few bodies towards me. "Don't you dare do that cute arrogance thing on me."

"Cute arrogance? Didn't know I had such a gift."

She scoffed loudly.

"Thought you had left, Abby," I told her honestly. "Haven't seen you all night."

"Well, you did tell me to stay away from you." The dirty look she was giving me fell for a moment. "I've been catching up with Dad."

Her look went from dirty to hurt in an instant. I knew then her dad had given her all the details.

"Abby, don't."

"Don't Abby me!" she hissed. "You were spying on me!"

"Wasn't like that."

"What was it like then? You only reported to him every second day?"

"Will you calm down?"

The judgment in her eyes was clear. "You know, all I wanted to do was find you and hope that you had a good reason for doing it!" Her shoulder hit mine as she went to leave.

Typical Abby. Things get hard and she runs away.

She was halfway up the stairs when I grabbed her wrist.

"Would you let me explain?"

"Let go of my arm, Kade." She glared over her shoulder down at me. "You're a liar."

"You said that you wanted a good reason?" I was about to do something stupid; I knew that. I had done a lot of stupid things. This shouldn't be terrifying, but to me, it was.

With her back to me, I brushed the hair off her shoulder.

Lowering my mouth to her bare skin, I softly kissed her, working my way up her neck.

I knew she hated herself for not pulling away from me.

So I had to tell her the truth, and fuck if I knew how things would work after that.

Wrapping an arm around her stomach, I pulled her against me. "I did what I did, Abby, because I love you."

Her breathing intensified. She twisted in my arms until we were face to face. Her silence was killing me.

"Say something, Abby." I needed to know what she was thinking. Her cold expression was scaring the hell out of me. If she turned away from me right now, that would be it. I would never try again.

Lowering her forehead against mine, "You're saying what I want to hear."

I didn't expect that.

"You think I'm lying?"

A hurt expression crept across her face. "Wouldn't be the first time."

"I'm not lying, Abby. I love you. Why else would I be here?"

"Because it is your home."

"I don't have a home, Abby. I don't belong to anyone, anything. I don't make roots. But I always come back to you."

She had built some pretty tough walls, and she wasn't letting me get through easily.

Bracing my shoulders, she pushed herself away from me. "I wish I could believe you." She took a step up, away from me. "But I can't."

Then that is when it happened. She turned her back on me and walked away, leaving me speechless, standing on a fucking staircase looking like a complete heartbroken loser. She didn't believe me.

I knew things were messed up. I knew I had stuffed up, but she was no innocent party in that either.

Fuck it. I wasn't letting her just walk away from me, from this, us. So I followed her steps and found myself looking at a familiar wooden door. I would make her believe me.

I knocked once, and the door flung open, I was ready to spill my heart, but her smiling face took me by surprise.

"What took you so long?" she smirked, holding the door open. "Thought you would have already pulled my door off the hinges."

"Was deciding if you were worth it." I stumbled out a fake confident lie.

Chewing her bottom lip, she took a step forward, grabbing my shirt and pulling me towards her.

I knew when her lips hit mine that there would be no more conversations, at least for tonight.

My hands ran down her sides as I kicked her door shut. Her curves were perfect and I had been dying to touch every inch of her. Now was my chance and like a greedy man on death row getting his last wish, I gripped her tightly, not wanting to let go.

Her lips tasted of sweet chocolate and vodka. Most likely her last meal. It bothered me she wasn't eating properly. But right now, as I claimed her lips, it wasn't the right time to give her a lecture.

I lifted her up and her legs locked around my waist. *Yep, right there.* That's where I wanted her. Her hands were going to the bottom of her tank top, but I was one step ahead of her. I ripped it off and tossed it to the ground.

Our kiss broke as I lowered her to the bed.

"God, you are incredible." The words tumbled out as I stared down at the sight in front of me. The black lace bra, her slightly burnt shoulders and cleavage. Her blonde hair fanned out, but that was nothing compared to the smile on her face, looking up *at me.*

"You know, Kade, you already have me. You don't have to compliment me."

Have her. Was she mine?

What did I do to deserve her?

"You sure about this?" I didn't want to believe that Abby was actually agreeing to be with me again. After everything I had put her through. Yet here she was. Putting herself on the line again.

I don't know what I expected her to say. Maybe quickly shatter off the bed. Heck, hide in the bathroom again when she realized how I wasn't worth the risk.

So you could have knocked me over when she started giggling.

"Seriously Kade, you expecting me to back out? I dragged YOU in here." She sat up on her elbows and looked me straight in the eye "Are you the one having second thoughts?"

No. Maybe I just couldn't believe my luck? But my lack of movement made her frown.

"You can't start something and not finish!" she sighed underneath me. "But if you're not up for it, maybe I'll just have to find someone else. Brad might still be up somewhere." I knew she was teasing, but that was enough to bring the caveman out of me.

"Like hell."

She giggled and ran her hand down my chest. "Lucky for you, I kind of have a thing for you."

"Good." I lowered my mouth to her ear. "Cause you're mine." And I meant that. Somehow, some way, I was going to make sure it stayed that way.

Chapter 29

Abby

"What are you doing?"

I quickly averted my eyes, feeling like the one who had just got caught out *because I had.*

"Nothing." I avoided Kim's eyes, knowing she didn't buy it. "What are you doing up so early?"

"Don't lie to me, you were totally checking Kade out." She gave me a knowing smile. "So you going to fill me in on what changed?"

She didn't realize what she was asking was impossible to answer. How can everything have changed between Kade and I, but yet some things still stayed the same?

I knew he loved me. He knew I loved him; and as for last night, well, nights like that changed everything for any girl. How had the man gotten so skilled?

I mentally hit myself for thinking that and then had a sudden urge to slap him. Because there is only *one* way someone gets that skilled.

Kim snapped her fingers in front of my face. "Abby, get out of the daydream and answer my question."

What was her question again? I frowned for a moment before remembering. "Oh right. Um, nothing changed. All is good, you know."

"If you are going to lie, at least put some effort behind it."

"I'm not lying. Reaper and I are good. Friends, but not friends, you know what I mean?"

"I don't think even a trained psychiatrist would know what you mean."

I rolled my eyes. "Why does it matter anyway?"

"Because," She took a step closer to me, lowering her voice. "You're currently giving that poor boy the sexy kitten eyes. I'm just interested in what he did to deserve them."

"I am not!" I was outraged. I *did not* do sexy kitten eyes. I grabbed her arm while pulling her away from the bar and out of sight of men eating their breakfast.

Kim giggled as I led her outside. "Gee, Abby, talk about an overreaction."

"Well, you accused me of something I don't do."

"Why, because you are above the sexy kitten stare down?" She couldn't hold back the laughter. "Gee, what happened last night?"

"Nothing."

"Lying again!" She pointed a finger at me. "You are on a roll this morning."

"We had sex, ok!" I blurted it out and slapped a hand over my mouth. Why the hell did I just say that to her!

Her expression went from amused to serious in a moment. "Abby, please tell me you are joking."

Okay, I wasn't expecting that reaction.

"No, I'm not." I crossed my arms, feeling defensive. "You can't lecture me, ok? It's not like you haven't done a bad guy before."

"I wasn't going to say that, but come on, Abby. This is Reaper."

"And you're hot for Trigger."

"Yeah, I am." Regret captured her face. "And you have no idea what I would do for him not to have this pull on me. All I'm going to say is, think about it before you get in any deeper. Men like them, like Dad, they live on this shit, you know. Pulling women in and making them theirs."

"Reaper's not like that."

"Really? Because from what I heard, he stalked you to the point of moving in with his brother."

How the hell did she know that! "Did Dad tell you that?"

"I may have been listening to your conversation with Dad."

Of course she was.

"Well, then you know why he did it. He did it for Dad."

"Yeah, that's my point. He was willing to listen to his president and break your privacy."

"Kim. Drop it." I wasn't getting into this with her. I wasn't about to justify my actions.

I could see that she didn't want to. It was clear she had more to say. Instead, she nodded her head and sighed.

"I guess we are all free to make our own mistakes, right?" She reached into her pocket, pulling out her phone. "I've got to go, but I'll see you later and Abby, if you want to talk about it, I'm here."

I don't remember a time in my life that I had heard Kim say that, and it was somewhat sad how much safer I felt hearing it.

"I'll see you later." I opened the pub door and headed back inside.

I suppose the moral of this story is I needed to be more careful when it came to Reaper. I couldn't be gawking at him. Though it was so hard to not admire his beautifully crafted body, especially in that black tank top. It was cruel seeing all that ink and muscle on display.

"Abby." Dad gestured for me to come to him.

The boys had been eating a late breakfast, or early lunch, for an hour. I was sure all the hot food was cold, and all the cold food was warm by now. I hadn't been listening to what was being said. I knew that it wasn't my place.

"Yes, Dad?" I made a point to not look over at Reaper, who had his arm draped over the back of a free chair.

"How long are you and Kim staying?"

My eyes slightly widened. How funny that he would be asking me the same question Reaper kept asking me last night. "I don't know." I gave him the same answer I had given Reaper. Because I really didn't know. We hadn't planned on staying longer than the weekend. But things were changing, I knew that, so did that mean I was ready to come back home?

"Well, I need to know." Dad reached for his beer and finished it. "Need to get shit in order."

I raised an eyebrow at him. "And what possibly needs to be ordered?"

"Yours and your sister's stuff has to be moved back down here, and I've got a few men riding up that way next week. They could take a van and load your shit up, bringing it back on the way through."

"I do not think so. I'm not having anyone just throw my stuff in a box." I wasn't letting anyone go through my things.

"Fine, I can get your Aunty to do it."

I didn't really like that idea either. I wonder if whore can stain things.

"Why does it have to be done now?" I crossed my arms, feeling cornered. "I don't see what the rush is. Kim and I might just be staying for a while here and then heading back up."

"Well, are you?"

"I don't know. I haven't spoken to her about it."

"Since when did you only do what she did?" Dad gave me a pointed look. "What's keeping you there, Abby? I thought you hated the place."

I hated being made to move there, yes, but I didn't hate it there anymore. I had friends and somewhat of a job.

But Dad was right, what was keeping me there? I guess he had the same answer as I did. Nothing.

"I thought you didn't want me back here?" I threw that question at him because that was the clear impression I got last night when he was going on about me following Reaper here.

"You're my daughter; of course I want you here." He seemed almost hurt at the suggestion. "Just didn't want you coming back for the wrong reasons."

I didn't like having a double-sided conversation in front of this

many people. But it was Dad. He didn't care who was listening.

"I guess you can tell Aunt Mandy to pack my things up then." I cringed at the thought of her touching my stuff. "But tell her to wear gloves."

"Abby, that isn't nice."

Shrugging my shoulders, I reached for the empty glasses on the table. My eyes caught Reaper's for a moment as I took the glass in front of him.

"Tell Kim I'm getting her to pack her shit up, too," Dad told me as I walked away and I paused, turning back around.

"Just because I am staying doesn't mean she is." Out of the corner of my eye, I saw Trigger shift in his seat. "Kim has a guy there, Dad. She might not be ready to walk away from that."

Call me a troublemaker, but I knew Kim would do the same for me. The only way to know if Trigger was interested in her was to see if he got jealous. She could thank me later.

"It's Kim. She will move on to another soon enough." Dad didn't look up from his phone as he scrolled through numbers.

"Come on, Dad. Do you really think Trent is like all the others? She's really taken with him. When you meet him, you'll know what I mean."

I didn't need to be a mind reader to see the jealousy building up in Trigger.

"That nerdy kid." He scrunched his nose up. "You don't think she actually likes him?"

Dad's outrage was so clear that it made me smile. The thought of a nerdy son-in-law was equal to having his own eyes poked out.

I shrugged my shoulders. "He's the only guy she has ever changed for, and you saw them, Dad. They are sort of cute together."

Trent and Kim just made my skin crawl. The dude was as boring as a wallflower. But he was serving a purpose.

"Fine. I'll ask your sister before packing her shit up, but I'm telling you right now, no way is that boy marrying her." Dad pointed a finger at me as if he were laying down the law.

"Well, I think that works out well because she just plans on screwing his brains out," I smirked, watching Dad's face roll in disgust, and headed towards the kitchen with the empty cups in hand.

My work there was done. Trigger thought he had competition now, and I knew that would make him pull his act together.

Placing the dishes in the sink, I nearly jumped through the roof when I felt a pair of hands grab my hips.

"So you're staying then?" Reaper's hot breath crept across my ear, causing every sensation in my body to come alight.

I pressed back into him. "I guess so." I slowly turned my head to the side to meet his eyes. "You ok with that?"

The corner of his lip twitched into half a smile. "Never wanted you to leave, babe." His hand slowly crept under my tee shirt.

My pulse began to race as his cold fingers grazed my stomach.

"You're lucky I didn't bend you over that bar for giving me those sexy fuck me eyes before." He nibbled my earlobe.

"I wasn't even!" I huffed. My eyes have never done nor will never do 'sexy kitten' or 'sexy fuck me' eyes.

Hearing footsteps coming down the passage, we jumped aside just in time for Brad to enter the kitchen.

"So do you want me to organize your car to be towed down?" Reaper faked a bored tone in his voice.

I thought about it for a moment. "Um, no actually. Would you be able to organize Drake to sell it?" I dried my hands on the towel.

"What, you're going to sell your beast?" Brad joined the conversation, getting a beer out the fridge.

"Yeah, time for a change, you know." I shrugged my shoulders, crossing my arms and leaning back against the sink. "Plus, I think

I want to get a convertible."

They both cracked a grin.

"Women." Reaper shook his head.

"What's wrong with a convertible? They are sexy and have the added bonus of having no roof when you want it that way," I defended my choice.

"They leak, always have problems with the roof not going down right, and if you kill someone, there is no boot space." Brad listed the reasons on his fingers.

I scoffed. "This is coming from a man that owns a motorcycle."

Brad shot me a wink, striding out of the kitchen, leaving Reaper and me alone again.

Reaper pushed himself up off the table, and I took a step closer to him. It wasn't fair for a man to be as attractive as him.

"So you really don't like the idea of a convertible?"

He shrugged his shoulders and brushed the hair from the side of my face. "Just didn't see you as the convertible type of girl. But you can get whatever you want."

I ran a hand down his arm. "Means I won't have room for a dead body." I joked.

A smirk captured his lips, and he dropped his mouth down to my ear. "If you have to kill someone babe, it means I'm not doing my job right, and I'm never planning on that happening."

Tingles spread across my body and before I could say anything, he slapped my arse and gave me a wink before walking out of the kitchen, leaving me speechless. *Oh god, what have I gotten myself into?*

Chapter 30

Abby

"So you're moving back here?" Kim stood in my doorway, arms crossed with a very unimpressed look on her face.

"Yeah, I am."

"Didn't think of telling me that this morning?"

"Does it matter?" I didn't really see how it would affect her. "I told Dad just because I'm coming back doesn't mean you are."

Rolling her eyes, she closed the door behind her. "Yes, it does."

"Kim, I'm a big girl. I can look after myself."

"I don't doubt that but…" She looked torn as if she knew what she was about to say was going to offend me. "I don't want to leave you here with no one to talk to. Especially when I'm the one who convinced you to come back here."

Was she feeling guilty? I chewed on my bottom lip, stopping myself from smiling.

"Kim." I gripped her shoulders, looking her straight in the eye. "You don't have to feel responsible for me. If you want to stay, stay. If you want to go, go. But before you make your decision, I need to tell you something."

She frowned, "Ok. What?"

"It's about Trigger."

She rolled her eyes and sighed. "What about him?"

"I may have made it sound like you and Trent were still dating."

She scrunched her nose up. "Why on earth would you do that?"

"To see if he was jealous, and he was."

She moved to go sit on my bed. "Trust me, he isn't jealous. Jealousy would be the last emotion he would feel when it came to me. He might have shown some interest, but I doubt it was jealousy."

"Ok, what makes you say that?" Clearly, she knew more about this situation than I did. I thought I had read pure jealousy on Trigger's face. Had I read it wrong? No. Not possible.

"He's dating someone."

"What, a club whore?" I laughed at the thought, "Come on, Kim. Screwing isn't dating; you know that."

"No. She's a real woman, has no connection to the club." The disappointment in her voice was noticeable. "I thought he was lying about her, but this morning I went and checked her out for myself. She's real."

That couldn't be possible. Trigger dating a good girl? I just didn't see it.

"Who is she?"

"Some chick that works down at the council. I thought maybe he was with her for the club, you know, but she works the desk. She wouldn't have any influence."

I couldn't help but frown. "So what was with his reaction last night? He was clearly into you, Kim. Maybe this girlfriend of his is just to make you jealous."

"His reaction last night was because he didn't want me here." She looked up from her hands. "He told me. He said that I could ruin everything."

"Please, you couldn't ruin anything when it comes to him. He is more than able to do that on his own."

"Still. He doesn't want me here."

"Since when did you do what Trigger wants?" I couldn't believe what I was hearing. She was willing to back down because she didn't want to hurt him, or worse, ruin his relationship.

"I don't want him to hate me." She smiled sadly at me. "I know this sounds stupid, but I would rather be his friend than nothing, you know?"

"Then be his friend." I went to sit beside her. "Stay, and then at the very least you can show him what he is missing out on."

Trigger wasn't a clear-cut type of guy. Which made me think that this 'relationship' of his wasn't clear-cut either.

Kim sighed, looking around the room. "You so have to redecorate this room if you are staying here."

"Funny, I was thinking the same thing." I grinned at her, "So are you going to stay?"

"I wouldn't be a good sister if I left you here by yourself with Reaper, would I?"

Laughing at her, I couldn't help but think about how much I had changed since I left this room. I just hoped I didn't fall back into old habits.

***

"You going out in that?" Dad's eyes widened slightly, his nostrils flared. "It's a bloody bra, Abby. Put a top on."

"It's a sports bra, Dad, and I'm going for a run. Not like I'm heading down the street." I felt highly annoyed at him. All I wanted to do was go for a run, and he had to be hovering around the gate.

"What are those? Underwear!" He pointed at my shorts.

"They are Loren Jane, Dad. Hardly underwear!" I snickered at his overreaction. While I knew a few of the guys were giving me a once over, there was only one pair of eyes I wanted on me, and he wasn't here. In fact, I hadn't seen him since morning.

"Can I go now?" I huffed at him while clicking my phone into my armband.

"Not till you get changed."

"Dad. Back off." I wasn't letting him stomp all over me again. "I'm going for a run. I have my phone. Call me if you need me."

I turned my back sharply and headed out the gates. After all, what could he do? Stop me? Doubtful.

Putting my headphones in, I started to quicken my pace. Time to have some me time, and I really needed it.

***

I was sweaty, I was hot, and I really needed a drink. Bursting into the clubhouse, I headed straight to the bar, reaching over for a scoop of ice and some water.

I gulped it down at an incredible rate while still listening to my music. I was in such a rush to get a drink I hadn't even stretched or taken my headphones out. Which I suppose led me to a humiliating moment when I finished my drink only to realize that the end of the bar was full.

My chest heaved and I still hadn't managed to get control over my breathing, taking out my headphones, then Trigger decided he wanted to be a smart arse.

"Lose your top, Abby?" He made a point to stare at my chest for a few moments.

I slapped my glass down on the bar and ignored him.

"You know, babe, I could get you a sweater if you want." Some greasy, dirty man on a bar stool smirked at me.

I walked past them, not bothering to give them a response. It was when he slapped my arse that I got mad. Spinning on my heel, I slapped the man's hand away.

"Don't touch me," I snarled.

"Come on, darling; that's no way to talk to a bloke."

Who was this man? Usually, the guys had respect for Kim and I. Clearly this guy didn't know who I was or more importantly, who my dad was.

Trigger leaned back against the bar, looking amused and not seeming to want to step in.

The man reached out for me again, and I was quick to push him away. "I said leave me alone!" I picked up his half empty beer and threw the contents in his face.

In hindsight, it was a stupid move. So I suppose I shouldn't have been surprised that the man went from flirting to furious in a second.

"Apologize, bitch!" He grabbed my wrist, twisting it tightly.

"Let go of me!"

Trigger must have thought he better step in, as I saw him move out of the corner of my eye.

"I think you need to be taught a lesson," he snarled in my ear and pulled me forcefully into his chest. I was sure my wrist was inches from snapping in half. Then just at the man went to unzip his jeans, his grip on my hand was ripped away.

I thought it had been Trigger; I was wrong. Reaper sent one punch into the guy's jaw and another into his stomach, causing him to hunch over. Gasping, I took a few steps back, trying to get out of the way before I ended up in the way of one of his swings.

Reaper didn't look furious. He was controlled, which for some reason was more terrifying.

I cradled my wrist in one hand while tears threatened to spill. It was throbbing, and it was a sinister type of pain. I didn't want them to see me cry, so I turned quickly and ran out while cradling my wrist. I was wiping away tears when I ran into Brad at the top of the stairs.

"Holy shit, Abby, what's wrong?"

"Nothing. Just please move." I went to sidestep him, but he only blocked me off.

"Did you hurt yourself?"

I shook my head, letting the tears run down my cheek. "Please Brad, move."

His eyes were glued on my wrist. "Come on, let me take you to get that looked at."

"I just want to go to my room!" I stomped my foot. Why did everyone think it was ok to try and stop me from what I wanted to do?

"Abby. It looks broken." His voice softened. "Let me take you to go get it looked at?"

I couldn't go back through the bar. I didn't want Kade to see me like this. I didn't want Dad to see me like this either because I was sure I would get an *'I told you so.'*

Glaring down at the carpet. "I can't go back through the bar."

"Fine, we will go out the side exit." He didn't question as to why, and I was grateful. So I followed Brad back down the stairs, crying and holding my wrist.

Chapter 31

Abby

I knew I never had the best luck, but this, well, this just sucked! I stared down at the white cast on my wrist. This was the most unattractive thing I had ever seen.

"Now come back in about six weeks, and we can have a look to see if it is ready to come off." The doctor finished writing a prescription and handed it to me. "These painkillers do cause drowsiness, so best not to drive while taking them."

I nodded my head, feeling very sorry for myself.

"Now miss, before I let you go." The doctor went and pulled the curtain around the bed. "I want to ask you one more time, how did this happen?"

He wasn't buying my 'I fell' story. It most likely didn't help my case either that a large, overbearing tattooed monster called Brad brought me in.

"My wrist breaking was my fault. No one else's." And I wasn't lying; it was my fault. I shouldn't have walked around the club in my gym clothes. I should have taken my dad's advice. It was my fault I was here.

He frowned and while he nodded his head, accepting my answer, I knew he hadn't believed it.

"Well, then you are free to go." He pulled the curtain back, and I gathered my things off the bed.

"Thanks, doc."

I took another look at the hideous cast on my arm. God, I looked like I was back in primary school. Walking out into the waiting room, I spotted Brad immediately. Just his appearance made him easy to spot, but what had made it easier was the way everyone was leaving the seats next to him empty.

It seemed people had taken to standing rather than sitting next to him.

"Brad." I waved at him, his head snapping up.

I watched the color drain from his face. "Please tell me it isn't broken." He was out of his seat, coming at me immediately. "You ok, Abby?" He placed a hand on my shoulder, looking concerned.

"Yeah. I'm fine. Just sucks I'm stuck with this for months." I realized that close to nearly everyone in the waiting room was staring openly at us.

I suppose seeing him actually being concerned and caring had shocked them.

"Can we go?" I asked him, shifting my handbag on my arm, which he then immediately took off me.

Now that did make me smile.

"Yeah darling, I parked the van around the corner. Not too much of a walk for you."

"I broke my arm, Brad, not my leg," I smirked at him.

Cracking a grin, he answered, "Righteo smart arse, let's go."

The thing about Brad that most people didn't know was unlike a lot of bikers, he had a good, caring heart. He just didn't show it often.

"Talked to your old man before," Brad said, walking beside me and I cringed.

"Great. What did he say?"

"He wanted to know what happened." He gave me a sideways glance. "Didn't realize something had happened, Abby. Why didn't you tell me Mavis attacked you?"

"So that's his name." I groaned, realizing now Dad knew the whole story. I couldn't just fib to him. "So Dad is furious then?"

"Nah, he was just concerned. Wanted to know if it was broken or not."

"Well, it's broken."

"Yeah, I can see that. Why didn't you tell me? If I had known

197

Abby, I would have…"

"Stop, Brad." I gripped his arm, shaking my head at him. "There wasn't anything you could do. Reaper was already laying into the guy, and it was my fault. I shouldn't have been wearing what I was wearing."

Anger boiled in his eyes, "Don't be stupid, Abby. You should be able to wear whatever the fuck you want without getting attacked. What happened shouldn't have happened. Simple. And it's been dealt with."

"What does that mean?" I didn't like the sound of violence, but I knew that was the only language my dad spoke clearly. "Did Dad hurt him?"

Brad scoffed, "He would have if he got a chance. Reaper apparently beat him to it."

My stomach twisted, and nerves filled me. "Is Reaper ok?"

Brad gave me a blank expression, "It's Reaper, of course he is ok. The man didn't even land a punch on him."

I felt relief that Reaper hadn't been hurt because of me.

"Dad's going to be so mad. He hates it when his guys fight, and I caused it, which will only make him more furious."

"Mavis is a wild one, Abby, just rides between clubhouses. So Roach will be ok about it."

We stopped at the van, and I smiled as Brad opened the door for me. Such a gentleman.

"Thanks." I smiled up at him, "And thanks for bringing me here too, Brad, and for waiting. I owe you one."

"Nah darling, you don't owe me a thing." He winked and gave me a push up into the van.

It was now that I realized I wasn't that unlucky. In fact, I was actually lucky to have run into Brad tonight because I don't think any other guy would have stopped what he was doing and taken me to the hospital. Well, forced me to go to the hospital.

Chapter 32

Abby

I was all about new experiences. Well, I was all about them now that I had grown up. Even I would admit that as a teenager, I was very sheltered. Still, there are some new things I didn't want to experience, such as a broken wrist.

Kim was giving me a sideways smirk.

"Shut up." I pointed a finger at her after catching her expression in the mirror. "You can't say anything."

"I hadn't said anything." She crossed her arms, giving me a cocky smirk. "Can't believe Dad hasn't said anything yet."

"I don't see that as a bad thing." Seriously, if I could avoid a lecture from Dad, I would. "In fact, I'm making an effort to avoid him."

"I'm sure he has noticed," she arched an eyebrow at me.

"Come on. Don't make me feel bad about it." I huffed and put my hands on my hip. "It is more than acceptable to give him some space, you know? That way, he is less likely to kill me."

"I think he is more worried that you want to kill him."

Surely Dad wouldn't be thinking that I was avoiding him because I was mad at *him*. I was scared he was going to throw me out.

"I guess it's been a few days," I grumbled. Maybe I should stop being invisible.

"Have you seen Reaper?" She made an effort to not sound overly interested.

Just his name sent my stomach into a knot. "No, I haven't."

"What, not at all? Since it happened?"

Why did she sound so outraged?

"He left that morning Kim. Wasn't like I could take him down."
It was true. He had ridden out that morning.

I couldn't lie and say it hadn't bothered me. He hadn't even checked to see if I was ok. He had just left.

"So he didn't even see if you were ok? Before he rode out?"

God, why did she have to have that tone in her voice? I knew it was screwed up; I didn't need her making it more obvious.

"I got back from the hospital, and he was gone." I shrugged my shoulders. "It's not a big deal."

"So when is he back?"

"Today." I met her judging eyes. "Well, that is what I've heard."

"Uh huh."

"Don't say uh huh like that. It's not a big deal. God, it's just a broken wrist."

Sure, I was downplaying it. I knew it was just a broken wrist, and it wasn't that big of a deal. Still, the fact that Kade hadn't even thought about seeing if I was ok before he left bothered me.

"Well, it's past ten, so he must be here any minute then," Kim smirked while heading for the bedroom door. "Oh," she paused, holding the door open. "Go see Dad before he gets back."

Since when did she become the one giving the good advice? I really wasn't enjoying this change of roles.

***

"Dad, can we talk?" I stepped into his office, closing the door behind me.

He looked up from his newspaper, a morning coffee in hand and a burning cigarette leaning on the ashtray.

For a moment I saw relief wash over his face, and he folded the paper up. I moved to sit in the chair across from him.

I noticed his glance drop to my plastered arm.

"How's the wrist?" His smile formed into a frown.

Well, that was getting to the elephant quickly.

"That's kind of the reason I'm here." I swallowed sharply. "Dad, I'm sorry. I should have listened to you. This is all my fault, and I'm sorry for ignoring you."

Dad's face twisted quickly into shock and disbelief. "You got nothing to feel sorry about, Abby. This was my fault. I'm the one who should be saying sorry to you."

"I'm the one who walked around half naked in your bar! I was asking for trouble."

"No woman, no matter what she is wearing, should be attacked. *Especially you.*"

I could hear the protective father coming out in his voice.

"Still, Dad, I was the one walking around like bait. It's my fault, and I'm sorry for embarrassing you like that."

He huffed. "The only embarrassing thing about this is I wasn't the one to wring the bloke's neck."

"Yeah, sorry about that too. Getting Reaper involved. I know you hate it when the boys fight."

"He was defending you. I would have done the same thing. Should have been what Trigger was doing instead of egging it on."

My eyes widened slightly; I hadn't expected Dad to know about that.

"You should know better than anyone, Abby. There isn't anything that goes on around here that I don't know about."

Yeah, I suppose I should know that by now. Guess it was a miracle that he didn't know about my relationship with Reaper yet.

"About Reaper and you…"

God, I spoke too soon.

"Um yeah?" I faked a frown. "What about us?"

"Want to tell me what is going on between you two?"

"Nothing."

He gave me a pointed expression.

"I'm serious, Dad. Nothing is going on between him and I. I just… well, it is going to sound stupid."

"Try me."

"I feel safe around him." I met Dad's examining eyes. "That's all, I swear."

I was leaving out a lot of details, but I suppose I wasn't lying either. The foundation of the relationship I have with Reaper was built on trust. I trusted him. I felt safe with him.

Dad slowly sighed, seeming to have accepted my explanation. "You got plans for today?"

Change of subject, which meant that awkward conversation was over.

"Not sure. Kim is heading into town, something about needing new clothes. I'm not in a shopping mood."

"So you're planning on hanging around here then?"

"Is that a problem?" Did he want me to leave? I couldn't be sure.

"Reaper's heading back in this morning with a few blokes. It might be for the best if you weren't around."

So he wanted me to leave.

"So that explains why you gave Kim that heap of cash yesterday," I smirked. "How long do you want us gone for?"

He picked the cigarette up from the ashtray and finished it.

"You can come back tonight, just make it late."

Great. Now I had to think of something to keep me occupied all day.

"I'll head out soon then."

He nodded his head. "I'll see you when you get back."

"Yep."

Being made to leave felt way too familiar. Maybe if I was going to stay in town, I should think about getting my own place and stop living with the old man and his drunken crew.

I pulled out my mobile and dialed Kim's number. Looks like I was going shopping.

***

"What about this one?" Kim held up a black dress. "It's shorter."

"I don't know if that is necessarily a good thing," I advised her while searching in my handbag for my buzzing phone. "I thought you said you wanted to look classy?"

Kim shopping for something that wasn't trashy, slutty, or didn't show half her breasts was a challenge, one she wasn't succeeding at.

I think every blood vessel in my body ran ice cold when I finally found my phone and saw the name on the screen.

A text message from Reaper.

Not once had he messaged me.

Not once in the whole time that we had been doing, well, whatever our relationship is, has he ever messaged me.

Had something happened?

I stared blankly at my phone for a good few minutes while multiple theories ran through my head. Finally, I decided to just see what it said.

Where are you?

There were a few things that floated to my mind as I read his three little words.

One, he actually spelled correctly.

Two, he had noticed I wasn't in the clubhouse.

Chewing my bottom lip, I decided it was better to keep my response short and sweet.

Shopping

I suppose you can't get any shorter than one word.

My phone buzzed again.

Why?

He had a very good point. He knew I didn't like shopping. It wasn't like it was a hidden secret that I despised it. To give him a real answer to that question, it was going to take more than a few words.

Dad wanted us out of the clubhouse for a bit

I pretended to help Kim look for a new dress while waiting for his reply. When five minutes had passed and I had heard nothing, I realized maybe he wasn't going to write back. Wasn't like I had given him much to go off.

My doubt disappeared when my phone buzzed again.

Hear your wrist is broken?

I frowned instantly. Hadn't he already known that when he left? Unless he had left before anyone had told him.

Perhaps he didn't even know I went to the hospital?

You left

I wanted to add, *'and it really bothered me that you pissed off without a word,'* but I thought it was better to just keep that to myself.

Not by choice. Are you coming back here tonight?

His little explanation didn't really answer any of my questions. But then again, I wasn't sure if I could answer his question either. I glanced over at Kim, who was still going through racks and racks of dresses.

I had a strong feeling that she had no plans of heading back to the clubhouse tonight, and it wasn't like I had anyone else to be with.

I don't know

I decided to just write back the truth because I had no idea what the plan was. I knew Dad didn't want us back early, and I knew Kim didn't want to go back tonight at all.

I want to see you

I smiled instantly reading that. I wanted to see him too. Hell, I've wanted to see him every day since he left. But I couldn't be all needy and tell him that. I had to play it cool.

I'll be back when I'm allowed to

And that was the truth. As soon as Dad let us back, and Kim wanted to go back, I would be there. Until then, I just had to stay away. He didn't write anything back, and I sort of didn't expect him to. Sighing and putting my phone away, I spotted Kim and headed towards her. I really wish this day was over already.

Chapter 33

Abby

He was wearing a tank top, with long open sides that showed off his tattooed side piece and part of his back piece. Leaning on his bike, a pair of thick black sunglasses blocked his marvelous eyes, which I could spend hours staring into.

He had a half smile on his face while he listened to some man who I hadn't seen before. In fact, he was so focused on their conversation that he hadn't even heard Kim pull in, which was saying something.

"Get the boot, Abby," Kim grunted while readjusting her shopping bags. "Seeing as you aren't getting any shopping bags."

Rolling my eyes at her pointed remark I closed the boot and followed slowly behind her.

As far as I was concerned, there was no rush to go inside because once I was in there, I wouldn't be able to gawk at the sexy god beast known as Reaper.

"Oh, hey Abby. How's your wrist, love?" Cameron asked, I hadn't realized it was him Reaper was speaking to.

Reaper's head turned in my direction, and I watched his smile fall. Well, that hurt.

"It's all right." I lied. It was aching today, and I think it had something to do with the fact Kim thought having a broken wrist was no excuse to not be able to help her carry her bags at the mall.

"You're the only girl I know who could pull off a cast, darlin'." Cameron attempted to make me feel better. "Good to see you girls are back too, your old man thought you had split."

Funny, because he was the one who had sent us away for the day.

"What's with all the extra bikes?" I nodded my head at the new row of motorbikes.

"Upgrades," Cameron smirked, and I knew behind that confident smirk there was a story.

I glanced at Reaper, hoping he would say something, but he didn't. I could literally feel my heart pump a few extra beats. He just filled my mind with fantasies.

"Did they fall off the back of the truck?" I asked, wanting to keep some sort of a conversation flowing.

"You ask a lot of questions for someone who is meant to be keeping her nose clean." Cameron gave me a challenging smirk.

I shrugged my shoulders.

I glanced at Reaper, hoping he was going to say something, but he didn't. Which made me standing here awkward.

"Abby?" Brad walked out of the garage with grease on his forehead. "Thought that was your voice." His face softened with a smile.

He had been so kind to me the other night, which reminded me.

I opened up my handbag and pulled out a small plastic shopping bag. "I got you something," I said, taking a few steps towards him. "I really hope it fits."

I noticed his belt looked really worn and I knew he hated shopping so when I saw it, it was a bit of an impulse buy.

I immediately started to second guess myself when he pulled it out of the plastic shopping bag.

"Um. It was kind of an impulse buy. If it doesn't fit you, I can um take it back. You don't have to like, wear it if you don't want to."

There was this thing about Brad. He didn't smile much or laugh. Actually, when it came to it, bikers just aren't really a happy bunch, so smiling in general doesn't happen.

Which is why I was slightly stunned when I saw a big grin on his face.

"Thanks, Abby." He honestly liked the belt and wrapped it

around his waist, checking if it fit. Which it did.

"As long as you like it."

I could feel the scorch of Reaper's glare.

"Thanks, miss." He gave me a wink while threading his old belt out and putting the new one on.

"Well, I'm gonna head inside. Dad might be looking for me."

An awkward blanket had just wrapped around me, and I did the only thing I knew how to do, run.

Brad was throwing his old belt in the trash when I headed inside. Was it stupid of me to expect Reaper to speak to me?

He messaged me, acted like he wanted to talk to me, then becomes a mute when I do show up.

That is so totally him.

Chapter 34

Abby

There is a reputation that comes with a motorcycle group, and it isn't the most desirable one. Unless of course you want that reputation, and most of the boys liked it.

People openly stared: some out of interest, others out of anger, and most because they were jealous.

Jealous of the freedom.

When it came down to it, the guys stood for everything a typical society didn't. At the end of the day, they were a brotherhood, one very large family.

What they did was no one's business.

But because they were considered outlaws, they were judged, but they weren't judged as harshly or as openly as supporters or people they saw as *'living off the dirty cash.'*

I should be used to it by now.

It shouldn't bother me as much as it did.

Why the hell did we have to order out again? I threw a dirty look at the middle-aged couple who was giving me a distasteful look.

Right now, I was furious at Cameron for scaring the delivery driver. Because of his stupid prank or whatever he did, the restaurant won't deliver to the clubhouse.

So guess who got sent out to get their stupid darn food?

Me.

"Will it be much longer?" I asked the cashier. Who had told me they would only be a minute half an hour ago.

I placed this order two hours ago because I knew it was a large one.

"It won't be long." She glanced behind her, not even bothering to go check. Her bored and unhelpful tone was clear.

Stupid blonde haired, wide-eyed, teenager bitch.

I heard the boring bell tone of the door opening. I was ready to give this unhelpful mole a serving of bitch.

"Abby, what the fuck is taking so long?"

Only one man would storm into a pizza shop with that demanding voice.

My expression hardened. "Why are you here, Reaper?"

He hadn't come with me. Even though I had hinted *several times* before I left for him to join me.

Instead, the thickheaded monkey stayed behind and played poker with a cheap woman on his lap.

"Your dad wanted to know why the hell it takes an hour to pick up pizzas."

"Oh, and he thought that was a job for his VP, did he?" I had no doubt that Dad would have sent someone down to check on me, but I doubted it would be Reaper.

His cold-stoned unbiased expression broke for a moment, and his eyes shone with curiosity.

My head snapped back to the boring menu board. I swear I was going to go back there and ask the cook myself how much longer he would be!

Pizza parlors weren't known for overwhelming space. Reaper took a noticeable (well, noticeable to me) step closer to me, placing a hand on my hip. He pushed me back until I was firmly against his chest.

The thing that annoyed me most was now I had the cashier's attention. Well, Reaper had it.

My back was tense, and I was sure if I didn't have my fingers tightened in a clenched fist, they would be shaking.

My hair was brushed to one side, and he took the opportunity presented to him.

"You mad, babe?"

His tone was tainted with slight amusement.

Mad?

No.

Not me.

I crossed my arms tightly, losing my clenched fists.

As smooth as a snake, his fingers slipped under my tee shirt, lightly tracing my skin, sending a heat wave through my body.

"Stop it." I forced out and cocked my head up to meet his smoldering eyes. "I mean it."

My wavering tone took any power from my words, and I watched him smirk with triumph.

"Why don't you go do something useful and get our pizzas," I snapped at him and pushed his grip off me.

I was sure the blonde would actually go out the back and check for him.

"Order 21."

What a surprise.

"You can head back to the club." My eyes sliced through his. "Tell Dad I'm safe."

The cashier was stacking the pizzas up. I knew I was going to have to make two trips, and I would have preferred *that* than to have what happened.

"I've got it, babe." He took the stack of ten pizzas while I paid the bill and got the remaining five.

It was after eleven at night, and this was meant to be a late tea, which now has turned into midnight drinking food.

His black sleek beast was parked next to the old pickup I had taken. Funny how no one ever seems to park that old thing.

When the pizzas were safely inside, I closed the old rusty door, which led to one of the main reasons I didn't want Reaper to help because at that moment, there was an awkward silence.

"See you back at the club." I murmured and walked around Reaper.

"You pissed I didn't talk to you this afternoon?"

"Nope."

"You brought Brad a belt, Abby. The blokes haven't got off Brad's back all night about it."

I wouldn't lie and say I hadn't heard the digs or the sly remarks. I could defend my actions to Kade, but I felt like I *shouldn't* have to. He was the one walking around all night with that woman under his arm then on his lap.

I knew even if I mentioned it, he would just say *nothing happened*, or *nothing was going to happen* and give me that demeaning look.

I slammed the car door and didn't even give him the pleasure of a heated conversation with me. Because I knew what would happen, what always happens. He would make me feel silly, and I would end up caving.

Chapter 35

Abby

Kim was standing out front as I pulled in, smoking. Why was she outside? Wasn't like Dad didn't allow smoking inside.

"Hey." I said, getting out of the truck. Reaper had passed me on the way here. My eyes flashed to his bike. A gentleman would have stayed and helped carry the bloody pizzas in. But this was Reaper. He was most likely thinking about the woman he had on his lap all night. *Yeah, he really loved me.*

"Reaper said you needed a hand with the pizzas?"

Well, what do you know, he sent Kim to do his job.

"Um yeah, thanks." I opened the passenger side door and started taking them out, handing them to Kim.

"Trigger's left."

"Where to?"

"His girlfriend's. At least that is what the guys are saying." Kim swayed on her feet.

"You're drunk." I laughed. I should have expected it. Kim wasn't coping when it came to Trigger. Like at all. I was waiting for her to do something outrageous. Come up with some stupid plan.

I closed the door with my butt and we walked back to the clubhouse.

"So what have you been doing apart from knocking off Dad's top shelf liquor?"

She paused at the clubhouse door, thinking. "Um, I have actually made friends."

I pushed the door open. "With?"

"KIM!"

Two bikers I had never seen before greeted Kim like she was their best friend. Both were tall, slim build, but muscular and of course were covered in tattoos.

"Them." Kim grinned and then like me started dishing out the pizzas.

I avoided Reaper's table and his brunette friend.

I wondered where Dad was, then I spotted him at the table Kim was giving pizzas to. Looks like he was busy gambling like the rest of them. Smoking, drinking, and gambling. Yeah, one hell of a Saturday night.

"So come meet the boys." Kim grabbed my elbow and slowly pulled me along. I wouldn't lie and say I hadn't noticed Reaper's eyes on me. Was he paying any attention to the cards? Or the brunette?

"This is Darren and Collins." Kim introduced us. "And we are polishing off this bottle of Jack." Her eyes lit up as she reached for it. "Though they're cheating. They have drunk way more than me." Kim swayed on her feet and I guided her to a stool.

"So you must be Abby?" The one with the neck tattoo turned to me.

"And you are? Darren or Collins?"

"Collins." He grinned. "The eldest."

"And he won't let me forget it." Darren pushed a shot glass in my direction.

"Brothers?" I assumed.

"By blood." Collins threw back a shot. "You still drinking, Kim?"

Kim was busy playing with an empty glass. How much had she had to drink? But her ears picked up the sound of more and she pushed her empty glass towards him.

"It's still early days, guys." She gave us a loose grin and I knew that grin, that grin told me she was in for the long haul. I knew then I'd be dragging her drunk ass to bed.

***

The hours ticked by and the shots didn't stop. We moved on from that bottle of Jack. We were throwing back straight bourbon. The drinks didn't stop flowing and the conversation was just as good. These boys could really talk, they were from up north and were just here for the night.

Darren and Kim were play fighting while having an arm wrestling competition. Kim kept losing and asking for a rematch, saying it didn't count.

They were too busy laughing and drinking to be serious, even though we all knew Kim was trying her hardest.

I had watched the brunette get more and more feely with Reaper over the past hour. Every time she kissed his neck, I did two shots. Collins said I was outdrinking him.

So when Collins wrapped an arm around my waist and pulled me into his side, I didn't stop it.

That's when Reaper started giving me daggers. Good, I was under his skin, because he was under mine. I also knew he was paying way too much attention to our conversation cause when Collins said he didn't have a bed yet and Kim said he should sleep with me, Reaper had an overreaction to a losing hand.

"You know what, we should play something I can beat you at." Kim dismissed her losing arm wrestles.

My face lit up hearing that. "POOL! We should play pool!"

Kim's face lit up the same as mine. "Yep, let's play pool."

"Doubles," I added.

Darren nodded his head, but it was Collins's evil smirk that made me know he was going to add to the terms.

"Strip pool." Collins added. "And Abby gets to pick the teams."

Kim and I shared a look. A smart mind would remind me that I was wearing a cast because I had been wearing very little near a biker. But I had had more than a few and this actually sounded like fun. Plus I had a secret weapon.

"Ok." I grinned and turned in Collins's arm, facing him. "I know how badly you want to play with me, Collins."

His eyes lit up at the double meaning, and he pulled me that inch closer to him. I made sure to say it that much louder, just to ensure Reaper didn't miss it.

"But I'm totally picking Kim," I added with a cheeky grin. "So you ready to lose your clothes, Collins?"

"Sweetheart, you will be losing yours. And if I win, you're sleeping with me tonight," Collins said as we walked past Reaper's table.

"Deal."

"Looking forward to it. Look at Kim, she can barely stand." Collins laughed at me. "Should have picked me, sweetheart."

I just grinned. They had no idea what they were in for.

I sucked at pool. Sure, I could hold myself in a game, but I had more misses than good shots.

Brad was at the pool table and as Collins explained how we were all going to get a show, the boys jumped off.

"Really, Abby?" Brad said to me, handing me a cue with a knowing smile.

"Have you seen Dad by any chance?"

"Yeah, lucky for you, he's already headed upstairs with Linda."

"Ta." That's all I needed to know. I winked at him. Brad was one of the few that knew my secret weapon.

Kim walked towards me and I steadied her when she got to my side. Word about the game spread, and the boys actually stopped playing poker for the first time this evening to watch.

I guess boys would stop anything if there was a chance they were going to see nudity.

Kim leaned on my shoulder.

216

"So how drunk are you?" I asked her.

She just grinned at me. "Past drunk."

"Do you know Trigger is here?"

Her eyes went wide. "What, where?"

I lowered my voice and whispered in her ear. "Behind you. Guess that girlfriend of his didn't keep him entertained."

I was aware of the fact Reaper was now leaning against the brick pillar, watching with that stupid brunette under his arm. I seriously wanted to rip that girl's hair out, or drag her out the back. But what annoyed me the most was, why did club girls always have to be so young and happy? Seriously, are they all so happy to be used and ditched?

She was laughing and giggling under his arm. Reaper wasn't funny. So I don't know what she found so entertaining.

"Ok, some rules!" Collins cleared his voice, making everyone look at him. "Shoes and socks don't count."

All the boys cheered with agreement.

Kim was looking over my shoulder. No guess needed to know who she was staring at. Then she snapped back in the moment and had a killer look on her face.

"Fine then, vests don't count." Kim took a beer from a member and threw it down, and the girls cheered in agreement. Kim stumbled towards them. "No rings, no sunglasses, or belts. Clothes only."

Darren just laughed and nodded his head. "It's on, Kim."

Ok, maybe I was confident, but I wasn't *that* confident.

"You can break, too." Kim smiled and my eyes widened slightly. I gripped her arm and dragged her backwards.

"You better be bloody drunk, Kim." I whisper-yelled at her.

"Four shots baby girl, and you are all mine." Collins rounded the table and winked at me.

I gave him a confident smile, but I was starting to doubt our plan, especially because Kim just let them break!

My eyes went from Collins to Reaper. He was furious. One look at him and I could tell. *Time to feel how I feel, Reaper.*

The game had brought out every biker, even the ones that were busy feeling up the girls down the back. The other pool tables were empty now, all players more interested in this game. The boys were wanting a show. The ones that had always wanted to see us naked were now here, hoping.

Hope all you want, fellas.

Kim and I had already kicked off our sandals. We weren't wearing jewelry and we were ready for the game.

Collins gave me a wink and then broke. Everyone was watching as the balls went around the table. Collins let out a deep rumble of laughter as one ball went into the pocket. Darren whacked Kim on the butt, and all the other lot cheered.

Kim and I looked at each other.

The crowd started to chant. Kim and I had to hold up our end of the deal.

"Bras." I told her over the chanting.

Kim nodded her head and did the same as me. I unclicked my bra under my tank top and then threaded my arms through. My eyes flickered to Reaper's just in time to see him crumpling up his beer can while glaring at me.

As if saying, *don't fucking dare.*

I couldn't help but smile at him as I dropped my bra on the ground.

Kim handed me the cigarette. "Ok, your shot Abby."

I sucked on the cigarette lightly and handed it back to her. "So we are stripes, right?"

She nodded her head.

"What's that, Abby, don't know your pool that well?" Darren laughed at me.

"You won't be laughing when you're butt naked." I sneered at him. "Let's see how well that back tattoo was done."

"I'm interested if you have any tattoos, Abby. On that fine body." Collins leaned back and watched me bend over the table. I giggled at his obviousness.

"Where the fuck is Roach?"

Reaper's voice caught my attention.

I looked over at him smugly. "Asleep." I answered his question and because I knew I was going to miss anyway. I didn't even have a look at the balls, taking my shot while keeping my eyes locked with his. I knew I had missed by Reaper's reaction.

"Nice try, Abby." Collins patted me on the shoulder. "Now let's see what you look like topless."

"I think you are counting your chickens before they hatch, Collins."

"Only three pieces of clothing on your body, sweetheat." Collins threw an arm around my shoulders and pulled me into his side. "But there will be nothing when we are finished with you."

I shrugged his arm off me just as Darren sunk a ball.

I looked at Kim. Ok, maybe we were in trouble.

Collins laughed "Ok, how you getting out of this one, Abby?"

"Undies," Kim said and started to work her way out of hers.

"Maybe this wasn't the brightest idea we have had." I shook my head at her while getting one leg out and then pushing them down my right leg.

Kim swiped another beer and took the cue off me. "Hope you boys are ready to get naked." She stumbled to the table, spilling her beer on the velvet.

There was something that not a lot of people knew about Kim. I don't think even Trigger knew. She was a master of pool, but only when she was drunk. Brad knew because we had once played this trick on him.

"Don't miss, Kim." Darren taunted her.

"Never," she said, taking her eyes off the ball and sinking one. "Start showing us skin, boys."

"Come on, Collins. Strip." I took his beer off him.

He gave me an amused look but nodded his head, taking his shirt off. God, the boy was fit.

"Don't get so happy, Abby. I'm only one shot away from seeing what's under those tiny clothes of yours."

Kim had another shot, and all the girls in the room cheered when she sank another.

"Yeah, but in order for that to happen, Kim would have to miss." I laughed as I watched him take off his pants.

While all the men in the room were groaning. Collins just smirked at me, pointing a finger.

"You set me up."

"Me? Never." I shook my head. Do I do it? Had I pushed the point home to Reaper enough? Or did he need to be shown I could have anyone I wanted? He wasn't the only one with options. I glanced at him, and my eyes hardened as I saw his lips locked with the brunette's. While he was kissing her, his eyes were on mine. Fuck it. "After all Collins, I need to know what I'm working with later."

Kim lined up another ball. While her and Darren were discussing all the ways he was going to get her back for this, Kim just shrugged her shoulders and told him she would still be asleep when he rode out later, so he was all talk.

I noticed Trigger's expression darken when Darren said they still had hours before that happened.

"Ok, no pressure or anything, but if you don't sink this, we are in trouble," I whispered in her ear and she shooed me away.

As if it was easy, Kim sank a ball down the other end of the table, and all the men in the room groaned with disgust.

I turned to Collins, smiling. "So are you a man of your word?"

"Fucking oath." Collins handed me his beer and pulled down his boxers. It must have been at the same time as Darren.

"WHY ARE THERE NAKED MEN IN MY BAR!?"

Dad had appeared for the end of the show, looking like his furious self. It would have to be after three in the morning. Why he had surfaced, I didn't know.

"Roach." Collins quickly pulled his boxers up.

"We were just playing strip pool." I answered for Dad.

His eyes narrowed on me. "Was Kim drunk?"

"Not was, Dad. Am." Kim picked up her undies, still wobbly on her feet.

Dad pinched the bridge of his nose and attempted to calm himself down. "Bed now. The two of you."

"Whatever you say, Dad." I picked up my undies as well.

"*Dad.* Roach is your father?" Collins looked at me as if I was completely insane.

"Yeah. Night, Collins. Have a safe trip home." I shot him a wink, and Kim was giving Darren a good night kiss when I looked back at Reaper. Had I made my point?

"Girls, bed!"

Kim grabbed my arm, giggling, and for the first time in days she was actually having a good time and not crying over Trigger. Sure, she was so drunk she could barely stand, but she was happy, at least for the night.

The crowd had broken up and the boys were either heading to bed too or ready to hit the cards again.

I hoped Reaper had gotten the message. If he could fool around, so could I. And I hoped it hurt him, as much as it hurt me to watch.

***

"You girls need to get a life." Dad sat across from us with a serious expression on his face. It was middle of the afternoon and all three of us were still hung over.

"Get a life!?" My mouth dropped open. He could not be serious right now, and where had it come from!?

"I'm not working." Kim crossed her arms stubbornly. "I won't be some chick on a register." Screwing her nose up, she clicked her tongue. "Why do we have to anyway?"

I couldn't believe my own father had told me to get a life. Seriously, my dad, telling me to get a life! He hadn't meant it in a nasty manner. I knew that.

"Still don't see how getting a job equals to getting a life," I grumbled, adding to Kim's argument. I wasn't keen on the idea of getting a job.

"Can't have you girls just hanging around here all day," he grunted, "being on my back twenty-four seven. If you two are moving back, you need to get jobs. Support yourselves."

I opened my mouth, and he pointed a finger at me.

"Working the bar doesn't count."

Well, there goes my only option. I folded my arms and swung back in the chair.

"So you just want us out of your way?" Kim leaned forward in her seat. I knew that face. It meant her twisted riddled mind was coming up with a plan.

And if I knew Kim, it would be better than a fucking nine to five job.

He grunted with a short head nod while reaching for his freshly poured whiskey.

"What about if Abby and I headed to university instead, would you support us then?"

I nearly choked on my own breath.

"Kim," I growled. She better shut those fat lips before she locks us into university.

But before I could say anything. Dad gave Kim the nod of approval, sealing the deal.

Chapter 36

Abby

The Shields. When it came down to it, they were one terrifying family. All four brothers were sworn members, though one brother died a year back. But what was more terrifying was their sister. Amber Shield.

When it came down to it, she was intimidating. It wasn't just her reputation and a sharp tongue, it was her beauty. Those haunting eyes, beautiful figure, and styled hair.

How had she managed to get the complete darn package?

Her boyfriend and President, Jackson, was nearly as scary as Reaper. He also had a reputation that would scare many men and women from him. I swore he had done the most time, and he was still so young.

Whatever the reason for their visit, Dad didn't want us here.

"They've been in there for two hours," Kim whispered, looking over her shoulder at the closed doors.

"Wonder why they are here." I leaned on the bar, staring at the closed door as well.

"You shouldn't care." Kim's words were clipped. "I just want them to hurry the hell up so I can finish my argument with Dad."

I rolled my eyes. That was so Kim.

"The whole point of the argument was he wanted us to leave before they got here. So I think it is fair to say that fight is over, Kim."

She huffed "Still. He can't just keep throwing us out every time he feels like it." By the tone of her voice, she was still going to argue with him anyway.

"Whatever Kim," I sighed, "just don't bring me into it."

"Wonder if they are staying here." Kim's eyes shot around the room, and she leaned in closer to me. "Have you noticed how light we are on guys since they got here?"

She did have a point. The open living was feeling even bigger than normal because there weren't bulky bikers taking up space.

My eyes slowly drifted over to Reaper and Cameron, who were at the end of the bar. They had just come back in after doing 'men's stuff,' as Cameron told us.

Trigger had taken off in a fit of rage as soon as Dad went in the boardroom. Of course, Kim and him were able to share a few more threats before he stormed out.

God, those two were getting unbearable. It was crystal clear to everyone else what the real problem was between them. Neither of them would admit to liking the other.

"I'm going to take a piss. Come get me if he comes out." Kim jumped off the bar stool. She had been acting like a cat waiting for the mouse to come out for the last two hours.

I suddenly decided I was thirsty, and it just so happened to coincide with when Reaper went around the bar. Cameron had slopped off in the direction of the kitchen, which left Kade and me alone.

"Want to pour me one while you're at it?" I leaned on the bar. I couldn't lie and say I wasn't feeling the sexual pull he had on me. The man just did weird things to my hormones.

His eyes were emotionless when they locked with mine.

"Thought you weren't talking to me."

"Never said that." I sipped my beer. "You were the one with the problem, if I remember correctly."

He scoffed but kept his words unspoken.

"Do you know what that is all about?" I nodded my head to the boardroom.

"So that's why you're talking to me again." His lips twitched with a small smirk.

I gave him a pointed look. "I was always talking to you."

"You should get your sister and take off for a bit." He finished his beer. "Before your old man comes out."

"I don't see why it is such a big deal they are here. It isn't like I haven't met the Shield boys or Jackson before."

"It's not them you should be worried about."

I didn't need his stupid warning. I knew to stay out of Amber's way.

An awkward silence slowly fell between us. I didn't know what to talk to him about. The man I had made love with the other night. It was easygoing and I usually felt able to speak freely with him.

But when we are out here, in the real world, he had such a hardened exterior that it left me baffled on how to talk to him.

"Kade, I mean… Reaper. Can I ask you something?" My words tumbled over each other, causing my cheeks to flush.

His unbiased expression didn't waver. "What?" His eyebrows arched with what I guessed was interest when I didn't speak straight away.

I was still trying to word it in a way that didn't make me sound like a whining teenage girl.

Taking a deep breath, I locked my eyes with him, mustering some fake confidence.

"What are we?" I finally said. Sure it was soft, and he might have struggled to hear it, but I did say it.

When his mouth opened, my hopes skyrocketed. Finally, I was going to get a label to put on us. If we were in a relationship, that meant we needed boundaries. It also meant I was his.

My luck being as it was, of course, this would be the very moment the boardroom doors opened, which killed the conversation completely.

I couldn't stop the frustration from showing on my face, and I turned on my stool.

She didn't look any less threatening, and the boys didn't look any more thrilled to be here.

"Do you want me to clean out some of the rooms, Dad?" I spoke loudly across the room. Seeing as they had killed my conversation, I might as well kill their silent whispering.

Dad turned sharply. He seemed taken back by me being here. Had he expected us to take off?

Maybe I should have taken Reaper's warning.

When Dad's eyes didn't glow red, I assumed I was in the clear. Though I was making sure I was out of here when Kim came back. I wouldn't be wearing her mess.

"Amber, you staying?" Dad grunted in a kind type of way, causing my eyes to widen for a second.

Was Dad scared of her too?

She was looking directly up at Jackson. What were the chances of two of the most feared criminals in our society dating one another? Together, they created a ruthless and powerful couple.

"Suppose we'll stay." Amber's eyes flickered over to me. Her head tilted to one side as she silently judged me.

"Well um, I'm going to go get the room ready." I slid off the bar stool.

"And I'll go help. What was your name?" Amber's eyes were locked on me and even though she was staring at me; I didn't think it was possible that she would want to speak to me.

"Abby. My name's Abby." I felt like a complete retard saying my name twice, but it had already slipped out before I could stop it.

"I'm going to help Abby get our rooms ready." She seemed set on the idea.

"Since when did you get rooms ready?" Cole asked dryly.

"Since now," Amber said sharply while giving him a pointed expression.

I swallowed sharply as nerves consumed me.

Well, this was going to be interesting.

Chapter 37

Abby

Just keep cool Abby, don't freak out. I tumbled through the cupboard, pulling out a stack of sheets. I could feel her eyes on me. Why had she wanted to come with me? Why wouldn't she just stay with her brothers?

"Need a hand?" Amber's cool voice spoke behind me.

I turned around, shaking my head. "No, it's fine."

Shrugging her shoulders, she began to rip the old sheets off.

"So what happened to your wrist?" She scrunched her nose up, looking at the pillows, and then dropped them on the ground. "Sports injury or what?"

At least something good was coming out of having a broken wrist. Suppose it was a great conversation starter.

"No actually, an outta town member was staying here and yeah, he broke it."

"On purpose?" Her eyebrows arched.

"Yep."

"Did you break his neck?" By her tone, I could tell she wasn't joking.

"Um, no."

"Well did you at least land a good punch?"

"No."

She scoffed and shook her head. "Well, I'm sure Reaper didn't let him get away unharmed."

My blood was flooded with cold ice. "Why would you say that?" I stopped what I was doing and looked her directly in the eye. "Do you know Reaper?"

Her face was expressionless until a smirk graced her lips and turned into a knowing smile.

"Does Roach know you two are together?"

I scoffed loudly. "Sure, because that would make Dad's day." I threw the top sheet across the bed, and it floated down. "Doesn't matter anyway, we aren't together."

"You don't have to lie to me." Her tone was free from judgment. Was it possible that I saw Amber's softer side?

"I'm not lying."

"Fine, let me rephrase that. I don't like being lied to." Her voice hardened, and her haunting eyes locked with mine. "So how about you try that again, though this time look me in the eye."

How did she make a simple thing like eye contract terrifying?

"We aren't a couple. He told me he loved me, and we kind of have this," I frowned, feeling my anguish towards him rise. "Well, I don't know what it is. A pull to each other, I guess."

She sighed while slipping her arms out of her leather jacket and placing it on the freshly made bed.

"You know when I first met Jackson, I didn't even know who he truly was." Her eyes danced with the memory, and I nervously sat next to her on the bed.

"How could that be? You both belong to the same club."

"I wasn't brought up in the club."

"But you have such strong ties to it." I looked at her, puzzled. How could she live and breath this way of living if she wasn't born into it? You didn't just adopt this lifestyle; you were *born* into it.

"I was in a different crowd, a gang actually. Though to me, it felt like family." She shook her head. "I suppose I was stupid and young and thought that was what it felt like to have a family. My dad," Her tone weakened, and she swallowed sharply. "My dad was a busy man."

"Surely not too busy to notice what a great daughter he had."

Shrugging her shoulders "I don't know, but I wasn't bringing this up to talk about dad or the gang. I'm bringing it up because I know what it is like to have a connection with someone early in life. Hell, I met Jax in high school." A full smile took her lips, and she turned her head to look at me. "Do you love Reaper?"

Deep deep down, I knew what my answer was. Still, I had never voiced it.

"I don't really know what love is," I whispered.

"There are different types of love. But love isn't something you find, or know. Love is the reaction that consumes you when you're with your other half. It is blinding, it is selfless. I would die for Jackson because the pain of losing him would surely rip apart my heart."

"Is love really that intense?"

Shrugging her shoulders, she gave me an honest smile. "I don't know. All I do know is if you want to really be by Reaper's side, you need it to be that strong to survive."

"What if his love for me isn't as strong as the love I have for him?"

"I'll tell you something, but you can't repeat it," I could hear the importance and nodded my head.

"Reaper is ruthless, heartless, and I've seen him do things that no man should be capable of. Yet, he has only been driven to that point because of his respect for the brotherhood. I don't know if he loves. Hell, I questioned if the man had a heart once. But if he does truly love you, he will stop at nothing until you're his."

I felt terrified and excited all at once. How was it possible for her words to make me want to be closer to him than ever before but yet terrified me to the point I was ready to run?

"He's kind. He does have a softer side," I mumbled. "And I can handle myself. I know my broken wrist doesn't give me much credit, but I would never let anyone rule me."

"Of course not. It's not in our blood." She winked, standing up. What did she mean our blood?

"Can I ask you something, Amber?"

"Sure, why not? It's not like I can be anymore softer."

"How did you handle the other women? Do you just turn a blind eye?" I knew what club life meant. I knew that they would always be around. That temptation for him. I wasn't stupid; I had seen how wives and marriages were looked upon in this type of life.

Hell, it was like the biker had a wife and mistresses, just like Kings once did.

"Jackson slept with another woman," she spluttered out, causing me to just stare at her. What the hell do I say to that?

"I um... well.... umm."

"You can stop." She wiped away the awkwardness. "I'm only telling you this because all couples go through rough periods. But at the end of the day, if he loves you and you love him, you'll work it out."

I nodded my head. "Life just keeps throwing me in his way."

"Maybe life keeps placing you in his path because clearly he is meant to be sharing that path with you."

I had never looked at it like that.

Chapter 38

Abby

There are some decisions that make themselves; then there are others that require more thought. Then, of course, there were those decisions that were impossible to make.

Like right now. As I stared across the common room from behind the bar, cleaning glasses, leaning back on the chair, smoke in one hand, beer in the other was the man that was slowly driving me crazy.

After that conversation with Amber, it had caused me to rethink what I was doing with Reaper. I knew he would never change. He would always be that scarred, scary, and loyal guy to the club.

I glanced over at Amber, who was whispering in Jax's ear. Jax might be sitting around a table full of blokes, but all his attention was on Amber as she spoke to him.

If that was love, then fuck knows what Reaper and I have.

"You staying for the fireworks?"

My eyes bounced up and locked with Brad's. He was only wearing his leather vest, displaying his tattoos and scars. It seemed to be the outfit of choice tonight, with most of the other guys also shredding their top layers off. Guess it was a hot night.

"Don't know." I began to put the clean glasses away. "Don't see why Dad is making a big deal out of the Shields being here anyway."

"Isn't just the Shields, the North Landers and Westies are here, too." He pulled up a stool and sat down. "Wanna get it off your chest, darlin'?"

My head snapped to look at him. "Just because some girls are using the heat as an excuse to strip doesn't mean I am." Did he not know me better than that?

He smirked. "Was talking about whatever was on your mind."

Oh. Well, that's awkward.

"Got nothing to say."

"Amber being here doesn't change anything between you and your old man, right?"

I frowned. "Of course I know that."

"Then why is your sister getting high out the back and you're here scrubbing glasses that usually just get thrown out anyway?"

"Why would there be a correlation at all between them?"

We were our own people, or did people just forget that ALL THE TIME! We are twins for fuck's sake, not the same person!

He shrugged his shoulders. "Just thought you two were taking it hard finding out about Amber being your half sister."

I blinked. I blinked again, then my fingers curled into fists.

"My what?!" I hissed across the bar at him.

He gulped. "Fuck, you didn't know."

"Clearly." I snapped, storming off around the bar and heading for my dad's bedroom.

I could bet he was in there smoking a joint and getting laid. He only ever cared about himself. Everything was making sense now. Why he was so mad when we were here. Why he didn't want us to meet her.

I didn't knock on his bedroom door, I just twisted the doorknob and walked in.

The whore squealed and tumbled off the bed while Dad cursed.

"ABBY!" he roared when he realized who it was.

"You're a LIAR!" I screamed in his face, not even caring that he only had a sheet wrapped around him. "WERE you EVER going to tell me that I had half sister? Hell, what about the boys, how many children have you fathered?!"

"YOU'RE OUT OF LINE, GIRL!"

"DID MOM KNOW THAT YOU WERE SLEEPING

AROUND BEHIND HER BACK?!"

"BACK DOWN ABBY, YOU'RE TALKING SHIT ABOUT SHIT YOU KNOW NOTHING ABOUT!"

Angry tears were spilling down my cheeks, which I was wiping away just as they dropped.

"HOW COULD YOU LIE TO US ABOUT THIS?"

"I DIDNT!"

"FUCK YOU." I spat in his face and spun on my heel. He was a lying bastard just like every other biker outlaw.

"ABBY!"

I was at the bottom of the stairs and bolting through the crowded common room when he grabbed my arm, nearly ripping it out of its socket.

His face was still red with rage, but he had somehow found a moment to put a pair of pants on.

"LET GO OF ME!" I roared at him, not even caring that the filled common room had quieted.

Why would they want to talk when they could listen and watch the president yell at his daughter.?

"You aren't leaving till we talk this through."

My mind was swirling with questions and anger, but I couldn't have this conversation with him because I didn't want to hear his excuses.

I stepped in closer, glaring up at him. "Why would I want to hear anything that came out of your mouth when I know that while my mother was dying, you were off making another family. You're a pig. A cold-hearted arsehole!"

I didn't see it coming, but I felt it when the back of his hand whipped across my cheek at the same time he let go of me.

"I don't want to see you again." Pure boiling red rage was behind his words, and with fresh tears filling my eyelids, I turned and sprinted out of there.

Chapter 39

Reaper

He didn't have to say it. He didn't even need to say he regretted it. Because as soon as his hand whipped across Abby's cheek, the impact of his reaction hit him immediately.

All eyes were on him, which meant everyone could see Abby being slapped down by her father; even all the guests saw it. What the fuck was the man thinking!?

My first instinct was to storm over there and block the slap for her, but I thought her old man would have kept a lid on it. I was wrong.

Kim, who was flirting with some bloke I hadn't seen before at the pool table, had dropped to her feet and bolted out after her sister.

Now there was just an eerie coating in the air. Roach stood at the same spot, breathing heavily, while nearly all the women glared at him and half the bikers were even giving him a dirty look.

Bottom line was you aren't meant to hit women. Though the girls do tend to get roughed up sometimes by their parents. But when it came to Abby, Abby was untouchable.

No one should ever hit her.

Especially because she was mine.

Downing the rest of my beer and kicking back the chair I had been sitting on, I wasn't letting Roach get away with this.

"Take a seat, Reaper,"Amber's enraged eyes locked with mine, "You will only make things worse. Getting into a punch on with her old man will only ruin any chance you two have together."

Amber spoke calmly, but her eyes were burning with a boiling rage. I was surprised she could keep the clear anger she had inside her out of her voice.

"Why do you care?" I kept my tone in check, knowing Jax's eyes were on me, along with her brothers.

"Because I'm guessing it was me who caused that fight." She planted her hands on her hips. "And I don't let others fight my battles."

"He hit her."

"He slapped her. Which is even more demeaning, which is why he won't get away with it."

The deadliness in her words would send terror down a normal person's spine.

"So you want to go head to head with Roach then? Cause no offense Amber, you've got more bark than bite. At least I'll get some punches in."

"When will you ever learn," she took a step closer to me, rising to her tippy toes and whispering in my ear, "Words burn and slice deeper than any physical punch."

Her soulless eyes met mine once more before she spun on her heel and headed in the direction Roach had stormed off in.

Fine. If she wanted to take on the old man, she could. I was going to find Abby. My stomach twisted, remembering the pain in her eyes. Amber better bloody well give Roach what he deserves.

But right now, I needed to focus on finding Abby before she fled town and I never saw her again.

Chapter 40

Abby

I hadn't thought it through; I just ran and kept going. I didn't stop when I heard Kim's screaming voice behind me. I ducked around the corner and hid in a bush when I heard the roar of a familiar motorcycle.

I didn't want to be dragged back there. I never wanted to see Dad again. I cupped my cheek and flinched at the touch.

He hadn't gone easy on the slap; he had put his full force behind it.

After running for what felt like hours, I stumbled to a stop and slumped down at the bottom of a driveway.

I had nowhere to go.

I had no money.

I had no car.

I had only what I was wearing, and I wasn't dressed for this chilly night.

I didn't even have anyone to call, even if I did have my phone on me.

The clouds thundered above and the rain wasn't far away. Which only confirmed to me that tonight still could get worse.

Why had he kept Amber a secret for so long? Did that mean the boys were my step-brothers? I gagged at the thought of how many times I had admired Troy and Tyler with their tops off.

The crying was slowing to a small stream now, but it was my cheek that really hurt.

"Excuse me, but you're blocking my way," a voice said from behind me. I wasn't in the mood to be nice.

"Then walk around," I snapped back.

"Sure, if you want me to drive over you."

Pushing myself up from the ground, I let out a long sigh. "Think you would be doing me a favor if you did."

He adjusted his suit jacket while his eyes examined me in a manner I hadn't experienced before. His chiseled features and combed back black hair told me this man had money, and I noted the Bentley parked behind him.

He swallowed sharply and took a step towards me, his eyes still examining mine. "I'm assuming by the red cheek and tears you have had a break up with someone."

I scoffed loudly. "You would be half right, half wrong. But what does it matter anyway? You're just a stranger, and I was just a girl standing in your way." I took a noticeable side step out of his driveway. "Night," I muttered, turning my back to him and beginning to walk in the opposite direction of the clubhouse.

I really needed sleep. Not to mention a plan. I groaned internally. I really needed Kim. She knew how to handle these situations so much better than I.

A car pulled up beside me, window winding down. "Do you want a lift?"

"My parents always told me not to get in the car with strangers." Actually, that was a lie; Dad always said get in then pull the knife and rob them. Being a minor, you don't get charged as harshly.

Never got to do it, though.

"My name's Cody Marks, as in Mark Flets. My favorite color is blue, and I have a dog called Cobber." He gave me a challenging smirk, "Now you know more about me than most of the people I see every day."

Chewing my bottom lip, I came to a stop and leaned over into the car.

"I'm not a hooker."

"I wasn't asking for an hourly rate."

"I don't have money to give you for fuel."

"Did you miss the part where I said I was Cody Marks?"

Of course I knew who Cody Marks was, but I found it hard to believe he was offering me a lift.

"The whole problem with you giving me a lift is I don't know where I am going."

He leaned over closer to me "Then it doesn't really matter where you end up, does it?"

He had a point, and by that challenging, charming grin, he knew he had the upper hand.

"Fine. But if your hand comes over to my side of the car, I'm cutting it off."

He laughed, popping the locks and letting me in.

I wasn't sure if I was making a bad decision or not, but when I look back at my track record…

Chapter 41

Abby

Whether it was the heat from the Jacuzzi or the expensive cider I was drinking, I was sure that this was what heaven was like.

"Chocolate strawberries be alright?" Cody stepped off the porch. His smirk teased me, "I guess you will just have to suck the chocolate off."

I ran my tongue across my bottom lip and tilted my head slightly, "Is that so?"

He shrugged his shoulders while he stalked over to me, giving me a very long and nice view of his chiseled muscles.

"Who knew you were so toned under that jumper earlier?" When I first met him, all I took in was his frustrated glare, which was fair enough because I was blocking his driveway.

"Who thought that the girl crying at the end of my driveway blocking me from a boring meeting would be the highlight of my night?" He poured me another cider, and my hand shot out through the bubbles to take it.

"And here I was thinking I was going to spend the night in a gutter drinking some bad-tasting scotch."

It did turn out Cody Marks wasn't a serial killer or anything that his reputation was.

Sure, he had the bad boy image down pat. Tattoos, scars, upper body strength and that cocky grin, which just oozed bad boy.

So like the young hormonal, angry teenager I was, things continued to snowball until I was in my underwear in his jacuzzi.

Screw the tattooed, controlling bikers. What was wrong with an old school gangsta?

"You're thinking too much, darling." He dropped to his knees in front of me, his eyes locked on mine. "Wanna tell me who made that beautiful cheek of yours bruised?"

It was so twisted I wasn't even sure if I had deserved it or not. God, I must look like a mess to Cody; one broken wrist and a bruised face.

"Do you know that saying," I swam to his corner, pulling myself up to the curb. "If you play with fire, you get burnt?"

He scoffed. "Everyone knows that one."

"Well, what do you do when you are born the flame, and everyone that gets close gets hurt. Or worse, they push me away before they burn."

"You got a broken heart, sweetie." He lightly stroked my cheek. "I can hurt them for you. You know *who I am,* don't you?"

I knew who he was.

I knew what he was capable of.

He just didn't realize that the Reaper already had my heart in his clenched fist.

I brought my wet hand through his hair, pulling his head down to me until my lips were inches from his.

"I don't need protection, and I don't need a lover." My words were sweet and seductive, and I could see the sexual pleasure cross his face.

"Then what can I do for you?"

The one thing I had wanted someone to do all day

I reached around my back, unclipping my bra. "Take my mind off everything." And when he slipped into the Jacuzzi, I knew there was only one name that was going to be on my mind in a few minutes, and that wasn't Kade's.

My legs wrapped around him as we floated in the middle of the Jacuzzi.

"I have one more request," I whispered in his ear while my fingers ran up his back. "Get me to scream your name, and only yours."

His eyes had darkened with the challenge before he drove

forward, taking my lips.

Chapter 42

Abby

I strongly believe that there is someone up in that darn screen using my life as a source of entertainment. I sank deeper under the bubbles.

Things had been heating up between Cody and I, and then what happened? Only the most unthinkable.

My dad showed up!

Here!

Out of all the fucking places in the world, he turns up here at this time of night!

Cody got out as soon as he noticed who it was, and they had moved around to the back porch. I still wasn't sure if I should continue to hide in the jacuzzi or if I should make a run for my clothes and hightail it out of here.

I was creeping to the edge when their conversation started to get louder. Shit. They were coming this way. I turned my back and pulled as many bubbles around me as possible.

"I'm telling ya Marks, shit won't be clear next time." Dad's voice was hard and so easy for me to pick out. "I don't take shit like this."

"Neither do I, which is why we have the problem with your shipment," Cody said back with just as much ice in his voice.

My eyes widened. Cody Marks wasn't scared of Roach. I learned something new every day.

"Your drugs drying up is one thing, but I hear you got problems with your men, Roach. If that shit is impacting our business, you know what needs to be cleaned up."

So this was how business went down. Talk about ruthless and cold-hearted. I knew Dad dealt with that side of things; it wasn't all about riding loud bikes. But to hear it so bluntly and loud… it was disturbing.

"You got a pair of ears in that tub, Marks." Dad's voice hardened, and I immediately went stiff. He knew I was here, or at least he knew a blonde was in here.

"Don't worry about it Roach, I got it handled. Pity, though, seems like a nice kid."

My blood ran cold, and suddenly I didn't care if Dad saw me half naked or not.

I jumped out of that hot tub as if it was burning me and blotted with a towel.

"Great, shit's gonna get messy now, it's easier just to drain the hot tub after you kill them," Cody said with a boredom in his voice.

"Dad." I swallowed sharply, pushing my wet hair to the back. He seemed to still be in shock, which was fair enough. How many times do you see your daughter drop out of a man's pool after asking that girl to be killed?

The bullet in that gun was for me.

"What the fuck are you doing here, Abby?" Dad's moment of shock had gone, and he was in full-on rage mode now. Great, another reason for him to fight with me about. I guess at least I wasn't going to be shot in the head.

"Your daughter!" Cody looked outraged. "You fucking with me?"

"No, I'm not, but I bet you were about to," Dad snarled and reached into his vest.

"Dad, nothing happened, trust me. You stopped it, and I just want to go home, so please just take me home?"

Only hours ago I couldn't get farther away from the clubhouse, and now I was begging to go back.

I stopped in front of Dad, rising on my toes, making eye contact with him. "I'm sorry. I fucked up. Don't kill him. Take me home, please."

There was a calm voice that Kim and I used on Dad when shit got seriously fucked up, and right now stopping Dad from killing this guy counted as a serious situation.

"Fine, get your clothes." His eyes scorched mine for a moment as I scrambled off to find the pieces of my clothes.

Why couldn't I just have a normal teenage life? You know, the one where you spent your night on Facebook stalking the guy you were never going to talk to or search "weheartit."

But no.

I had to be a biker bitch who is creating drama when I'm not getting into drama.

I had a strong feeling that the lecture I was getting off Dad for this one was going to be a long one.

Chapter 43

Abby

"Cody Marks!" Kim jumped on my bed, waking me up. "I just don't believe it. I've been trying to get on that for years." She shrugged her shoulders. "Maybe it was the whole cast thing that did it for him."

"Shut up, Kim," I groaned while trying to push her off the bed with my feet. I failed miserably.

"Have to ask," she sniggered, "did you wrap the cast in plastic first?" She broke out into uncontrollable laughter.

Why did the thought of my broken arm and sex in a hot tub amuse her so much? The woman was insane!

"Piss off, Kim!"

"Bubbles, alcohol, no clothes, and a plastic bag!" she stuttered out while rolling around on the end of my bed, laughing her head off.

"If you don't get out, my cast is going to give you a facelift."

"Have to ask." She positioned herself with one elbow, "will there be a plastic bag involved."

I threw a pillow at her.

For someone who wasn't a morning person, she really was laying it on thick this morning!

"How do you know anyway?" I snapped, pulling myself up into a sitting position.

I hadn't seen her this morning or last night when I did the walk of shame back into the clubhouse followed by a furious father.

So how on earth does she know?

"Dad told me."

"Liar."

"Fine, I overheard it."

"Overheard him telling it to who?"

A satisfied smile bloomed into a full-blown grin. "Reaper."

I groaned instantly, falling back into the pillows and putting one over my face.

This just had to happen, didn't it? Now Kade is going to think I'm over him or something or worse, he will do something stupid and start screwing his way through the club meat.

"I have to find him." I threw the blankets back.

Kim pushed the blankets away from her. "Who are you going to find?"

"Reaper, of course!"

Was she that thick? I had just tightened my jeans button when she got off the bed.

"Well, if you are going to go tell him it was a big mistake and you were hurting or some other bullshit like that, you should know this." She stood, hands on hips, blocking my bedroom door. "Men have two emotions: love and hate. They either love something to death or they hate something till it's dead. Reaper cares for you, Abby, and I don't think you fully understand what the power of that love can do to a man."

"Reaper doesn't love me; he loves the idea of having a woman. Which is why I'm going to go tell him we are finished. Completely and utterly finished."

She tilted her head to the side, examining me before stepping out of my way.

"You were never a good liar, Abby," Kim said before letting the door swing open.

I wasn't lying.

It was over with Reaper.

It had to be.

I swallowed sharply while marching down the hallway. I would not let any man tell me what I can and can't do.

***

The one day that I actually want him to be around, he isn't. That was just my luck. I groaned to myself, leaving the empty boardroom, which was the last place I could think of where he might be. It turned out that that decision was a terrible one because guess who I walked into on my way out?

Roach.

To say I was avoiding him was an understatement.

"Abby." His tone was softer and perhaps gentler. "Been waiting for you to poke your head out of your room."

"What, couldn't come to me?" I glared down at my sandals.

"Didn't think you would want to see me, darling." He gently cupped the side of my face, bringing my head up to look into his eyes.

The regret boiled within his eyes and his face twisted with guilt.

"I'm sorry darling, I know you can't forgive me for this yet, but I wanted you to know I'm sorry."

Sorry.

Did it even fix it?

Why do people think they can do awful things and then just throw a *sorry at the end of it* like all is forgiven?

I found myself counting my breaths. I didn't want to yell at him, but I wasn't ready to forgive him either.

So I did the next best thing. I deflected.

"Have you seen Reaper?" I asked in an unemotional tone.

He eyebrows arched. "Why?"

"He owes me something?"

"Money?"

"No."

"A ride?"

"No."

"Then what does he owe you?"

"If you must know, answers." I crossed my arms defensively. "So do you know where he is or not?"

Dad let out a big grunt. "Should have expected that," he muttered more to himself before he walked around me and into the boardroom.

I turned sharply, "That didn't answer my question."

"Tell me the question you want to ask him, then I'll tell you where he is."

"Screw it. I'll find him myself."

And I had every intention to until his rough grumpy voice stopped me.

"He's in jail."

"WHAT!" I couldn't believe he had waited that long to tell me! "What the hell for?"

Dad's eyes weren't judging me, but the look within them told me whatever he was thinking about was me. For a split second, his lips twitched into a small smile.

"He laid a few punches on a man, police got called, no big deal. He'll be out by tomorrow."

"No big deal." I stared at him blankly. It sure as hell was a big deal! "I'm going to see him."

"And I didn't expect you not to."

I spun on my heels, striding through the common room and collecting my handbag off the table as I headed out the door.

Reaper knew better than to throw punches, especially at people that weren't part of the brotherhood or underworld.

That told me that the citizen he hit really deserved it.

"ABBY!"

I spun around, seeing Dad following me. "When you get back,

we are talking about last night."

I nodded my head while silently groaning. Suddenly I wasn't in a rush to come back here at all. Maybe I should trade places with Reaper.

Chapter 44

Abby

Bailing him out was one thing, but having to deal with the lecture he gave me on the way home was making me regret it.

Should have let him and his opinions rot in that cell.

"Pull in, would you? I need smokes." Reaper pointed to the closest supermarket.

I could've been a bitch and keep driving but this was me, I was the *nicer* twin after all.

Automatically, the eyes snapped on to us. I followed in Reaper's large, dominating shadow. He was only wearing an old singlet under his leather vest, which was covered in patches.

I smiled as I watched people move out of the man's way. If there was one thing about this town, they knew to avoid the Reaper.

His reputation was that well known to the general public now; that said something.

"Hey, I've seen you around campus." A boy I had never seen before suddenly stood in my way.

"I don't know what you are talking about." I was honest with him and my eyes were back on Reaper as he was at the counter.

"My name's Sebastian." His hand shot out.

"And I still don't know you." I looked at his hand and walked back outside.

A lady walked past me, giving me a look while holding a cross around her neck. What made me more furious was she was my age. If she thought she could openly insult me and get away with it, she was wrong.

I spun on my heel and walked out the automatic doors, catching her slim figure and boyfriend only a few meters ahead of me.

"Oi!" I screamed up at them.

They both turned to look back at me.

"You got the guts to say what you said behind my back, but do you have the guts to say it to my face? Cause this is your chance."

She pursed her lips and took a confronting step forward.

"I said, there is one of Satan's sluts." She crossed her arm, and only now did I notice she was part of a group; a group that was now standing behind her, each glaring at me. *The filthy slut.*

"And she belongs down below," she snarled. She might dress like a lady, but the woman wasn't scared or backing down.

"Funny," I took a confident step closer to her, meeting her glaring eyes. "Because I swore your man said he was putting me in his spank bank."

Her mouth fell open, but her boyfriend went bright red.

"If it helps you for later," I twisted, giving him a seductive smile, "I'm really skilled when it comes to sucking and swallowing."

"Then once you finish daydreaming about her, I'll come and give you a face lift." Reaper's arm wrapped around my stomach, pulling me back into him, declaring I was his.

How much of that had he heard?

"Excuse us," he added before turning us around and heading back towards the truck.

"Wanna tell me what that was about?" he asked while lighting up a cigarette.

"Just living up to their expectations."

He scoffed, handing me the cigarette for a drag. "You're beautiful Abby, you aren't any club whore, so don't let any of them get you down."

I swallowed a thankful smile and climbed into the truck.

How could one nice word from him make up for all the shit stuff he does?

"Been meaning to ask, how's the wrist?" he asked once we were heading up the highway.

I still hated the cast; it was sweaty and ugly. "Still there. Been meaning to ask you," I gave him a quick sideway glance "What got you locked up?"

His expressionless face turned to a heated expression immediately.

"Someone crossed a line, and that is all you need to know."

"I hate that." I snapped, shooting him a sharp glare, "When you block me out like that? Just deflect the question and yet when I do it, you won't stop till I give in."

He winked. "That's just the way it is darlin'."

I pursed my lips. Maybe I wouldn't let it just be that way anymore. I didn't have to tell him everything, or anything really.

Something Kim said earlier rang in my mind. *We can't depend on them.*

She was right, and as of tomorrow, I was doing something about it. I wouldn't spend my life asking questions, getting half answers and dodging bullets. I needed a backup plan for myself.

I needed something outside the club.

I knew now; I needed to talk to Kim.

***

"You and I need to talk." I closed Kim's bedroom door behind me. My sudden invasion startled her, and she snapped her laptop closed.

"Would it kill you to knock?" she snapped.

"Like you ever do!" I jumped on her bed, wriggling my way up to the top. "We have some serious decisions to make."

She gave me a mocking expression. "Since when did I become the smarter twin?"

"We need to get our own source of income because we can't just rely on Dad always being there, and I refuse to get chained to a

252

biker."

"Funny how you see marriage as being chained," Kim pointed out. "I'm already one step ahead of you."

She opened her bedside drawer and pulled out a folder. Suddenly I was nervous and felt nauseated knowing what Kim had signed us up for.

"Guess what, sis," Kim said with a broad smile on her face and the open folder in front of her. "We're going to university!"

Chapter 45

Abby

I stared at her. Then I stared at her a bit longer, then I swung a closed fist, which she narrowly ducked.

"YOU DID WHAT!" I screamed while launching across the bed at her, again narrowly missing her.

"Would you let me explain myself and put your fists down!" She skipped across the room. Any minute now and she was going to be in my grasp.

"THIS EXPLAINS THE BOY AT THE SUPERMARKET!" I exclaimed, pointing a judging finger at her. "He *had* seen me around campus, but he had mistaken *me for you*."

"Boy, what boy?" Her ears pricked up at that.

"His name was Sebastian. Now tell me what the hell you enrolled us in."

"Was it Sebastian Woodbeam?"

"I don't know what his last name was." I snapped. "What is it you enrolled me into?"

Even since I left school, I never planned on heading back.

"Culture studies for you, and I'm finishing off my nursing degree." Her voice suddenly sharpened. "We need to chop off the anchor called a biker man like you said." She crossed her arms. "We need to think long-term, Abby. We can't just be leeching off the club for the rest of our lives. Especially when they are known to like younger women."

I scoffed, "Come on, it isn't like Reaper would just drop me for a younger girl."

She gave me a deadpan expression. "Name one biker who hasn't moved on once their old lady has aged?"

I opened my mouth then shut it.

"Ok, at least we agree on that one."

"I am always thinking one step ahead." She smirked confidently. "So between Sebastian, Reaper, and Marks, you do have some men drama on your hands."

I rolled my eyes. "There is no drama."

"So tell me." She jumped on the bed, crossing her legs. "What are your theories on why the Shields are still here?"

"Don't know and don't care."

"Liar."

"It will be club business; it always is when it comes to these types of things."

There was some loud screaming from downstairs that stole both our attentions. As quickly as it floated to our ears, we both ran to the door and down the stairs following the screaming.

"YOU CAN'T JUST GO SHOOTING PEOPLE UP!" Amber screamed at her brother Troy.

"Fuck off, Amber; you've done enough damage here." Troy filled his guns.

"We need to find out who did this first, brother." Jackson placed a large hand on Troy's shoulder. "If we don't know who did it, we could end up fighting the wrong club."

"I want BLOOD!" Troy roared in Jackson's face. "AND YOU ARE TOO MUCH OF A COWARD WHILE MY SISTER RULES YOUR DICK!"

Tyler was getting involved now, and the three of them were yelling. Then Dad got involved, and Cole.

They were all too busy to notice Amber take the keys off the table and slide out the front door.

I poked Kim and pointed at Amber. Not only was Amber crying, but she was sneaking away from the drama.

Where was she going?

Should we follow?

I took one step down, then Kim grabbed my arm. "This isn't our fight, Abby. Leave it be."

Chapter 46

Abby

The Shields left, but not before doing damage to our charter; and by that I mean they turned my dad into a grumpy beast. Heck, yesterday he snapped at Kim for repainting her room.

I was no fool. I knew my dad had a bad reputation, and that came with a bad temper. But normally we (Kim and I) were shielded from it.

But that wasn't the case since the Shields left abruptly last week.

So right now as Dad was giving me a lengthy lecture about a scratch he found on the car that he just bought me, I was only half listening.

"I said I was sorry, ok, Dad? I can't help it if someone opened their door and hit the side of it while I was in the supermarket." I defended myself while standing up. "Now if you are done yelling at me, can I go before I'm late for my first day of university?"

University plus me still left a sour taste in my mouth.

Dad grunted. "Fine, leave."

He didn't wish me good luck.

He didn't even question why we were going to university.

Like I said, when he wasn't treating us like we didn't exist, he was yelling at us over shit that didn't matter.

Reaper had left last week with the Shields to 'sort' something out. He didn't give me the details, and because he left so quickly, there is still a giant question mark hanging over our heads on what we were.

***

"I still can't believe you talked to me into this." I grumbled, getting out of the car. Kim couldn't wipe the grin off her face.

"Come on, Abby, you know this is the right thing to do." She grabbed my arm, locking her familiar eyes with mine. "We can't lock our future down to being a biker's babe. The money they bring in is dirty, and you and I both know that if they get caught, we will be left high and dry."

When did she become the sharp one?

I still had my eyes locked on her when they widened and flashed over my shoulder. Frowning, I turned to see what caught her attention.

Sebastian.

"Hey," I said as he approached.

I could see why the girls found him handsome. He had this rough, sexy appeal to him.

"Thought you didn't attend university." He stood next to me with half a grin on his face.

"I didn't." I nodded my head at Kim. "She signed us up, so I wasn't lying the other night."

"Twins." His eyes flashed between the two of us. "Talk about double trouble."

"Trust me. She is here for the books." I smirked over at Kim, who was giving me a dirty look.

"Well, you stood me up the other night, so I think it is only fair that I give you the tour of the campus." He ran a hand through his freshly styled hair.

Darn, this boy was hot, and that fact hadn't gone unnoticed by my sister.

"Seeing as we are both new, do you mind if I come?" Kim fluttered her eyelashes and gave him the classic seductive smirk.

That boy was going to be putty in her hand soon.

His eyes locked with mine for a moment, and I swore I saw regret flash across them.

"Sure, why not." He nodded his head and began to lead us into the building.

Kim grabbed my arm and pulled me in close. "Whatever you do, don't fuck up with him. Sebastian is the king of this place. His dad owns a million hotels or something." Her grip tightened on my arm. "Don't get on his bad side, ok?"

"Ok." I ripped my arm from her grasp and hissed under my breath back at her. "You're the one acting like a patient from an insane ward."

So what if Sebastian had money and a good reputation? As far as I was concerned, he hadn't done anything to earn my respect, and I wasn't going to hand it over to him as Kim had.

Chapter 47

Abby

I would admit, there have been numerous occasions when I have wanted to kill my sister, and right now was one of them.

I continued to glare at the bald-headed man as he gave his lecture. If the point of his lecture was to bore us to death, he was succeeding.

"I would love to say it gets better, but it doesn't."

I turned to look behind me, only to see the handsome face of Sebastian. I hadn't even realized he was in this lecture. Actually, now that I recall, I don't remember seeing him again after he gave us a tour.

"I thought you were in the second year?" I questioned him with a hushed tone, not wanting to score the attention of the rest of the hall.

"I am."

"Then why are you here?" Curiosity stirred within me because I knew if I had a choice, I wouldn't be here.

A wide grin captured his lips and charm filled his eyes. "Why do you think?"

Surely he wouldn't be hanging around the back of this lecture hall just on the off chance he would run into me. Would he?

"You're an odd one to figure out, Sebastian," I finally said, turning fully in my seat to look up at him. The only good thing about these halls is they are so large, you never get stuck sitting next to someone.

"Not that hard, babe, if you think about it." He winked and much to my dislike, I let my cheeks blush red.

He moved to the edge of his chair, leaning over closer to me. "So are you finished with this lecture or do you want to continue to play flappy bird?"

If my cheeks weren't red before, they definitely were now.

"Depends." I literally couldn't think of anything else to say.

"Come on, admit it, anything would be better than this."

He had a point, yet it wasn't in my nature to just give in. But when it came to him, I felt unsure. Scooping up my handbag off the floor, I stood up quietly and exited the lecture hall, knowing very well I was being followed.

Chapter 48

Abby

Sebastian had trouble written on his forehead. I knew that, yet I continued walking beside him down the empty halls.

"You don't seem that interested in social science?" He broke the ice between us.

"Can someone be interested in social science?" I gave him a pointed look.

"Point taken."

I slowed to a stop, turning to look at him. "So is there a reason why I should have ditched it and taken a stroll of the hallway with you instead?"

"Always straight to the point."

His charming grin wasn't getting him off the hook.

"Well?"

He took a noticeable step forward, entering my personal space, and surprisingly I didn't mind.

"You don't like waiting, do you?" The smirk in his voice was enough to cause me to smile.

"Waiting for what?" I tilted my head to the side, looking up at him, slowly rising onto my tippy toes.

Then he did something I didn't expect nor did I think he was capable of.

In one flash moment, he gripped each side of my hips, my legs automatically wrapping around him and before I could take a breath, he had my back pressed against the wall.

His mouth captured mine while he carried all of my weight easily. His tongue slid into my mouth. My chest rose quickly as my heart rate skyrocketed when his hand ran under my shirt, still being able to hold me easily with one arm.

The man knew what he was doing. Our long kiss broke for a moment as he trailed kisses down my neck, and I couldn't stop the gasp that escaped my lips.

I was gasping for breath when he gently placed me back down to the ground, but my mind was still high from the dose he just gave me.

"Been wanting to do that since I saw you." He grinned, winked, and just walked off down the hall.

Leaving me standing here, stunned, confused, and really really turned on.

***

"Dinner." Kim knocked and opened my bedroom door. "Dad wants us to come down tonight." She rolled her eyes, and I closed my laptop.

I climbed off my bed, grabbing a jumper and following her out.

"You've been really quiet since we got back from university." It seemed my muteness hadn't gone unnoticed.

My mind was consumed by that stupid kiss and the way he caused such a reaction out of me.

A pair of snapping fingers in my face caused me to come back to the moment.

"Sorry," I grumbled and followed Kim into the dining room. "Just a lot on my mind."

She gave me a 'not buying it' look over her shoulder. "Whatever you say."

I took a seat next to Kim; I hadn't meant to do it on purpose, but when I looked up, I was directly across from Reaper.

Great.

Wasn't hungry anymore.

His eyes were as sharp as razor blades, slicing away the layers I had put up to keep him out.

Kade had a way of getting under my skin. He had a way of changing my mind but most of all, he had a strong pull on my heart.

When it came to him, I just melted.

"How was university, girls?" Dad grunted from the top of the table.

"Just thrilling," Kim replied with attitude and a fake smile.

I just shrugged my shoulders. The only thing that I truly remembered wasn't something I was bringing up at this table.

"Really?" He put his knife down, swallowing a mouthful of food. "Cause I heard one of you broke into office drawers and stole secure test papers and the other was busy playing tongue hockey in the hallway."

He knew.

My eyes flickered to Reaper, and I knew instantly, he knew too.

Crap. Why did I feel bad? We weren't a couple. Suddenly a blanket of guilt wrapped around me.

"I was just making sure the place was up to snuff." She lowered her voice slightly, smirking at me. "Guess Sebastian's charm worked on you."

I wanted to hit her.

Right after I hit myself.

Because she was right, he just wanted me under his thumb, and now he had me.

I dodged every question and finished my plate as quickly as possible. No way was I hanging around to listen to their grumbles and jokes.

What I hadn't counted on was Kade following.

"You going to pretend like it didn't happen?" His voice was raw and tainted with anguish.

I dropped my plate in the sink, turning to look at him. "Depends, are you going to pretend that you aren't sleeping around on a ride out? I remember you clearly telling me sex was nothing more than a need, and you didn't care who gave it to you."

"Don't twist my words, Abby."

"I'm not."

"I told you," his voice lowered, and he made his way closer to me, "I loved you. That fucking means something, doesn't it?"

I slowly nodded my head. "You did say you loved me," I took a steady breath in. "But that doesn't mean you have a claim over me. When you're ready to admit it to the world, I'll be yours. Till then, guess I'm just one of the whores you use."

His hand wrapped around my wrist, "You aren't a whore."

For a moment, there was softness in his eyes.

"Thanks."

His grip loosened and I walked out, leaving Reaper behind me.

We both knew he would never make a relationship with me official. Because that would give him a weakness and if there was one thing The Reaper couldn't have, it was a weakness.

Chapter 49

Abby

"You messing around with that Sebastian boy is only going to bring trouble," Kim spoke smugly while sitting on my bed, watching me get ready.

I scoffed loudly. "And you messing around with Trigger isn't going to bring trouble?" I poked my earring in before grabbing my clutch.

"I can handle Trigger."

"And you're saying I can't handle a common university boy?"

"No." She jumped up off the bed. "I'm saying you won't be able to handle how Reaper reacts to you dating a common university boy."

My lips pressed together. "How he reacts doesn't get to influence this."

She chuckled. "Get a grip, Abby. You wouldn't even be dangling this university meat in front of Reaper's face if you had his full attention."

"Sebastian is not meat!"

"You're right. He's a dead man walking once he gets involved with you."

I huffed loudly and snatched the top she was holding. "Don't you have your own problems to deal with tonight?"

By problems, I meant Trigger. She had made the rookie mistake and stayed home when he didn't go on the run this morning with the rest of the boys.

Which meant he was in charge.

Which meant no Dad around.

Which meant Trigger and Kim had the whole place to

themselves once I step out those gates.

"The prospects are here," Kim snapped.

"Yeah, because they are really allowed inside and all." I rolled my eyes. She was kidding herself. We both knew that her night was heading in one direction, and that was Trigger's bed.

"Reaper didn't go."

I froze on the spot and slowly turned back to look at her.

"Kim, please tell me you are joking?"

Her grin turned into an evil smirk. "Not joking. He stayed back to straighten out the books or something."

"Darn it, Kim! Why are you only mentioning this now?"

"Because I thought it would be funny to see your reaction, and it was clearly worth it."

I groaned immediately. Kim and I couldn't leave the clubhouse freely at night. It was just a protective thing Dad put in place. The only way we got around it was if we were going out with someone else.

But it wasn't like I could go up to Reaper and be like, 'hey, can you let me out the gate so I can go on a date?'

"Guess your night plans just got squashed," Kim smirked at me before leaving the room.

I groaned again. Not only had I just spent an hour getting ready, but now I had to go and suck up to Reaper to get out.

Great. Just great.

The chances of me heading out tonight were zero.

Chapter 50

Abby

I took a sharp breath in, straightened up, and walked into the kitchen where I knew Reaper was.

I was not letting him ruin my night. I would not let him control me. I repeated this over and over in my head until I laid eyes on him, then my mind just went blank.

He sat frozen in one of the kitchen chairs, glass in one hand and smoke in the other, and he was just staring at the bottle in front of him.

Suddenly, if I made it out didn't seem to matter as much.

"Are you ok?" I stood across from him.

His drunk, smoky eyes slowly drifted up in my direction.

"You look nice," his alcoholic tongue said while he refilled his glass.

Had I missed something important that would turn the stone cold Reaper into this mess in front of me?

"Again, I repeat, are you ok?" I attempted to get eye contact with him, but his eyes were glazed over from the liquor. "Kade?" I dipped my head to his level.

His expression was distant, but it was the glaze that covered his eyes that concerned me.

"You're heading out, Miss Harrison, don't let me stop you," he mocked and slid his key to the gate across the table in my direction.

Still, something within me stopped me from reaching out for it. I had the heels on, the short clingy dress, the beautifully curled hair and makeup were done perfectly. I was ready for a night out. Yet my heart wasn't ready to leave Kade sitting like this.

So I pulled out the chair next to him.

"Tell me what happened." I turned in the chair to face him, well, his body at least. His eyes hadn't lifted from the shot glass from when I walked into the room.

"Leave, Abby." He poured his glass. "Leave before my ugliness ruins you."

Ugliness?

What was the man talking about?

He reached for his glass and I was quicker, covering it with my hand.

"Kade, what is wrong? You know there isn't anything I can't handle."

I had heard stories darker than the one he was likely to tell me.

Turning his head to the side, he looked at me, and for a moment, I swore I saw the pain in his eyes.

"You're a good girl, Abby. Go have fun." The corner of his lip twitched up. "Don't let me stop you."

He clearly hadn't realized, or maybe he didn't get it, it wasn't him stopping me; it was me.

I wouldn't let myself leave.

Opening my clutch, I grabbed my phone and sent Sebastian a very respectable cancellation message. When it came to boys like him, me canceling would only turn him on more and make him chase me harder.

Lifting my hand off Kade's glass, I reached across the table, grabbing an empty glass and pouring myself a drink.

"I still remember the first time I met you." I opened up. "How you and those gray eyes pulled me in. I remember clearly how heartbroken I was when I thought you had left me in the motel room. Then when I saw you at Drake's that morning,"

I ran my finger around the edge of the glass while my mind was pulled back to memories that could never be forgotten.

"You've always been there. Sometimes in the shadows, other times in my face, but you've always been there." I gently lifted his head and held it in my hands, making his eyes look into mine. "Now it is my turn to be there for you. There isn't anything you can or could do that would make me turn my back on you. That's what unconditional love is, Kade, and that is the type of love I have for you. So just tell me, what's wrong?"

For a few moments, the glaze lifted from his eyes. "You would understand."

I nodded my head.

"You could justify it for me."

Again, I nodded my head.

"You could give me an excuse out, and I don't deserve that." He gulped down the remaining of his glass. "Maybe that is what's truly fucked up about it."

"Kade, you are being very hard on yourself."

"This unconditional love you have for me," He lifted his head from my hands and turned to face me on his own. "It's the same thing I have for this club."

I swallowed sharply. "I know that."

"So everything I do for it, to keep the brotherhood together, is out of love."

"I suppose."

"So the two men that I just put in the ground was out of love." His eyes hardened, "The fact that I just put a bullet in a man's head that I've known my whole life, that I once faithfully looked up to as a brother, father, leader, is out of love?"

I opened my mouth then closed it because I knew he wasn't finished yet. I could see it boiling up inside him.

"I'm soaked in his blood," he slightly opened his leather vest, displaying the bloody shirt. "and his brother's blood."

I took a steady breath in, finished the alcohol in my glass, and pushed my chair back.

I walked around him and then gestured for him to take my hand.

"Where are we going?" He glanced at my hand then back at me.

"To handle it."

Standing there, I wasn't sure if he was going to take it. He reached for the bottle first and then took my hand, linking our fingers together. I led him away.

**

I turned the taps of my large en-suite shower and then adjusted the temperature. When Dad had the renovations done, he made sure that us girls got the best and largest en-suite. In fact, my en-suite matched the size of my large bedroom and walk-in wardrobe.

But right now the half drunk, barely standing Reaper wasn't taking in the fine tiling and double-headed shower or the extremely impressive spa.

I slipped out of my heels and sighed. Taking the bottle from his hand, I placed it on the basin. It was like he was numb, or he just couldn't give a fuck what happened to him right now.

I slowly removed his leather vest, which was covered with patches showing his commitment to this club. I respectfully folded it and placed it on basin next to the bottle. Then I unclipped his gun holsters, laying them beside the vest.

I unbuckled his belt, then let his bloody jeans fall to the ground. My fingers were coated in thick crimson blood as I lifted his shirt off, then dropped it to the floor.

The bloody clothes now lay in a pile.

Reaper still had his dog chain around his neck and boxers on. I swallowed sharply and lifted my arm. Slowly, I dragged the zip down, freeing me from the dress and leaving me standing in front of him in my strapless bra and see-through panties.

I reached for his hands, intertwining our fingers together while walking backward into the shower.

Right now I didn't care about what had come between us, right now I only cared about this moment, and at this moment he needed me, more than he even knew.

The warm water sprayed across our bodies, and he gently pulled me into him until we were chest to chest.

Our hands separated, and I wrapped my arms around his neck as he lifted me up and guided my legs around his hips.

The steam encased us as our lips were naturally drawn to each other's. The hot water washed away his drunken shadow, and he kissed me with more passion.

I placed my mouth to his ear. "Don't hold back."

I was giving him permission to fuck it out of his system, and he knew that was exactly what I meant by saying *don't hold back*.

Chapter 51

Abby

Some of the best moments in life are ones where the reality has been twisted, and for those few beautiful tainted hours, reality has no place. The past, present, and future don't matter because you're in this black hole, escaping the death grip of reality and all the consequences it brings, and sometimes it only takes a small thing to pull you back to reality.

I was warm.

Warmer than normal, and I kept my eyes closed, enjoying it. My body was bathed in this nice comfortable warmness. Slowly, I opened my eyes, and the heavy tattooed arm wrapped around me answered why I was so warm.

I rolled over onto my back.

Reaper's face was clear of an expression; he looked calm, peaceful. He didn't look anything like the broken mess that he was last night.

Now reality was slowly coming back, but it wasn't because of me. It was because of a buzzing phone.

I slipped out of his grasp and tiptoed to the bathroom. It didn't take a second to realize it wasn't my phone ringing, it was his. I pulled it out of the bloody jeans pocket and then wiped the blood on the towel before glancing at the caller ID.

Automatically, I dropped the phone when I saw the word *Roach*.

Lucky for me, I dropped it when I walked into the bedroom, and it landed on the carpet.

"Dropping it won't break it."

My head snapped up after I picked it up.

"Um sorry. It's…um… my dad." I quickly walked across the room and handed the phone to him.

Seeing as Dad had kept ringing, it gave me the impression he wasn't going to stop till Reaper answered.

After giving him the phone, I walked to my wardrobe to get *anything* to cover myself with.

I hovered in there for a bit longer, not wanting to overhear their conversation. No need to make an awkward situation more awkward!

When I was wearing jeans and a black tank top, I wandered back into the bedroom, only to be surprised by an empty bed.

It was when I heard noise coming from the en-suite that I put it together.

I leaned against the doorframe, waiting for him to come out. Then when he did, I had to take a sharp breath. With no top on, leather vest, and stained jeans, how was it possible for a man to be that darn hot?

The tattoos covered his chest, only highlighting his defined muscles. I literally had to drop my eyes to the ground before he saw how turned on I was getting seeing him like that.

"I should…" My words dried up, what was I saying again? Oh yeah. "I'll make sure no one is in the hallway for you."

I was already walking towards my bedroom door before he could answer.

I doubted he wanted to be seen coming out of my room.

"Abby, about last night." His rough voice and the fact he was now standing behind me sent my skin alive with prickles.

"Don't worry about it." I turned quickly, cutting him off. "Seriously."

He had made no promises, and I hadn't expected anything of him. It was a one-night thing that I only wished was an every night thing.

I faked a small smile, "You better go before Dad calls again."

Knowing Dad, he would be barking at Reaper to do something.

He nodded his head, and I poked mine out the door just to check it was clear and when it was, I opened the door wide for him.

He didn't look back, and I didn't linger around waiting for him to. Instead, I closed the door and cursed softly.

It's official, I'm hooked on the Reaper.

***

"Breakfast smells good," I said, walking into the kitchen to see Kim.

She looked me up and down, "Your sex hair looks good too."

My expression dried. She was lucky that no one else was in here.

"Shut up, Kimberly."

She smirked and flipped a pancake. "So want to explain why I didn't see you sneaking out to go meet the university boy?"

"Want to talk about how I have excellent hearing and heard you and Trigger tripping up the stairs?" I nabbed a pancake and started to pull it apart before eating it.

She scoffed and kept her words to herself. Which turned out to be a good thing cause as luck would have it, our dad just so happened to walk into the kitchen that very minute.

"Why are you girls making breakfast?" He gave us a stern look.

Usually, we would only help out around the club when we wanted something or we had done something wrong.

"I'm eating, not making." I put the rest of the pancake in my mouth.

"And I just felt like doing something nice." Kim gave Dad the biggest fake grin I had ever seen. "Just like you, Dad, you do nice things all the time for other people, don't you?"

Yep, she wanted something.

"The answer is no," he snapped immediately, but he was more than happy to start picking at the food Kim had made.

That bacon did smell good.

"You can't say no before I ask," she threw back. "Anyway, it's not even a major thing."

I stayed silent. Sometimes I just felt sorry for Dad; we knew how to play him so well.

"Fine, what is it?" He gave in, pulling out a kitchen chair and sitting in front of the bacon and eggs. I handed him a plate.

"My car is acting up again," she started, "Well, actually, it left me broken down in town."

I knew where this was going. I scoffed and crossed my arms. She gave me a sharp look, but she didn't have to worry about me ruining this for her, she can do that all on her own.

"So I may have borrowed another car to get home."

Dad's eyes snapped up and locked onto her. "You did what?"

"It was a bucket of shit." Kim's voice went higher, defending her actions. "But now I don't know what to do with it."

"It's that blue thing in the driveway, isn't it." Dad connected the dots, then pointed a piece of bacon at Kim. "You said you were done with lifting cars, Kim."

"It was a one-off."

"I can't have hot cars parked in my fucking garage!"

"That's why I'm telling you, so you can get rid of it."

They started to enter into a longer argument about the car, which I tuned out. My cast was giving me hell today, and I knew it was because I hadn't covered it up last night in the shower. Thank the lord it was coming off today, though.

A pair of fingers snapped in my face, and I was brought back to the moment.

"What?" I snapped at Kim.

She gestured her head to Dad.

"You not all here this morning, Abby?" Dad frowned. "The arm giving you trouble?"

I shook my head, "No, I was just thinking about how it was coming off today."

"Is that today?" Kim was actually surprised.

"Yep. So no more plastic or plaster jokes from you." I smirked at her and began to back out of the kitchen.

"Oi, kiddo." Dad stopped me. "I need to ask you something."

"Yeah?"

"You see Reaper last night?"

My stomach dropped and I nodded my head.

"What was he doing?"

"Last time I saw him, he had a tight grip on a bottle of Jack Daniels."

That was true, kind of.

***

The day was hot, and it engulfed me when I stepped out onto the lot.

"Taking the cast off today?" Brad popped up out of nowhere and was at my side.

I grinned, "Yep, no more plaster."

"Want a lift into town? I can take you."

"You heading into town, Reynolds?" Reaper stepped out from the shed, his eyes on Brad.

"Wasn't gonna," Brad stared back at Reaper, "but I can."

"Well I am, so I'll take her." His tone was hard and blunt. Like there was no argument, and I sure as hell wasn't giving any input.

"Um well, let's go then." I gestured for him to get his ass moving because I was not missing this appointment.

I gave Brad a smile and thanks. My stomach twisted into a tight knot. I was kind of hoping Reaper and I wouldn't be having any time alone. I didn't want that awkward conversation.

Seems like I wasn't going to get a choice about it though.

It felt like my arm was a feather, free and light and awesome. I had gotten used to how heavy the cast was but now it was gone, my arm had turned into a feather.

"Want something to eat?" Reaper asked when we stepped out of the clinic.

Guess now was time for that awkward conversation.

"You got time for that?" I asked, pulling my sunnies down and following him to his bike.

I was so used to the way people stepped out of his way now that I wasn't even fussed by the glances and staring.

He mounted his bike and handed me a helmet. "I've always got time for you."

It wasn't the sweetest thing he could say, but it was pretty darn close to it.

I gripped his shoulder, throwing my other leg over the bike.

Just touching him sent lust through my blood. I didn't know what to say back to that, so I said nothing and just linked my arms around him.

Chapter 52

Abby

You don't dance with the devil and not get burnt. In saying that, you have to be in hell to be able to dance with him in the first place.

I snuck a sideways glance at Kade as we waited in line. It was noticeable how people were giving us a wide birth, and I wasn't the only one giving Kade sideway glances.

I wonder if it annoyed him how people just openly stared at him.

"What you want?" He looked down at me.

"Salad." I looked up at the menu board, "with chicken."

He scoffed. "I should have expected you to eat like a rabbit."

"Rabbits don't eat chicken," I snipped back.

I leaned on the counter, letting him rattle off our order. It was when he added eating in that my ears pricked up.

Here I thought we would stuff in the food and head back to the clubhouse. It seems Kade had other ideas.

I followed him to a booth while chewing on my bottom lip. I *really* didn't want this to be awkward.

"Won't the boys be missing you?" I slid into the booth across from him while keeping an unemotional expression on my face, hiding the embarrassment and nerves real well.

After what we did last night, it was hard not to blush or turn bright red.

"Doubt it." He twisted the top off a bottle of Coke. "Look, might as well just fucking get to the point about last night-"

"Don't," I stopped him. "You don't have to say anything. I don't expect anything from you or that it changes anything."

"Abby, stop." His eyes locked with mine. "What happened last night does change shit."

Great. Just what I didn't want.

"It doesn't have to." I pressed. "Seriously Kade, I don't expect anything from you."

He leaned across the small table, "You're not getting it, Abby. I was struggling to keep away from you before; now that is impossible. I want you. I want you as mine and mine alone. I am willing to take on the punching from your old man to claim you as mine."

My mouth opened.

My mouth closed.

I just blinked at him. Suddenly I was a mute.

"The girl that never shuts up is silent." He arched his eyebrows at me.

Reaper had just put a claim on me.

He wanted me.

Me.

"Dad won't like it." I finally found my voice. "Not to mention we still have the same problems. I won't turn a blind eye to you sleeping with other women on the road."

I wouldn't be one of those girls that just accepted it.

"I wouldn't disrespect you like that. Plus your father would have his gun at my temple if he thought I was sleeping around on you."

"So you really are going to tell Dad?"

I didn't believe it. Surely he didn't have the guts for that. Dad was, well, Dad. He wouldn't take the news lightly and be all *yeah that's fine.*' I felt the nerves bubbling in my stomach.

Though this was Reaper.

"If you want me to."

I arched an eyebrow "What is that supposed to mean?"

He shrugged his shoulders. "Is that what you want?"

A smile twitched on my lips, "Why don't you just come out and ask me out?"

"I already did. You're the one not giving me the answer."

It wasn't often that you would see amusement or playfulness in Kade's eyes apart from right now.

I slid out of the booth and went and sat next to him. His arm naturally wrapped around me and I curled into his side. This felt so right.

"I've always wanted to be claimed by a reaper," I whispered in his ear, causing him to smirk.

His hand ran up my thigh and he lowered his voice. "You're mine now, Abby Harrison."

Tingles spread across my skin at the deadly, alluring sentence.

Chapter 53

Abby

If it wasn't impossible, I would swear someone had set my morning up to fail. First I slept in, then I burned my forehead with the hair straightener. It was around this point that I realized close to everything I owned was dirty.

It was by a complete miracle that I managed to scramble an outfit together. Then when I thought my morning was turning around, I went to start my car and what do you know, a flat battery. Which then, of course, led to me having to ride in Kim's rubbish-filled car to university.

I swear it would kill her if she cleaned it.

So it was fair to say my nerves were red raw and I wasn't in the mood for anything else to happen.

Kim and I were both already running late for our lecture when she thought it would be a bright idea to stop and get a coffee from the canteen.

"Would you just chill, it's a boring lecture anyway." Kim rolled her eyes and was walking slow on purpose.

"I hate the way they stare you down when you enter late," I grumbled.

She shrugged her shoulders, not caring whatsoever.

We turned the corner and was suddenly confronted by a brunette and a gang of females.

I side-stepped them.

Only to have the brunette match my step.

I sighed heavily.

Kim was already in a bitchy mood; she had been fishing for an argument with me all morning.

"Can I help you?" I spoke dryly to her, meeting the brunette's bitchy eyes.

I had never seen her before, so it was highly doubtful I had managed to piss her off. But considering how this morning was going, maybe I had and I didn't even know about it.

"Harrison sisters." She stared down at us, her tone unfriendly. "I thought it was just a rumor that you were attending, but yet here you both are."

Kim was keeping unusually silent beside me.

Clearly we were at a disadvantage. She knew us while we didn't have a fucking clue who she was or her gang of friends behind her.

"As great as it is to know your eyesight works, we really have somewhere to be." Kim moved forward. Finally, I wasn't in the mood for a confrontation.

"Didn't take you as one to care if you were late for a lecture." The brunette made a point to step forward, staring Kim down further. Did this bitch want a fist in her face? Cause Kim would be more than happy to give her one.

"What do you want?" I broke their staredown.

The brunette's eyes flicked across to me. "I want you both to fuck off and go back to where you came from."

The bitch just said what?

Kim grabbed my arm and pushed me back behind her.

"And why would you care if we furthered our education?" Kim's voice was full of interest.

Who gave a fuck why, just punch the bitch so we can keep moving.

"You both aren't welcome here." She made a point to glance over Kim's shoulder at me. "And as for you, stay away from my brother."

"I don't even know your brother," I snarled back.

"I saw you with Sebastian, and I don't know what your game is, but I'm telling you now, stay away from him."

Sebastian was related to this thing.

"Fine, I'll stay away from him. Now get the fuck out of our way."

Kim let go of my arm only when they stepped out of our way.

"You should really just turn around and head to the office. I've heard un-enrolling is a lengthy process," she said as we walked past her.

She wasn't worth a word back, so I just pinched my lips together and gripped my textbooks that bit harder.

We were nearly at our lecture hall when Kim thought it was safe to speak.

"That was interesting." She dropped her coffee cup in the bin. "Have you ever seen her before?"

"No, and it wasn't interesting." It was just another thing to make this day that bit suckier.

"I'm going to find out who she is." When Kim put her mind to something, she wouldn't stop till she got answers. So I had no doubts that she would indeed rip apart anything and everything till she got her answers.

I was about to enter the lecture hall when she started to walk off.

"What, aren't you even coming in?" I asked.

She spun on her heels, grinning. "Nope. Got better things to do now."

"Whatever," I murmured. This was just like her. Sign us up for the university, slack off, and lose interest.

I wasn't in the mood to argue with her. It was barely after ten in the morning, and I already felt drained as fuck.

***

I let out a steady and relieved sigh as I stepped into the

clubhouse. For the first time all day, I felt the stress lift.

Finally home.

"Abby, your old man is looking for you," Brad said when I walked past the bar.

I stiffened immediately and stared wide-eyed at Brad.

"Was he angry? Did his head look like it about to explode?" I asked in a rush. Had Reaper already gone to Dad about us?

I begged Reaper last night to wait a few weeks, let me at least warm Dad up to me having a boyfriend. But this was Kade; he did shit when he felt like it, not when others wanted him to.

Brad frowned. "No. He looked normal."

I let out long breaths of air. Maybe he hadn't gone to Dad yet.

"Where is he?" I asked.

"He's in the garage with Reaper."

My stomach sank, twisted, and then was filled with pins and needles.

"Thanks." I turned on my heels and headed for the garage.

This was either going to go really well or really terrible,

I strode across the car park quickly, but I didn't take a steady breath till I heard laughter coming from the garage. I opened the door and relaxed when I saw Dad and Reaper laughing and working on a motorbike just like normal.

"Hey, Dad." I stepped over the tools and made my way towards them.

My eyes met Reaper's for a moment, and I wanted to grin like an idiot when I saw a softness fill his eyes when they locked with mine.

"You feeling alright, little one?" Dad placed his can of beer and spanner down. "Heard you had a bad morning."

"Who told you that?"

"Cameron told me you were kicking your car and cursing about a hair straightener or something."

Oh, that.

"Just a bad morning." I smiled guiltily. Fine, so sometimes I overreact.

Dad's phone started ringing, and he glanced at the screen. "I've got to take this, but I'll be back in a minute." He answered the phone and walked off in the direction of the door.

Wasn't till it closed firmly that I walked closer to Reaper.

He tucked the stray hair behind my ear and saw the mark on my forehead.

"You alright?" His voice was soft and kind, everything that his personality shouldn't be and what others thought he was incapable of being.

"Just had a shit day." I linked my arms around his waist and rested my head against his leather vest. "Then this chick all up in my face this morning just topped it off."

"What chick?" His voice spiked with interest, and he peeled me back from him to look down at me. "Something happen?"

"Just university bullshit. Some girl has taken a disliking to Kim and me."

"Why?"

"Guessing cause of the club." I shrugged my shoulders, "That, or she doesn't like anyone getting close to her brother."

"Why would you be near her brother?"

"The other night when I was all dressed up, and I found you in the kitchen and yeah well, I was heading out to meet him."

"So you were dating him?"

"No. I *was* going out on a date with him." I let go of him, feeling his rage beginning to boil. "And before you go off and make a big deal about it. It didn't happen and was going to mean nothing. Just something to fill my evening."

His jaw was still clenched, and he was just staring blankly down at me.

I sighed. "Kade, I spent the night on top of you, literally. Would you just not make a big deal out of nothing?"

I watched as he calmed himself down. It was when the door opened that we jumped apart. Now I was furious that we had wasted those few moments we had alone.

"Want to go out for tea, little one? Kim's willing to if you're coming."

"Is it just us three or everyone?" I crossed my arms, not feeling in the mood for an outing.

"A few of the others might join us."

That was Dad saying it was an open invitation and others were coming.

"I'll go," I glanced over at Reaper, "if Reaper goes."

Dad's eyes narrowed slightly and bounced between us.

"Why does it matter if he comes or not?" Dad pressed for an explanation.

"Because he owes me a beer, and not a beer that I've poured."

Dad accepted that and nodded his head, "Well Reaper, you coming?"

I swear I felt his glare for a moment. He didn't like going out in groups. I didn't know why but if he came, that meant my evening might turn out better than what my day was.

Reaper grunted a yes, and I didn't hide my grin this time. I didn't even care that Dad gave us an odd look.

***

It turned out that Dad had booked the restaurant. Which worked out in my favor because no one noticed that Reaper and I snuck away. I twisted the lock on the disabled toilet, finally giving us privacy.

"You know you could have just said no to going out for tea and we wouldn't have to be forced to make out in a fucking toilet," he complained.

"Who said anything about making out?" I arched my eyebrows at him. "In fact, I think we left things with you being mad at me."

He scoffed.

"Anyway, this is all part of my plan." I brought it back to point.

"That being?" He crossed his arms, not hiding his disgust of having to be in here.

"If Dad starts to notice that I feel safe around you and that I want to be around you, it will make it easier when you go to tell him about us."

"Abby, I'm gonna get a punching anyway, so no point having fucking plans and crap."

I crossed my arms stubbornly. "You know, I'm starting to think you just want to get a punching from Dad."

He stepped forward, pinning me against the wall.

"And I'm starting to think that you're missing the point of us being alone." His hands landed on my hips. "So sweetheart, want to continue plotting or," he kissed my neck, "do you want to make the time we have worthwhile?"

My plans melted instantly as his hot lips slowly went up my neck. But it was me who stole his lips as soon as they were free. Kissing him like I always kissed him—hard and passionately.

I wrapped my arms around his neck and he lifted me up with ease. His lips left mine and he kissed me down my neck, over my collarbone.

I was gasping from his touch.

"Kade?' I managed to say something as his hands roamed my body.

"Mm."

"We have to get back."

As much as I would love to stay in this very position, with Kade exploring my body, I knew we would be missed.

He groaned and slowly lowered me to the floor.

"It's killing me not being able to touch you. To have to watch you sit next to other men." He leaned his forehead against mine and looked like a man in pain. "I want you on me. Sitting on my lap. Eating off my plate. Which reminds me, you aren't eating."

"I am eating!" I ordered food.

"You are fading away."

"I am not."

"Abby, don't force me to make you eat."

I rolled my eyes. Maybe I hadn't been eating as much as I should be, but it wasn't like I was starving.

"Fine, I'll make sure to eat more tonight." I said, hoping that would settle it.

He nodded his head, "Let's go." He let go of me but took my hand.

Holding hands, we walked down the passage. Then just before we walked out into the restaurant, he pulled my hand up to his lips and kissed it before letting go.

I missed his touch immediately. I frowned at the ground as we walked back to the table.

"Reaper, got your beer, bro," Brad said. He was sitting next to Reaper's empty chair at the top of the table.

I walked around and sat directly across from him and Brad. Dad was at the top of the table like normal, Kim was on his right, followed by me and Cameron and the rest of the table.

I noticed my food had come but I wasn't interested in it. My mind was on Reaper and all the things we could be doing instead of playing nice with the club.

"How's your steak, Abby?"

I looked up. Had I heard him correctly? He was actually speaking to me, in public. In front of dad. My eyes were locked on Reaper as he waited for my answer. He was sipping on his beer, like he had all the time in the world to wait for my reply.

He was going to make me eat.

Narrowing my eyes at him, I picked up my knife and fork and cut into it. "It's overdone." I said and then put my knife and fork down.

"Send it back."

Was he serious?

"It's fine, I'm not hungry." I gritted my teeth and gave him a pointed look to drop it.

"I'll send it back for you." Reaper went to get up.

"No, it's fine. I'll eat it!" I didn't want to make a big deal out of this. I just wasn't hungry. But knowing he was watching me and also Dad was now, I cut off a piece and put it in my mouth.

Wasn't till the juices filled my mouth that I realized I was actually starving.

God this was good.

Why had I stopped eating meat?

I was chewing on a bit of steak when I caught the smile on Reaper's face. Yeah, maybe he was right. This once.

Chapter 54

Abby

They say that couples balance each other out, like yin and yang. That the bad things one does is balanced out with the kind things the other one does. If this is the case, Reaper and I were screwed.

"Kim, how do you know this is even her car?" I hissed down at her, while Kim did artwork on a black sedan that she swore was the brunette's.

The last thing I needed was a rant off Dad about this.

"I'm done." Kim stood up proudly, ending my watch. I glanced at the poorly drawn penis and the scratched words, *sit on this, bitch.*

I handed her back her handbag, and we started to weave our way out of the car park.

Kim found out that the brunette was named Viven Westbrook. I was more than annoyed when I found out that it was indeed Sebastian's little sister.

I wondered why he had gone out of his way to befriend me and she had gone out of her way to scare me off.

"I swear if that bitch has tipped our lockers again, I'm going to lose it," Kim grumbled beside me.

Over the past week, Vivien had been doing childish things to get to us. It was amazing what influence she had across the university. Her shitty deeds ranged from the canteen lady ignoring us, to our lockers being tipped, teachers refusing to answer our questions. The one thing that really got to me was Sebastian wouldn't even acknowledge me.

Not that I wanted his attention in a romantic way, it was just the point of the matter.

"Well, I'll see you at lunch." I said, parting ways with Kim.

"Don't do anything stupid between now and then."

Kim was ready to go head to head with Vivien; I was the one holding us back.

It was going to take a lot more than some childish pranks for me to break.

***

My locker door was shut forcefully in my face, my hand just escaping injury.

"Defacing my car? Really?" Vivien was once again in my personal space, her face curled with rage.

"I'm starting to get sick of you in my face." I turned to face her. "Actually, I'm starting to get over you in general, Vivien."

Her eyes widened slightly when I said her name.

"Why can't you and your club whore of a sister go back to sucking cock for a living already?"

She sure had a mouth on her.

I glared back into her rage-filled eyes. "Why don't you just get the point and leave us alone?" I kept my tone controlled. "Because we aren't going anywhere." I took a dominating step closer to her. "So back the fuck off."

She looked intimidated before her eyes filled with an uncontrollable rage. "You and your sister will be leaving this campus."

She shouldered me firmly before storming off up the hall.

I gritted my teeth for a moment and thought over her threat. She wasn't going to stop anytime soon. Which meant two things, we would either have to step up and take her on or just continue to ignore her as much as possible.

I sighed heavily. Still was going to take something more than what she was doing to get me to sink to her level.

***

"So you're letting this bitch walk all over you?" Kade looked at me with disbelief while he continued to stroke my bare back. I had snuck into his room just after midnight—boy, did he get a surprise when I slid into his bed.

He told me I was lucky I didn't get a bullet in the foot. I told him he was a drama queen, and who else would be wanting to sneak into his room but me?

"Do you know her? Vivien Westbrook, does that ring any bells or something? She is acting like I've personally attacked her."

He frowned for a moment while I got distracted tracing the tattoo that ran down his arm.

"There is a family of Westbrooks that live on the border of town; she could be related to them. The man owns a chain of hotels or something."

That could be them. But still, I hadn't done anything to them.

Kade reached out for my face, tracing down between my eyebrows. "Don't frown baby girl; it doesn't suit you."

"Do you have to ride out tomorrow?" I dropped my head on his chest and sighed. "Can't you just not go?"

His stomach rumbled with laughter before he flipped me on my back.

"I'm sure your dad would love that. Sorry Roach, can't make the ride because I'm going to stay home and bang your daughter."

I slapped his arm. "Seriously, bang? Couldn't you be a bit more romantic?"

He smirked before giving me a quick kiss on the lips. "I won't be gone for long."

"A week is a long time."

"You'll be so busy taking it up the ass from this Vivien chick that you won't even notice."

I playfully glared at him. "Not funny."

"Neither is letting this woman walk all over you. Take a stand, Abby."

"It's childish."

He shrugged his shoulders. "She's acting like you're pissing on her territory or something."

I just loved how blunt Reaper was with words.

"But I'm not even. It's not like I'm selling drugs on the corner of her beloved campus or something!"

"Maybe it's got nothing to do with you personally; maybe it's the club." He played with my hair, his softer side showing. "You wouldn't be the first taking a punching for being linked to the club."

I sighed again "I don't know. But Kim isn't going to stop till she gets to the bottom of it."

"Good." He lowered his lips to my neck, "Cause I've got a better idea of how we can be spending our time now."

I didn't have to ask what that *better idea* was.

Chapter 55

Reaper

She was literally killing me this morning. What was she thinking wearing a dress like that? Didn't she realize that dresses like that cause men to lose control?

"Didn't you sleep last night or something?" Brad shouldered me, giving me a weary look.

I knew I looked like shit, and no, I didn't sleep cause I was too busy spending every waking moment I had with Abby in my room.

"Something like that," I muttered back, still walking beside him down the lot towards Roach.

"I can't be fucked riding for a full week," Brad complained.

I wasn't exactly jumping for fucking joy about it either. Leaving Abby for a full week, by herself, shit is bound to go wrong, and I won't be there to help clean it up.

"Thought you two were hitting the road early," Roach barked as soon as we were in range.

"Slept in," Brad replied dryly. "But we're going now. That's what we came to tell ya."

He nodded his head, then his eyes landed on me. "I want a word with you before you head out." His tone was unfriendly and blunt. But when wasn't it?

"Good thing we didn't head out on time then," I grunted back at him.

The two other guys in the shed walked off, and Brad headed towards his bike, giving Roach and I space.

"You got anything you want to tell me?" Roach's eyes were hardened, and he was clenching that spanner so tight his knuckles were going white.

What the fuck. Had Abby said something?

"You knew this ride out was important, yet you still managed to not give a fuck. Wanna tell me why you are suddenly more interested in something else other than this club, this family?" His voice rose with rage, his eyes boiling with it.

Sure, I knew I had been letting things pass that I normally wouldn't. I had my mind on Abby all the fucking time, and it was affecting my role in the club. Guess if there was a word for it, it would be distance.

"Just had other shit on my mind. I'm getting my shit sorted. Won't happen again," I lied. Cause things won't go back to normal, not after I tell him what I am planning on telling him when I get back.

He nodded his head. "Hope the long ride clears that head of yours."

"Yeah well, I'll see you in a week." I turned and walked off.

This ride wasn't going to clear my head; it was going to fill my head with worry. I knew Abby could handle herself, but that still doesn't stop a man from worrying about his girl.

Abby

"Guess what I found out?" Kim barged into my room. Why knock when you can just burst in? I closed my laptop, not seeing the point of yelling at her about knocking because she would just turn around and do it again.

"What Kim?"

"I found out why Vivien is so hell bent on scaring us off."

"That didn't take you long." I was surprised at how quickly she had worked it out. "So what is it?"

"Vivien Westbrook is scared of us." Kim's tone soured, "Her dad owns a chain of hotels and as for that Sebastian, he's bad news."

I smiled at her choice of words because the men we hung around weren't bad news at all.

"So why has she got it out for us? Because she hasn't been acting like she is scared of us."

"She and her brother are suppliers."

"Suppliers?"

"Of drugs, you idiot, get with the program," Kim snapped, frustrated by my lack of knowledge.

"What drug suppliers? Seriously?"

Sure, the girl looked like she had attitude, but she didn't look capable or should I say involved with that side of life.

Kim nodded her head. "They are the main supplier for the campuses."

My mind slowly started to catch up. "So she would have thought that we'd be stepping on her toes."

"That's what I thought at first. They'd be concerned that we would start supplying. But-"

"Go on, don't stop; you have me hooked now."

"I think they are more concerned with us finding out about it."

I frowned. "Why?"

"They're dealing ice, Abby. We both know what Dad thinks of that drug."

Ice was a drug Dad had no interest in. In fact, he hated it. His younger sister, our aunt, got hooked and overdosed on it when she was young. She died when we were really little.

"And Dad doesn't use outsiders; they deal directly," Kim added.

"So they are being supplied with it from who? Another club?"

She shrugged her shoulders. "All I know is whoever is supplying them is doing it behind Dad's back, and they clearly have guts."

It made sense now. Why she was trying to scare us off. She thought we were going to take her trade, but more importantly find out they were dealing in the first place behind the club's back.

"Dad's going to be furious."

"Furious? He'll take heads off for it!" she exclaimed. "It could start a war. Abby, we have to handle this."

"And how exactly do you plan on us handling this?"

"By making her see who she is really dealing with," Kim smirked. "Right now she only see us as a threat, but once she realizes that we aren't just some little club whores but are in fact the fucking princesses of this club, she will back off."

"That might get her off our back, but what about the supplying issue?"

Kim's eyes widened and her face soured; I knew that look too well. That look meant she had a plan.

I was outside smoking when Kim found me. I was not in the mood for games. If anything, I was in a foul mood because Reaper had left. And all I wanted was him.

"We need to take care of Vivien." Kim said, taking the cigarette off me. "And how is that?"

"By reaching out for our half sister's advice." Kim handed me her phone. "Her number is sitting there; you just need to dial."

"Why would she want to help us?"

"Because we are family and that is all the club is about. She won't turn her back on this."

Kim had a point.

"Fine, I'll call her."

"Good. Cause she might be able to give us more details on our new enemy." Kim finished the cigarette and dropped it to the ground, stomping on it. "Smoking doesn't suit you, Abby. You're meant to be the good twin, remember? Tell me how that turns out."

"Where are you going?" Wouldn't she want to hang around and see what Amber said?

"I have to go see Trigger. I won't be long."

"Whatever." I shot at her while hitting the dial button. This was either going to go well or she would hang up on me.

"Hello?" Amber's voice answered.

"Hi, Amber. You might not remember me, but I'm Abby. Abby Harrison. I just have a few questions for you."

There was silence for a moment on the other end of the phone.

"I was wondering when you were going to call. It took you long enough."

Chapter 56

Abby

"I'm not calling to ask for a sisterly chat. I just need to ask you a question."

"Sisterly chat," she scoffed. "Fine, what is your question?"

"Do you know Vivien Westbrook? Or the Westbrooks in general?"

My question was met with dead silence. I was about to give up and hang up just before she finally answered.

"I know her sister."

"And?"

"And the Westbrooks once had a strong connection to the club. Let's just say that connection got cut. Vivien and her brother Sebastian are the only ones that are still acknowledged within the family."

"What did you do to her sister?"

"It's a small world, sometimes you step on toes. I don't remember what I did, all I know is it caused her dad to stop acknowledging her as part of the family."

"Well, now I'm copping heat for something you did."

"Is Vivien giving you trouble?"

I paused before answering. Should I really be telling her anything? I suppose what was the harm, wasn't like she was going to ride down here and sort it out for me.

"She's threatened by us, and well, I'm not sure how to handle it." I was honest. I wasn't one to go to her level and play dirty. But at the same time, I was born with a backbone; it was time to use it, and I knew that.

"You want my advice?" Amber's tone was crisp, no bitchiness

within it. "Handle it the way our blood knows how. We don't take shit from others. So give it back to her, just do it better."

I smiled slightly to myself. "Thanks."

"If you need anything else," her words broke for a moment. "You can call me."

I think that was Amber's way of extending an olive branch.

She wasn't shutting us out.

"I might take you up on that."

"Well, I should tell Reaper that when he gets back, his woman might be a changed one." Amber's words surprised me.

"Reaper is with you?"

"Didn't he tell you where his run was to?"

"No."

"Well, I guess it doesn't matter where the guns are going as long as they get to where it's needed. Nice speaking to you, Abby." The dial tone followed after her goodbye.

So it was official. We had to handle Vivien the only way we knew how, and that was dirty.

***

At the moment, Vivien only saw Kim and me as a threat. But as of this morning, that was all going to change.

My grip loosened around Brad as we slowly came to a stop outside the campus. Just as I hoped, Sebastian and Vivien were out the front.

Kim was on the back of Trigger's bike and behind him was Cameron and a few of the other boys. They were going for a 'ride' today, and we had convinced them to drop us off on their way.

The reason?

To give Vivien the fucking message that she isn't just fucking with us, they are fucking with the club.

301

Brad braced the bike as I climbed off, and I yelled a thank you over the roar of his motor.

Kim was walking towards me, and then together we faced the campus entranceway, which had every pair of eyes on us, including the two pairs that we wanted.

"Vivien, Sebastian, morning." I stopped, smiling at them, with Kim at my side. "The car was getting serviced; boys gave us a ride."

"Good thing that you live so close to a mechanic," Sebastian smirked across at me.

"Having so many men around all the time does help." I met his determined eyes. "But guess that is expected when you live in a clubhouse."

Kim and I were both wearing club supportive tee shirts. Time these idiots got the message they aren't just fucking with us, but with all the deadly men that wear these colors as well.

"Nice choice of tops." Vivien looked us up and down. "Really makes it clear who you support."

"It's not supporting, love." Kim stepped forward, giving her a determined look. "It's our blood, our family." Kim faked a friendly grin directed at the both of them. "Would hate to find out someone is threatening them."

"Good thing everyone knows not to fuck with Satan's Sons then," Sebastian snapped, losing his cool. "See you both later." He gripped his sister's arm, and they turned sharply and walked off.

Kim and I shared a look.

They had gotten the message.

I couldn't help but smirk as Kim and I walked off.

"They're scared," Kim smirked back at me.

"So they should be."

No one fucks with the Harrisons and gets away with it.

Chapter 57

Vivien Westbrook

"They know, Sebastian." I kicked his leg as he lay on the couch, not caring at all. "Sebastian, would you at least listen to me!"

We hadn't spoken about it at school, but we were home now, and this had to be addressed.

He lazily looked up over his phone at me. "Calm down, Vivien."

"This is all your fault! If you hadn't gone kissing one of the brats, I wouldn't even have stepped in and threatened them!"

"Chill, would you? Abby had no idea why I was chasing her, and she wouldn't have found out because I would have blocked it. What happened this morning is all on you."

"And how did you come to that conclusion, dumbass?"

"You're the one that harassed them."

"I'm the one taking a stand before Dad finds out! So yeah, go ahead, blame me for acting and trying to get rid of them!"

"Before I find out what?"

I went stiff and slowly turned around to see Dad standing in the doorway. Fucking Sebastian should have warned me or shut me up; he would have seen Dad standing there!

"Nothing."

"Has the Harrison situation been dealt with?" He looked directly at me.

Of course he would be expecting answers from me, not his golden son.

"No." I crossed my arms. Fuck it. I wasn't sugarcoating it. "If anything, shit got serious. They know. Which means it is only time till the club finds out. Then we end up with our throats cut and our house shot up."

"I love how you place the house shooting at higher importance than our throats being cut," Sebastian piped up.

Dad's expression hadn't changed. His normal hard expression remained. "Get rid of the girls before they open their mouths. I don't care how you do it. Just get it done."

And just like that, Dad turned his back and walked out. Turning his back on us and the problem. He expected me to handle this. Well, I was done handling it.

"I'm done. My way didn't work, as you pointed out. So you deal with it," I snapped at Sebastian and then stormed out.

If Dad was so concerned about his trade through the universities, then he eventually has to step up and deal with it; till then, Sebastian can deal with it.

I was done.

Abby

I wouldn't say the week had been uneventful, but it had been a long one without Reaper around. Not that I was telling him that. I wasn't giving him that to hold over my head.

But my week was coming to an end as of now, and I couldn't stop the grin as I heard their bikes ride through the gates.

"You could at least pretend not to be jumping for fucking joy that he is back." Kim gave me a sideway glance. "Dad's going to pick up on you two being together."

I rolled my eyes. "He won't be picking up on anything because I'm telling him myself."

Her eyes widened. "Are you insane?"

"Questioning my sanity levels when you're back with Trigger?"

"I'm not back with anyone." She glared at me. "We're just friends."

"With benefits."

"Depends what you class as a benefit," she muttered under her breath, clearly not expecting me to hear.

"Didn't expect you girls to be down for tea tonight." Dad sat on a bar stool, beer in hand.

"Why?" I walked towards him to sit beside him. "We get hungry too, you know."

Dad's eyes locked with mine. "Sure, that is the reason. You and I need to talk, girly."

I swallowed the needles of nerves; he only called me girly when I was in trouble.

"Can we do it after tea?"

"No." He put his beer down. "Now. Come on."

I glanced at Kim, only to see her smirking. Great, well, she wasn't going to help me.

I remained silent while following him across the room and into his office. I did a quick run through my mind, and I couldn't think of anything I had done to piss him off.

Nope, nothing. Couldn't come up with a thing.

He closed the door and I still remained silent, taking the seat across from his giant chair.

"You better start talking, girly."

"About?"

"Why you're chasing the Reaper." He drew out a long breath. "I'm not blind, sweetheart."

Suddenly my stomach dropped. "Well, I guess it was going to get out eventually."

"End it."

My mouth dropped. I hadn't expected his decision to be so final so quickly.

"No."

"I mean it, Abby."

"And I mean it too, no. I'm not breaking up with him."

I was trying my best to be firm, but I was going up against one of the hardest and meanest men, and that wasn't just me thinking that.

"The Reaper is my Reaper for a fucking reason, Abby. He had no weakness. He's cold."

"I'm a weakness to you."

"And I fucking take that on board with everything I do."

"Reaper wouldn't put me in harm's way."

"Being with the man puts you in more fucking harm than just being my daughter. There are more men that want that man's head than mine. That's why he is called the fucking Reaper. He kills, Abby."

"Stop it, Dad."

"I've watched him gut a man with a knife."

"Stop it."

"He's a killing machine. My killing machine."

I stared at him blankly. "And I love him."

Dad's eyes bulged and the veins running up his neck stiffened. "Take that back."

"Sending him to another charter, threatening me, threatening him, it isn't going to work because I'm in love with him. My heart chose him, not me. Don't you think I know how stupid it sounds to be in love with a man that is known for only coldness?!" I blew out a hot breath. "But it doesn't change anything. I love him. The good and the bad."

Dad grunted. "There is more fucking bad in that man than any good."

"That's your opinion."

"He is my Reaper."

"And I love him."

Dad cringed. "Stop saying that."

"It's not a joke, Dad, and I want your blessing." I crossed my arms stubbornly. "You know that with him looking over me, there is no chance any other man or woman could hurt me. You know he would die before letting someone hurt me." Or so I hoped.

Dad glared back at me as his mind clicked over what I said. Then he just stood up, surprising me completely. Had this conversation ended it?

"I've seen that man screw through women. I won't be letting you be another one of his girls."

"I won't be."

"Darn straight you won't be, because I'm going to make sure of it."

I gulped. What did that mean?

"If you punch him-"

"I'm not punching up your pretty boy. I'm fucking telling him straight what being with you means, then we can see what he decides."

They were going to talk.

Talk.

I don't know how I felt about that.

Chapter 58

Abby

"YOU!" Reaper came at me, pointing a finger. Taking in his red cheeks and narrowed eyes, I knew what had happened.

I slipped off the stool.

"Don't you fucking dare run away." His furious voice followed me.

He didn't even seem to care that the bar and dining room was full; meaning we had every pair of eye on us.

I had managed to scramble up the hallway away from their ears just in time when Reaper's hand gripped my upper arm, pulling me to a stop.

"Got something to tell me?" he grunted.

I had run through how this was going to turn out a few times and each time it didn't end well, and so far Reaper's reaction was leaning me towards that becoming a reality.

"About that," I said overly sweetly.

His eyebrows shot up. "Don't fucking downplay it, Abby. I nearly didn't leave that boardroom with my head attached."

"Oh, don't be a drama queen. I highly doubt Dad was swinging an ax in there."

"You know what I fucking mean."

"Stop cursing." I crossed my arms and huffed. "I thought you would be relieved that you didn't have to pull the trigger on the problem."

"Pull the trigger? Pull the fucking trigger! That is exactly what you did, but you pointed that gun in my face."

"Fine then. What did Dad threaten? Come on, spit it out, what has you running so scared?"

If he couldn't handle Dad, then there was no way we would ever work, and I was beginning to think maybe I was just fun to him and he didn't want serious.

"I'm not running."

"Fine. What has you so..." I gestured a hand at him, not even knowing how to explain his reaction, "overreacting."

He glanced up the hall then back at me before running a hand through his hair. He grabbed my hand, letting go of my arm, and pulled me along the hall till we reached his room and he opened the door for me. One would think he was a gentleman; if only he wasn't dragging me in behind him.

"Kade, would you just tell me what Dad said?" I huffed, closing the door after us. "If you are having second thoughts about being serious, you should have told me earlier."

"I told you that I would handle it," he said. "I told you that."

"Yes, and I was more than happy for that to happen until Dad dragged me into his boardroom and made me explain what was going on."

"He gave it to me; then he backed off." Kade collapsed on the edge of the bed. "He told me that your safety was in my hands now. He basically handed me you."

I shifted awkwardly from foot to foot in front of him. Wasn't that a good thing? Or was it not? Then it hit me; no, it smashed into me hard. What if Reaper didn't want me? What if it was the chase he wanted and now... well, now he caught me.

"You don't want that." My stomach twisted immediately.

"I can't keep a fucking pet fish alive. How the hell am I meant to be able to protect you and keep you safe?"

"I'm not a fish or a child." I snapped. How dare he! "I can and do look after myself."

Now I knew what Dad had done. Dad didn't punch Reaper; he did something scarier than that. He gave Reaper responsibility.

"You either want me, or you don't. You either love me, or you don't. It's crystal clear cut, Reaper." I stormed across the room.

"Let me know when you've made your mind up."

For me, it wasn't a hard decision. While for him, well, who the fuck knows?

***

"You're in an extra pissy mood," Kim noted the obvious as we left our last class together.

Reaper hadn't got back to me last night. He hadn't even bothered to check to see if I was ok. He was a typical selfish biker, and right now I hated his guts.

"Don't want to talk about it."

"Doesn't have anything to do with what happened with Reaper chasing you down the hallway last night?"

Pursing my lips, I didn't give her an answer. She would only find it hilarious.

We had reached our lockers when my bad mood just clicked to completely furious.

"Again with spray painting the lockers," I spat angrily, seeing the word 'whore' sprayed across our lockers.

I stuffed my handbag and textbooks in the locker and slapped it shut. "Fuck this. I'm over it." I was over Vivien's little childish pranks.

"Abby, where are you going?" Kim was hot on my heels as I stormed down the hall, and I wasn't planning on stopping till I was face to face with Vivien fucking Westbrook.

***

I slapped the can out of her hand to get her attention. Of course

310

I would find her in the canteen. But the mood I was in, I didn't care about the attention we were about to get.

"You got something to say to me?" I got up in her face.

I had taken her by surprise, so it took her a moment to understand what was happening.

"I thought I sprayed it clearly." Her eyes narrowed, and she was willing to take me on. "Can't read?"

It was one comment. That was all I needed, then I let my right hook free, straight into her face.

Chapter 59

Kim

I didn't usually feel bad for my sister, but right now I felt that and kind of guilty as Dad screamed down the walls at her.

Everyone was silent in the bar, all listening to the booming voice of my dad yelling at Abby. I had captured a few pieces of sentences such as 'club image, suspension, and disappointment' as well as a lot of cursing.

Abby had gotten three good punches in, taking Vivien to the ground. Vivien hadn't even laid one on Abby. I had never seen my sister so red raw with anger. It took two teachers to pull Abby off Vivien, and she didn't need my help to take down the bitch.

I cringed, hearing Dad roar at her.

Even the boys in the bar were sheepish. My eyes flickered over to Reaper, who was staring directly at Dad's office door. Actually, his eyes hadn't left it since he found out who was in there.

I wondered again what happened between the two of them last night. Whatever it was, I think it had something to do with why my sister was in such a pissed-off mood this morning.

"So your sister punched someone up?" Trigger dragged a stool and sat in front of me while I cleaned glasses.

"Yeah, something like that." I glanced at Trigger's bloody knuckles. "Looks like Abby isn't the only one punching things or people."

Trigger weakly grinned at me. "What can I say, self-defense?"

"I doubt it."

"How was your day?"

"I spent the day with a hormonal motherfucker." He glanced over his shoulder at Reaper. "Swear that man only has anger inside him."

"Sounds close to my day. Only Abby doesn't normally punch first."

"Yeah, that's your job, isn't it?" He smirked at me.

I cracked him a beer and handed it to him. "Yeah, meant to be."

This was the new Trigger and me, trying to be friends. It was hard to be friends with someone you felt something stronger for.

Dad's office door burst open and out walked a very pissed-off looking blonde.

"Excuse me," I said, putting the glasses down and walking around the bar.

"Kim, you ready to go out?" Abby pretty much shouted across the room.

"I didn't know we were going out." I looked her up and down; I had never seen her so furious.

"Well, I don't want to damage the club's image," she shouted over her shoulder and in the direction of the open door.

She then did one thing I never expected to ever see my sister do.

She took off her leather jacket and ripped off the white tee she was wearing that had the club logo on it and tossed it in the direction of Dad's office door.

Standing there in a bright pink lacy bra, it was nothing compared to the 'I don't give a fuck' look on her face.

She threaded her arms through her jacket, then her fiery filled eyes landed on me. "Are you ready Kim or not?"

"Yep. Good to go." Who knew where we were going?

Reaper stepped up and stood in her way, and automatically her arms shot up.

"Don't touch me," she hissed, then stepped around him and made a beeline for the exit. When I heard the thumping of Dad's boots, I scrambled for the car keys.

"I'll see you later," Trigger said as I walked past him.

"DON'T YOU GO OUT THERE AND MAKE MORE

FUCKING TROUBLE!" Dad roared from his office door

"Oh fuck off." Abby spun on her heel and fired at him. It was me who was quick to block her and push her out the door.

"God, do you want to go another round with Dad?" I hissed at her while she stomped across the lot towards my car.

"Where are we going anyway?" I asked.

She shrugged her shoulders. "Somewhere where there is liquor and men."

"So basically here then."

She glared over her shoulder at me. "Real fucking funny."

Chapter 60

Abby

There are times in life when you wish that you could just fast forward through them. You wish that you could just escape the pain and headache that is sure to be brought on.

I thought getting drunk would help.

I thought escaping the clubhouse for the night would help me.

But it hadn't.

Now I stared up at my ceiling, feeling dizzy and lightheaded. Kim had managed to get us out for the night, and I smashed the drinks back quickly. She literally had to hold my body weight as we came home in the early morning hours.

And now, well, now my body was paying me back for it.

I rolled onto my side, the room still spinning. A sharp knock on my bedroom door caused me to groan. Any noise seemed to be ripping through my ears with blades at the moment.

"Come in," I answered. There was no way I was getting out of bed to answer that door. My head was spinning badly enough without adding movement to it.

I heard the door close and when the person stepped into my line of sight, I regretted letting him in.

"What do you want, Reaper?" I was feeling too sick to even bother putting emotion in my voice. I was weak and exhausted; I didn't have time for a fight with him.

"To see you." He crossed his tattooed arms and let out a long sigh. "You really did a good job last night, didn't you?"

"Fuck off Reaper, I'm not in the mood." I was also more aware of how little clothing I was currently wearing while lying on top of the bed.

"What was last night about?" He pressed me with more

questions.

"Why would you care?" I slowly sat up, "That would mean responsibility and caring, and we both know how much you hate both."

His hollow eyes locked with mine. "Abby, you know there is more to it than that."

"Whatever. I don't care."

I did care. I cared a fucking lot. I wanted to be his girl, and he ran away scared of being responsible.

He pulled a bottle out of his pocket and placed it on the bedside table. "Take some, it will help with nausea."

"I'm always nauseous around you." I snapped at him. "Now fuck off."

"You're more of a bitch than normal."

I gave him a mocking expression. "Well, it's not like I got my heart squeezed till it exploded and now I am forced to pretend like nothing ever happened."

"You know it's not like that." His voice was firm. "I love you, Abby, but you being with me puts a fucking target on you."

"Oh, don't give me that crap. I was brought up with a target on my back being a President's daughter. So why don't you just admit it, Dad scared you off by making you responsible for my safety."

"Your Dad just laid out the facts."

I scoffed loudly. "How kind of him. I thought we were on the same side. Clearly, a talking to from my father is enough to scare you off."

"Just take the tablets and sleep it off, Abby." His voice lingered with a warning.

"Fine. I'll get over it. But you had your chance, and you didn't want to be with me. So from now on, we are nothing. Not friends, not enemies, nothing, got it?" I couldn't stand to be his friend. It was going to be hard enough seeing him with other women.

"How about we talk about this when you don't smell like you drank the bar dry."

"How about we just never talk again."

"You're fucking childish."

"Me. ME!" I scoffed loudly. "I was the one ready to have a relationship with you, and you are the one acting like a child by backing out of it."

"There is more to it than that."

"Well guess what, I don't want to hear it."

He ran his hand through his hair and groaned. "I wish I didn't fucking care about you; this would make it all a whole lot fucking easier."

"Oh yes, poor you for once in your life, you're experiencing an emotion."

"I heard you decked a girl at the university yesterday."

Way to change the subject.

"I punched her. I didn't deck her."

"The story is being told differently."

"Well, I don't care what others think."

"Yeah you do, Abby."

I felt my stomach beginning to boil with rage. "If I was that self-centered, I wouldn't have put my heart on the line for you." I wiped a tear away. "Can you just leave, please? You're just making me feel worse."

He shifted his weight from side to side before he did something I wasn't expecting; he sat next to me on the bed.

"Do you know why I am called the Reaper?" He made sure to lock his eyes with mine.

"Because you're Dad's right hand. You clean up dirty business."

"Dirty business," he muttered more to himself then shook his head. "I kill people, Abby. I'm the Reaper of death. I can't count how many bodies I've put in the ground. The worst thing is, I don't care. I can put a bullet through anyone, and I wouldn't feel an inch of guilt. So tell me how a girl like you, perfect, pretty, and drop dead fucking gorgeous wants to be with a soulless beast like me?"

He still didn't see it. He still didn't understand.

"You don't get to choose who you fall in love with, your heart does, and mine has always belonged to yours, ever since you saved me in that alleyway." I placed a hand on his. "But you don't feel the same, because if you did, you wouldn't be looking for an excuse to get out of loving me."

Maybe that was he was trying to scare me off. Maybe the love that he thought he felt wasn't love at all.

He stayed silent.

I lifted my hand off his. "You should go."

He let out a long sigh before standing up. "I didn't want this to turn out like this." Regret covered his words. "I'll let you sleep."

I watched him get up, and just when I thought he was leaving, he turned back around to face me.

"This, you and I, we aren't over."

"We are if you can't move forward."

He left. Just like that, he walked out of my room, leaving our relationship in the air. Heck, who was I kidding? It was over, and I just didn't want to accept it.

Chapter 61

Abby

Reaper disappeared, literally. Dad had sent him out on a run. Not seeing him was worse than not seeing him at all. Call it stupid, but I thought we would just make up and things would go back to semi-normal, but that can't happen when he wasn't anywhere to be seen.

"So you ready for university?" Kim poked her head in my room. "Your suspension ends today, right?"

"Yeah, it does." I finished applying my makeup and turned to face her. "But I'm not going back just yet."

She frowned, "Why?"

Because university sucked.

"I made plans for today."

She crossed her arms. "Abby, do I have to give you another lecture about hanging out with him?"

"Brad is fine. It isn't a big deal."

"Where you two planning on going?"

"Picking up a motor in Linton. See, told you it was nothing serious. We're just hanging out, friends. I promise that is it."

"I'm your twin, dipshit. I can tell when you're lying," she scoffed and stepped into my room, closing the door behind her. Just what I didn't want, her poking her large nose into my business. What I did in my free time has nothing to do with her.

She really needs to back off.

"Making Reaper jealous is just going to cause drama. Do I have to tell you this again?"

"How can I be making him jealous when he isn't even here? Brad is a good guy."

"Not one man here is a good guy Abby." She rolled her eyes, crossing her arms. "You are just stirring the pot and when Reaper comes back, what do you think is going to happen when he finds out that you are making a move on one of his brothers?"

"Well, seeing I have no plans of ever telling him, I wouldn't know."

"Childish."

"Worrywart."

"Fine, go then, but don't come crying to me when this backfires in your face."

"Wasn't planning on it," I said just before she slammed my door close.

Brad and I had been hanging out a lot lately because he was the only one around. That and he is funny, like he comes off as a bad type of guy but has a good heart. I wasn't stupid. I knew he was dangerous, but if I could handle the Reaper as a lover, I'm pretty sure I can handle a badass as a friend.

This had nothing to do with Reaper; at least, that was what I was telling myself.

***

"No, I am telling you that guy was scared shitless." I laughed across at Brad as he drove the van.

"Got the price down, that is all that matters." Brad shrugged off his scary behavior from before.

I couldn't believe he had the ability to turn that on and off so quickly. To be honest, when he was arguing the price with the salesman, I was slightly scared of him for a minute.

"God, I hope you never do that to me." I exhaled sharply and crossed my legs.

He took his eyes off the road for a minute to look at me. "I'd never do that to you."

"Why, because I'm Roach's daughter?" I joked.

"No, because you're you. I would never treat you like that."

I smiled slightly at his kindness, "You know Brad, I don't know why people are scared of you."

"Got two sides, darling." He winked at me.

Two sides.

I chewed my bottom lip thinking that over. Reaper had two sides. Dad had two sides. I guess I was just lucky to be able to see their other side.

"You hungry?" Brad took a hand off the steering wheel and glanced at me. "Or are you in a rush to get home?"

Hurry to get home to Kim's judgment and Dad's short answers? Hell no.

"I'm in no rush."

"Then food is the next stop." He shot me a smile then his eyes went straight back to the road.

We had only locked eyes for a few moments, but I noticed a hint of happiness dance across his eyes.

Looking out the window, I wondered why it had taken Brad and I so long to hang out. Sure, he was five years older than me, but he had always been a part of my life. Even when I was little, he was around.

I snuck a glance at him. He had his sleeves rolled up, showing off his tattoos and toned arms. His black leather vest was worn in and covered in different patches.

I chewed my bottom lip, trying hard not to smile when I noticed he was wearing the belt I brought him.

His phone started buzzing in his pocket, and he reached in and pulled it out of jeans.

"Can you answer this?" He handed it to me. "Only got one point left, can't be caught on the phone while driving."

I took his phone and slid it across, answering it.

"Where the fuck are you?" A voice barked at me immediately, causing me to flinch away from the phone.

"Excuse me?" I shot back. Who the hell greets someone like that?

"Who the fuck is this?"

"Who the fuck are you?" I snapped back.

"Put Brad on the phone."

"Can't, he's driving."

"Tell him to pull the fuck over then, you dumb whore."

My mouth dropped open. How dare this stranger call me that!

"How about I just hang up instead?"

Brad kept glancing at me, frowning. "Who is it, Abby?"

I moved the phone from my lips, "Some rude cunt. He called me a dumb whore."

Immediately, Brad hit the indicator on and pulled over, snatching the phone from me.

"Who the fuck is this?" he barked into the phone.

Good, the rude man can get a dose of scary Brad.

"I told you, Reaper, I'm fucking out of town picking up a motor." Brad's voice was hard and blunt, but hearing that hadn't caused my blood to run cold. No, the word *'Reaper'* caused my blood to run cold.

I hadn't even picked up on his voice.

"No, I'm not fucking pissing off with a woman, I'm with Abby," Brad continued to talk to Reaper.

Reaper must have thought Brad was slacking off when really he was doing what he told them. I had just tagged along.

"Abby Harrison, what other Abby would I be talking about?" Brad snapped.

My stomach twisted.

"We'll be back when we are fucking back, and you better have an apology for Abby when you see her." With that said, Brad

322

hung up the phone and indicated to get back on the highway.

"Sorry about that, Abby."

"It's fine."

"It's not. Reaper has been more hormonal than normal lately. You're no whore."

"Thanks."

I didn't know what to say. Was it my fault Reaper was in a bad mood? Or was it because he had just come back from a long trip?

I made myself stop thinking about him. He was a waste of time. Even though everything inside me was screaming to send him a message, I didn't.

He couldn't handle me.

I was too much of a risk for him.

Reminding myself of these facts stopped me from thinking about him further.

"So back to food. I'm hungry." I changed the subject before Brad asked a question or I let Reaper's harsh words get to me.

I guess Brad was right about having two sides. It seems I had just heard the other side to my Reaper.

***

We had pulled into a twenty-four hour dinner and taken a booth up the back away from all the people who were openly staring at us.

That leather vest sure did bring attention to us.

I sat across from Brad and placed my elbows on the table, resting my head on my hands.

"I wonder how long it takes for them to make a burger here," I grumbled.

"I'm sure they won't be long," Brad said while playing on his phone.

"Hey, can I ask you something?" I asked Brad, grabbing his attention.

"What?"

I don't know if it was because I had been with him all day, but I felt relaxed, and I felt like I could ask him anything, so I was going to before the feeling went away.

"Do you still talk to Linda?"

Linda was his girl for years, but she started out as a club girl, and everyone knew that you didn't make a club girl your official woman.

An emotion covered his eyes for a moment, and his jaw clenched slightly. "No. She moved upstate, she's married now. Heard she was knocked up as well."

I was surprised he gave me an honest answer. "Do you miss her?"

His eyes locked with mine, and I saw the regret and then it was gone. "Not anymore." He smiled at me. "How can I be missing her when I've got you entertaining me."

I grinned. "Glad I can help."

"It would never have worked between her and me," he opened up. "She hated the club, what it stood for."

"But she chose to be a part of it." I frowned.

He nodded his head, "When she was young and stupid, she decided to become a club girl. She said she always regretted it."

I couldn't understand why. We were a family, a tight family.

"She asked me to pick between the club and her, and well, you know how that ended," he added.

"She should never have put you in that position. If she knew you for real, she could never do that. You and the club aren't separate; you're together. You wouldn't be who you are without the club."

He grinned, looking up from the salt and pepper shakers. "And that is what would make you the perfect woman."

I brushed my blonde hair to the side of my face, "Not everyone would think that." Reaper didn't see it like that.

"Well whoever he is, he doesn't deserve you."

My eyes bounced up from the table and met his again. "He sees me as a responsibility. Like I'm something he has to protect, and it is too much work."

"Sounds like a wanker."

I laughed, "You could say that. As well as stubborn, immature, and hot-headed."

"Nothing would ever happen to you anyway, Abby. You got a lot of men standing in front of harm's way before there was any chance of you getting hurt."

It was official, Brad had a soft side, and I grinned across at him. "Thank you."

He shrugged his shoulders, "It's just the truth."

"He thinks that the bad things that define him could hurt me."

"A man is defined by his choices. But he has to know you aren't going to wait forever. Or are you?"

Was I going to wait for Reaper to change? To accept me? To change his mind? When I really thought about it, I realized just how stupid I was being.

"I'm not."

"Not what?" Brad frowned at me.

"I'm not waiting for him anymore."

"Sounds like a smart idea, darling." He smiled at me kindly.

And just like that, I made a decision. I wasn't waiting anymore.

Chapter 62

Abby

We didn't get back till late, and half of me believed that was because of Brad. He seemed to be in no rush to get back and did the actual speed limit the whole way home.

Now we were here, I didn't want to go in.

"You alright?" Brad gave me a questioning look as I stayed strapped in the van.

"Yeah just um," I unclicked my seat belt. "Not really in a rush to see my dad."

"Thought things were good between you two?"

"It was." Then I recalled how he scared Reaper away from me. "But when it comes to him, you never know."

"Yeah well, I'm gonna get an earful from Reaper." He unclicked his seat belt.

"What for?"

"For taking all day."

"What does it matter anyway, wasn't like he was around today."

He frowned for a moment. "Reaper rode in last night. Surprised you didn't hear them."

He was back.

He had been back since this morning.

I swallowed my anger quickly. "Nope, must have slept through it."

"Yeah well, he's acting like a dick at the moment." Brad climbed out of the van, and I was quick to follow, scooping up my handbag off the floor before slamming the van door shut.

God, it was cold. The freezing air whipped through me as we walked across the lot.

"Thanks for letting me come today." I gave Brad a smile. I was honestly thankful to get away from this place.

The corner of his lip twitched up. "Surprised you wanted to come."

"Any excuse to get out of this place." I suppressed a smirk. "Plus you aren't bad company."

He scoffed, "Glad to hear I don't bore you."

"You could never bore me."

We shared a simple smile before he opened up the clubhouse door for me. Was it wrong of me to like having Brad's attention?

"Where the hell have you been all day?" Kim roared from across the bar; her face went from calm to furious in a second.

"I've been with Brad."

"So you thought you wouldn't answer your phone?"

"We were out of range for a bit. God, Kim, calm down, it's not like someone died."

The anger melted off her face. "Dad's in the hospital."

Hospital. Dad. Dad didn't go to the hospital. Ever, period.

"What happened?" I was more aware of the glum mood that stained the air now. All the boys were quiet and sitting randomly around the room, drinking silently.

"He had a heart attack." Kim's voice wavered with emotion. "He was on his bike when it happened. He's messed up, Abby, like real bad."

"Why aren't you at the hospital?"

"Because I've been there all day, I just came home to get changed and try to track you down."

"Well, I'm going back up with you."

"I can take you," Brad spoke up. I had forgotten he was standing next to me. "You girls don't look right to drive yourself."

"Thanks." I looked up at him. "Well, let's go."

Kim walked around the bar, looking like hell. "Reaper is up

there; he has been keeping us updated with any changes."

"Has there been any?"

"No, he's still in surgery."

Stepping back out into the cold night, my stomach twisted tightly. Dad never got sick. He was Dad, strong and untouchable. Suddenly I was regretting giving him the cold shoulder for the last week. Hell, I was regretting putting him under extra stress.

All I knew as I climbed back into the van was it was going to be a long night.

***

He was standing, looking like a guard in the middle of an empty waiting room. At the sound of our footsteps, his eyes shot up and immediately locked onto mine. His eyes were scorching as if he was yelling at me through eye contact.

"Any news?" Kim asked, dropping her handbag on the plastic chair and sitting down next to it.

Reaper shook his head but still managed to not break eye contact.

"Why didn't you tell us Dad was in the hospital when you called?" My voice was firm and strong, the complete opposite of what I was feeling right now.

"Would it have made you get here any quicker?" he fired back at me with a harshness lingering in his words.

"Just would have been nice to know." I crossed my arms and continued to stand next to Brad and didn't make a move to go towards him.

"How long has he been under for?" Brad asked, moving from my side and taking a seat.

"Five hours," Reaper muttered back and finally broke eye contact with me.

Feeling freed for some reason, I went and sat next to Kim. She was a nervous wreck, which kind of surprised me because I would have thought I would be the one having a breakdown and stressing out, not her.

Brad gestured with his head to Reaper. "Wanna go out for a smoke?"

Something was telling me that these two had unfinished business and something to talk about.

Reaper nodded his head and followed Brad out of the waiting room.

"Wonder how long it is going to take." Kim tapped her long nails on the armrest. "You would think they would have something to tell us by now."

I leaned back in the seat. "They'll come and tell us when they can." I knew we were in for a long night.

Because if there was one thing you could bet on when it came to a hospital visit, it was never quick.

***

Thirty minutes had passed and the boys still hadn't returned. Nothing had changed; we were still waiting. Well, Kim had gone from sitting to pacing, so apart from that, nothing had changed.

"That's it, I need a smoke." She whipped around to look at me and went towards her handbag. "Fucking useless hospital."

"No news is good news, remember." I attempted to be positive, but it was only met by her rolling her eyes.

"I'll be outside. If anyone comes, come get me." She walked out of the room, leaving me alone in the empty waiting room.

I was alone for a total of five minutes before he walked in.

Immediately I wished Kim was back.

"Can we talk?" Reaper stood in front of me.

I dragged my eyes up to meet his. "Didn't realize we weren't."

"I'm sorry."

I blinked up at him, keeping a plain expression on my face. Had he really just said that?

No; I must have heard him wrong.

"Abby, answer me." He dropped down to his knees in front of me. "Say something, anything."

If you took away the outfit, removed the outlaw and the fact he was covered in tattoos. Then maybe, just maybe, he would look like a desperate man asking the girl he loved to forgive him.

Pity this was Reaper we were talking about.

"Don't worry about it," I blew out, finally giving him something.

"Abby, don't be like that."

"Like what?" I forgave him, didn't I! "I said everything is fine, so don't worry about it."

"I was a dick."

"What's new?"

"I got scared."

"I know."

"Then can you at least try and forgive me?"

"I already have."

"Like fuck you have, I know you."

He was right, I hadn't forgiven him. But what was there to forgive? He didn't want responsibility for me. Well, he doesn't have responsibility.

"You and I were never going to work. You said that multiple times. I was just stupid enough to think that a cold-hearted bastard like yourself could have true feelings for me." I let rip some of my anger. "But I was wrong. So that's that."

He pursed his lips together, his eyes hardening. "We aren't over."

330

"You're right because that would mean something would have actually had to have started."

"Don't fucking act like that."

I crossed my arms. "Could you just go back outside? Or fuck off back to the clubhouse. You don't need to be here."

"I'm here for you."

"I don't need you."

He groaned and stood back up. "You're being difficult."

"What did you expect?"

"Well, I sure as fuck didn't expect you to start chasing another man right away."

I frowned for a moment, then made the connection. "Brad and I are friends, nothing more."

"We were friends once."

I scoffed. "We skipped friends the first time we met."

Brad and Kim walked in, ending our conversation. Well, it was more of an argument.

"Any news?" Kim asked, stuffing her cigarettes back in her handbag.

"No." I stood up. "I think I need some fresh air."

"You ok?" Brad frowned at me. "Want me to come with you."

"No, I'm fine, just need to get out of this waiting room for a bit." And away from Reaper.

"I'll come." Brad offered.

"I'm fine." I smiled at him and touched his shoulder lightly before I passed him and headed for the exit.

Maybe the fresh air would help me think clearer. Maybe then I could process the fact that the Reaper had said sorry to me.

The question was, should I believe it? Or was I just asking for more drama?

Chapter 63

Abby

I was putting out my third cigarette when out of the corner of my eye, I saw Brad striding across the car park towards me.

"Thought you might need a new pack?" he said smugly.

Sure I had been out here a while, but I just wasn't in a rush to head back inside to see Reaper.

"Any news?"

He shook his head. "Nope. Kim wanted me to check on you."

"I'm coming in." I sighed and stuffed my hands in my leather jacket. It was a chilly night, and the wind was ripping through me. That should have been an encouraging reason for me *to* go inside.

"Wanna talk about it?" Brad walked slowly beside me as we headed back to the hospital.

"Not really."

Had he picked up on something?

"Look, Abby," He gripped my hand lightly, stopping me. "Your old man being sick is a stressor. If you need someone to talk to, I'm here."

Oh, he was talking about Dad. Thank fuck for that.

I smiled weakly. "Thanks. But Dad is strong; he'll pull through this." I was trying harder to convince myself of that than Brad.

The hospital doors slid open, and I walked into the last person I wanted or expected to see.

"You have to be fucking kidding me." Vivien's eyes narrowed nastily at me immediately.

"Vivien," I said dryly. "Always a pleasure."

"How dare you. HOW dare YOU come here!" She sharply shoved me backward.

"What the fuck!"

"You have the cheek to come here after what you did. If you think you and your mutt of a family will get away with this, you're wrong."

"Again, WHAT THE FUCK!" I shoved her back. I had no idea what she was talking about, and I really wasn't in the fucking mood to play a guessing game with her.

"You know what, you stupid club whore!" Fury covered her face, her sharp eyes wanting blood.

Brad's arm whipped up between us, and he gently held me back.

"Back the fuck off." Brad stepped in. He wasn't the gentle, laughable, or friendly Brad right now. His facial expression was hard, his voice dripping with controlled rage.

"Yeah, get someone else to fight your fight. What a surprise," Vivien snapped, seeming not fussed that Brad was standing there looking like a foaming bulldog ready to bite.

"If you've got something to say, spit it out, bitch." I felt my control over my rage for her boiling over.

"Like you don't know! Like you have no idea that Sebastian is in here beaten nearly to death because you went and told your father."

I hadn't told Dad anything; the less the club knew about their business, the better. But right now she was digging her own grave.

"That's not on us."

"As if."

"Believe it or not Vivien, but I'm sure Sebastian has pissed off more people than just me."

"Vivien," An older man in a business suit stood behind her, likely her father.

"You must be one of the Harrison sisters." He stood at his daughter's side, forcing a false polite tone.

"Your daughter needs to back the fuck off." I looked him directly in the eye. I wasn't scared of him, and he couldn't intimidate me, especially with the beast standing beside me.

His face clenched, and he took a dominating step forward. "Just let it be known that the Westbrooks don't back down from a fight. What you did tonight, little girl, will cause a chain of reaction that your tiny whore mind couldn't possibly wrap around."

How fucking dare he.

I opened my mouth but was pushed back behind Brad before I could say anything.

"You're threatening the wrong girl."

The man laughed sharply. "The threat wasn't limited to her. It was directed at the lot of you bottom feeders. Now if you'll excuse us, I have a son to see."

Brad didn't say anything. Instead, he let the awful bad-mouthing man walk around us. Vivien made sure to give me a smug expression before following.

Grinding my teeth, I stepped up my pace, heading back in Dad's direction.

"You've got some explaining to do, Abby." Brad glanced down at me, his eyes still holding anger.

Thanks to Vivien.

"If I said it was nothing, would you believe me?" I looked back up at him.

"No."

"If I said I was handling it, would you believe me?"

We paused at the waiting room door before entering.

"You don't need to be handling shit. That's why you have us. So if you've got something, Abby, you bring it to us. Not fucking go behind our back playing Robin Hood."

Rolling my eyes, I pushed the waiting room door open, ending that conversation.

"Dad's out," Kim pounced immediately. "He's in room four. I've been waiting for you."

"Well, let's go then."

She linked her hand with mine, and I followed her back out.

Now I had two bikers to try and avoid. My night was really getting better by the moment.

***

Tubes ran down each of Dad's arms; I had never seen him look so weak, so pale. He lay there, eyes shut, barely breathing. The only noise in the room was the continual beeping of the monitor to his left.

Kim and I sat on each side of him, both holding one of his hands. His touch was so cold, and all I wanted to do was warm him up.

The doctors had come in and given us a detailed, perhaps over-detailed debrief of Dad's condition. The only words that really stood out to me were that he was still in bad shape and that they had done all they could.

"You think he can hear us?" Kim glanced across at me, teary-eyed.

I shrugged my shoulders.

I didn't know.

If anything, I was still in shock. I had never seen Dad like this, and it terrified me.

"You girls want anything?" Reaper's voice was soft and came from behind us.

Kim wiped her eyes and shook her head.

"No." I turned to look at him and Brad, who were leaning against the wall. "You two don't have to stay here, it's late, and I don't know about Kim, but I'm not planning on leaving him anytime soon."

"We're here for the night." Reaper's eyes locked with mine. "Though we do have to give the boys an update."

I nodded my head and just when he was about to step out, there

335

was a knock on the door.

It quietly opened and Trigger stepped in. His eyes searched the room till they landed on Kim.

"How's he doing?"

Her face melted with relief, and I couldn't help but smile gently at her. I knew what she was feeling right now, relief and safety, what I used to feel when my eyes landed on Reaper.

"He's stable but still in a bad state," Brad answered for us.

Trigger moved across the room till he was standing beside Kim, and he dropped down to his knees. "I just got back and heard, sorry it took me so long to get here."

Kim cupped his face with her free hand and smiled. "It's ok."

He wiped away a tear that was running down her cheek, and while they shared a romantic moment, I glanced back at Reaper, only to find his eyes zoned in on me.

"I think I need another smoke." I let go of Dad's hand and stumbled up to my feet. "And some fresh air."

Kim nodded her head. "Do you want me to come?"

"No, stay with Dad; I won't be long."

"I'll come out with ya. It's too late of a night to be by yourself out there." Reaper stepped forward, giving me a look that I knew I couldn't argue with.

Nodding my head, I scooped up my bag and walked out the door he was holding open for me.

Pausing, I looked back, locking my eyes with Brad.

"Can you come too? We should finish that conversation from before." I didn't have to add anything else than that for him to know what I was talking about.

Dad was sick. Right now would be a perfect time to strike an attack on his club. I wouldn't have them going in blind. They needed to know the details, and if Vivien's dad's threat was serious, then that made it more important that I tell them.

I wished I could have talked it over with Kim first, but right now she couldn't deal with any more worry or stress. I had to handle it myself.

So I was going to, by telling the two men I trusted everything I knew.

Chapter 64

Abby

"All this time, you said nothing." Reaper spoke harshly to me. "What the fuck were you thinking, keeping this shit to yourself?"

I had told both of them everything I knew; well, everything Kim and I had known. It was fair to say I was getting the third degree for keeping my mouth shut.

I crossed my arms and stepped out of a nurse's way as we stood in the passageway outside Dad's room.

"Keep your voice down or we'll be thrown out," I hissed back at him.

He scoffed loudly, but it was Brad's intense, furious eyes that had me feeling like I was trapped.

"I'm telling you now," I defended my actions.

"Because your old man is on his fucking death bed and you're feeling guilty." Reaper ripped through me, not caring about my feelings. "You've started a shitstorm."

"No, I found out about a shitstorm." I corrected him and forced my emotions back. I wouldn't let Reaper see me scared.

"Do you know who gave the kid the beating?" Brad asked, and I shrugged my shoulders in response.

"He's a dick of a guy. Sure he has an arm length of people wanting to give him a beating."

"So while Abby was being threatened, what the fuck were you doing?" Reaper turned to face Brad.

It wasn't Brad's fault. The last thing I wanted was to turn brother onto brother.

"There wasn't much he could do," I stood up for him.

"Back down Abby, don't need you defending me." Brad turned

to face Reaper head on. "You got something you wanna say, brother?"

"Just saying if someone was threatening Abby openly in front of me, they wouldn't be walking out of the hospital but getting a bed instead."

"Would you two stop it?" I snapped in between them. "Fighting between yourselves does nothing. I wasn't hurt; it wasn't a big deal. Now can we just focus on what we do next?"

"Nothing." Reaper's eyes flickered back to me. "You do nothing. This is club business now."

"Oh, really, and how is the club going to handle it when the President is in the hospital and the Vice President is a dickhead?"

Reaper narrowed his eyes at me.

"Not your concern."

"It is my concern because I have to go to school with these arseholes."

"The threat will be handled, you don't have to worry about it."

"You say that, yet I still don't believe you."

"Learn your fucking place!" Reaper roared down at me, taking a dominating step over me. "You don't get a fucking say. You aren't a member. We put up with you because of your old man and guess fucking what, right now he's lying on his back, and the only place you have the right to be is by his fucking side. So back the fuck off and get the fuck in line, Abby."

My stomach clenched tightly, and tears slowly coated my eyes.

I wrapped my arms around me and let my eyes fall to the ground, staring down at the patterned carpet.

I wished Dad was awake.

I walked around Reaper, and my hand landed on the handle of the door. I slipped back into the room, and by what I caught of Kim and Trigger, I had walked in on a moment.

But I didn't care.

I couldn't stay one more moment near Reaper.

I sat in the plastic chair and went back to holding Dad's hand. If he was awake right now, he would have given Reaper a straight punch to the face for talking to me like that. I wiped away an angry tear and kept my eyes planted on Dad.

I never thought Reaper would speak to me like that. Sure, I had heard him speak to others like that, harshly, his words as sharp as knives. But I hadn't ever expected him to speak to me like that.

Guess I was as stupid as he made me out to be.

"You ok?" Kim asked.

I didn't pull my eyes away from Dad. "Fine."

"You're crying."

"I just want Dad to wake up."

Trigger moved from Kim's side and whispered something before leaving the room quietly.

"He'll wake up, Abby; he's strong, and he won't let a heart attack take him out."

I nodded my head, pretending the tears that slid down my cheeks were for Dad and not out of embarrassment.

***

Kim had drifted off to sleep; how, I didn't know. I still hadn't been able to take my eyes off Dad. I watched intently, waiting for his chest to rise each time. I knew the next twenty-four hours were important; the doctor had made that part crystal clear.

I just wanted him to wake up.

The door opened quietly.

I squeezed my eyes shut tightly. *Please don't be Reaper.*

A hand fell on my shoulder, and my body stiffened immediately.

"You ok?"

I relaxed. It was only Brad. "Yeah, I'm fine." I twisted to look up at him. "Didn't think you were still here."

340

"I gave Reaper a spray for talking to you like that." He dropped to his knees beside me. His voice deepened as he tried to speak quietly.

"I don't care." I cared a fucking lot.

"Shouldn't have gone down like that."

"I don't care." I kept my eyes on Dad's rising chest.

"Abby," his voice softened, and he gently turned my head to look at him. "I care, and I'm sure as hell your old man would have cared."

I stared back at him, keeping my eyes empty of emotion. "I don't care."

I kept saying it, but that still didn't mean I meant it.

Reaper's words had whipped across me, and it hurt; it still hurt.

"Your old man being sick puts a lot of pressure on him. He walked away from a President patch; he never wanted the responsibility of it again. Suddenly he has it fucking dumped on him, and the safety of the President's daughters is on the top of his list."

"Don't make excuses for him." I turned my head back on to Dad. "Anyway, I don't care."

Brad's leather crackled as he moved. "He'll wake up." He still had his hand on my shoulder, and when he didn't lift it, I was glad.

Because right now I was scared of losing my dad.

"I hope so." My voice was barely above a whisper. Tears filled my eyes for the second time tonight. "The last time we spoke, I was yelling at him."

"Most of Roach's conversations involve yelling."

"But I started it." I glanced away from Dad, meeting Brad's smooth, kind eyes. "I can't even remember what it was about."

Brad ran a hand through his messy black hair and sighed slowly before he did something I hadn't expected. He dipped his head, locking his eyes with mine. "Stop beating yourself up." He cupped my cheek. "And fucking stop crying because it doesn't suit you." He wiped away a tear with his thumb.

I smiled weakly. "When did you become so soft?"

A smirk spread across his lips, "Can't stop the charm when a pretty girl is involved."

I didn't know what I could call the feeling that engulfed me hearing that, but it was something that softened me and stopped my stomach swirling with nerves, and somehow, it gave me some relief.

Chapter 65

Abby

It had been twenty-six hours since Dad had come out of surgery, and he still hadn't woken up.

"You girls need to go home, shower, get some sleep, and come back. You heard the doctor, it could be days before he wakes up," Trigger attempted to reason with us.

The boys had left and came back this morning.

I hadn't acknowledged Reaper, even though his presence in this room was causing me to suffocate.

"Trigger has a point, Abby," Brad backed him up.

Kim had gotten a few broken hours of sleep last night. I couldn't. The chair was uncomfortable.

I was too busy watching the nurse check Dad to look at them. But I would bet they were giving us a pleading smile to go with their convincing words.

"I'm fine," I said, clipping my words. I didn't want to talk to them. I was tired and angry.

"So am I." Kim gave them her answer.

"You know," the nurse turned to look at us, "I could arrange for another bed to be brought in here and perhaps if the girls really don't want to leave, you could bring them a change of clothes. There is a full en-suite to the left, you both are more than welcome to use it."

I blinked continually at her. Why hadn't we thought of that?

"I like her idea better." Kim said and twisted in her seat. "Could you organize someone to bring our clothes up? Cherry or Red could do it."

There was a heavy sigh behind us. "Better than nothing," Trigger muttered. "We'll organize it."

"Abby, I need to speak to you."

I didn't need to turn around to know who was speaking to me. I knew that voice better than I knew my own.

"I'm not leaving Dad."

"It will only take a minute, I promise."

"Your promises don't mean shit."

Tension started to fill the air, and I was sure everyone was feeling it.

"Go, Abby. I'll come get you if Dad moves or opens his eyes," Kim said, trying to defuse the tension.

"Fine." I dragged the plastic chair back and stood up, walking past him and out the room.

What could he possibly have to say to me? Yell at me some more?

He followed me out, closing the door behind him.

"Wanna walk with me to the waiting room?" His voice was softer, kinder. I glanced at him and he sure as hell looked a lot less stressed compared to last night.

He might have calmed down, but that didn't mean I had. He had hurt my feelings, and I felt like a damn two-year-old admitting it.

"What do you want, Reaper?"

"You normally call me Kade."

"You hate your first name." I crossed my arms and kept stride with him.

He lightly grabbed my arm. "Not when you say it."

It was like I was dealing with a completely different person compared to last night.

"What do you want?" I pressed when we entered the empty waiting room.

He sighed. "I need you to go see this Sebastian kid."

"Thought it was club business now."

"Abby." He growled my name, using it as more of a warning.

"Don't be difficult."

"You know what, Reaper? Maybe that is what I want to be, after how you spoke to me last night."

"I said I was sorry."

"No, you didn't, and I don't want to hear it now."

"Really? Because it sounds like you're holding onto it."

"Maybe I just don't like being spoken to like a piece of shit."

"If you weren't being so difficult, I wouldn't have had to pull you in line."

"And what line is that? The line of a President's daughter? Am I only allowed to talk when spoken to?"

"Abby, stop it; you're being stupid." Annoyance flickered across his eyes.

Normal people would be scared of Reaper. His dominating strong shoulders, strong jaw line, everything about him just caused women to look at him. So it didn't surprise me when two nurses were openly checking him out.

For fuck's sake, why was I jealous?

He's a prick. A stubborn, annoying, selfish prick. I crossed my arms.

"Fine, I'll talk to him. Are we done now?" I drew the conversation to a close.

He leaned against the wall, his stone cold eyes running up and down and examining me.

"I don't like you pissed off."

"Then here is an idea, don't piss me off."

"I'm sorry."

"Yeah, I've heard that before."

I doubted he even meant it. He snapped at me last night and just thought that it was ok? Well, it wasn't. I needed him on my side last night. I needed him, the way Kim had Trigger, reassuring her. Instead, I had Brad, and I still didn't know how I felt about that.

My eyes dropped to the ground while my mind went wild with thoughts of Brad and what last night could have meant to him.

"Abby." He gently cupped my chin, lifting my head. "I'm really sorry about last night. I was freaking the fuck out and took it out on you. I'm sorry." Honesty lingered through his words, and the soft smile he gave me just was the cherry on top.

I should be happy with that.

But I wasn't.

"Ok."

He frowned, "You still don't believe me, do you?"

"If you've done it before, what is stopping you from talking to me like that again?"

"My word. I'll never speak to you like that again. Fuck, Abby, you know how I feel about you."

I pulled away from his hand and took a step back, "Well, sometimes feelings change. I'll talk to Sebastian, can I go now?"

He stepped out of my way with a hurt expression on his face. "Sebastian is on ward four."

I walked quickly down the hallway and back to Dad. Maybe it was because I was so tired and angry that I couldn't take his word. I don't know. All I knew was I wanted my dad to wake up.

I needed him to wake up.

***

I felt a bit more refreshed after a few hours' sleep on the spare bed and a shower. Now that I was thinking clearly and didn't look like complete shit, I decided I might as well handle this business with Sebastian now.

I knocked on the room, and when I heard a weak come in, I entered.

His eyes widened when they met mine.

346

"Abby Harrison, what did I do to deserve your visit?" He straightened up in bed, clenching his right side.

"I think you know why."

"My sister told me that they ran into you."

"And did you correct them, or are they still under the impression that it was us?"

"I corrected them. Wasn't your fault I got my ass handed to me."

"Your sister opened up a shitstorm by doing that." I dragged a chair to his side. "Really, she couldn't have picked worse timing to lose her shit."

"Heard you were with a patched member when they confronted you. Any chance of damage control?"

"Nope." I crossed my arms. "The boys are handling it now."

"Which means they'll be knocking on my old man's door soon."

"Most likely."

"So why did you come here? I know that kiss was something, but I didn't think it was good enough for you to turn your back on your club."

"It wasn't, and I'm not. I'm here under club orders."

"What, to give me a warning?"

"No, to find out who really gave you that beating."

"It was a drunken fight I picked in a pub. Sorry, the story isn't more eventful."

"You lost badly."

He cracked a grin, "Yeah, I fucking did."

Sighing, I leaned back in the chair, feeling some stress lift from me. "Did they break much?"

"A few ribs, swollen face, as you can tell."

"Could be worse then."

"Yeah, they could have broken my arm or leg, I guess. Still, hurts like a mother fucker."

"The ribs always do." I remembered when I broke one of mine

when I was little. I fell from a tree that I wasn't meant to be climbing, and Dad was so mad.

My stomach twisted thinking about Dad. God, I wanted him to wake up.

"So why are you in the hospital? Apart from visiting me, of course?" Sebastian asked, his face covered in pain for a moment when he moved.

I doubted he would care, hell, he would most likely be pleased to hear it. Still, I found myself wanting to tell him.

"My dad had a heart attack."

"Shit Abby, how bad?"

"Bad." My voice croaked with sadness. "He still hasn't woken up."

"You should be with him, not wasting your time up here with me," Sebastian said kindly. "I know I'm charming and all but seriously, you should be with your dad."

"I will be. I just had to check on you first." I forced a small smile.

"Hope he recovers."

"No, you don't."

"Nah, I do." His voice was serious, "Nothing worse than losing a parent." He sounded to be speaking from experience.

"Thanks." I got up from the chair. "Hope you recover quickly, Westbrook." I patted his leg, and he tried to give me a charming grin.

"Yeah, same to your old man, Harrison."

I opened his door and slipped out.

Well, that was handled. Now it meant I had to report back to Reaper. Well, maybe I didn't have to do it face to face.

I pulled out my phone while walking to the elevator.

Spoke with Sebastian was a drunken pub fight.

I sent the message and pressed the elevator button.

"You look cold."

348

I glanced to my right. A young doctor was standing next to me, looking me up and down.

He was right; I was cold because Red hadn't packed a fucking jumper.

"You don't," I responded blankly and entered the lift. To my disappointment, so did he.

"You're Jed Harrison's daughter, aren't you?"

"How did you know that?"

"I'm one of his doctors. We spoke late last night?"

"Sorry." I felt rude immediately. "I couldn't take my eyes off Dad last night."

"I'm due to do my rounds soon, so I'll be seeing you shortly. Perhaps this time I'll leave more of an impression." He smiled at me.

The lift doors sprung open, and he smoothly walked out.

Why did that feel like he was hitting on me? I frowned. Maybe I was just thinking that lately about every male I was near.

God, I needed a good night's sleep, or at least my brain did.

***

"Abby, look at me. Tell me why you did it." Dad looked down at me, hands on his hips.

"Because I wanted one." I looked up at him, close to tears. "Kim dared me."

"If you want something, you tell me next time, you don't steal it." He huffed. "Just because your sister dares you to do something, doesn't mean you do it. Got it?"

This was all over a lollipop I took from the corner store. Wasn't like the grumpy old man caught me. No, Dad did, when I was sucking on it in the backseat.

"You're my little girl, and you want for nothing," He dropped

349

to his knees, looking me in the eye. "So next time, kiddo, you open your mouth and tell your old man you want a lollipop."

"Ok, Dad."

"Now give me a hug." I wrapped my arms around him tightly, and he easily lifted me off the ground, standing back up. "And stop crying. Harrisons don't cry; we make others do the crying."

I wiped my eyes and nodded my head.

For some reason as I walked back to Dad's room, that memory bounced into my mind. What I would do right now just to have a hug from my dad.

I turned the corner, and immediately I knew something was wrong because Kim was banging on Dad's door, screaming.

"Kim!" I yelled, breaking into a run. "Kim, what's wrong?" I attempted to pull her away from the door as she banged on it with closed fists, tears streaming down her face.

"Kim, what the hell happened?" I forced her to look at me.

"I don't know. One minute he's fine and then next he started jolting and then the machines started beeping." She spoke in a rush, sobbing, "Then they pushed me out of the room, and I don't know. I don't know what's going on."

I wrapped my arms around her. "It's ok. It's ok. Just, just keep breathing. Breathe through it, Kim."

Her head dropped to my shoulder, and her body shook as she sobbed.

I glanced over Kim's shoulder, watching the doctor who I had just shared a lift with running toward us.

I pulled Kim out of his way, and he didn't give me a second glance. He went straight into the room. I could hear a lot of beeping, rushed voices, and then the door shut and then all I could hear was Kim's sobbing.

I hugged her tightly, and tears slowly ran down my cheeks.

He wasn't meant to die.

He can't die.

350

I couldn't face the world yet without a parent.

I couldn't face this world without my strong dad behind me.

The doors burst open, and Dad's bed was rushed out. I pulled Kim and me out of their way just in time.

"What's happening?" I asked anyone, everyone who was rushing Dad's bed down the hall. I let go of Kim and jogged after them. "Please don't just take him, tell me what's happening!"

"There has been a complication; he needs to go back into surgery. I'm sorry Abby, I don't have time to explain it to you right now." The young doctor spun me a quick reply just before the lift doors slid shut, leaving me standing there staring at the metal doors.

A complication.

My body went numb with fear.

"I'm sorry, Dad," I whispered to myself as I let the tears fall freely; sometimes Harrisons do cry.

Chapter 66

Abby

Sometimes numbness can overcome you to the point you lose track of time and day, what is happening. Your grip on reality loosens. I stared out the hospital window, down at the busy street, watching the people live their lives while mine crumbled apart.

Kim was whimpering, sitting in the corner. We hadn't called anyone. I couldn't bring myself to say it. I knew as soon as I spoke on the phone my voice would crack and I would lose my self-control again.

I barely had a grip on the tears.

"Are you going to call the boys?" Kim wiped her nose and looked at me. "They should know."

They should know what? That Dad was losing his fight? That he had been rushed to surgery and we had no fucking idea why apart from knowing there was a complication?

I pulled my phone out.

Staring at it.

I should have made more of an effort to make sure Dad had his heart medication. I should have stopped him smoking. I should have made him stop drinking so darn much.

I collapsed in a chair.

Who was I calling again?

My mind was flying from one thing to the next. Right. The boys needed to know.

Just as I was about to scroll down the list of names, a name popped up on the screen.

Brad.

I answered.

"Abby, just checking how things are going?"

I stayed quiet, letting the tears slid down my face.

"Abby?"

I cleared my throat. "He's back in surgery." I could only string a few words together.

"I'm coming." What followed was a beeping. I pulled the phone away from my ear.

"They're coming." I looked across at Kim, and she nodded her head.

"I've been thinking," Kim moved a seat over, sitting next to me. "We should call the Shields."

That wasn't a terrible idea. They had a right to know. Doubted they would care, but they did have a right to know.

"I'll call Amber," I said.

Kim nodded her head. "You should do it now. Just in case."

I knew what she was referring to. Just in case Dad didn't make it. Then they knew he was sick before he passed.

I was so numb now that it wasn't even causing me to cry.

I reached for my phone and scrolled down to her name.

The ringing tone followed.

"Hello?"

"Amber, it's Abby Harrison."

"I know, I saved your number." Her voice wasn't hard or cold. She sounded perhaps friendly.

"Dad's had a heart attack." I was straight to the point. I couldn't be bothered with small talk.

"How bad?"

"He's just had another attack; he's been rushed into a second surgery."

"Are you ok?" Her words were genuine, kind, and caring. "And Kim?"

"No."

353

"We'll ride out this afternoon."

"You don't have to."

"I said we would be there; we will be there."

"Thanks."

"Abby, he's a strong man. Don't give up on him yet."

"Thanks." I felt like a frozen record.

"I'll be seeing you soon," Amber said before she hung up.

"They're coming." I sighed. Kim dropped her head on my shoulder, and we sat in the empty waiting room.

"I just want him to be ok," she whispered.

"I know."

***

Brad entered first, followed by Reaper and then Trigger. Trigger went straight to Kim, dropping to his knees in front of her.

She broke out in tears immediately and wrapped her arms around him.

"You ok, Harrison?" Brad stood in front of me, "Fuck, you look freezing."

He pulled his leather vest off and peeled his jumper off. "Arms up, Abby."

I did as he asked and he threaded the jumper on. His scent engulfed me, making me feel safer for some strange reason.

"Come on Harrison, no tears," he said, wiping them off my cheek. "He's a fighter, and he hasn't given up yet."

"It's been hours." My voice was dry, and the numbness I felt could be heard within my tone.

Reaper moved behind Brad, and my tear-stained eyes landed on him. The pity he was feeling for me could be seen across his face.

Then someone stepped out from around him, someone I wasn't

expecting.

"Drake." I couldn't believe my eyes.

"Hey, baby girl." He walked towards me, and Brad stepped to the side. "Heard you were having a rough time."

My throat tightened, and that was it. As his arms wrapped around me, I broke down, and I cried and cried into his shoulder.

He just held me tighter, and I squeezed the life out of him as I wailed into his shoulder.

And it was in Drake's arms that the grief I was feeling overtook me.

Reaper

I watched Abby cling to Drake, crying into his shoulder, and I was forcing myself not to rip his hands off her. I knew it would be hard seeing them together, but I had made the decision I would rather see her leaning on Drake for support than fucking Brad.

Cause her and Drake were only friends.

Brad and she could become something more.

Which would be happening over my fucking dead body.

She was mine.

It was fucking killing me, not knowing how to help her right now. I wasn't good with words like Drake. Didn't have the smooth words like Brad either. When it came down to feelings and emotions and crap, I fucking sucked.

Which meant right now, I was useless to her.

The only thing I could do was protect her from the fucking pieces of shit known as the Westbrooks. I could do that.

I could run the club for her old man, but I couldn't give her what she needed now.

Because I wasn't even sure what she needed.

A hug?

Fuck if I knew. I ran a hand over my head and took a step away from them. I needed a motherfucking smoke and a hard drink.

She pulled away from him, wiping her eyes. "How did you know?"

"Kade called me," Drake answered her, and I cringed hearing my real name.

Still, don't know why I liked it when Abby said it but when anyone else said it, it made me cringe.

Her swollen eyes landed on mine, and she almost looked thankful. First time in days she hadn't looked at me with anger or given me this empty expression.

I wanted to say something, anything that would cause her to keep looking at me like that, keep her from going cold on me again.

But I had nothing.

"Harrisons?" A doctor stepped into the room. Immediately Kim and Abby sprang up from their seats.

The doctor's eyes landed on Abby, and they softened. "Jed has been moved to the ICU. He's recovering but needs to be closely monitored."

"So he made it." Kim seemed amazed.

The doctor nodded his head "Your father is a strong man. But his heart can't take much more, if he has another attack like that, we won't be able to do much. Which is why we will be monitoring him extremely closely."

Abby sighed in relief and closed her eyes. That would have taken some stress off her.

"Can we see him?" she asked, opening her eyes and looking calmer.

"Of course, I'll take you myself." The doctor smiled kindly at her, but there was something about that smile I didn't trust.

You had to be fucking kidding me.

She had a motherfucking doctor chasing her now as well?

What the hell was it with this woman causing men to follow her and drool over her?

Great, another one to deal with.

At least he was a citizen, and if there was one thing about Abby, it was she never went for a straight-cut type of guy.

Chapter 67

Reaper

You don't get to where I am in life without doing a lot of shit you shouldn't. When I took the Vice President patch, I never thought for a moment of being the President for the mother charter. I was happy to sit back and back up when required.

I had only come back here to be with Abby.

That had backfired in some ways, but we were making amends till I lost my shit at her the other night.

Now I had a club to run, men to pull in line, and a woman who was leaning on every other man but me.

And it was all royally fucked up, thanks to myself.

"The girls are coming." Brad hit my arm, pulling me from my thoughts.

Abby and Kim were walking down the hallway towards us.

"Abby looks like hell," Drake muttered beside me.

"What did you expect?" I gave him a clipped reply.

Trigger was the first to make a move and went for Kim.

"You alright darling?" he asked her, taking her hand.

Abby just stood beside them, Brad's jumper hanging down around her knees.

"They said we should go home and come back in the morning." Her voice was weak and drained. "He's in the best hands here, and there is nothing we can do, not while he is in the ICU anyway."

"Well, that settles it then, you girls are coming home, eating, and getting a good's night sleep." Brad smiled gently at her; she attempted to smile back at him, but it didn't light up her eyes like normal.

"Let's go then," I said, wanting nothing more than to get out this darn hospital and its dying patients.

Hospitals freaked me the fuck out.

Guess that didn't help the situation now.

We all crammed into an elevator; Abby stood in front of me next to Drake. Took everything inside me not to reach out for her and pull her back towards me.

Then I thought fuck it, what was the worst she was going to do, push me away?

I threaded an arm around her waist and pulled her back against my chest. To my surprise, she didn't fight it. Instead, she melted back into me.

The elevator door chimed, and everyone started to file out, but Abby didn't make a move.

She turned in my arm to look up at me. "Can I ride home with you?"

She wasn't angry with me. Her eyes didn't hold resentment or hate towards me. It fucking shocked me to the core.

"You sure you don't wanna go home in the van?" It was all I could string together.

"I want the fresh air."

"It's cold out."

"If you don't want me on the back of your bike, you can just say," she said, deflated.

"Never said that, hun. Always want you on the back of my bike, you know that."

Wasn't romantic or anything, but it was the truth.

"Then it's settled." She pulled away from me, and we quickly exited the elevator before it shut, locking us back in this hellhole.

She wanted to ride with me. I stared at the back of her head. Why? Was fresh air the real reason?

By the time we caught up with the others, Kim was climbing into the back of the van, Trigger had already taken off on his

Harley and Drake was in the van chatting to Brad.

"I'm going with Reaper," Abby said, walking towards my bike.

Kim nodded her head, not arguing or questioning why, and I just followed Abby.

I straddled the bike, bracing it while she climbed on. Her slim arms wrapped around me, and I had to admit that it was the first time in days I felt calmer and not on edge.

Kicking the beast alive, I took off slowly, keeping in mind that Abby had had zero to no sleep and was in a weak condition. Still, I was taking the long way home, enjoying her clinging to me for once.

***

"You alright? You look frozen," I questioned her while taking my helmet off.

We had taken the long way home. Still, it wasn't enough. I wanted more time with her. When it came down to her, I was fucking greedy.

"I'm fine. Just tired." She stared down at her feet, "Reaper, can I ask you something?"

"You can ask me anything; you know that." I climbed off my bike, and we both slowly walked towards the house.

It bugged me that she wouldn't look up from the ground. She was reminding me of her sixteen-year-old self.

"Are you going to yell at me like that again?" Her long blonde hair flicked to the side, and she finally stared up at me. "Like I'm just another one of the many girls you have?"

That's what she thought? That I saw her as one of the many?

"I don't see you like that. I was just having a fucking bad day, and somehow you ended up wearing it." It still didn't sit right with me. "I'm sorry, Abby."

She started to chew her bottom lip, most likely keeping what else she wanted to say to herself.

"Can I ask you something else?" She tested the waters like she was scared I was going to fucking snap at her or something.

I gently gripped her lower arm, pulling her to a stop beside me. "I told you, Abby; you can ask me fucking anything, so spit it out. What's really on your mind?"

She let out a long breath and ran a hand through her unwashed hair. God, she looked tired.

"Will you stay with me tonight?"

I blinked blankly at her. Had I heard her correctly?

"You don't have to. It's just I kind of don't want to be on my own, and well, you're the only one I would want in my bed. But it's fine if you don't want to. Heck, I get it. It's not like we are a couple or anything." Her eyes fell back down to the ground, and I wondered what had happened to the strong, confident side of her.

She must be just that worn out she couldn't even put up a front.

"You sure you don't want Drake or Brad?" I wasn't saying it nasty or to start a fight. "You're friends with them, it would be innocent."

"And what, we aren't friends?"

"Never were, never will be. Hold you a lot higher than a friend, Abby; you should know that."

This time it was her turn to stare at me blankly. "Why couldn't you just take responsibility for me then? Why did you let Dad scare you off?"

If I had an answer, I would give it to her. But I didn't. Still didn't.

"I don't know-"

"You know I remembered what my last words were to Dad earlier," she cut me off. "They were about you. I was yelling at him, arguing with him about you."

"And that shit's on me, not you. Your dad loves you, Abby; he wouldn't hold it against you."

"But I do." She crossed her arms. "I care. Because I was fighting with him for what? You don't even really want me, do you?"

So this is what it boiled down to.

If I wanted her or not?

Of course I wanted her. I'd die for her. Fuck, I've taken on bloke after bloke to keep her as mine. She just didn't know about it.

"I love you, Abby." I took a step forward. The truth was all I had. "I've never been great with responsibility. Fuck, it is one of the reasons I am who I am today. Why I joined the club. But shit has changed when it comes to you. You are... fuck, woman, you're my everything, and I just didn't wanna screw you up by making you mine."

She breathed out. She breathed in. She stared at me blankly again. No emotion. No tears. No sign of fucking anything.

"I love you too, Kade." Her lips cracked into a small smile. "Now please take me inside where it is warm."

Just like that, the ice between us broke. She wasn't out of reach anymore. She knew how I felt and she wasn't yelling at me about it.

"I can do that." I threw an arm around her shoulder, pulling her into my side, and we continued to walk towards the house.

She was mine now.

Heck, she was always mine, it's just now, for the first time, I was openly declaring it.

Boy, I wasn't looking forward to when her old man woke up and found out.

***

You know how there are moments in life where you just wished

362

you could hold on to it for a bit longer and make the time tick slower to let that moment last longer without anything ruining it? As Abby slept with her head on my chest and one arm around me, that was exactly how I felt. I wanted the moment to last forever.

It hadn't taken long for her to close those beautiful eyes and fall asleep. She tossed and turned and didn't get comfortable until she rested her head on my chest and draped one of her slim arms across me like I was her teddy bear. I enjoyed every moment of it.

Still, I couldn't figure out why such a beautiful girl would want anything to do with me. I wasn't called the Reaper for no reason. I reminded most people of death, but she didn't care. She hadn't seen the men I killed or the blood on my hands. She saw through all that bullshit and still wanted to be with me.

She was perfect, and I was fucking lucky.

Abby

I slowly woke up, my eyes fluttering open. God, I was comfortable and warm. I moved to my side but was trapped under a heavy arm. My eyelids bounced open, and I recognized that tattooed arm immediately.

He stayed. I had thought he would take off as soon as I fell asleep.

I turned under his arm so I could see his face.

I ran a finger down his strong jawline. Kade really didn't know how handsome he was. My fingers lingered on the tattoo on his neck.

My stomach turned when I recalled the way he said "I love you" last night. It still took the breath from me. I had always loved him. It was unconditional, and I was still coming to terms with it.

His eyes sprang open, and mine looked into his deep gray eyes.

It was a love so strong that it was undying; impossible to

destroy. It was the type of love that filled novel's pages, which romance movies aimed to feature.

Every bone in my body ached with a warning; every muscle stiffened with fear at the thought of him. But like the stubborn person I was, I didn't listen to my own body's warning.

He was a flame, able to burn through me. He was the flame, and I was the moth; unknowing of the harm this man could cause within me or the power that he would one day hold over me.

If I knew then what I knew now, would I still let myself be drawn to him? I often asked myself this question.

But now as I stared into his misty gray eyes I had my answer. Yes, I would do everything the same because I loved him, and this love was worth every torment I would face for being with him.

Every torment, every second glance, and every argument I was sure to have with my father. It was all worth it.

"Morning." I smiled, and for a split second for the first time in days, my mind wasn't on Dad.

Till I remembered.

"Morning," his hand ran down my side and stopped on my hip. "How are you feeling?"

"Fine," I stretched out. "Wonder how Dad is."

"I'll get dressed and take you up if you want."

Frowning, I answered. "I'm sure you got more important things to do." Like running the club.

"You come first."

A sly smile spread across my lips, and my fingers danced down his arm. "Even Dad never put us in front of the club."

"I'm not your father."

"Good." I grinned and leaned forward. "Cause I sort of like kissing you." I curved into his muscular body.

"Fuck woman, you trying to kill me? Cause you're doing everything to stop me from letting you out of this bed."

I laughed, and it sounded so unfamiliar hearing it. "You never change, Kade."

His grip on my hip tightened. "Not when it comes to you."

"Seriously, you don't have to take me to the hospital today. I can get Brad to take me or Drake."

"Wanna explain what's going on with you and Gitz?"

I cringed slightly, hearing Kade refer to Brad as Gitz. "Nothing."

His thumb gently rubbed my cheek. "Ain't nothing, sweetheart. He's fallen hard for ya."

"No, he isn't." I scoffed, finding it slightly amusing. "Seriously Kade, you're worrying over nothing. Next thing you will be telling me Drake has come back because he is in love with me."

"Nah, he knows fucking better. But that doctor sure as fuck doesn't."

I couldn't suppress my grin. "You jealous, Kade?"

"You're mine." It was the rough growl that rumbled through his body as he said it that caused my body to freeze in chills.

My fingers ran down his chest, and I leaned my forehead against his. "And you're mine." It was the first time I had said it out loud.

"Yeah darling, I am." His hand slipped underneath my tee. "Fucking wishing you didn't have to get up right now."

I smirked; I had him just where I wanted him.

Pity I had to get up.

"Oh fuck, I forgot to tell you." My hand froze on his chest. "I called the Shields. They are on their way down."

His eyebrows shot up. "And you're just telling me that now."

"I forgot."

"Well, now we have to get up. Got to deal with fucking Jackson Johnston today."

"They aren't that bad."

"Amber's a bitch."

"Kade." I slapped his chest, "Don't call my half sister that."

"What? Are you saying that you aren't slightly scared of her? She's only five foot something, and I've seen men buckle at the knees under her intense glare."

"Well, she's coming." I finished the conversation. "So we better get up."

"Yeah, darling, we better." He brushed the hair from the side of my face and pushed it behind my ears.

He was acting so sweet and caring. It made my heart crumble. If only others got to see this side of him. But then he wouldn't be just mine.

Chapter 68

Abby

The Shields arrived that day, and they stayed for a solid week. During that time, Jackson and Troy helped Reaper deal with 'club business.' Amber, however, didn't leave the hospital. Dad woke up four days into the week.

It was beyond relief.

He was stable. He could barely move, but he was stable and talking.

And two days after waking up, I could bet Reaper was wishing he hadn't woken up cause he was bossing him around like anything.

Kind of made me smirk a lot, seeing Reaper being bossed around like a girl.

I think Dad was more settled knowing Jackson was there to back Reaper up.

But after Amber said her piece with the old man, they left.

Leaving Kim and me to deal with one grumpy old man.

"I told you, the one under that." Dad pointed at the stack of magazines with his walking stick.

Kim sighed and dug the right mag out.

"Can't wait to get the fuck out of here today," Dad grumbled, flicking through the pages of a car magazine. "Sick of these four fucking walls."

"Well, at least you aren't sick of us." I put my feet up on his bed.

"Where's Reaper today?" he snapped at me.

"How am I meant to know?"

"Because you're fucking him," Dad roared out me.

How had Dad taken to mine and Reaper's relationship? Well,

seeing as we didn't tell him and just started acting like a couple in front of him, maybe not the wisest move to do considering his health, but still, that didn't stop us.

"Thanks for putting it so nicely." I glared at him while searching in my handbag for my phone. "You know, Dad, you could at least pretend to be happy for me."

What else was Dad sick of? Family time.

"Yeah, I'm over the fucking moon that my VP is hitting my daughter up."

"I came to you about it first. Your attempt to scare him off just failed." Much to my happiness.

"Never trust a man that would go behind a man's back and screw his daughter."

"Then you must be really hating on Trigger now, too." I glanced across at Kim with a smirk. About time she got some heat for their relationship.

Her eyes scorched mine before she turned to look at Dad. "We aren't in a relationship."

"That's even fucking worse," Dad grunted, throwing the magazine down. "He just wants to ruin you."

"Dad, you really should be proud. Wouldn't you want us with men that can protect us?" I pointed out.

"I protect you."

I rolled my eyes, "Well, someone else to be able to protect us."

"Don't need no one else. Never have. Never will."

"Well, I needed Trigger when you were lying there like a corpse!" Kim defended her actions. "So Dad, yeah, we do need someone else apart from just you. I am going to get some fresh air." She pushed the chair back, dragging it on the tiles.

She slammed the door after herself.

I think all this family time was getting to us. I leaned back in the chair and sighed. My mind slowly drifted back to something Amber had said before she left.

"See you're still chasing the Reaper." Amber crossed her arms, standing next to me.

"It's not chasing when you already have him." I highlighted that important fact and went to sit down. "What do you have against him?"

"He's called the Reaper for a reason. He leaves a trail of bodies behind him. He's not the guy you cuddle up with at night. He's the type of guy you lock the fuck out." Her words were firm.

"He's not like that to me."

"Clearly, because you wouldn't be with him if you really knew him."

"You know Jackson has a reputation, yet you're still with him."

"I've known Jackson nearly my whole life. Hell, I've been by his side while he built that reputation." She scoffed and sat down beside me. "Look, if you want to chase the Reaper, by all means, don't let me stop you but just remember, he isn't sunshine and rainbows. He has another side to him and until you see that side, you don't really know him."

Was she right? Did I not really know him? I had thought I had seen it when he came home covered with all that blood. Wasn't that another side to him? Or was she referring to him killing? I swallowed sharply. Yeah, that was something I couldn't wrap my head around.

"Dad?"

"Umm?" He was looking down at his phone.

"Do you think I know Reaper enough to be with him?"

His eyes flashed up and locked with mine. He was silent for a while, thinking.

"He lives the life of the road; you'll never really know the full him." Dad put his phone down. "You'll only know as much as he let you."

"I've seen his soft side, his hard side, but what if there is another side to him that... that I can't love?"

He huffed and straightened himself up on the bed. "I don't want you loving any man, BUT Reaper is a straight cut man. He breathes the club, loves nothing, and leaves no weaknesses. So he bloody well must love you to let you be a weakness."

"Great, I'm a weakness."

"Or a strength." Dad's eyes zoned in on mine, and I saw a torn expression. "You be the pillar. The home he comes back to. That shit keeps a man sane. That's what I lost when I lost your mother. But what I gained when you girls came and lived with me."

I suppressed my smile. "So you do love us hanging around, old man?"

He grunted, and I knew that was Dad's way of saying yes.

***

I was exhausted, hungry, and worn the fuck out.

Of course, that didn't mean everyone else was. The club was in full swing of a welcome home party for Dad, and it was loud, so loud.

The drinks were flowing, the music was pounding, and the laughter was deafening.

Dad was on a bar stool, enjoying every minute of it.

Kim was under Trigger's arm, and they were keeping to the shadows, whispering and stealing kisses.

I hadn't seen Reaper once.

I wasn't even sure if he was here.

Kim and I had brought Dad home to this massive party, and not once had I seen my boyfriend's face.

I finished the remainder of my beer and sighed while sitting at the end of the bar, watching the party unfold. Just couldn't find myself wanting to be a part of it.

I glanced at my watch, and it was after midnight. I was starving, and the food here wasn't doing anything for me.

I pulled the van's keys out of my pocket. I was craving a hamburger from the hamburger cart.

Well, it wasn't like I was going to be missed if I was to leave. So I quickly weaved in and out of the crowd and made a beeline for the van once I hit the lot.

I was nearly at the van when I did a double take. Spinning back around, my eyes landed on a familiar bike.

Only one bike I knew had a detailed Reaper painted on it.

If his bike was here, where the hell was he!

My stomach curled as my mind was flooded with possibilities, all which were bad.

What if he was in there cheating on me?

What if he was in there bashing the skull of a man in?

What if he wasn't in there at all and was off with another woman?

I pulled my phone out and dialed his number. If he knew what was good for him, he would answer the fucking phone.

But he didn't.

I was torn between tearing the clubhouse apart looking for him and going to go get a hamburger.

"You look confused."

I closed my eyes and slowly turned around. All my worries eased.

"I didn't know where you were." I opened my eyes looking at Kade.

"Been in the garage." He titled his head to the side, "Where did you think I was?"

"Trust me; you don't want to know." I shrugged my hoodie on and did the zip up.

"Where were you going?"

"Hamburger cart."

"Want me to drive?"

"First, tell me what you were doing in the garage?" Something was eating at me like he was keeping a secret from me.

"On the phone with Jackson, finishing some shit up. Couldn't hear fuck inside and people kept coming out to fucking talk to me out here."

"Why didn't you come and see me when we got back?"

"What is this? Twenty fucking questions?" Kade snapped at me. "Look, if you've got something to say Abby, just fucking tell me."

"Were you cheating on me?" I crossed my arms, faking confidence. "You said yourself you didn't do relationships."

He closed the gap between us and lightly took my hand out of my pocket.

"Trust me, woman; I wasn't cheating. Who the fuck would I want other than you?" He dipped his head and met my eyes. "You're you, for fuck's sake. You seen yourself?"

I smiled lightly. "Is that your way of saying I'm good looking?"

"You know you're good looking, and you're all fucking mine. Now give me the keys. Going to get my girl a hamburger."

Smirking, I handed the keys over. "You're kind of sweet when you want to be, Kade."

"Don't call me sweet." He wrinkled his nose up at it, and I laughed, following him to the van.

I was wrong. I didn't need to know if I could love every side of him. I already did.

Chapter 69

Abby

We all make mistakes we can't come back from. There was an unspoken rule that bound each man to the club. Some would call it a duty. I would call it blind faith in something that was only ever going to offer them a short life and a bloody death.

Still.

I understood it.

Could understand it.

Till today.

Today my faith in this club and what it really stood for was shaken.

Earlier in the day

I rolled over in Reaper's arms, feeling safe and at home. There was nothing like waking up in his arms every morning. His strong, tattooed arms that held me out of love and protection. I lifted my head from his chest and glanced at his sleeping face.

It was like he was a part of me and without him, something was missing. My stomach couldn't settle; my blood pumped with nerves. Only in his arms did I feel safe and this feeling left.

He breathed heavy but remained sleeping. I traced a finger down his tattooed chest. The ink only helped define each strong muscle.

If I had to describe Reaper in one word, it would be strong.

Nothing shook him, scared him.

I hooked a leg over him and slowly pulled myself out of his arms and straddled him.

His eyes slowly opened. "Now I could wake up to that every

morning." He smirked.

I grinned foolishly down at him, wearing only one of his overly large tee shirts.

"I missed you." I leaned down and quickly kissed his lips.

"I've been sleeping beside you all night." He arched his eyebrows at me as if I was mad.

"Like I said, I missed you." Our hands interlocked, and his arms flexed as he took my weight, and I leaned down to kiss him.

"You're a strange woman at times, Abby."

"You wouldn't have it any other way."

"True." He kissed my forehead.

At this moment, everything was perfect. He, I, we were perfect. Happy and content. I didn't want to face the day. I didn't want to leave this bed.

Just as I thought it, his phone buzzed on the bedside table.

"Don't get it." I pleaded, not wanting our moment to be over just yet.

He cocked his head to the side. "Could be important, babe."

"Could also ruin our morning."

He scoffed and reached for it anyway, letting go of my hand. Sighing, I dropped off him and lay at his side.

"Roach," Reaper answered the phone, and I automatically rolled my eyes. Of course it would be my father ruining our moment.

He hadn't really taken to Reaper and I being in a relationship that well. He ignored it. Like you ignore a fly buzzing around. He treated us like that.

"I'll be there in ten." Reaper hung up.

"What was that about?" I asked, already expecting a 'nothing or don't worry about it babe' response.

"Your old man wants a word." He ruffled my hair as he got up. "Stop looking so stressed; frowns don't suit you, babe."

"Ever get that feeling where you just know something bad is

going to happen?"

"No."

"Well, I've got that feeling." I slipped out of bed and searched for my clothes. "Just promise me today you will be extra careful."

He shook his head as if I was a mad woman. "Fine hun, I promise I'll be extra careful."

I tightened up my jeans and took off his top, tossing it to the bed and threading my arms through my bra.

"I mean it, Kade. I have this…"

"I know, bad feeling." He cut me off and strolled around the bed, doing his pants up. "Stop stressing over nothing. Fuck Abby, the day has only just started."

"And I wish it was over," I muttered while picking up my top. "Did Dad say what he wanted?"

"Something about a job."

I arched an eyebrow. "Well, that doesn't sound dangerous at all."

He rolled his eyes, picking up his keys and wallet. "Promise ya, nothing will happen."

Still, my stomach rolled with warning, and my nerves were raw with a knowing of an unseeable threat coming.

I nodded my head. I couldn't ask any more from him.

"You coming out with me or staying in here?" He asked with a hand on the doorknob.

"Coming." Like hell I was staying here to worry.

"Righteo, let's go then." He held the door open for me and slapped my butt as I walked through.

"Perv," I threw over my shoulder, only to catch his smirk.

God, he was relaxed today, while I was a bundle of nerves.

"Finally, you're up." Kim greeted us as we came down the stairs.

"Didn't realize you were waiting for me." I eyed her. What did she want?

"Can I steal your woman for a bit, Reaper?" Kim batted her eyelashes at him.

"She's all yours."

I glared up at Kade for a moment, "Stay safe," I grumbled at him.

"Yeah yeah, enough with the lovey dovey shit, let's go." Kim linked her arm through mine and dragged me off in the opposite direction.

"Want to explain the dragging, Kim?"

I snuck a glance over my shoulder, watching Kade walk into Dad's office and close the door.

"Can't say yet." She pulled her car keys out, and her eyes told me all I needed to know.

She was up to something, and I was about to get involved whether I wanted to or not.

"Let's go for a drive, sis." She held the door open for me, and I sighed.

Well, at least this would distract me from my bad feeling; at the very least I could count on Kim to do that.

***

"You have to be fucking with me." I stared at her blankly, unable to believe what she was saying.

"It's a fucking good idea." She crossed her arms stubbornly. "Admit it."

"I'm not admitting to anything because you're fucking crazy. As if the club is going to let us do that!"

"We need to earn our own, and we can't do that if we are restricted by the club."

"So going off and forming our own gang is the solution?" I

looked at her, gobsmacked.

"It won't be a gang. We are simply stepping in and taking charge."

"In charge of criminals!"

"We are surrounded by them every day. What's the difference?"

"The difference is, we aren't leading them. We aren't pulling jobs, for that matter, we aren't organizing jobs! Kim, you're crazy if you think we could even pull this off."

"The Hellbound need someone to step up. I was talking to Amber about it while she was in town. Blake is still serving time, and we would have her backup."

"So this is what you two were whispering about. Please tell me she said you were crazy. Dad would lose his shit."

"Dad wants us under his thumb, controlling everything we do. He doesn't think we have it in us to step up and take charge, and he's wrong. It is in our blood."

I sighed and pulled the coffee closer to me. "Dad won't allow us to do this. The Hellbound are viewed as scum in his eyes."

"That's what they are at the moment. But think of what we could do with all those men and women. We could pull real jobs." She leaned in, "Bank jobs, security runs, the lot. All they need is someone telling them how to do it."

"And what makes you think we would have any idea how to handle that crap? Last time I checked, all we do is pour beers and clean up bikers' spew. We aren't the criminals."

"But we could be." She really believed this could happen. "I can't do it without you. Heck, I won't do it without you."

"Why? What have I got to offer you?"

"You have a fire inside you that is uncontrollable. When someone pisses you off, you turn into a machine. I need that fire on my side."

"I'm not ruthless."

"You can be."

"When I don't have a choice and am pushed to it!"

"Will you just think about it?" Her eyes pleaded with me. "Please."

It was madness. Complete and utter madness.

"I'll think about it." But that was all that was going to happen. Thinking. Like hell I would ever act and become a ruthless leader of the Hellbound. I was surprised Amber thought we had it in us.

"That's all I ask." She leaned back in the booth, seeming pleased with herself. "No rush on the answer."

I scoffed but kept the words to myself.

The answer was no. Never going to happen, but if she wanted to wait a few days to hear it, fine.

Reaper

There are times when you think life is going great. Then it pulls out a sharp knife and stabs you in the motherfucking back.

Roach butted out his cigarette. His eyes judged me coldly. But that wasn't why he dragged me in here. That wasn't why he pretended to call me in here about a job.

He wasn't shoving these jobs down my throat out of fucking love for the club.

"You want me on the road?" I spoke with a harshness in my tone "Why?"

"You're the Reaper, and I need you fucking reaping. You don't get paid to sit here."

I leaned forward on the seat, "Don't fucking bullshit me. I know why you are doing this, so fucking spit it out."

"You think I was gonna sit back and watch my daughter be your only weakness and a walking fucking target for your enemies?"

He was taking her away from me.

No.

He was sending me away from her.

"So what, you planning on taking the VP patch with it cause it looks fucking weird to have your Vice President on the fucking road cleaning up the scum?"

"Having the Reaper as my Vice President has made this club stronger. So no. I'm not taking the patch. You simply are going back to doing what the fuck you're meant to be doing. Which isn't fucking my daughter and putting her in harm's way."

"I wouldn't ever let anything happen to Abby."

"If you really meant that, you wouldn't be fucking her."

I had once convinced myself that I was protecting her by staying away from her. Then I fell hard for her, and nothing could keep me from her.

Not even the fear of Roach.

Blind, numbing rage crept through me, "This is bullshit."

"No, this is, you do as I fucking say." He smugly stood up and glared across at me. "My girls were off limits. You crossed the fucking line, boy, and now you'll pay."

I stood up, challenging him. "You can order me off, but that won't change a fucking thing between me and your daughter."

"Distance does a fuck load. Remember your place, boy."

"Maybe you should remember I'm the fucking REAPER. ME. I'm the one men are scared of. I'M THE FUCKING ONE THAT TAKES AND CHOOSES."

"You're not a President or a fucking nomad now. You do as I fucking say. ME!" He roared back at me, gripping the table. "I say you are cutting the fucking list; you're cutting the list."

"You know Roach, there is nothing more dangerous than a man with nothing to lose." It wasn't an empty threat. If he wanted to have a fucking showdown, then I'd give him a fucking showdown.

"I won't forget this." I threw my arm across his table, wiping it

379

of its contents. "This is fucking BULLSHIT!" I roared on my way out, slamming his door behind me.

If I were still President, this wouldn't be fucking happening.

If I hadn't walked from my charter.

If I hadn't gone fucking soft.

Then this wouldn't be happening.

I had no choice. I was up against a fucking hard wall, and I had no fucking choice. He had the power, and I was fucking powerless. He could send me away, and I had no fucking choice.

It came with my name, who I was. The Reaper.

The list needed cutting, and now I had been called to do my duty. That meant time on the road. That meant time away from Abby.

Who was I fucking kidding? Abby and I were over.

The Reaper didn't come back laughing and fucking loving. I came back harder than I left. I come back a bit more soulless. I come back more Reaper than Kade.

Abby

Walking into Reaper's room, I closed the door softly behind me. I could hear him in the wardrobe.

"You were right." I tossed my leather jacket on the bed. "There was nothing to worry about. Unless you count what Kim told me. Seriously, you won't believe what she told me."

He walked out of the wardrobe, and immediately I knew something was wrong. Ice slowly melted through my body as I stared at him.

"What happened?"

He grunted and dropped the packed black bag on the bed. "Your old man happened."

"What's that supposed to mean? Did he threaten you?"

"Abby," His voice was thick with emotion, and he pulled me across the room, sitting me on the bed. "I can't be with you anymore."

He didn't just say that.

No.

No, he couldn't have just said that.

"What did you say? Because if you're fucking breaking up with me, you can forget it." I wasn't letting him. We had come so far.

"I'm leaving."

It was an automatic reaction. I didn't even think about it. My hand whipped across his face, slapping him. My eyes filled with tears. "You fucking promised me. YOU PROMISED ME!" He said he loved me. He said it was forever. He said he needed me as much as I needed him and now what, he was leaving?

"HOW CAN YOU DO THIS TO ME!"

His head slowly turned back to face me, taking the slap as if it was nothing. "I don't get a choice."

"Don't lie to me. Everyone has a choice. Everyone makes them. If you're leaving, it's on you, no one else."

"I've been called to do my job. I don't get a fucking choice in the matter. Your old man wants the list cut. He wants me on the road. He gets me on the road. It is as simple as fucking that."

"You're putting the club before us." I shook my head in rage. "You said you loved me. How can you say those words and not really mean it?"

"I do love you. I fucking care more about you than anything else in the world. But your father made a choice. He doesn't want me near you, so I'm hitting the road."

"You're letting him win." Furious tears slid down my face. "You're the fucking Reaper for god sake, stand up against him."

"I CAN'T!" he roared, getting up, not keeping his anger in check. "I'm under his fucking orders. It's my duty, Abby. My duty to cull the list. I'm the Reaper. It's my job and if the

381

President wants me to do it, then I have to step up."

I didn't know who to be mad at. I didn't know who to blame for my breaking heart.

"It was all just a lie, wasn't it? You never wanted a relationship." I stared at him, my eyes shining with breaking pain. "You are the Reaper. Cold-hearted, and you get what you want. You always have. So blaming my father won't get you out of this. I don't believe you. You deceived me from the start; I was just too stupid to see it."

I got up from the bed, the ice that floated through my body slowly melting as boiling rage replaced it.

"I hate you for doing this to me." I wiped my angry tears away. "For breaking my heart, again."

He stood there in silence, just watching me. His eyes flashed with splintering rage, but he kept silent.

"What, nothing more to say?" I cocked my head to the side. "No more excuses."

"I never expected you to understand." He picked up the black bag and my heart squeezed tightly. "This is my life. The club is all I have."

"That's a lie. You had me."

"And I couldn't have fucking both, could I?"

"Just because you're leaving didn't mean you had to end it. Last time I checked, distance didn't mean ending."

"I don't come back the same man." He muttered more to himself, zipping the bag, then he looked up, locking his eyes with mine from across the room. "I wish I could give you what you want, Abby. But I can't."

"All I ever wanted was you."

"Your father doesn't want you to have this life." He strolled across the room till he stood in front of me. Gently with his thumbs, he wiped the tears away from under my eyes. "I should have never chased you. The hurt you feel now is on me. I'm sorry."

"You're sorry." I snorted and crossed my arms. "Well, that does so much."

"I love you, Abby. Always will." He dipped his head, holding my eyes with his. "I'll never stop loving you."

What could I say to that? I placed a hand on his hard leather, close to his heart. "Then don't go." Don't leave, not again. I wasn't sure if I could deal with it again. Every part of me ached when I wasn't with him. I lost the point to living without him. Without him, I was nothing.

Nothing but an empty shell.

"You'll be ok," he reassured me and wrapped an arm around my back and pulled me into a hug. "You're stronger than you know. You don't need me."

"I'm heartless without you," I spoke, just before another wave of tears took over and I cried into his chest.

"Come on baby girl, no more tears. You're killing me here."

I sniffed back my tears and pulled away from him. "What did you expect? When you ride out of that lot, you're taking a part of me, and I don't know if I can live without it."

"You were always too young and sweet for this type of lifestyle. You deserve better. You deserve a man that can put you first, and I can't do that. Not now."

"I mightn't deserve you, but you're all I ever wanted, Kade. Always will be." I stepped out of his embrace. "But I get it. Club comes first."

"I'm the Reaper. It is who I am. I'm the one that does the shit others can't stomach. I'm sorry that you fell for the wrong guy."

He leaned across me and opened the door.

"Do you have to leave tonight? It's the dead of the night." My stomach twisted with the realization that this was it. He was leaving and wasn't coming back. I couldn't fix this.

"I'm sure our paths will cross again." A dim smile traced his lips. "Maybe then you'll have found a man that deserves your heart."

I closed my eyes, letting the tears fall.

Then he walked past me, and I didn't reach out to stop him. Instead, I let him walk through the door and down the hall.

I let him go.

That's what he wanted, wasn't it?

He had deceived me from the start, or maybe I had deceived myself into thinking we could actually be together.

Was that the goodbye I really pictured us to have?

Didn't what we had deserve a better goodbye?

Without overthinking, I spun the bedroom door back open and sprinted down the hallway, down the stairs, through the crowded bar, and out the clubhouse doors.

My eyes landed on Reaper's back; he was still walking to his bike.

"REAPER!"

He turned and then caught me with both arms, lifting me off the ground.

I curled into him, holding on for dear life. Taking in his strong scent for the last time and the safety of his arms.

"I lied." I whimpered into his chest. "I could never hate you."

"Shhh." He ran his hands down my back. "I know. I know, Abby."

"I just didn't want you to leave and I..." I pulled away from his shoulder, meeting his eyes. "I love you, Kade. Please don't go."

"Got to, babe. But," He leaned his forehead against mine. "I love you too. Always will."

I didn't want to let go, but I knew I had to. So I slid down his body, pulling my arms from around his neck and cupping his cheeks. "You don't know how much I need you. How much I need to breathe the same air as you. I won't make it without you."

"You have before. I know you can." His grip on me loosened, and he held me by my hips. "I'll be seeing you again, Abby."

"Yeah, I will be seeing you too." I kissed the side of his cheek and pulled away. "Don't go and get yourself killed now."

"I'll try my best not to."

My eyes dragged across his motorbike and then slowly back up to him.

"I love you, Kade."

"And I love you, Abby." He dipped his lips and kissed me with the force of a hurricane.

Like it was our last kiss. *Because it was our last kiss.*

Then he pulled away, and I watched with a stomach filled with knives as he rode off into the darkness. And when the taillights of his bike disappeared, my heart froze.

***

"Did you send him away?"

I had stormed into Dad's bedroom. The whore that was on him screamed and pulled the blankets over herself.

"DID YOU SEND HIM AWAY?" I screamed from the end of his bed. Not caring he was busy. Not caring that he most likely was furious at me for being in here.

"Get the fuck out, Abby."

"Answer me!"

"YES!" He threw the blankets off him, pulling up his pants. "I fucking sent that fucker the hell away from you."

"How dare you." I shook my head, full of rage. "I love him. Sending him away isn't going to change that."

"No," he arched his eyebrows. "I can fucking promise you that it will change him. You will be the last thing on his mind when he returns. He'll be back and searching only for the bottle like he always does."

"You're a monster." I saw my father in a completely different light.

"I'm a fucking president, and he is under my fucking control. MY CONTROL! And I can fucking promise you that I will never let you be with one of my men."

"I hate you," I spoke with such force and when his hand whipped across my face, causing blood to spill in my mouth, I didn't even care.

Instead, I turned my head to look back at him.

"Don't you ever fucking say that." His eyes bulged as he pointed a finger at me harshly.

"You can't control my life, and I promise you now that what I do next is on you. You caused it." Tears of pain stung my eyes and I whipped around, strolling out of his room, slamming the door behind me.

He could have his club.

He could have his whores.

But from now on, he didn't have me.

***

We all make mistakes we can't come back from. There was an unspoken rule that bonded each man to the club. Some would call it a duty. I would call it blind faith in something that was only ever going to offer them a short life and a bloody death.

Still.

I understood it.

Could understand it.

Till today.

Today my faith in this club and what it really stood for was shaken.

I brought a closed fist to Kim's door and knocked.

"Fuck, you look like shit," she said after opening the door and letting me in.

"Thanks." I sank down on the edge of her bed.

"What happened?" She crossed her arms, looking at me with worry.

I dragged my eyes off the carpet and met her curious eyes. "Reaper left."

Her eyes softened. "I didn't see that coming."

"Dad sent him."

Her mouth dropped open in understanding. "I'm sorry, Abby."

It didn't matter, my heart was broken. Nothing could heal it. The man I loved was miles away now, and he wasn't turning around.

He was gone.

"This shit with the Hellbound, is it for real?" I asked her.

She sighed, nodding her head, and sat beside me. "I wanted you to come around on it, but I didn't want it to be like this."

"Well, you wanted me ruthless." I stared into her eyes, "I'm hollow now. So I'm ready." I stood up. "If you're serious about cutting ties with the club, then let's do it."

"We'll need to find somewhere else to live."

"That won't be hard."

"If we do this," she stood up, "there is no going back. We can't just patch things back up with them after we do this."

"I don't ever want to patch things up." I felt an emotion I couldn't even explain swallow me. "I want out. So if you're still serious about it, let's do it."

She sighed, running her hand through her long blonde hair before giving me a firm look.

"Didn't want you doing this for the wrong reason."

"There was never going to be a good reason to do this."

"I'll call a meeting with Blake." She looked unearthed about it, and I wondered what had made her make this decision.

"Good. I'll pack my shit."

I turned my back on her and walked out of her room with a new objective.

That objective was to be someone, someone that my father thought I couldn't be.

I was stronger than he thought. Taking Reaper from me, took my heart. And a heartless soul was a dangerous one.

Did I have it in me to be a soulless monster and help Kim run this gang? I don't know. All I knew was I had nothing to lose, and when you have nothing lose, there isn't much stopping you from risking it all.